The Mountain Between Us

Also by Cindy Myers

The Mountain Between Us

CINDY MYERS

KENSINGTON PUBLISHING CORP.
www.kensingtonbooks.com

KENSINGTON BOOKS are published by

Kensington Publishing Corp.
119 West 40th Street
New York, NY 10018

All Kensington titles, imprints, and distributed lines are available at special quantity discounts for bulk purchases for sales promotion, premiums, fund-raising, educational, or institutional use.

Special book excerpts or customized printings can also be created to fit specific needs. For details, write or phone the office of the Kensington Special Sales Manager: Attn. Special Sales Department. Kensington Publishing Corp., 119 West 40th Street, New York, NY 10018. Phone: 1-800-221-2647.

Kensington and the K logo Reg. U.S. Pat. & TM Off.

ISBN-13: 978-1-61773-823-4
ISBN-10: 1-61773-823-9

First Trade Paperback Printing: November 2013
First Mass Market Printing: October 2014

10 9 8 7 6 5 4 3 2 1

Printed in the United States of America

*To Loretta Myers, a wonderful
mother-in-law and friend*

Acknowledgments

Thank you to Rocky Mountain Fiction Writers for your unwavering support and the many friends I've made in this wonderful organization. A special thanks to the Hand Hotel for hosting the writers' retreats where much of this book was written. Mike, Stella, and Richard, I couldn't have done it without you. The same goes for the writers who are regular parts of the retreat—you keep me going!

Thank you to the many people at Kensington Publishing who work behind the scenes to make this book possible, with special thanks to my editor, Audrey LaFehr, for her continued support of my stories.

As always, the people and places of Ridgway and Ouray, Colorado, inspired my writing. I can't think of a more beautiful and special place.

Finally, thank you to my husband, Jim, for his unwavering encouragement and love. You are the best.

CHAPTER ONE

Maggie Stevens stared out the front windshield of the Jeep, at the mountainside ahead painted with golden aspen, maroon rock, and purple aster—as if fall were playing a game of "top this" with summer, decorating itself with even more beautiful color. A lot of people probably came to this overlook above Eureka, Colorado, to try to deal with life's big questions, to let the hugeness of the mountains lend perspective.

Really, she'd only driven up here because the cell phone reception was best.

She glanced at the plus sign on the little plastic strip in her hand again. "Maybe the test is defective," she said into the phone. "Maybe that's why it was for sale at the dollar store."

"You bought a pregnancy test at the dollar store?" On the other end of the line her best friend, Barb Stanowski, sounded very far away.

"I certainly wasn't going to buy it here in town." If anyone had seen her with her purchase at Eureka Grocery, the news would have been all over town before she even got back to her place. So she'd driven half an hour up the road to Montrose. "And I couldn't bring myself to pay ten dollars for something I was going to pee on. Besides, I needed three of them."

"Three?" Barb was laughing again.

"I wanted to be absolutely sure. What if they're wrong?"

"All three of them? Not likely. How are you feeling?"

"I told you. Sick. Scared. And kind of elated." Her first husband had refused to consider the idea of children. When he'd left her shortly before her fortieth birthday, she'd resigned herself to never having the baby she'd always wanted. Then she'd met Jameso and now . . .

"Any physical symptoms?" Barb asked.

"My breasts are really sensitive. I've been throwing up, but not just in the morning. Yesterday, Janelle brought onion rings with my lunch. I love her onion rings, but one whiff of those and I had to leave the café. And Rick told me I was glowing."

"Your boss told you you were glowing? Have you been around any leaking nuclear reactors lately?"

"He was teasing me." Rick Otis, editor and publisher of the *Eureka Miner,* made a hobby out of getting people's goats. "He said I must be in love, because I was positively glowing."

"You are in love, aren't you?"

"Yes, maybe. I mean, yes, I love Jameso, but he's not exactly responsible father material." Handsome, sexy, unpredictable Jameso Clark, who'd roared into her life on a motorcycle on her very first night in Eureka. He'd made her feel alive and sexy and hopeful again after the emotional wreckage of her divorce.

"How can you say that, if he cares about you and the baby?" Barb liked Jameso. She'd liked him before Maggie did, and continued to see qualities in him Maggie couldn't.

"He'll probably freak out when I tell him about the

baby." Maggie shuddered. She pictured him climbing on his motorcycle and riding away, out of her life forever. "I do love him. I think he's great, but I don't have any illusions about him. He's a part-time bartender slash ski instructor slash mountain guide, whose most valuable possession is a motorcycle. He's estranged from his family, and he probably suffers from post-traumatic stress, though he won't admit it." Jameso refused to talk about his time in Iraq and turned away if she tried to question him.

"I think you're underestimating him," Barb said. "This may be just what he needs to turn his life around. He'll probably make a great father."

"What about me? What kind of mother will I be?" Maggie allowed herself to give in to the panic a little. "I don't know anything about children. I've never spent any time around them. I'm forty years old. I'll be ready to retire when this baby graduates college." She closed her eyes, fighting a wave of dizziness.

"Calm down. Lots of women in their forties have babies these days. And you've always wanted children. You'll be a great mom."

"Barb, I'm scared." She opened her eyes again, shifting her gaze until she found the top of Mount Winston. How many mornings now had she awakened to the sight of that towering peak since coming to Eureka from Houston five months ago? She'd come here intending to stay a week—two at the most—gathering her late father's effects and trying to learn as much as she could about the man who'd walked out of her life when she was only a few days old. But the mountains had pulled at her, refusing to let her leave. Of all the things her father had left her, his greatest gift had been that new perspective on her life and the chance to start over with a different vision.

Was a baby part of that vision? Apparently, it was. Was it possible to be so thrilled and terrified at the same time?

"Oh, honey, I know," Barb said soothingly. "I was

scared when I found out I was pregnant with Michael, too. But you'll get over that, I promise."

"What if I screw this up?"

"You won't. You and Jameso will make the most beautiful baby, and you'll love it in a way you've never loved anyone in your life."

"What if Jameso can't handle this and he leaves?" Her husband and her father had bailed on her—why should she expect any better from Jameso?

"If he does, you'll manage on your own. You have a lot of people to help you."

She put her hand on her stomach, trying to imagine a life growing in there. She couldn't do it. It was the most wonderful, impossible, surreal thing that had ever happened to her.

"Where is Jameso right now?" Barb asked.

"At work at the Dirty Sally."

"He gets a dinner break, doesn't he? Go tell him."

"No, I can't tell him at work." The Dirty Sally Saloon was the epicenter of Eureka's highly developed gossip chain. If Jameso really did flake out on her, she'd rather it didn't happen in front of the whole bar crowd. "I'll tell him tomorrow. He's off in the morning and we're supposed to drive up to the French Mistress to check on the new gate I had installed." The French Mistress Mine, another inheritance from her father, had turned out to contain no gold, but it was producing respectable quantities of high-quality turquoise. Work was shutting down for the winter and Maggie had installed an iron mesh gate to keep out the curious and the careless.

"That's kind of romantic, telling him at the place you first met."

"That's Jameso—Mr. Romance."

"You don't give him enough credit. It's going to be all right. I promise."

"I hope you're right."

"Of course I'm right. Don't you believe me?"

"I believe you." Maybe it was talking to Barb, or maybe it was sitting here, letting the beauty of the mountains soothe her. Such a vast landscape made her feel small, and her problems small, too, in comparison.

She said good-bye to Barb, then started the Jeep and carefully backed onto the highway. She had about eighteen hours to figure out how to tell Jameso he was going to be a father. And about that long to let the realization that the thing she'd always wanted most was finally happening—and she'd never felt more unprepared.

Fall always felt like starting over to Olivia Theriot. The first sharp morning chill in the air and the tinge of gold in the leaves made her want to buy a new sweater and sharpen a pack of number two pencils. She'd turn to a blank page in a fresh notebook and start a new chapter in her life.

One of the chief disappointments in being an adult was that fall didn't bring new beginnings that way. No new clothes, new classes, new friends, and the chance to do things over and get it right this time. While she'd sent her thirteen-year-old son, Lucas, off to school with a new backpack and a fresh haircut, she felt more stuck than ever in a life she hadn't planned.

"I've got a bad feeling about this one."

"I feel that way so often I've thought of having it put on a T-shirt." Olivia slid another beer toward the man who'd spoken, a part-time miner named Bob Prescott who was the Dirty Sally Saloon's best customer.

"You're too young to be so cynical." Bob saluted her with the beer glass, then took a long sip.

Next month, she'd turn thirty. To Bob, who had to be in his seventies, that probably felt young, but most days Olivia felt she'd left youth behind long ago. Maybe it was having a kid who was already a teenager. Or having lived in at least fifteen different places since she'd left home at fifteen. Or maybe this used-up feeling was really only dismay that nothing in her life had worked out the way she'd planned. Back when she was a starry-eyed twenty-something, her dreams of happily ever after had certainly never included single motherhood, a job tending bar, and sharing a house with her mother in a town so remote it didn't even make it onto most maps.

She pinched herself hard on the wrist. Time to snap out of it. At this rate she'd end up crying in her beer, like one of her sloppiest customers. "What do you have a bad feeling about, Bob?" she asked. In the four months she'd worked at the Dirty Sally, Bob could be counted on for at least one outrageous story or proclamation a week.

"This winter." Bob shook his head. "It's going to be a late one. We should have had snow by now and there's scarcely been a flurry. Mount Winston's practically bare and here it is into October."

"It has been awfully dry." The other bartender, Jameso Clark, moved down the bar to join Bob and Olivia. Tall, with dark hair and a neatly trimmed goatee, Jameso was something of a local heartthrob, though lately he seemed to have settled down with Maggie Stevens. "It's not looking good for an early ski season."

"You working as a ski instructor again this year?" Bob asked.

"Of course."

"Aren't you getting a little long in the tooth to play ski bum?" Olivia asked.

Jameso's eyes narrowed. "I'm only two years older than you. And there are plenty of guys who are older than me, a lot older, who work as instructors or on ski patrol."

"But it's not like it's a real job. Not something a man can support a family on."

"Who said anything about a family?" Jameso's voice rose in alarm.

She never should have brought it up. Now he was going to get all pissy on her. "Things just seem pretty serious with you and Maggie. I thought you two might get married and settle down."

"What if we do?" Color bloomed high on his cheeks. "That doesn't mean I can't keep skiing. Maggie likes me fine the way I am."

"Forget I said anything."

"You won't be teaching anybody to ski if we don't get snow," Bob said. Olivia didn't know if he was deftly cutting off their argument or merely continuing with his current favorite topic, oblivious to what had just passed between her and Jameso. Whatever the reason, she gratefully picked up the thread.

"I can't believe you two are moaning about the lack of snow," she said. "Why would you even want the weather we have right now to end?" She gestured out the front window of the bar, where a cluster of aspens still held on to many of their golden leaves. The sun shone in a turquoise blue sky, the thermometer on the wall showed sixty-four degrees, and the breeze through the open window at her back was dry and crisp. Olivia, who'd lived all over before coming to this little corner of the Rockies, had never seen such glorious weather.

"The weather's good, all right," Bob said. "Too good. We need a good snowstorm to send all the tourists packing."

She rolled her eyes and started emptying the contents of the bus tray into the recycling bin.

"What about you, Miss O?" Jameso asked. "Have you decided yet if you're staying in Eureka for the winter?"

Olivia fixed him with a baleful glare.

"What?" He held up both hands in a defensive gesture. "I just asked an innocent question."

"You're the sixth person who's asked me that question in the past week. I'm beginning to think people are anxious to see me gone."

"You've got it all wrong." Jameso leaned his lanky frame back against the bar and grinned in a way most women probably found charming. "Maybe we're anxious to see you stay."

"People say if you can survive your first winter in Eureka you're likely to stick around for good." Bob regarded Olivia over the rim of his beer glass. "You strike me as the kind of woman who's got what it takes to stick it out."

This passed for high praise from Bob, who regarded most newcomers to town with suspicion—herself and Maggie excepted. Olivia suspected his approval of her had more to do with her ability to pull a glass of beer and the fact that her mother was the town's mayor than with her potential as a mountain woman.

"I don't see what's so special about winter here," she said, going back to filling the recycling bin with the bottles from last night's bar crowd. "The way you people talk you'd think Eureka's the only place to ever get snow."

"It's not just the snow," Jameso said, "though we get plenty of that. We measure storms in feet, not inches. But snow here in the mountains isn't like snow in the city. Some of the roads around here don't get plowed until spring. Avalanches can block the highway into town and cut us off from the rest of the world for days. Most of the tourists leave town, so everything's quieter. The people who stay are the ones who really want to be here, and everybody pitches in to help everybody else."

Olivia wrinkled her nose. "You make it sound like some sort of commune."

"That's community—the two are related," Bob said. "You find out who your friends really are when your car breaks down on a winter road or you run out of firewood with two months of winter left."

"Lucille has gas heat, and I don't plan on exploring the hinterlands this winter," Olivia said.

"You laugh now, but you'll find out soon enough if you stick around," Bob said. "Folks around here look after each other."

"I can look after myself. Thanks all the same." Olivia had a hard enough time getting used to everyone in town knowing everyone else's business—knowing *her* business. How much worse would it be when there were fewer people to keep the busybodies occupied? She was tempted to get out of town while she still could, but her son, Lucas, liked it here, and though her mother, Lucille, would probably never admit it, Olivia thought she liked having them here in Eureka, too.

Besides, she didn't want to give certain people the satisfaction of thinking she was running away from them.

She hefted the recycling bin onto one hip and headed out the back door, to the alley behind the bar where the truck could pick it up this afternoon.

"Let me help you with that." Before she could react, two strong arms relieved her of her burden.

She glared up at the man whose broad shoulders practically blotted out the sun. "What are you doing here, D. J.? I thought I made it clear I didn't want to see you again."

A lesser man might have been knocked off his feet by the force of her glare, but Daniel James Gruber, too good-looking for her peace of mind and far too stubborn by half, never flinched. "Which do you think is heavier?" he asked. "These bottles or that grudge you're carrying around?"

If he thought her feelings about him were the heaviest thing in her heart, he didn't really know her very well.

But, of course, he didn't know her. If he had, he never would have left her in the first place. So why had he tracked her all the way to middle-of-nowhere Eureka, Colorado? And why now? "Go home, D. J.," she said. "Or go back to Iraq. Or go to hell, for all I care. Just leave me alone."

"Mo-om!" The shout was followed almost immediately by a boy with wispy blond hair, large ears, and round, wire-rimmed glasses. He wore cutoff denim shorts, a too-large T-shirt, and the biggest smile Olivia could remember seeing on him.

"You don't have to shout, Lucas," she said. "I'm right here."

"Mom, you gotta come out to the truck and see the fish I caught."

"Where were you fishing? You know I told you not to go off in the mountains by yourself." Almost two months ago, Lucas had fallen down a mine tunnel on one of his solo expeditions, exploring the surrounding mountains. Ever since, Olivia had been haunted by worries over all the ways this wild country had for a boy to get hurt— mine tunnels and whitewater rivers, boiling hot springs and treacherous rock trails. Lucas had never been a particularly rambunctious boy, but he was still a boy, with a boy's disregard for danger.

"I didn't go by myself. D. J. took me."

She could feel D. J.'s hot gaze on her, though she didn't dare look at him. If she detected the least bit of smugness in his expression, she'd leap up and scratch his eyes out. How dare he think he could get to her by playing best pal to her son!

But she couldn't tell him what she thought of him now, with Lucas standing here. The boy idolized the only man who'd ever really taken an interest in him. The man she'd been so sure would make such a good father.

She bit the inside of her cheek, the pain helping to

clear her head, and managed a half smile for Lucas. "Go ask Jameso to give you a soda and I'll be out to look at your fish in a minute," she said.

She watched him go, his shoulders less rounded than they'd been even three months ago, his head held higher. He'd shed the hunched, fearful look he'd worn when they first arrived here. That was the real reason she couldn't leave Eureka, at least not yet. As improbable as it sounded, Lucas was thriving here, roaming the unpaved streets of town and the back roads beyond, as if he'd lived here all his life.

"He's a great kid," D. J. interrupted her thoughts. "I'm not hanging out with him to get to you, if that's what you think. I like spending time with him."

Since when had he developed this ability to know what she was thinking? Too bad he hadn't been so tuned in before he skipped town. "You're just prolonging the hurt," she said. "Isn't it enough that you broke his heart once?" That he broke *her* heart? "You should go now, before you make it worse."

"There's unfinished business between us. I won't leave until it's settled."

"It's settled, D. J. It was settled when you walked out the door six months ago." She started to move past him, but he took hold of her arm, his touch surprisingly gentle for such a big man, familiar in the way only someone with whom you'd shared the deepest intimacy could be. No matter that they hadn't been lovers in months, her traitorous body responded to him as if he'd last held her only yesterday, her skin heating, her heart thumping harder.

"I'm not letting you off that easy," he said. "I've decided to stay. At least for the winter. Maybe if we spend a few months snowed in here together you'll let go of that grudge long enough to grab hold of what you really need."

"And you think you're what I need? Of all the self-centered, arrogant, male things to say."

"All I'm saying is, you don't have to carry all your burdens alone. Let me help."

She wrenched away, rushing into the bar and out the front door, past Jameso and Bob and Lucas, who sat on a stool next to Bob, sipping a soft drink from a beer mug. She wanted to jump in her truck and drive and keep driving without stopping until she was a thousand miles away from here.

But she'd already learned moving on wasn't the answer. You couldn't ever really run away when the thing you were running from was yourself.

"I'm a lot of things, but I'm not a magician. I can't pull money out of thin air or make this budget stretch to cover one thing more." Lucille Theriot, Eureka's mayor, stood behind the front counter of Lacy's, the junk/antique shop she owned, trying her best not to lose her temper with the older woman across from her. Cassie Wynock, town librarian and perpetual thorn in Lucille's side, thought her family's deep roots in the town entitled her to anything she wanted. Today, she wanted new shelves for the library, an item not in the town's very tight budget.

"We ought to have plenty of money," Cassie said. "The Hard Rock Days celebration this year was the biggest it's ever been. I know for a fact the Founders' Pageant sold out." She patted her hair, preening. The play devoted to telling the story of the town's origins had been written and directed by Cassie, who'd also taken a starring role.

"The extra money we took in from Hard Rock Days doesn't begin to make up for the money we aren't getting from the state and federal governments this year. We've had to really tighten our belts. I've already warned people not to expect plowing of side streets this winter."

"People around here can do without plowing. They can't do without the library."

Lucille was trying to think of a suitable response to this bit of skewed logic, perhaps by pointing out that if the streets weren't plowed people couldn't get to the library, when the cow bells attached to the back of her front door jangled. She looked up, hopeful of a customer who would necessitate cutting her conversation with Cassie short. Instead, Bob Prescott shuffled in.

"Afternoon, ladies," he said, touching the bill of his Miller Mining ball cap.

Cassie wrinkled up her nose. "You smell like a brewery."

Bob did have a faint odor of beer about him, but this was nothing new. He spent most afternoons propping up the bar at the Dirty Sally. "Stop by the saloon any afternoon, Cassie, and I'll buy you a drink," Bob said. "I predict it'll do wonders for your disposition."

Considering Cassie's disposition was almost always bad, Lucille doubted alcohol would help. "What can I do for you, Bob?" she asked.

"You're interrupting a private conversation," Cassie said before Bob could reply.

"I was explaining to Cassie how the town budget is so tight this year we've decided to forgo plowing side streets for the winter," Lucille said.

"I say we set up snowmobile-only lanes and forget about plowing altogether," Bob said. " 'Course, you won't have to worry about that at all if we don't get snow."

"And I say new library shelves are a matter of liability," Cassie said. "The old ones are falling apart. If we don't replace them, someone could get hurt."

Lucille met Cassie's defiant look with a skeptical one of her own. Were the shelves in such bad shape? Or would Cassie see to it that they did start falling apart, even if she had to remove a few bolts to do so? She looked like a prim old maid, but Lucille knew she had nerves of steel.

Coupled with her outsized sense of self-importance, it could be a recipe for trouble.

"I'll have someone come down and examine the existing shelves for safety concerns," Lucille said. "Maybe we can reinforce them somehow." She turned to Bob. "Can I help you, Bob? I just got a nearly complete set of 1970s-era *National Geographics* and two solid brass spittoons in stock if you're interested."

"Nah, I'm here on official business, Madam Mayor." He propped one elbow on the counter and leaned against it, his customary posture at the Dirty Sally.

"Official business?"

"You might say it relates to your conversation with Cassie. I've got an idea for a fund-raiser for the town. Something to liven up the quiet weeks after the summer tourists have left and before the ski crowd shows up."

"We don't get a ski crowd, Bob," Lucille said. "That's over in Telluride. The best we can hope for is a few folks who stop on their way to and from the slopes."

"They're all tourists to me," he said dismissively. "What I'm talking about is entertainment for the locals and a way to bring in a little extra cash for the town coffers."

Lucille leaned back, arms folded. "Let's hear it." Bob's past ideas—all of them voted down by the town council—had included boxcar derby races down the steep main road leading into town, hiring a burlesque troupe to "liven up" the Independence Day celebrations, and letting tourists pay to be a miner for the day and work Bob's claims with a pickax and shovel.

"Let's start a pool on when the first snow will fall," he said. "Charge five dollars a guess and the person who gets closest to the date and time wins half the money. The town keeps the other half."

"I'm certain city-sponsored gambling like that is illegal," Cassie sniffed.

"She's right, Bob," Lucille said. "We can't do something like that. It was a good idea, though."

"Humph. Nothing to stop me from doing it, is there?"

"You can't run a gambling operation of any kind without a license," Lucille said.

"Tell that to the weekly poker games in the back room of the barber shop."

Lucille covered her hands with her ears. "I didn't hear that," she said loudly.

The door opened again and a distinguished-looking man with tanned skin and silver hair and moustache entered. Lucille's heartbeat sped up and she fought the urge to smooth her hair or check the front of her blouse for lint. "Hello, Gerald," she said, aware that her voice had taken on a musical lilt.

"You're looking lovely as usual, Lucille." He smiled, showing perfect white teeth she suspected were caps, but who cared? Everyone was entitled to his or her little vanities.

"Who are you?" Bob demanded.

Gerald's smile never faltered as he turned to face the old man. "I'm Gerald Pershing. Who are you?"

"I'm Bob Prescott. I live here."

"In this store?"

Bob looked as if he'd bit down on a walnut shell. He scowled at Lucille. "He a friend of yours?"

"Mr. Pershing is visiting from Texas," she said.

"Him and half the state, feels like." Bob gave Gerald a last dismissive look, then stomped out.

"So nice to meet you, Mr. Pershing. I'm Cassandra Wynock, the town librarian." Cassie extended her hand, palm down, as if she expected Gerald to kiss it. Her cheeks were pink and while she didn't exactly flutter her eyelashes, the suggestion was there.

"Nice to meet you, too, Miss Wynock," Gerald said.

He shook the offered hand but didn't linger over it. Lucille fought back the urge to toss Cassie out onto the sidewalk by her ear. It had been years, but she recognized jealousy tightening her stomach and lending a sour taste to her mouth—a particularly ugly and useless emotion.

"I stopped by to see if you'd be free for dinner tomorrow evening."

Cassie's frigid silence alerted Lucille that Gerald was speaking to her. Her cheeks heated, and she busied herself straightening the stack of newspapers on the counter, avoiding his gaze. They'd had lunch once already—not a real date, just two acquaintances running into each other at the Last Dollar Café and agreeing to share a table. But the encounter had left Lucille feeling sixteen again. Well, maybe not sixteen. Some of the ideas she had when she thought about Gerald wouldn't have entered her head at sixteen. Maybe twenty-six, then. Old enough to know what's what and young enough to get it.

But who said she was too old to get it—whatever "it" turned out to be? Sex? Companionship? Love? Aware of Cassie staring at her, she smiled at Gerald. "Dinner sounds wonderful."

"About those shelves . . ." Like a Rottweiler who'd grabbed hold of Lucille's shirttail, Cassie refused to let go.

"I'll send someone over to the library tomorrow to take a look at the shelves," Lucille said, glaring at her.

Cassie ignored the look, offering her schoolgirl smile once more to Gerald. "I was telling the mayor the library is in serious need of new shelving. The ones we have are a danger to the patrons."

"That does sound serious." He looked sympathetic, but his eyes found Lucille's and he lowered one lid in the suggestion of a wink.

Lucille coughed. It was either that or burst out laughing, and laughing at Cassie was never a good idea. She had friends in county government who could make Lucille's life uncomfortable. Right now, thanks to Gerald's sympathy, Cassie looked triumphant. "You've got to find room in the budget to replace those shelves," she said.

"Submit your request in writing and the town council will take it under consideration at our next meeting," Lucille said. "But if the money isn't there, it isn't there."

Cassie sniffed. "It was so nice to meet you, Mr. Pershing," she said, transforming immediately when she faced Gerald once more. "Do stop by the library. I'd love to show you around."

"If you're sure I won't be injured by falling shelves."

"I . . . well." Cassie sniffed again. "Well!" Then she hurried away, glaring at both of them over her shoulder just before she pushed out the door.

Lucille collapsed against the counter, laughing. "Gerald, you are too wicked," she said.

"It is a persistent fault." He leaned across the counter toward her, intimately close, his mouth mere inches from hers, eyes shining. She felt a thrill, the excitement of being the center of attention to the person she most wanted to be with. "You are amazing," he said. "Running a business and taking on the responsibility of overseeing the whole town . . . I don't see how you do it."

"It's not as if this business is particularly demanding. And I don't run the town—the town council does that. I'm more of an administrator."

"Still, it's a large burden for one person, especially in these perilous financial times."

Gerald had a formal, flowery way of talking that some people found off-putting, but Lucille saw it as part of his charm. He behaved like a man from an earlier, more courtly era. "The lack of money does make the job a little more stressful," she admitted. "We don't have enough money for essentials, much less extras like Cassie's library shelves."

"Much like many a personal budget, I suspect."

"Yes, I know a lot of people are hurting, which is why I hate to cut any services residents depend on."

He straightened, his expression more serious. "In my work I see it often."

Gerald had told her he was involved in investments some way. "Is your business hurting, too, with the economy?" she asked, then felt stupid for even asking. Of course it was. Whose wasn't? Even receipts at Lacy's—the kind of place people shopped when they were strapped for cash—were down.

"On the contrary. I don't like to brag, but I'm doing very well for my clients. I was lucky enough to discover a few investments that have actually grown, despite the economic difficulties in other sectors. In fact . . ." He paused, his eyes searching hers. She nodded, encouraging him to continue. "I would never presume to take advantage of your friendship," he said. "But I would love to help you out of your difficulties. I could show you some areas where the town might think about investing, where you could realize a solid return on your money quite quickly. It might be enough to help you out of your current difficulties."

The idea seemed crazy, but definitely tempting. Right now the town had its small surplus in certificates of deposit with the Eureka Bank. "I couldn't make a decision like that on my own. The town council would have to approve."

"Of course. And there'd be no obligation." He smiled, blue eyes sparkling. God, he was handsome. "I'll bring some material to dinner with me for you to look over. You can let me know and if you like, I can make a presentation to the council."

His interest in her problems touched her. She'd been alone so long—raising her daughter with little help from Olivia's father, coming to Eureka after Olivia left home, and making a life for herself here. She'd enjoyed living on her own terms, being independent. She scarcely knew how to lean on someone else anymore, but it was a surprisingly good feeling. As if the time was finally right for a little romance in her life.

CHAPTER TWO

Maggie didn't say much on the drive up to the French Mistress Mine the next day, letting Jameso carry the conversation. She gazed out the window at scenery that still took her breath away, despite its familiarity. Mountains like jagged, broken teeth jutted against a sky as blue and translucent as the finest turquoise dug from the French Mistress. Aspen glowed yellow against the darker green of conifers on the flanks of the mountains, the road a red-brown ribbon wound between the peaks. The truck engine whined as Jameso shifted into low gear to climb a steep grade.

"Most years there'd already be a foot of snow up this high," he said. "Bob's saying we might not get any snow at all before Christmas. Telluride's making snow on a few slopes, but it's not the same as the real stuff. It ices up too much."

A native of Houston, Maggie wasn't sure how she felt about snow. The longer it held off, the better, she thought, though Jameso didn't share that opinion and she wasn't in the mood to argue with him.

"You're being kind of quiet this morning," he finally

said as he turned his truck onto the dirt track that led to the mine. "You feeling okay?"

"Just a little queasy." That was true enough. Between the winding mountain roads and her misgivings about the news she had to give him, it was a wonder her breakfast was staying down.

"Are you coming down with something?" He took one hand off the steering wheel and laid it on her forehead. "You don't feel like you have a fever."

"I'll be fine." She blinked back sudden tears. His palm on her forehead had been cool and slightly rough, yet the gesture itself had been quite tender. The kind of gesture she could imagine a father making toward a daughter. Or a son. She swallowed hard. If she burst into hormonal tears here, Jameso might freak out and run the truck right off the side of the mountain. For the sake of her unborn child—and her own dignity—she had to keep it together.

"Let's go by the house first and check on things," she said.

Her father's house—her house now—was a three-room miner's shack with no two windows the same size. Solar panels, a wood stove, and a cistern provided all the comforts of home. Though her father had lived here year-round for years, the road wasn't plowed in winter and Maggie had no desire to commute to work on a snowmobile, so she'd relocated to a place in town, next door to Jameso.

Three weeks ago, they'd come up to the cabin and drained all the water lines, emptied the refrigerator, and closed everything up tight for the winter. But she felt the need to revisit the place as long as they were here. It had been the first home she'd ever had that was hers alone. She'd gone straight from her mother's house to her husband's apartment. Living on her own had been a heady sensation—a privilege she hadn't been willing to give up when Jameso asked her to move in with him. Judging by the look of relief in his eyes when she'd turned down the invitation, he wasn't ready to give up his independence either, which didn't bode well for their baby.

"I'll go around back and make sure marmots haven't gnawed the insulation off the pipes," Jameso said as he and Maggie climbed out of the truck, parked on the only semi-flat stretch of dirt in the yard.

"Marmots?"

"They like the way the insulation tastes, for some reason. Porcupines like to gnaw foundations, but since the cabin's built on rock, you don't have to worry about that."

"Between potential avalanches and rock slides, lightning storms and attacks by wildlife, it's a wonder anyone ever even tried to live up here," she said.

"Nature's always trying to take back its own," he said, and disappeared around the side of the cabin.

Maggie climbed the steps of the front porch, the grayed boards creaking beneath the soles of her boots. The house perched on the side of the mountain, the back porch jutting into space. She knew strong bolts kept the foundation anchored firmly to the rock, but on her first visit here she'd been sure she was in danger of sliding down into the canyon. She hadn't known anything about her father, Jake, then, but his choice of a place to live seemed to confirm the picture his lawyer had painted of a first-prize eccentric.

Maggie had spent the first night in the house—divorced, unemployed, and absolutely unsure of the future—disappointed that her inheritance was this ramshackle house and a mine that produced no gold. Yet, she'd found everything she needed to get back on her feet right here in this mountaintop cabin.

Jameso came around the side of the house. "The pipes are okay."

"Do you remember that first night we met, when you drove up here on your motorcycle?" she asked.

"You threatened me with a stick of firewood."

"You accused me of trespassing." Jake hadn't told many people he had a daughter, so when Maggie told Jameso the cabin was hers he'd thought she was lying.

"I was a goner from the moment I met you." Jameso closed the gap between them in a few strides. "You were so beautiful—and clearly scared out of your skull, but determined to be brave. Even without the firewood, you knocked me for a loop." He kissed her, his lips firm and warm against hers.

She turned away, heart fluttering wildly. *It's just the altitude,* she told herself. They were above 10,000 feet in elevation, where the air contained less oxygen, making breathing more difficult.

"Is something wrong?" Jameso's dark brows drew together, giving him a foreboding look.

"I'm just"—she looked around for some excuse that would explain her attack of nerves—"it's just sad, that's all, closing the place for winter. I really enjoyed living here. I felt like a real mountain woman." For the first time in her life she'd made her own decisions, done what she wanted. She'd come to understand why Jake had chosen to live here, surrounded by sky and mountains.

"Jake would love knowing that. This place was always special to him."

Jake had been a larger-than-life figure to everyone who knew him. The people in Eureka had filled Maggie's head with stories of things he'd done—both heroic and awful. These stories had kept company with the fantasies she'd built up over the years about the father who was only a smiling young man in a photograph to her. He'd walked out on her mother when Maggie was three days old, but before she'd died, Maggie's mother had forgiven him. Maggie had spent months uncovering Jake's story, and though she still didn't know it all, she had learned how his experiences in Vietnam had left scars that wouldn't heal—psychological wounds that made it impossible for him to stay with the ones he loved the most.

"Do you ever think much about Iraq?" she asked Jameso.

"Iraq?" His expression darkened. "Why are you talking about that now? What difference does it make?"

"I was just thinking how Vietnam messed up my dad's life so much."

He compressed his lips into a thin line. "I'm not your dad. Come on." He took her arm and they started down the path toward the mine.

The air held a winter chill at this altitude, and the wind blew from the north as they headed up the path. Maggie drew her coat tighter around her. "I'm surprised we haven't seen Winston," she said. Her father had tamed the bighorn ram by feeding it cookies, and Maggie had continued to hand out the treats.

"He's probably found some pretty little ewe to cozy up with for the winter," Jameso said.

"No more Lorna Doones."

"No, but something better." He looked back over his shoulder at her, his gaze smoldering.

She smiled in spite of herself. Jameso was an incorrigible flirt. And maybe Barb was right about him being a romantic. His declaration at the cabin just now had been unexpectedly tender.

They reached the new gate at the entrance to the mine, which Maggie had ordered to replace the old barrier after Lucas Theriot squeezed through the bars and fell down a mine shaft. "Looks good," Jameso said, giving the heavy iron a tug. The gate had narrower mesh at the bottom and wider spaces at the top to let the bats who lived in the mine fly in and out.

"That should be good, then." Jameso started to turn away and Maggie grabbed hold of his shirt and pulled him back.

"What?" His gaze searched hers, questioning.

"There's something I have to tell you." She opened her purse and he took a step back, as if prepared to run.

"What are you doing?" she asked.

"I had a woman pull a gun on me once after she said those words."

The image surprised a laugh from her. "No guns, I promise." She took out the little cardboard box that held one of the pregnancy tests and shoved it toward him.

He stared at the box but didn't take it. "What is it?"

"It's a pregnancy test. It came back positive."

"A pregnancy test?" He'd gone very white beneath the dark beard stubble.

"A *positive* pregnancy test. I'm going to have a baby. Your baby. Well, *our* baby."

He didn't say anything. He didn't even look at her, just continued to stare at the box in her hand, his mouth slightly open.

"Dammit, say something," she said.

At last, he raised his gaze to hers. "I . . . I . . ."

Then Jameso Clark, modern mountain man, ski instructor, rock climber, and all-around tough guy, sank to his knees and keeled over in a dead faint.

Olivia had the noon-to-happy hour shift by herself on Thursday. This late in the season it should have been slow, but three couples from Texas came in and all the women ordered dirty martinis, forcing Olivia to use the last of the olives. When lawyer Reggie Paxton came down from his law office next door in search of a Diet Coke, Olivia recruited him to man the bar while she went to the Last Dollar Café next door to borrow more olives.

"Do you want garlic stuffed, pimento stuffed, Kalamata, black, or green?" one of the café owners, Danielle, asked, surveying the metal shelves in the pantry behind the kitchen. Petite and curvy, her dark hair in two ponytails worn high on either side of her head, she reminded Olivia of the heroine of one of the anime novels she'd been fond of a few years back.

"Pimento stuffed," she answered. "One jar should be plenty. We don't get that much call for martinis. I'll pay you back when we get our next grocery order."

"No problem." Danielle handed over the jar of olives.

"Hey, Olivia. You're just the woman we wanted to see." Janelle, Danielle's partner in business and in life, leaned around the door. Tall and willowy, her white-blond locks cut short and wound with a pink bandana, she resembled a Bond girl, complete with an alluring German accent.

"Me?" Olivia clutched the jar of olives to her chest. Her high-school principal and more than one former boss used to say the same thing when they were about to chew her out, but Danielle and Janelle were both smiling.

"We've decided we want to paint a mural on the back wall of the dining room," Danielle said. "Something depicting the history of Eureka."

"We don't want to paint it," Janelle corrected. "We want to hire someone to paint it for us."

"That's a good idea," Olivia said. Not that she'd ever given the décor of the restaurant much thought. And she didn't care much about the history of the town, though Lucas was into that kind of thing. He'd spent much of the summer researching local Indian tribes and mining and stuff.

"So you'll do it?" Danielle asked.

"Do what?"

"Paint the mural. We'll pay you, of course." The dimples on either side of Danielle's mouth deepened along with her smile.

"You want *me* to paint a mural in the restaurant?" Olivia almost dropped the olives, she was so surprised.

"Sure," Janelle said. "D. J. said he thought you'd be interested."

"D. J.?" Her head swam. Why had D. J. been talking to the café owners about her?

"We told him we were looking for an artist and he recommended you," Danielle said. "He said you were really talented."

"I've always admired the jewelry you make and the T-shirts you paint and stuff," Janelle added.

Olivia fingered the dangling earrings she'd beaded, then smoothed the front of her T-shirt, a plain white T she'd decorated with a painting of a columbine. Just last week a tourist had asked where she could get one like it. But instead of thanking Janelle for the compliment, what came out was, "D. J. said I was talented?"

"He did," Danielle said. "So, will you take the job?"

The thought of having a whole wall to cover with paint—and in such a public place—both intimidated and excited her. She'd always had a secret dream of making a living as an artist, but she'd never told a soul. How had D. J. known?

Both women stared at her, expressions expectant. "Okay. Do you know what you want?"

"We thought you could work up some drawings for us to look at and we'll pick one," Danielle said.

"And tell us your price," Janelle added.

"I guess I could do that." Could she? She hadn't a clue how to begin, but she wasn't about to pass up a chance like this.

"No hurry," Danielle said. "Maybe some time in the next week or two."

"Okay." Numb, the jar of olives still clutched tightly to her chest, she turned to leave. "Thanks."

D. J. was just climbing out of his truck in front of the Dirty Sally when Olivia came down the walk from the café. Still basking in the warm glow of the girls' flattery, she forgot to be angry at him.

"Hey, Olivia," he said.

"Hey, D. J."

"You're looking happy about something," he said, following her into the bar. The three couples from Texas were still at their table near the front window, laughing about something. Bob had showed up and sat at the bar, talking to Reggie. Everything was the same as any other afternoon in the Dirty Sally, but for Olivia everything was different.

She turned to face D. J. "Thanks for suggesting me to Danielle and Janelle to paint their mural," she said.

"They gave you the job, then?"

"Yeah, I'm going to do some drawings and get back to them. I figure Lucas can help me with the local history stuff."

"He told me he did a bunch of research for a project in school."

"His teacher's idea to keep him out of trouble. He's so damn smart." Pride for her kid mingled with her own sudden happiness and she didn't even try to hold back a smile.

"He is that. I'm glad you're going to paint the mural. You deserve to have more people see your talent."

"I can't believe you even noticed." For the first time in a long time she let herself meet his gaze. "It's not like I was always painting or anything."

"No, but you couldn't sit still for five minutes without doodling some little drawing, and you always put your own artistic touch on things, like that shirt you're wearing. I'll bet you painted that."

"Yeah." She smoothed the shirt again, once more uncomfortable with the intensity of his gaze. She set the olives on the bar. "Well, thanks anyway for recommending me."

"You're welcome. I just came from the county offices. I got a job driving a snowplow."

"What do you know about driving a snowplow?" Until he'd moved to Connecticut, D. J. had spent most of his life in Texas and Oklahoma, where they never got enough snow to plow.

"I drove heavy equipment in Iraq. A snowplow is just another big machine."

Snowplowing jobs were some of the best paying in the county, or so the guys who propped up the bar said. The work involved early hours and long treks into the mountains to clear high passes. At least one plow driver was pushed over the side each year by avalanches. Most survived the trip, but a monument up on Black Mountain Pass testified to all those who hadn't made it.

She pushed such macabre thoughts aside. "Bob says the snow is late this year, so you might not have any work."

"I'll find ways to keep myself busy."

She couldn't look at him anymore. He made her feel too weak-kneed and uncertain. "Yeah, well, thanks again. I better get to work."

"I'll see you around." He turned and strode out of the bar, a big man with broad shoulders and a cocky attitude that alternately drove her crazy and melted her heart.

Only after the door closed behind him did she wonder why he'd stopped by the bar this afternoon. He hadn't stayed to drink. Could it be he'd stopped to see her—to tell her about his new job, maybe, or to try again to persuade her to end the hostilities between them? Just because she'd been civil to him, she didn't hope he thought that meant they could be friends. She wasn't ready—would never be ready—to be that close to him again.

She retreated behind the bar and put the jar of olives on the shelf. "Thanks for holding down the fort, Reggie." The stocky, bearded lawyer looked more like a biker than an attorney, but she couldn't picture some dark-suited legal brain fitting in in this town that had made a virtue of informality.

"No problem. If I ever decide to give up the law, I can start a second career as a bartender."

"If you do, I'll have to start drinking somewhere else," Bob said. "Having to look at you every day would spoil the taste of the beer."

"I imagine you wouldn't be the only one to complain," Reg said. "Olivia here is a sight better looking than I am, I'll agree."

"Where have you been anyway?" Bob asked. "Reg doesn't have any idea how to put a decent head on a draft beer."

"I had to run next door for a jar of olives."

"Olives!" Bob's expression grew more sour than usual. "Fruit and vegetables don't belong in liquor."

"Now, Bob. Some people like to feel they're getting a little more sustenance with their drinks," Reggie said.

"That's what the pretzels and popcorn and beer nuts are for."

"Janelle and Danielle have asked me to paint a mural on the back wall of the café." Reggie and Bob weren't her first choice for confidants, but she couldn't keep the news to herself anymore.

"A mural?" Bob asked. "What of?"

"They want something depicting the history of Eureka."

"That's a great idea," Reggie said. "Congratulations."

"I'd like to see that," Bob said. "Give me something to look at over my eggs beside last year's feed calendar."

Olivia waited, but neither of them said anything about it being odd for the girls to hire her or acted surprised that she'd been the one to get the job.

"Guess this means you're staying in town after all," Reggie said.

"Yeah, I guess it does."

"Say, maybe you can help me with my new project," Bob said.

His words brought her back down toward earth. Even though she hadn't been in town that long, she'd heard enough about Bob's "projects" to make her wary. "What's that?"

"Janelle and Danielle said I could start a pool at the Last Dollar for folks to guess when the first snow will fall in Eureka. But I need somebody to make up a chart with all the dates and names. Maybe you could do that for me."

"Uh-huh. How much are you paying?"

"I'm not paying anything." Bob assumed a look of martyred superiority. "This is a civic project to benefit the town. I thought maybe you'd do it out of a sense of community."

Olivia opened her mouth to tell him she didn't have a sense of community, that she wasn't really part of the town, she was only passing through. But that wasn't exactly true anymore, was it? The people in Eureka were involving her in their lives whether she wanted them to or not. Just last week one of Lucas's teachers had asked her to volunteer at some harvest festival thing the school was having. And today Janelle and Danielle had asked her to paint the mural. People treated her as if she belonged here.

Her stomach fluttered at the thought. Olivia Theriot, citizen of a hick town like Eureka, Colorado? Six months ago, if anyone had suggested such a thing, she'd have laughed them out of the room.

How scary was it that now she actually—sort of— liked the idea?

"I'm fine." Jameso sat up and clutched the side of his head, which had hit the ground hard when he fainted.

"You're not fine. You passed out." Maggie pried his

hand away from his face and frowned at the golf-ball-sized knot rising above his temple. "Your head must have hit a rock."

"I'm fine," he said again more forcefully. "It was just the shock, that's all. You shouldn't spring a thing like that on a guy all of a sudden."

"What was I supposed to do?" She sat back on her heels. "Suggest a game of twenty questions? Guess what I've got cooking in the oven?"

He stared at her belly, the lines on his forehead forming a deep V. "Are you really pregnant?"

"No, I made it up to scare you. Yes, I'm pregnant. Three pregnancy tests all came up positive."

"When's it due?" He still wasn't smiling, and she wasn't sure she liked the way he said "it," as if he was referring to an alien or something.

She stood and stared down on him, at the crooked part in his hair and the cowlick at the crown. Would her baby have a cowlick like that? "I won't know for sure until I see a doctor. I have an appointment in Montrose next week. But I'm guessing around the first of June."

"Wow."

"Is that all you can say? Wow?"

"What do you want me to say?"

That he was happy. Thrilled, even. That he loved her. Instead, he couldn't even look her in the eye.

"You could come up with something better than 'wow.' " She turned away, arms folded across her chest. She'd so hoped he wouldn't disappoint her this way; though obviously, she'd been delusional. He was a man, and men disappointed her. At least all the ones she'd been involved with so far. Why should Jameso be different?

"Now you're angry." He got his feet under him and stood. "You're not giving me enough time to absorb the information."

"Take me home," she said.

"This is a big shock," he said. "I never thought."

"Did you think I was too old to get pregnant?" She was eight years older than Jameso, something that had worried her from the beginning, though he and Barb had both told her it didn't make any difference. But maybe it had. Maybe he liked her being older because he'd thought it made her safe from complications like this.

"I never thought about it one way or another." He put his hand on her shoulder, the touch almost tentative. "When we made love, the last thing on my mind was babies."

She hadn't been thinking about babies then either. Jameso Clark, naked, did not bring to mind images of cuddly infants in diapers. She fought to ignore the rush of heat at those memories. "You'd better think about it now," she said. "It's happening."

He bent and kissed her cheek, the softness of his goatee brushing her face. "I just need a little more time to think."

To think about what? Was he going to ride off on that motorcycle and never come back—the way her father had run away after she was born? Jameso had been Jake's best friend in Eureka. She'd heard enough stories to see how much the two men had in common. Maybe an aversion to parenthood was another thing they shared.

She cradled her stomach and closed her eyes. She hadn't planned on being a single mother, but she could do it if she had to.

"What's wrong?" Jameso asked, his face growing pale again. "Are you in pain?"

Only in my heart, she thought. "Take me home," she said again.

"Maybe you shouldn't be alone. Do you want me to call someone?"

She noticed he wasn't offering to stay with her himself. She met his worried gaze with a freezing look. "No, you don't need to call anyone. I'm pregnant. I'm not ill. And I'll take care of this baby just fine. By myself."

Without waiting for him to answer, she stalked ahead of him toward his truck. She didn't need him. She'd done fine without her father. Without Carter, her first husband. She'd do fine with this baby. Barb was right. She had a lot of friends. She had a whole town that would help her.

CHAPTER THREE

Lucille sat at the old-fashioned dressing table and tried not to notice the lines feathering out from the corners of her eyes and along the sides of her mouth as she put the finishing touches on her makeup. Those lines hadn't been there the last time she'd been on a date. Then again, she was pretty sure Reagan was president the last time she had a date, and all her dresses and tops had big shoulder pads.

Gerald obviously didn't mind a few lines. After all, he looked older than she was and he'd asked her out. She picked up a pair of earrings and held them up to her cheek. She'd borrowed them from Olivia's room, thinking the long beaded dangles matched her outfit, but now she wondered if the long strands of beads emphasized the length of her face—or worse, that they looked too young. As if she was trying too hard.

"What are you doing?"

The mirror reflected Olivia, who was leaning in the doorway, frowning. The girl frowned too much. All right, she was a grown woman, but she'd always be a girl to her mother. "I have a date," Lucille said. "I was trying to decide if these earrings look ridiculous."

"Those are my earrings."

Lucille laid them aside and reached for her usual pearl drops. "Yes, and I think they look much better on you."

"Who are you going out with?" Olivia moved into the room and stood at Lucille's shoulder.

"His name is Gerald Pershing. He's visiting here in town."

"I know who you're talking about. He's been in the Dirty Sally. He drinks scotch. Dewar's with water, no ice."

Lucille shouldn't have been surprised; everyone made it into the town's only bar eventually. Even teetotalers ventured in to eat burgers or grilled cheese sandwiches on Tuesday nights when the Last Dollar was closed.

"What did you think of him?" She kept her voice light, but held her breath as she waited for the answer, watching Olivia's face in the mirror.

Olivia wrinkled her nose. "He's too slick and charming. And those teeth have got to be caps."

"There's nothing wrong with a man who cares about his appearance."

"I guess not. But I don't trust him." She looked her mother up and down. "I don't remember you going out with anyone since I've been here."

"I haven't dated anyone in years." She swiveled on the vanity stool to face her daughter. "Any advice?"

"Don't sleep with him on the first date, but if you do, make him wear a condom. You probably don't have to worry about getting pregnant at your age, but you don't want to catch some nasty disease."

Lucille suspected Olivia was trying to shock her mother. The young woman had certainly dated her share of men in the five months she'd been in town. Maybe she'd slept with a few of them. Though, come to think of it, she hadn't gone out with anyone since D. J. had arrived in Eureka. "I'll remember that," she said drily.

"Where's Lucas?" Olivia asked.

"Up in his room, reading, I think. Where have you been?" Lucille couldn't help noticing that Olivia's truck—D. J.'s truck—hadn't been parked in its usual place outside the Dirty Sally when she passed on her way home.

"Out."

Just like that, the wall was up—the one Olivia had always been good at putting between herself and her mother. Lucille knew better than to fight her. She turned back to the mirror and tugged at a stubborn curl over her left eye. "There's frozen lasagna if you want to fix that for your and Lucas's dinner. Don't wait up for me. I might be late." The smugness she felt in saying these last words was probably immature and unbecoming, but it felt good nonetheless. How many times over the years had Olivia said those words, leaving her mother home to worry and wonder?

Not that Lucille expected her daughter to worry, or even wonder. She doubted Olivia cared much about her mother's social life.

"If you need anything, call me."

The words, the ones she herself had spoken countless times—almost always to Olivia's back as she walked out the door—startled her. She studied her daughter's reflection in the mirror for any sign of sarcasm but saw none. She swiveled the stool around again and stood. "I'll be fine," she said. "Gerald's a nice man."

"They all seem nice at first."

She recognized the cynicism, too—one part her own despair after her marriage to Olivia's father, Mitch, crashed down around her and one part the result of Olivia's own tumultuous relationships with the men in her life. "When you're young, it can feel that way," she said. "Getting older makes you a little more forgiving."

Olivia straightened, arms uncrossed. "Forgiveness is overrated."

She left the doorway, her footsteps making a faint, shuffling sound as she retreated down the hallway to the stairs. If Lucille had thought Olivia would listen, she'd have told her forgiveness hurt less than holding a grudge. But she knew sometimes holding a grudge was all that held you up. After Mitch left, the anger was all that kept her going sometimes—the desire to prove to him how much she didn't need him. It had been years before she realized he hadn't been watching, that he'd stopped caring long before she did.

Whatever D. J. had done, he'd hurt Olivia badly. Lucille liked the serious young man, and Lucas practically worshiped him, though Olivia could scarcely stand to look at him. But when she did, Lucille recognized the longing there. Her love hadn't yet burned out. Lucille remembered the words D. J. had said when they'd met—the night Lucas was trapped in the French Mistress Mine. How he'd loved Olivia the first time he saw her.

It was a foolish, romantic notion—that love could bloom from just one glance, like a spark setting a forest fire. But it was an idea Lucille wanted to believe in, for Olivia's sake and for her own. She was tired of being cynical and scoffing. After so many years alone, she wanted to believe in the possibility of love.

Olivia watched the red convertible pull away, her mom in the passenger seat, laughing at something the silver-haired man behind the wheel had said. Honestly, a convertible! Could this Gerald character be any more of a cliché?

"Where's Grandma going?" Lucas joined her at the window, watching the retreating car. He'd shot up over the summer, until he was almost as tall as she was. Soon he'd overtake and pass her. His father had been tall. Still was, she guessed. She hadn't laid eyes on him in eleven years and didn't care to, but if he'd died, someone would probably have notified her.

"She's going on a date," she said.

"A date?" Lucas's eyes widened behind the round glasses.

She turned and headed for the kitchen. Lucas followed. "Who's she going on a date with?"

"A guy named Gerald Pershing. He's visiting in town."

"Does he know she's the mayor?"

"I imagine he does."

"It seems funny to think of Grandma dating."

"Because she's the mayor?"

"Because she's Grandma." He tilted his head to the side, thinking. He reminded her of an owl, eyes magnified behind the glasses, tufts of blond hair sticking up like feathers. Except he looked less babyish these days, more evidence of the man who'd one day be breaking through. She wanted to shake him and tell him to stop. She'd barely gotten the hang of being a mother to a little boy; she hadn't the slightest idea how to cope with someone older.

"I guess Grandma is kind of pretty," he said.

Lucille wasn't classically pretty; she was too tall and raw-boned for that. But she had a striking quality and an elegance she'd grown into. The face that had looked back at Olivia in the dressing table mirror this evening had indeed been beautiful.

"Yes, I guess she is," Olivia said. She took the lasagna from the freezer and flipped the package over to read the directions.

"We should eat the fish I caught," Lucas said.

"Your grandmother can cook the fish tomorrow. Tonight we're having lasagna."

"D. J. told me how to cook it. He said to stuff it with lemon and butter and wrap it in foil and bake it."

When they'd been together, D. J. had done most of the cooking. He was much better at it than she was. "That sounds good," she said. "I'll let your grandmother know."

She set the oven for 400 degrees and slid the block of frozen pasta from the package.

"D. J. is going to teach me how to tie flies. You use real bird feathers and stuff."

D. J. again. Lucas would talk about nothing else if she didn't change the subject. "Janelle and Danielle are hiring me to paint a mural on the back wall of the Last Dollar," she said.

"That's cool." Lucas helped himself to a banana from the basket on the counter. She started to tell him he'd spoil his supper but bit back the words. One banana wasn't going to dull his appetite; he ate everything in sight these days.

"You're not surprised they asked me instead of some professional artist?" she asked.

"You're as good as any professional."

He thought that? Really? She couldn't hold back a grin. "I'll need you to help me decide what to draw. I don't know much about the history of Eureka."

"You should put in the Native Americans who first settled here—the Uncompahgre. And the gold miners." He made a face. " 'Course, Miss Wynock is going to want her family in there somewhere."

"Miss Wynock?" Olivia couldn't place the name. Not a patron of the Dirty Sally, then.

"The librarian. Her family supposedly founded the town. It was all in the play I was supposed to be in at the Hard Rock Days festival."

Of course—that Miss Wynock. How could Olivia forget? The woman had been a tyrant about that damn play, and she'd practically busted a blood vessel when Lucas had failed to show up to play his part in the Founders' Day Pageant. He hadn't made the play because he'd been trapped in the French Mistress Mine up on Mount Garnet. Olivia had been too worried about his absence to pay much attention to the play.

Right now she couldn't imagine anything more boring than a bunch of historical people painted on a wall. She wanted something bright and interesting—something that captured the wild, beautiful nature of this corner of the world. "If I'm painting this mural, I guess I get to say who's in it and who isn't," Olivia said. "Well . . . and Danielle and Janelle, since they're paying for it."

"Then they probably don't want Miss Wynock's grandfather in their mural," Lucas said. "I don't think they like her much."

"They don't?"

Lucas tossed the banana peel in the trash and looked around the room, she suspected for something else to eat. "Nobody much does," he said. "She's kind of a grouchy old lady, though she does know a lot about history. She helped me find books about Native Americans and stuff."

"So she likes you."

He shrugged. "I guess."

Olivia was intrigued by the idea of a friendship between the grouchy librarian and her son, whom she'd always thought of as socially awkward. Not that Lucas wasn't a sweet boy, but he was so damned smart he put people off, spouting knowledge about everything under the sun. And he wasn't afraid to challenge adults if he thought they were wrong. No one liked their errors pointed out to them this way, especially by a kid.

"Do you like her?" Olivia asked.

"She's not so bad, really. Just kind of bossy. And I think she's lonely."

Olivia's chest tightened—in sympathy? Or maybe empathy? She'd had her share of lonely nights, but who hadn't?

She knew a lot more people who were alone than to-gether—her mother, Bob, and most of the other regulars at the Dirty Sally, to name a few.

Even D. J., she guessed. Though if he was alone, it was by his own choice. She'd never asked him to run off to Iraq. He could have stayed with her if he'd really wanted.

Better to be alone than with someone she couldn't de-pend on.

"You could put Jake Murphy on your mural," Lucas said.

She forced her thoughts away from D. J. "Who's Jake Murphy?"

"He's Maggie Stevens's father. He owned the French Mistress Mine and lived in that cabin up on Mount Gar-net. I guess he was kind of a hermit."

"Why would I want to put a hermit on the mural?" she asked.

"He won the Hard Rock Mining competition three times, and I guess he did a lot of other stuff."

"And he was a hermit."

"Well, yeah. I mean, he lived way up on the mountain by himself. I guess a lot of the pioneers did that kind of thing—came here to get away from the city and people and stuff."

So much for Bob's boasting about the sense of com-munity in Eureka. The real driving force behind the town was independence—all those miners who staked their claims on mountaintops and dug for gold. They weren't banding together for a common dream. They were each out to get their own.

They were all loners. And probably lonely, though maybe that was beside the point. She had a theme for her mural. She'd do a tribute to independence—all those sin-gletons who didn't need anybody else to succeed.

* * *

Eureka's only steak restaurant closed after Labor Day and the owners returned to Arizona for the winter. So Gerald drove Lucille to Montrose, to a new French bistro off the square. They were one of only two couples in the place on Friday night, which, Lucille reflected, probably had more to do with the economy than the quality of the food. She was sure of this when she saw the prices on the menu. She might have suspected a man from Eureka of trying to impress her, but Gerald probably ate at fancy restaurants every week back home in Texas. He was clearly a man who enjoyed the finer things in life.

"You look beautiful tonight," he said, once they were seated and had placed their orders. He lifted a glass of the French wine he'd chosen. "Not that you aren't always lovely, but it's such a pleasure to see you dressed up."

She resisted the urge to put a hand to the collar of the silk blouse she'd pulled from the back of her closet. "Thank you. I don't have much occasion in Eureka to wear fancier clothes." And she never thought of herself as a fancy clothes type of person. Jeans and prairie skirts, flannel shirts and sweaters were both comfortable and practical, and good enough for her.

"Not even in your duties as Madam Mayor?" His eyes twinkled in amusement. Tonight he wore a western-cut suit of gray wool with black felt lapels and collar, and a cream silk shirt and string tie with a silver and turquoise slide. His black felt hat had a matching silver and turquoise band. He left the hat on while they ate—a habit Lucille had noted in Texans.

"The mayor's job in Eureka consists mainly of presiding over the town council meetings, juggling paperwork, and wrangling with the state over money."

"Ah, money." He nodded sagely. "A concern for everyone these days."

"Let's not talk about that right now," she said. She

wanted to believe Gerald was interested in her for herself, that this was a real date, not a business meeting.

"Of course. We're here to enjoy each other's company." He reached across the table and took her hand. His palm was smooth and cool against her flesh. He trailed his thumb across her wrist, a feathery, tingling touch that left her breathless.

"How much longer do you plan to be here?" She wished she could take the words back as soon as they were out of her mouth. At her age, why couldn't she keep her anxieties to herself? What did it matter if he didn't plan to stick around? Couldn't she enjoy being with him right now, without worrying about what might happen later?

But the question didn't faze him. He continued to stroke his thumb back and forth across her wrist in the hypnotic way. "I'm self-employed," he said. "I make my own schedule. I can stay as long as I like. As long as there's something here that interests me. Or someone."

Surely he could feel the way her pulse raced at his words. And he definitely could see the hot blush she knew stained her cheeks. She tried desperately to think of some casual, even coy reply. Some flirtatious remark to show she played these kinds of games all the time. But words failed her. She had zero experience playing fast and loose with emotions, or pretending her attraction to him was of no consequence. She didn't do romance anymore and had no idea what was expected of her.

He released her hand and sat back, his expression impassive. She thought at first her silence had offended him, then realized the waiter had arrived with their food. She looked down at what might be the smallest chicken breast she'd ever seen, garnished with a single boiled potato, three spears of asparagus, and an artful swirl of sauce. Her stomach growled and she thought longingly of Janelle and

Danielle's overflowing platters of southern fried chicken or pot roast and gravy.

Gerald's *biftek* looked only slightly more substantial, but he sliced into it with gusto. "I'm seriously thinking about relocating to the area," he said as he dabbed delicately at his lower lip between bites. "Not to Eureka, necessarily, but perhaps to Telluride. The demographics there seem favorable for the investment services I offer."

In other words, he was looking for rich people with lots of money to invest. Telluride had plenty of those, and she could easily picture Gerald, in his ostrich boots and tailored suits, mingling with the rich and famous who filled what had once been a humble village favored by hippies, but was now a posh ski town and summer retreat for the elite.

So what was he doing having dinner with her? She pushed the thought aside. She wasn't rich, or one of the beautiful people, but why shouldn't Gerald be interested in her? She was smart, reasonably attractive, and there was definitely a certain . . . chemistry between them.

She smiled in what she hoped was an alluring fashion. "I hope you do stay around. I'd like to see more of you."

His expanded grin sent another surge of heat through her. "Do you know what I like about you, Lucille? What attracted me to you from the very first?"

"What is that?" Who wouldn't want to know the answer to such a question?

"You're a woman who knows what she wants. You're strong and independent, and you're not afraid to take what you need from life. You live on your own terms."

"How else would I live?" Everything he said about her was true, but it wasn't as if she'd had a choice to live any other way. Mitch had left her when she was twenty-two, with a daughter to raise and no money or education. She'd had to push forward and make her way the best she could, with no one to depend on but herself.

"In my business I meet plenty of women who are little more than beautiful ornaments. They're rich men's trophies who have put aside their own careers and ambitions for the promise of wealth and a secure future."

"Surely not all rich women are like that." She felt the need to defend her own sex. "Many of them have successful careers, and their own money."

"Some, yes, but not the ones I most often deal with."

"That says more about your clients than the women," she said.

He inclined his head in agreement and refilled their wineglasses. "Still, it's not often that I meet a female of your caliber. There's a definite sex appeal in an independent woman."

Well, he certainly believed in bringing things out in the open, didn't he, mentioning sex this early in the evening. She thought ruefully of Olivia's advice, said only half in jest: *Don't sleep with him on the first date, but if you do, make him wear a condom.* She gulped her wine, determined to drive out the images the words brought to mind. She most definitely was not going to sleep with Gerald tonight.

Not yet.

"This chicken is very good," she said, slicing what was left of the bird into ever-tinier pieces.

"Don't worry, Lucille. I won't try to rush you into anything." Gerald's voice was a velvety caress. "I merely wanted to make clear my interest in you."

He was a man. Of course he was interested in sex, she told herself. Still, he had his choice in women and he was telling her he'd chosen her. The knowledge made her feel shaky, as if she'd ventured out onto a thin shelf of rock on the side of a mountain. It had been a very long time since she'd been so daring.

"I'm very flattered," she managed to say after another

sip of wine. "Why don't we get to know each other a little better first?"

Over the remainder of the meal she learned he was divorced, with one grown son in Dallas and a grandchild on the way. He'd been in business for himself for twenty years, having worked for a large investment firm for fifteen years before that. He liked to sail, and had made several trips to Europe and Japan. He had a house in Dallas and another in Tucson, and made frequent trips to Vegas, where he did well at the poker tables.

"I think I owe my success with investments in my ability to assess risk and my willingness to take chances," he said as they sipped coffee over dessert. Well, Lucille had a child-sized serving of chocolate mousse while he sipped brandy with his coffee. "It's why I've succeeded—and helped my clients succeed—in spite of the current economic downturn."

"You mentioned you might be able to help Eureka?" Despite her earlier reluctance to talk business, it seemed a safer subject than the more dangerous—dangerous to her equilibrium, at least—topic that still lurked beneath all their small talk. "Do you work with city governments often?"

"I handle investments for more than a dozen small- to medium-sized communities in Texas and Arizona," he said. He leaned forward, elbows on the table, expression earnest. "I look at the funds you have available and your financial goals, and match that with investments that will give you a better return than any bank."

"How do you find such investments? I mean, if they're out there, why isn't everyone taking advantage of them?"

"I use my contacts in Europe and Asia. I find emerging industries, as well as successful established firms that are in need of investment capital and are willing to sell stocks with a very favorable rate of return. And there can be tax advantages as well."

He sat back. "I won't bore you with the details, but if you're interested, I'd be happy to make a presentation to your town council. I think you'll be impressed with what I have to offer."

Did she imagine the double entendre in his words? She almost laughed but managed to rein in what he might mistake for hysteria. "Why don't you work up a presentation for our board meeting next week? I'll put you on the agenda."

"Wonderful. In the meantime"—he stood and offered her his hand—"let's go for a drive."

The night was chilly, so he put the top up on the car. She sat primly on her side of the vehicle, belted in. But he drove with one hand, the other firmly clasping hers. On the outskirts of Eureka, he turned onto the road up Black Mountain Pass and pulled in at the overlook. The valley spread out before them, the lights of Eureka a scattering of glitter amidst the shadows of rocks and trees.

Lucille stared out at the scene, her breathing shallow, anticipation filling her as if she'd swallowed a helium balloon. The tension between what her mind wanted and what her body demanded pulled her taut.

"Look at me, darling." Gerald spoke in a whisper and caressed her cheek with one finger.

She turned toward him and his lips covered hers, gentle yet firm, leaving no doubt that he wanted her. She gasped with surprise and pleasure at the intense rush of feeling. Oh, God, had anything ever felt this good?

He deepened the kiss, exploring her mouth with his tongue, and she responded in kind, pressing her body to his, blood humming in her ears.

He cupped her breast, massaging gently. She trembled, the intensity of her feelings frightening her a little. What was happening to her? She wasn't some virgin who didn't know her own body.

She shifted, trying to put a little distance between

them, to clear her head a little. But he didn't take the hint. Instead, he deftly undid the top button of her blouse.

"Gerald, no." She pushed him away.

He smiled down at her. "Not very gentlemanly of me, I suppose, bringing you here to neck like a teenager. But you make me feel that way, wanting you so much I can scarcely control myself."

Though he'd probably intended the words as a compliment to fuel her passion, they reminded her of the boys of her youth, trying to convince her they'd die if she didn't give them what they wanted. Even then, she'd known there was no real emotion behind the words. The thought was enough to quell her passion. "It's getting late," she said. "I think you should take me home."

His smile didn't waver. He started the car. "Or we could go to my place instead. I have a very comfortable bed."

She laughed. Give the man points for frankness. "We hardly know each other."

"Never on a first date, is that it?" He winked at her. "The older I get, the more impatient I become, I suppose. But I won't rush you. I merely wanted to make my feelings clear."

"You have." She buckled her seat belt with a decisive *snap!* "I prefer to take things more slowly." When she did decide to welcome a man into her bed again, it would be one she knew well enough to be comfortable showing off her less-than-perfect body and rusty technique.

Which didn't mean Gerald wasn't a strong candidate for the privilege. But if he intended to stay in town for a while, they had plenty of time. Time for her to lose a few pounds.

And to buy a box of condoms.

* * *

Of all the men in Maggie's life at the moment, the one who was at the same time the most aggravating and the easiest to deal with was her boss at the *Eureka Miner*, Rick Otis. Within two days of taking the job as the paper's only reporter, she'd sized him up as bombastic, antagonistic, sarcastic, chauvinistic, and completely harmless. A thin man with a tonsure of graying hair and a slight paunch, he nevertheless managed to fill a space with his presence. Several times a week he ranted around the office about one issue or another, running his fingers through his hair until he resembled a demented professor. He swore and fussed and demanded Maggie write this preposterous story or that. She'd learned to focus on her computer screen and ignore him. As soon as he calmed down he'd rescind all previous orders for inflammatory stories and accept whatever she had chosen to write about instead with surprising equanimity.

He was also a relentless tease who took an inordinate interest in Maggie's personal life—particularly her romance with Jameso Clark.

"I just saw Jameso headed out of town on that hog of his," Rick announced the afternoon following Maggie's conversation with Jameso at the mine. Rick knew very well that Jameso's bike wasn't a Harley. It was a 1948 Indian Chief, a rare and prized model, at least according to Jameso. But since it annoyed him to hear Rick call his beloved vehicle a hog, Rick went out of his way to do so, even when Jameso wasn't around to hear him.

Maggie kept her gaze focused on her computer screen. She absolutely would not show she had any interest in what Jameso was up to. Rick would seize on the slightest show of concern on her part and nag her to distraction. He was very like a mad scientist in that respect, dissecting human emotion.

"Where's he headed?"

Where *was* he headed? Away? When her ex-husband

had shown up in town this summer, Jameso had responded by disappearing for two weeks. Running away—he said because his feelings for Maggie scared him. Looking at him, you'd never think a man like Jameso would be a coward, but there you had it. "I have no idea where he was going. I don't keep up with his schedule."

"You don't?" Rick moved to stand directly behind her computer monitor, the green plaid of his flannel shirt filling her field of vision. "I thought all women kept tabs on their lovers. To make sure they were following the straight and narrow and not getting into trouble."

"Since when do you know anything about women?" As far as she knew, Rick had no romantic interests in town. He made a show of ogling pretty tourists, and Maggie was pretty sure he wasn't gay, but he was also apparently celibate, or incredibly discreet, not an easy feat to accomplish in such a small town.

"I know enough about women to keep from getting entangled with them," he said. "Lessons learned the hard way, I might add."

"Oh." This was interesting. Rick rarely talked about himself. "And how is that?"

"Don't try to change the subject," he said. "We were talking about you."

"We were? I thought we were talking about Jameso."

"Same difference. You and he are a couple. Don't bother trying to deny it."

"I wasn't going to." After all, she lived next door to Jameso. They went out together often and regularly spent the night at each other's houses—things they never tried to hide. They'd had what Maggie saw as a comfortable—and comforting—relationship. Good conversation, great sex, no pressure.

But a baby had a way of exerting a whole new force on a relationship. Enough to tear them apart? She supposed that was up to Jameso.

"So when are you two getting married?"

Her heart lunged like a racehorse at the starting gate. "Married?" The word came out in a squeak. She took a deep breath, struggling to control her emotions. "What makes you think we're getting married?"

"Oh, come on, Maggie. You're not the type to fool around with a guy just for fun. And if you'd wanted to merely live with the guy, you would have moved in with him already and saved on the rent."

Part of her suspected Rick was deliberately needling her, but she rose to the bait. "How do you know what type I am?" she snapped. "You hardly know me."

"I know you married your first husband at nineteen and you'd probably still be married to him if he hadn't left you for that heiress or whatever she is. You're the kind of woman who finds a man and sticks with him like glue."

"That doesn't sound like love—it sounds like desperation." And desperation was a word that in many ways described her marriage to Carter. She'd been desperate not to lose him and in the process had almost lost herself. A mistake she intended to never make again. "I'll have you know I'm perfectly content being single. I don't need a man to make me happy." Even as she said the words her stomach fluttered, as if the baby inside of her—surely not big enough yet for its presence to be felt—was protesting this declaration of independence. Maybe Maggie didn't need a man, but did her child need a father?

Of course, Jameso wasn't rushing to her side to declare his undying devotion to his unborn son or daughter. She hadn't seen him at all since he'd dropped her off at her house yesterday afternoon with his plea for "time to think."

She fixed her boss with a firm stare. "Rick, butt out," she said. "You're my boss, not my personal counselor."

He held up his hands in a defensive gesture that didn't

fool her for a minute. "Hey, I'm only trying to help. We look after each other around here. It's the only way to survive."

"Meddling in my business is not looking out for me. When I need your help, I'll ask for it." And he'd turn blue if he held his breath, waiting for that day.

"You know where to find me. And speak of the devil . . ."

She followed his gaze out the front window in time to see Jameso ride past—a man in black leathers, with a black helmet, on a black and silver motorcycle. Dark and sexy. Something out of a romance novel fantasy. She felt betrayed by the warmth that pooled between her thighs at the thought—and the relief that surged through her, knowing he hadn't left town for good, at least not yet.

She shut down her computer. "I'll see you tomorrow, Rick."

"Say hello to Jameso for me."

She didn't dignify this with an answer.

Jameso's motorcycle was parked in front of his house. The narrow miner's cottage was the twin to hers, with a steeply pitched roof and tiny square front porch trimmed in Victorian gingerbread. His house was painted mossy green with white trim, hers pale lavender. A light glowed in his back window—the kitchen. She resisted the urge to walk across the yard and knock on his door. She wouldn't go to him. He would have to come to her.

In the house, she changed and surveyed her figure in the mirror on the back of the bedroom door. Her stomach looked no rounder, her breasts no fuller. If not for the persistent morning sickness and the three positive tests stashed in her dresser drawer, she might have thought the pregnancy was a figment of her imagination.

A knock on the door startled her. The weight and cadence of the fist striking the wood set her blood to humming with anticipation, even as she hastily tugged on a sweatshirt and yoga pants.

"Hello, Jameso."

He stood in the open doorway, still dressed in his leathers, his shaggy hair windblown, his eyes shadowed in the yellow glow of the porch light. He had looked very much like this the first night she'd encountered him on the front porch of her father's cabin. She'd been both afraid of him and drawn to him then, just as she was now.

"Maggie, I've been thinking." He strode past her into the living room, motorcycle boots striking hard against the worn wood floor.

Well, that's what he'd said he was going to do, wasn't it? She faced him, arms crossed, waiting. He wore the grim expression of a man about to make a grave sacrifice. Maybe she should tell him there wasn't anything romantic about a martyr.

He ran one hand through his hair, nostrils flaring as he sucked in a deep breath. Tension radiated like heat from the taut set of his shoulders and the compressed line of his mouth. If she hadn't been so annoyed with him right now, she'd have been concerned he was going to stroke out from his obvious anxiety. As it was, she felt he deserved every bit of agitation, considering the distress his attitude had caused her.

But she was completely unprepared for his next move. The floor shook as he dropped to one knee in front of her and gazed up at her with a determined expression. "Maggie, will you marry me?" he asked.

CHAPTER FOUR

Maggie stared at the man who knelt on the floor in front of her. He looked about as happy as a felon on his way to the hangman's noose. "You don't really want to marry me," she said. The truth of the words made her feel cold.

He blinked. "You're going to have my baby. Of course I want to marry you."

"Get up off the floor this instant." Honestly, he looked ridiculous down there. Who had decided a proposal should be delivered from the knees? Such a declaration should be made while looking each other squarely in the eyes.

He rose in a fluid motion. "I was just trying to do this right."

Doing it right would be declaring his undying love and passion for her, not proposing because he'd knocked her up and felt an obligation. "Getting married just because I'm pregnant would be the worst idea in the world," she said.

"We wouldn't be getting married just because you're pregnant. I love you, Maggie." His tone softened, almost pleading. "You know that."

Did she know it? He'd certainly said it before—usually immediately before, during, or after sex. And he probably did have true feelings for her. But the distance between "I love you" and "I'm prepared to make a commitment to spend the rest of my life with you" was the distance between the earth and the moon.

She kept her arms folded across her chest, a barrier between them. "If I wasn't pregnant, would you still have proposed to me?"

He had the grace to look at the floor between their feet. "Maybe not this soon, but . . ."

"And I wouldn't have said yes if you had. We've barely known each other five months. My divorce has only been final seven months. I'm not ready for marriage again—and neither are you."

He nodded. "So you're turning me down?" He'd obviously come here expecting things to go one way and thought if he kept bullishly pressing forward he'd eventually get the result he wanted.

"I'm turning you down," she said. "I don't want a man who only wants to marry me out of a sense of obligation."

His eyes met hers, sadness and confusion in their brown depths. "I want to take care of you and our baby," he said.

The earnestness of his words breeched the barrier around her heart, and she felt a lump forming in her throat. *Oh, God, please don't let me start bawling,* she thought. Tears had a way of derailing any serious discussion. Not to mention if she got too emotional he was liable to flee in panic—and she wouldn't blame him if he did. She took a deep breath, marshaling control.

"I'm glad to hear it," she said gently. "And you can do that. You don't have to be a husband to be a father, any more than I have to be a wife to be a mother."

He swallowed, his Adam's apple jumping in his throat.

"I don't know anything about being a good father. My own dad did a pretty lousy job."

He'd never said a word about his father before. All she knew about his family could be summed up in a few sentences: His mother lived in Florida, he hadn't seen any of them in years, and he rarely talked to them. She had the impression he had a sister somewhere, though he never talked about his father. She resisted the urge to ask for more details; now wasn't the time.

"I don't know anything about being a mother either, but I guess we'll learn. People do it all the time." She tried to sound more confident than she felt. There was only a person's life at stake here; she could think of a hundred different ways they could screw this up.

He wore his stubborn look again. "It doesn't seem right, letting my kid be a bastard."

This surprised a laugh from her. "Hello! This is the twenty-first century. Things like that don't matter anymore."

"They matter to me."

Who would have guessed such traditional emotion ran through the heart of an avowed rebel? "Jameso, it will be all right, really."

"What about your dad?"

Her father? What did Jake have to do with this? "What about him?"

"I know he ran out on your mom right after you were born. I want to prove to you I won't be like that."

This was why she loved the man—he had a talent for getting to the heart of the matter. "Then the way to prove it is to stick around. A marriage license didn't stop my dad from leaving."

"I do love you, Maggie." He held out his arms and she went to him, the tension draining out of her as his arms encircled her.

"I know. And I love you. But that's not enough." She'd loved Carter, too. At least in the beginning. But the love hadn't lasted. She wasn't sure it ever could. And she was certain that marrying someone because you thought it was what you should do, instead of what you wanted to do, was a surefire way to kill whatever passion they shared.

"So what are we going to do now?" he asked.

"We go on the way we have been, and we'll decide how to work things out when the baby gets here. We've got seven or eight months to figure it out."

He held her tighter. "That doesn't sound like long enough to me."

Or to her, but it was seven or eight months for her and Jameso to get to know each other better and to figure out if they had a future that went beyond a shared child. A thought occurred to her and she nudged his shoulder. "Did you buy me a ring?"

"A ring?"

"An engagement ring. Did you buy me an engagement ring?" After all, he'd said he wanted to do things right.

"Uh, yeah. I went to a jeweler's in Montrose this afternoon."

That answered Rick's question about what Jameso had been up to. "Let me see."

He stepped back. "Uh-uh. You turned me down, remember?"

"Oh, come on, let me see!" She might never wear Jameso's ring, but she could at least see what he'd picked out for her.

"Nope." He shoved both hands in his pockets. Was that where he'd stashed the ring? "If I hurry, they'll probably give me my money back."

"You can still show it to me."

"No, I don't think so."

The smug look on his face infuriated her, which was, of course, the whole idea. A bit of payback, perhaps, for her turning down his proposal? Though she still didn't believe he'd actually *wanted* to marry her, she could believe his pride had been hurt, just a little. "So you really aren't going to let me see the ring?"

"Maybe one day, when you change your mind about marrying me." He bent and kissed her cheek, then walked out, leaving her to fume and to wonder. He'd sounded awfully certain, as if she really would change her mind. Or as if he really wanted her to.

"Excuse me, I'm looking for Miss Wynock?" Olivia's voice sounded too loud in the hushed confines of Eureka Library. Everything smelled of old paper and furniture polish, and had the air of a place long shut off from the world, like a mausoleum or a seldom visited museum. Olivia herself hadn't been in a library since high school, though Lucas spent hours in them, in every city in which they'd lived.

The woman behind the front desk stared at her, round-eyed behind thick glasses. "Cassie's in the back," she said in a normal tone of voice. She pointed a finger toward the back of the room. "Over in periodicals."

Olivia tiptoed between low display shelves filled with fossils and old mining tools, past a bank of personal computers and shelves filled with videos and books, to an open section of armchairs and rotating magazine racks. A thin, gray-haired woman dressed in a gray skirt and a white blouse looked up at her approach. "Miss Wynock?" Olivia asked.

"Yes?"

"I'm Olivia Theriot. Lucas's mother."

"If he's done something wrong, I certainly had nothing to do with it," Cassie snapped. "The boy's too smart for his own good."

The woman's instant recognition of Lucas's name surprised Olivia, even though Lucas had said they were friends. She had a hard time picturing her sweet, curious son and this dried prune of a woman together. "Lucas hasn't done anything wrong. He . . . I need to do some research on the history of Eureka. He gave me a list of books to read. And he said I should talk to you."

"Oh, he did, did he?" Cassie drew herself up taller, looking pleased. She adjusted her glasses on her nose. "Let me see the list."

Olivia handed over the sheet of paper covered in Lucas's boyish scrawl. Cassie scanned the list, then raised her gaze to Olivia once more. "Why are you so interested in Eureka's history?"

"Janelle and Danielle at the Last Dollar have hired me to paint a mural on the back wall of the café. They want something with scenes from Eureka's history."

"They stole the idea from my Founders' Pageant at Hard Rock Days. Those two were certainly never interested in local history before."

"I don't know what inspired them." She was not going to get in the middle of a feud between the librarian and the café owners. "Can you help me with these books?"

Cassie looked her up and down. Olivia fought the urge to fidget, like a girl called into the principal's office. If this project hadn't been so important, and if she could think of any other way to get the information she needed, she'd have turned on her heels and left Cassie Wynock to stew in her own superior attitude.

"Come with me." Cassie motioned for Olivia to follow and set off at a brisk walk back toward the front desk. She breezed past the woman behind the counter and into an office with glass on two sides, which allowed the occupant to look out over the library. "Sit down." Cassie indicated the chair across from the desk.

Olivia sat. Cassie took the chair behind the desk and pulled out a thick brown photo album—the kind where all

the photographs are held in place by black adhesive trian-
gles at the corners. She turned the album around to face
Olivia and opened to a page with a picture of a stern-
faced man with slick-backed hair and a curling moustache. "This is my great-grandfather, Festus Wynock. He
founded the town of Eureka. Everything it is today is because of him."

Olivia peered at the photograph. Old Festus looked
like he'd eaten a sour pickle. She pointed to a photo on the
opposite page of an equally stern and imposing woman.
"Who's this?"

"That's my great-grandmother Emmaline. The dowry
she brought from her family paid for all the property my
grandfather bought. At one time he owned most of the
land in the area."

That much land would be worth a lot of money these
days. Olivia had been around people who had money—
Cassie didn't look like them. "Why doesn't your family
own all that land now?"

"Because he sold it." She snapped the album shut. "I
can show you these books about gold miners and Indians,
but all you really need to know is that my great-grandfather
put Eureka on the map. If anyone should go on your mural,
it's him."

"I'd still like to look at the books Lucas recommended,"
she said. "I have a few ideas of my own for the mural."

Cassie scowled at her, her eyes beady, like a wary ro-
dent. Olivia couldn't have guessed the woman's age; her
face was almost unlined, but she had the attitude of an el-
derly schoolteacher, prim and unbending. "I hope you're
not one of those modern artists who is going to paint a lot
of deformed people in weird colors and make us look
bad."

Olivia choked off a laugh. Deformed people? Really?
"Danielle and Janelle have final say on what the mural
looks like," she said.

"Oh, well . . . those two." Cassie waved her hand dismissively. "There's no telling what they'd think was appropriate."

Olivia started to say that being lesbian didn't exclude a woman from having good taste but decided Cassie wouldn't get it. "I don't have any intention of painting deformed people in weird colors," she said. Though if she painted Cassie Wynock, she'd be tempted to render her as a shriveled old witch with snakes for hair. The image amused her.

"What are you smiling about?"

"Nothing. Do you have a picture of Jake Murphy? I'm thinking about putting him in the mural."

The librarian's transformation was remarkable to behold. Her face paled, then turned a deep red, almost purple. She rose from her chair, and when she finally spoke, her voice shook with rage. "Jacob Murphy was a terrible person who doesn't deserve to be immortalized in any way, shape, or fashion. If you intend to put him on your mural, you'll get no help from me."

Whoever this Jacob Murphy was, he'd obviously done something to piss off the librarian. Olivia was beginning to like him more all the time. She stood also. "Maybe I'll come back some other day for those books," she said, and backed out of the room.

In the meantime, she had another idea for a person to include on her mural—not Cassie Wynock's sainted great-grandfather, but her great-grandmother, the woman who had put up with the old reprobate. If he was half as pompous as his great-granddaughter, his wife deserved a medal.

"I call this meeting of the Eureka Town Council to order." Lucille banged her official mayor's gavel on the front counter of the Last Dollar, aiming for the wooden striker that had come with the hammer, but missing and hitting the side of the cash register instead, setting up an alarming jangling. She winced, but soldiered on. "All council members are present and accounted for."

She nodded to the large front table where council members Doug Rayburn, Katya Paxton, Junior Do-minick, and Paul Percival sat with cups of tea or coffee amidst the miniature pumpkins and gourds the girls had provided as a centerpiece. Katya had a steno pad open in front of her, a mechanical pencil at the ready to take the minutes of the meeting. The only sounds in the room were the shuffling of feet and the creaking of wooden chairs as various townspeople settled in for the evening's discussion.

Katya cleared her throat. "Madam Mayor, perhaps you should read the first order of business."

"Oh, of course." Lucille consulted the agenda on the counter in front of her, though there was really no need. She'd written the agenda herself two days ago. "I'd like to introduce, uh, Mr. Gerald Pershing, with GP Investments. He has, um, a business proposition to make to the city."

She didn't miss the curious glances Janelle and Danielle exchanged from their seats in the first row of folding chairs. Lucille usually wasn't so tongue-tied.

Gerald strode to the front of the room and Lucille sat, thankful she didn't have to say anything else. She hated that Gerald flustered her so. Yet, she enjoyed the idea that after so many years a man could affect her this way.

"Thank you all for agreeing to hear me out tonight," Gerald began in his velvety drawl.

Afraid of betraying too much of her emotions if she fo-cused on Gerald, Lucille studied the council members and the members of the community as they listened to his presentation. Doug and Paul sat with arms crossed, jaws set, as if determined not to be swayed. Junior was more expressive, nodding from time to time as Gerald talked about the plight of small investors such as Eureka and his own experience helping people maximize their savings.

In the audience, Bob sat with his hands on his knees, legs apart, frowning at Gerald the way he did anyone he deemed an "outsider." Behind him, Cassie focused on Gerald, an adoring expression on her face. Janelle and Danielle looked thoughtful, while others variously looked out the window or watched Gerald.

Gerald was masterful, presenting impressive evidence of results he'd realized for towns as diverse as Flower Mound, Texas, and Peach Springs, Arizona. "Call and talk to the people there," he said. "They were in the same boat you were in, having to cut services to balance the budget. Now they think I'm a miracle worker."

Did he sound pompous to the others? Lucille wondered. But maybe that was a good thing. You wanted the man you entrusted with your money to be confident of his ability to succeed.

"What's so special about your company that we couldn't do just as well buying stocks or municipal bonds on our own?" Doug asked.

"Do you have years of investment experience?" Gerald asked. "Do you have contacts with emerging firms who are hungry for investment capital? Are you familiar with the markets in Europe and Asia? Can you find out about new opportunities before they reach the market?" He pointed a finger at Doug. "And most important of all, how well have you done investing on your own so far?"

"And you've got references for these other towns you've helped?" Junior asked.

"Absolutely. I'd be happy for you to contact any of them. But I must ask when you talk to them you don't mention the opportunity I'm about to offer you. It's something that's just opened up this week and it's only available for limited participation."

"Can you put that in English?" Junior asked, garnering laughter from the audience.

Gerald smiled. "I have a Swedish technological firm. They specialize in the development of medical equipment. They have a new line of hardware to be used in corrective surgery: appliances for use on children who are born with birth defects, for instance, or soldiers injured in war. It's absolutely cutting-edge stuff, but they need investors to bring it to market. The returns on this kind of investment stand to be enormous. When word gets out about this opportunity, it will be closed to new investors in a matter of hours."

"What if we need more time to consider this?" Paul asked.

"Not to worry," Gerald said. "I'm sure something else just as good will come along."

"But would something else give us the chance to help children—and soldiers?" Cassie spoke from the audience, and several around her nodded.

"I'll be happy to answer any questions you may have." Gerald surveyed them all, waiting.

When no one spoke up, Lucille rose. "Thank you, Mr. Pershing. We'll discuss your generous offer and get back to you."

He smiled warmly and strode from the café. As soon as the door closed behind him the room erupted in the clamor of a dozen voices speaking at once. "How can we pass up such a great opportunity?" "If something's too good to be true, it's too good to be true." "Is what he's proposing even legal?"

"Quiet, everyone." Lucille banged her gavel. "I'd like to poll the council."

The vote was two and two. Katya and Junior thought the town should invest at least part of their funds with Gerald.

"Lucille is a good judge of character, and if she trusts Mr. Pershing, I think we can trust him," Katya said.

"If we've got the opportunity to make some real money to help out the town, I don't see how we can pass it up," Junior added.

"It sounds too risky to me," Doug said.

"I agree," Paul said. "If this scheme of his is so great, how come I've never heard of anything like it before?"

"So you keep up with the financial news now, do you?" Junior asked.

"I think we should table a final vote until we can do more thorough research," Doug said.

"I think we should give the guy a chance and see what he can do for us," Junior said.

"Madam Mayor, what do you say?" Katya asked.

"I only vote to break a tie," Lucille protested.

"Looks like a tie to me," Bob said. "You know this guy better than anybody. . . . Do you think we can trust him?"

She felt the eyes of everyone in the room focused on her. What could she say? That she'd had one dinner and a lunch with the man? That he'd kissed her and felt her up and left her breathless? That she was drawn to him in a way she hadn't been drawn to a man in years? "I don't know him that much better than any of you," she said. "He's only been in town a little over a month. But I have no reason not to believe what he says. And the truth is, we need to find some way to put more money in the town budget, or this time next year we could very well be broke."

This last statement caused a new eruption of voices. Lucille banged her gavel. "Are we ready to take an official vote?"

This time the vote was three to one, with Doug joining those in favor of investing the city's savings with Gerald. As treasurer, Doug would make the arrangements for a trial sum, to be followed by additional money if the first returns were promising.

She was pleased, and not too surprised, to find Gerald's car parked in front of her house when she arrived home after the meeting. He stepped out to meet her on the front walk. "From the smile on your face, I'd say the meeting went well," he said, taking her arm and walking with her to the door.

"Oh, you think that, do you?"

"Lucille, dear, you have such an expressive face. And I've made a life's work of reading people's thoughts in their eyes."

"Is that a necessary skill for an investment counselor?"

"And for a poker player," he said. "The difference between the two disciplines is not as much as you might imagine. So I take it the town council voted to let me handle Eureka's investments?"

"Yes, Doug Rayburn, our treasurer, will be contacting you to make the arrangements."

"You'll be surprised what I can do for you," he murmured. Not waiting for an answer, he pulled her close for a kiss filled with more passion than she'd expected.

"Gerald," she said, somewhat flustered when he finally broke away.

He grinned, teeth glinting in the glow of the porch light. "Have I mentioned I find women in power incredibly sexy? Watching you tonight, presiding over the meeting, was an incredible turn-on."

She hoped the darkness hid her blush. "Honestly, Gerald. I can't think of anything less sexy than a town council meeting."

"It's all in how you look at it, I suppose." He stepped back, though his hands lingered on her arms. "You are an incredibly sexy woman, Lucille Theriot. And one day you're going to give me a chance to prove it to you."

He turned and walked back to his car, his posture so confidant, almost cocky, as if he'd already gotten what he wanted from her. She fumbled with her key in the lock, trembling from both the force of his embrace and his words. For so many years she'd pushed aside her sensuality, like the fancy dresses that collected dust in the back of her closet. It was something nice to have, but not necessary for her happiness.

Now Gerald made her think differently. Maybe in denying the sexual part of herself she'd been ignoring something essential, something that was as important to being a woman as her ability to multitask or her skill at balancing a budget. Something she now had a chance to rediscover, a better gift than all the money he might make for the town, and certainly a lot more enjoyable.

CHAPTER FIVE

Something about sitting practically naked on a paper-covered table in a doctor's office made Maggie feel like a five-year old—vulnerable and at the mercy of everyone who was bigger than her. She had to fight the urge to curl into a ball and suck her thumb. "You appear to be in good health, Maggie, so I don't anticipate you'll have any problems with the pregnancy," Dr. Racine, an obstetrician Maggie had selected from the phone book, tapped away at her computer keyboard. "Of course, being a first-time mother at your age does put you in the category of high risk. I want to order an ultrasound and some blood work. I'm going to write you a prescription for prenatal vitamins and I'll give you some instructions on diet. You want to eat healthy, but I don't want you to gain too much weight. And you'll need a nuchal translucency scan after twelve weeks, a maternal protein measurement, an alpha fetoprotein test and, of course, amniocentesis, and a CVS to check for chromosome abnormalities."

Maggie squirmed, overwhelmed by the onslaught of instructions. And here she'd thought her biggest concern would be which stroller to purchase. "All those tests—what are they looking for?"

"We want to make sure the baby is healthy and developing normally."

"Do you think it isn't?" Alarmed, she put one hand on her stomach, as if she could somehow protect the child growing inside.

The doctor swiveled around to face Maggie, her expression that of someone used to dealing with emotional mothers. "Your baby is probably fine, Maggie. But your age does put the baby at a higher risk for birth defects, so we want to check that out."

"And if you find something wrong?"

"Then we'll have other decisions to make. But you shouldn't worry about that now." She turned back to the computer screen. "What about the father?"

The doctor's words brought Maggie out of her fog. "What about him?" Did the doctor need to know Jameso's name for some form or other?

"Is he going to be involved in the pregnancy and labor?"

"Oh, uh, yes. Yes, he wants to be involved." Jameso had said he wanted to be part of his child's life, hadn't he? Though how involved, exactly, could he be in the pregnancy?

"There'll be childbirth classes for the two of you later, of course, but before then he'll probably want to attend the ultrasound, and I'd like to see him at at least a few of your prenatal appointments. Meanwhile, he can read this." She handed Maggie a booklet, *The New Dad's Guide to Pregnancy*. The cover showed an impossibly young couple on the front, both grinning like idiots at a baby in the father's arms.

Maggie felt nauseous, but not from morning sickness. She scarcely listened to the rest of the doctor's instructions, dressed hurriedly, and fled the office to the safety of her Jeep. This was really happening. She was going to have a baby. Jameso's baby.

With trembling hands, she dug her phone from her purse.

"Hello?" Barb had to shout to make herself heard.

"What is that roaring sound?" Maggie asked, raising her own voice.

"I think it's a compressor. The painters are spraying Michael's old room."

"I thought you just redecorated that room." Barb was perpetually redecorating her home in Houston's upscale Woodlands neighborhood.

"I did. I painted the walls lavender. I planned to use it as my meditation retreat. But now I have to paint it back white."

"Why?"

"Michael's moving back home. He lost his job and his girlfriend kicked him out."

Michael, Barb's only child, was nineteen, a college dropout who until recently had worked as a delivery driver for an auto parts manufacturer. "Oh, Barb, I'm so sorry."

"Me too. But hopefully it won't be long term. Jimmy's going to try to get him on down at the golf course." Jimmy, Barb's husband, was chief financial officer at a big oil company, though his true love—other than Barb, of course—was golf. He spent as much time on the links as he did in his office. "Meanwhile, this couldn't have come at a worse time. I should be decorating for our Halloween party. The theme this year is Attack of the Zombies."

"Sounds fun." Barb was a renowned hostess, throwing parties that regularly garnered mention in Houston's society news.

"It will be fabulous, of course. But how are you doing?"

"I just had my first appointment with the obstetrician."

The roaring sound of the compressor faded as Barb moved into a quieter part of the house. "How did it go?"

"I'm definitely pregnant. Six weeks. The baby is due around the first week in June." That seemed so far away. She'd have been in Eureka a year by then. "The doctor wants to do all these tests—for birth defects. I guess because I'm so old."

"You are not old!" Barb was a year older than Maggie.

"I'm old for a first-time mother."

"You'll be fine, and the baby will be fine. I know it."

When Barb said it, Maggie could believe it.

"I'm so excited for you," Barb continued. "What does Jameso say?"

"He asked me to marry him."

She had to move the phone away from her ear as Barb squealed. "A new baby and a wedding, too!" Barb said. "That's it, I'm booking the next flight to Colorado."

"I'd love to see you, but there isn't going to be a wedding."

"What do you mean there's not going to be a wedding? You said Jameso proposed."

"And I turned him down. I'm not going to marry him just because I'm pregnant."

"You think that's the only reason he wants to marry you?"

"I know it is. He said as much." The words stung, but they were the truth—no sense denying it.

"Oh, Maggie." Barb sounded deflated. "What are you going to do?"

"We're going to keep on going the way we have been. He says he wants to be a part of the baby's life and that's good enough for me." For now anyway. They'd see how things worked out.

"Good." In typical Barb fashion, she rebounded quickly. She was the most optimistic person Maggie had ever known. Then again, maybe it was easier to be optimistic if you'd lived a charmed life. Barb was a beauty who'd been a runner-up for Miss Texas, had pledged the top sorority at SMU, married into money, joined the Junior League, and become one of Houston's top hostesses and society volunteers. And yet she'd remained fast friends with Maggie since they'd sat next to each other at a fund-raiser for Children's Hospital. Barb never let position and money—or the lack of it—come between her and a friend. "We have so much to do," Barb continued. "We have to plan your nursery, and pick out names, of course."

"We?"

"You're going to need help. And you don't think I'm going to let you experience this momentous occasion without me, do you?"

"Of course not. I can't imagine getting through this without you."

"Good. Now, let's see . . . oh, yes, what are you going to wear?"

"Whatever fits, I imagine. And is warm," she added. Much of her pregnancy would be during the winter months. She had a sudden image of herself, swollen to the size of an exercise ball, swathed in a bulky sweater and sweatpants, a giant Nordic grape.

"I can see I'm going to have to take you in hand. There's a whole fashion industry today devoted to stylish clothes for the mother-to-be. You'll look fabulous."

"Barb, I live in a tiny town in the Rocky Mountains. Function trumps fashion any day here. We have dirt streets. If you can't slog through the mud or snow here, it isn't practical."

Barb made a *tsking* sound. "That doesn't mean you have to dress like a lumberjack. Leave everything to me. Now, for the baby's room. Or rooms? Will Jameso have a room for the baby at his house, too?"

Two nurseries? Maggie had a vision of the two of them passing the baby back and forth across the yard like a football. "I'm not ready to think about any of that."

"You should think about it," Barb said. "Those eight months are going to fly by."

"That still doesn't mean I have to do everything at once."

"Of course you don't. I can do a lot of things for you. And you'll want to assign some tasks to Jameso, to make him feel a part of things."

Wasn't he already a part of "things" by virtue of his contribution of half the baby's DNA? "You make it sound like if I don't give him a job he can't be the baby's father."

"Genetically, he's the father no matter what he does. Honestly, beyond contributing that sperm and holding your hand while you're in labor, there's not a heck of a lot for the dad to do until it's time to change diapers. I strongly suggest you put him in charge of those."

She tried to imagine Jameso changing a diaper and failed. "Did Jimmy change Michael's diapers?"

Barb laughed. "Are you kidding me? He didn't even want to be in the same room when I was changing them. You want to start off on the right foot with Jameso. Tell him since you're in charge of input—breastfeeding—it's only fair that he handles output—diapers. It's the kind of logic men appreciate."

"That would only work if we were living together. I'm not going to haul the baby next door every time he needs a clean diaper."

"Or she. You might have a girl."

Maggie imagined an infant in a little pink dress and matching bonnet and had to blink back tears.

"You ought to consider moving in with Jameso," Barb continued. "It would make child care so much easier."

"If we're going to live together, we might as well get married."

"An excellent idea. You probably still have time to accept his proposal."

"Barb, I don't want to be married."

"Ever?"

Maggie massaged the bridge of her nose, behind which a headache was beginning to throb. "I don't know. But I don't want to be married right now."

"Fine. But you're just making things difficult for yourself."

Something she was apparently very good at. "I have to go now. I have to get back to work." She'd lied and told Rick she was going to the dentist—only because she wasn't ready for the whole town to know about the baby. Not when she was still getting used to the idea herself.

"Wait," Barb said. "Don't go yet. Any other exciting news in Eureka?"

"The town council's decided to pull the budget surplus out of the bank and invest in foreign stocks, or something like that."

"They couldn't pay worse than the banks. I swear, I'd come out ahead these days if they'd go back to giving away free toasters when you opened an account."

"The Eureka Bank gives you a coffee mug with their name on it." She had hers in the cabinet at home, next to a matching one that had belonged to her father.

"I'd take a coffee cup. Anything's better than one third of a percent interest, or whatever they're paying these days."

"Tell your CPA husband to find you a better deal."

"I'm the best deal the man ever found, and believe me, he knows it. I have to go. The painters want me to inspect the work."

Maggie hung up and slid the phone back into her purse. Talking with Barb was always wonderful, but exhausting, too. Where did she get so much energy?

She drove, not to the paper or her house in town, but

up to her father's cabin. The mountainside was still bare of snow, though last month when he'd persuaded her to move, Jameso had assured her the road would be impassible by the middle of October, if not before. Maggie was grateful she could still make it up here. She kept coming back to this place because this was where what she thought of as the second chapter in her life had started. She'd begun to see herself differently here—not as an orphaned, unemployed divorcee, but as an independent woman who could do almost anything.

Did that anything include having a first baby at forty, with no husband?

She was surprised to see a familiar black SUV parked in front of the cabin. Olivia Theriot walked around from the side of the house, camera in hand. "Hi, Maggie," she said. "I hope you don't mind. I was taking pictures of your dad's place. I'm thinking of including him as part of a mural I'm working on for the Last Dollar."

"Jake?" Danielle and Janelle had idolized her father for his defense of them against some town bigots—and for the fireproof chicken house he'd built them after vandals destroyed their first one. But putting him on a mural seemed a bit much.

"Yeah, I'm painting a mural of the history of Eureka. Some people suggested I should include your dad. But I can't find a picture of him anywhere."

The only photographs Maggie had of her father had been taken when she was an infant. They showed a thin young man in an army uniform, not the larger-than-life character locals remembered. "Come by the paper," she said. "We have photos on file of Jake at Hard Rock Days."

"I heard he won the competition three times."

"He did." The trophies were stored under the stairs in the cabin, along with his army discharge papers, his divorce decree, and half a dozen unpaid speeding tickets.

"Thanks," Olivia said. "I will stop by."

She started to turn away. "Olivia?" Maggie called.

"Yes?"

"Have you been a single mom long?"

"The last ten years or so. Why?"

"I just wondered. I know it must be hard, but you've done a good job. Lucas is a great kid." He was the one, after all, who'd discovered the turquoise in the French Mistress Mine.

"Thanks." Olivia gave Maggie a curious look. "Why are you so interested?"

She abandoned her determination to keep the news secret. It wasn't as if everyone wouldn't know eventually. And maybe Jameso had already told people. "I . . . well, I just found out I'm pregnant."

"Really? Does Jameso know?"

"Of course he knows. I mean, I wouldn't tell anyone else before I told him."

"And he didn't freak out about it?"

"Why would he freak out?"

Olivia fiddled with the camera, maybe to avoid looking at Maggie. "No reason, I guess. He just doesn't seem like the daddy type, you know?"

"Yeah." She knew. Jameso with his hot motorcycle and ski-bum avocation. He was the guy women lusted after and men wanted to hang out with—not the type to tote a diaper bag and warm bottles. "He seems good with it," she said. Not exactly thrilled, but maybe it would be easier when she started to show. The baby was scarcely real to her right now, beyond an increased fatigue and nausea.

"Jameso's a stand-up guy," Olivia said. "I'm sure he'll pay support and everything, something my ex never bothered with."

"Right." She hadn't even thought about child support. Not that Jameso would be able to contribute much. His approach to finances seemed to be to work enough part-time jobs to pay a minimum of expenses and not worry about anything else. And with the money from the French Mistress and her job at the paper, she didn't really need a lot more.

She realized Olivia was the first person who hadn't assumed she and Jameso would marry. "He hasn't said anything about this at work?"

"No, he was probably waiting for you to make the announcement. Guys are funny about stuff like that."

Guys were funny, all right. She could never tell what they were thinking.

"I'm sure he'll do fine," Olivia said. "At least he didn't leave town right away or anything like that."

Maggie stared at Olivia. Was she remembering how Jameso had skipped town in the summer when Maggie's ex showed up? Or had she, like Maggie, pegged him as the unsteady type? "Do you know something about Jameso I should know?" she asked.

"No." Olivia stowed the camera in her purse. "Some guys are just the type to duck out on their responsibilities. But not Jameso. Like I said, he's a stand-up guy."

She hoped Olivia was right, but she didn't think she could count on Jameso sticking by her to the bitter end. Not when no other man had managed it.

"Well, congratulations." Olivia started backing toward the SUV. "And don't worry about the single mom thing. Women do it every day."

Yes, women did it every day. But that didn't mean Maggie had to. And she knew from her own fatherless upbringing how much a child needed a dad in her life. Maybe Barb was right. If she wanted Jameso to contribute more to the baby than his sperm, she'd have to think of jobs for him to do. Reasons for him to stick around. She'd start by putting him to work on the nursery. She'd let Barb design it and Jameso carry out Barb's decrees.

She smiled. The plan was genius. As tough as he liked

to think he was, Jameso Clark was no match for Barb
Stanowski. If he survived her ordering him around during
the creation of a nursery, staying with Maggie for the
birth would be a cinch.

By the end of the first week after the council meeting
at which they'd approved investing Eureka's savings with
Gerald's firm, Lucille and Gerald had been to dinner
twice and once to a play in Montrose. Townspeople had
pegged them as a definite couple, and Lucille had stopped
worrying about it. Gerald had been ardent and Lucille
had basked in his attention.

Tonight was their third dinner date, and by the time the
main course arrived she was feeling mellow from two
glasses of champagne from the bottle Gerald had insisted
on ordering. "What are we celebrating again?" she asked
as he topped off her glass.

"The final funds transfer came through today. Tomorrow I'll execute the buy order for the Swedish stock. This
time six months from now you can expect the city's funds
to have doubled."

"You sound awfully sure of yourself. I thought financial markets were notoriously unpredictable."

"Only when you don't know the business as well as I
do." He took her hand. "But let's not talk shop. This night
is for us to enjoy each other."

She had never met a man like him, with the soul of a
poet and the face of a Greek statue. He wooed her with
oysters and shrimp, expensive wine, and tales of the
places he'd like to show her—Austria and Paris and Thailand. He was handsome, intelligent, and besotted with
her.

But years of caution kept her from rushing headlong
into deeper intimacy. "You mentioned a son," she said.
"So I assume you've been married before."

"I've been married three times before."

Her shock must have shown on her face. He chuckled and took her hand. "I know it's a lot. I could have lied and not mentioned the two marriages that didn't produce children, but I believe in being honest."

"I appreciate that," she said.

He gently massaged her fingers, caressing the knuckles, kneading the flesh between each digit. "Don't think of it as three failed marriages. Think of it as proof that I believe in marriage and monogamy. And I've learned how to be a better husband from each of those unions. Next time I'm sure I'll get things right." His eyes met hers, a look filled with meaning. Her heart fluttered wildly and she had to look away.

"What about your marriage?" he asked. "I'm assuming there was only one."

"Yes, only one. Mitch and I were very young. I was only twenty and he was twenty-four. We were together three years; then he left me for someone else."

"It still pains you. I can read the hurt in your eyes."

"No one likes to be rejected." Her love for Mitch had died long ago, but the shame of him choosing someone else over her still burned, just a little.

"He was a fool," Gerald said, his voice gruff with emotion. Lucille felt the bands around her heart loosen another notch.

After dinner they walked out into a frosty night lit by a full moon. At the car, he stopped her and pulled her into his arms for a kiss. She snuggled against him and returned the kiss with a new fervor, giving herself up to the desire she'd resisted for too long.

"Well, well." He smiled down at her, a wolfish look that sent heat curling through her. "I like this new fire in you. May I claim a little responsibility for this passion?"

"You may."

He pulled her tighter against him, letting her feel the hard evidence of his desire. "What should we do about it?"

It was her turn to smile, a seductive look meant to singe him. "I think you should take me back to your place."

Olivia had filled most of a sketchbook with drawings for the proposed mural, sketching ideas, then ripping out the pages in frustration and starting over. She'd drawn faces and animals and scenery from imagination and from photographs, and had cried tears of frustration at her inability to translate to paper anything that was as good as the pictures that lived in her head.

In the end, she'd chosen three drawings: a miner with hammer and drill who looked suspiciously like a somewhat younger Bob Prescott, a pioneer woman who looked enough like Cassie to keep people guessing, and a boy who was clearly Lucas who held a fish for a shadowy man to admire. "The first two pictures represent the past and the boy represents the present and the future . . . tourism and all that," she explained to Janelle and Danielle as she handed over the sketches. She'd stopped by before her shift at the Dirty Sally, just as the café was closing for the evening.

"They're perfect," Danielle said. "Just what we're looking for."

"Of course I'll fill in with scenery from the area," Olivia said. "And animals . . . a burro for the miner, a bighorn sheep, and maybe an eagle. And the mountains, of course." She was babbling, but she couldn't help herself. She'd let this commission become a lot more important to her than she'd wanted to. Investing so much emotion in anything made disappointment that much harder to bear.

"It will be beautiful," Janelle said, returning the drawings to her. "When can you start?"

She had the job? It was that simple? She clutched the back of a chair, willing her legs not to give way in relief. "Next week, if that's okay. I'll need to buy some supplies."

"We'll write you a check for half the fee tonight and the rest on completion," Danielle said. "Does that sound okay?"

"Yes, that sounds wonderful."

"You can take all this down." Janelle indicated the skeletons, spiders, and other Halloween decorations that adorned the back wall. "And work whenever you like. The customers will enjoy watching you."

The idea of performing for an audience made Olivia nervous all over again, but she vowed to overcome it. She was an artist—being paid for her work!

While Danielle went to the back to get her checkbook and Janelle continued clearing the tables, Olivia examined the oversized poster she'd designed for Bob's betting pool. She'd cut snowflakes from white cardboard and placed them in a box decorated with more snowflakes. Participants in the contest wrote their name on a snowflake and pinned it to the grid on the poster, over the date they guessed would see the first snowfall of an inch or more in the street in front of the Last Dollar. To get around gaming laws, participants were asked to make a donation to the town funds for each guess they proposed.

"Here's your check." Danielle handed Olivia the first payment she'd ever received for her artwork. She was tempted to frame it. Then again, she needed the money for supplies. Maybe she'd frame a copy of it instead.

"Thanks." She slid the check into her pocket. "I'll be back in a day or two to start work." The girls said good night and Olivia headed down the sidewalk to the saloon, hugging her coat tightly around her against the cold. Eureka may not have seen snow yet, but winter was definitely here. Frost glittered on the windshields of the cars lined up in front of the Dirty Sally, and the moon shone like a 100-watt bulb in the impossibly clear night sky.

Jameso was behind the bar, which Olivia had spent a previous day draping with fake spiderwebs and glittery black spiders. He was talking with Junior Dominick and another man Olivia didn't know. She studied him with a new appreciation. Was he really okay with the idea of being a father? She waited until he moved away from the other men, then walked up to him.

"Congratulations," she said, bumping him with her hip. "Daddy."

Two spots of color bloomed high on his cheeks. "How did you find out?"

"I saw Maggie yesterday and she told me."

"She did?"

"Are you hard of hearing? I just said she did."

"I guess I thought she was trying to keep it quiet." He folded his arms across his chest. "I mean, until she started showing and all."

"She didn't ask me to keep it a secret or anything. Or would you rather people not know?"

"Me? No, I'm fine with it. I mean, it's exciting."

"You don't look very excited." In fact, he looked a little sick. "Are you worried?"

"No, why would I be worried?" He grabbed a bar towel and began scrubbing at an imaginary spill on the bar's mahogany surface. "It's a little scary, though. I don't have any idea what to do with a kid."

"Does that mean you wish she wasn't pregnant?"

"No! It's just a surprise, that's all." He stopped scrubbing. "But the idea's growing on me."

"Men!" She threw up her hands in disgust.

"What's that supposed to mean?"

"Meaning a baby is the most wonderful, magical thing in the world and all you can say is that the idea is growing on you."

"That's not fair. The way I see it, you women are in on the news from the start—the baby is growing in you. You can feel it, or the effects of it. All we have is the results on some plastic strip and an idea we can't feel or see for months. It's hard to wrap your mind around something like that."

"Especially when you never planned on being a dad in the first place," she said.

The guilty look in his eyes told her she'd hit a bull's-eye. "I wouldn't say never," he said. "But you have to admit Maggie and I are doing things out of order."

"So marry her already. You still have plenty of time."

He looked grim. "Neither of us is ready for marriage."

Something flickered in his eyes—hurt? Understanding dawned. "Did she turn you down?"

"This is really none of your business." He headed back down the bar to retrieve Junior's empty beer glass.

Olivia pondered this revelation as she bused tables. Why would Maggie turn down Jameso's proposal? True, they hadn't been together long, but they seemed crazy about each other.

Olivia would have married D. J. in a minute, back before he left for Iraq. She'd been expecting a proposal the night he told her he'd taken the job. Instead of planning a wedding, she'd watched him pack up to move overseas. And he hadn't understood why she was so upset.

Her life had pretty much gone to hell after that. Only desperation could have made her drive across the country to move in with her mother. She hadn't seen Lucille in six years before then.

But it had worked out all right. Better than she'd expected, actually. Lucas liked it here, and Lucille had mellowed with age. Or maybe Olivia was the one who had mellowed. She and her mom got along better now than they had all the years Olivia was growing up. Things had been good, at least until D. J. showed up, opening up the old wounds as surely as if he'd slashed her with a knife. She'd told herself she was almost over him and he'd proved her so wrong.

She set her mouth and swept the last of the glasses into her bus tray. She was strong. She could get through this and not give in. D. J. would eventually tire of his pursuit and go away.

The cowbells on the bar door jangled and Lucas came in, too-long sweatpants puddling around his ankles and his wrists showing white at the sleeves of his too-small parka. "Lucas, what are you doing here?" She checked the clock. It was after ten.

"Where's Grandma?" he asked, dropping into a chair at the table she'd been clearing.

"I think she has a date."

"With that Gerald guy?"

"I think so."

He pushed his lower lip out in a pout. "I don't like him."

Olivia didn't care for the guy either. He was too full of himself by far. But she couldn't say that to Lucas. "You're not the one dating him," she said.

"Is she sleeping with him?" he asked.

Olivia struggled to keep any expression from her face. Lucas was clearly trying to shock her; she remembered doing the same thing to her mother when she was his age. Behind her, Jameso laughed.

She glared at him. "This is a private conversation."

"And you wonder why I'm worried about being a father. It's a piece of cake, right?"

"Go away, Jameso."

To her surprise, he did. She turned back to Lucas. He slumped in the chair, picking a napkin to pieces. He needed a haircut and there was a rip in the shoulder of the parka. When had that happened? Part of the mural money would have to go to buy him a new one. Back to the question at hand. Was her mother sleeping with Gerald? She shook her head. Okay, no matter how old she got, that was not a question she cared to answer. "You should be home in bed," she told Lucas.

He looked up at her through a fringe of hair. "It's not a school night. Besides, the house is kind of creepy late at night when no one's there."

"I don't know what to tell you. I don't get off until two or three."

"I called D. J. and he said I could come stay with him."

She gripped the back of the chair so hard her fingers ached. This was why there ought to be exceptions to laws about beating your children. Not that she'd ever really hit Lucas, but right now she fought the urge to strike out at something. "Why?" she asked, struggling to keep her voice even. "Why did you call D. J.?"

"He's my friend. He said to call him anytime I wanted."

But D. J. was not *her* friend. She did not want him involved in their lives.

Right on cue, the man himself walked in. He wore a desert camo jacket and a black watch cap, a hero to the rescue. "Hey, Lucas." He patted the boy's shoulder and handed him a bunch of keys. "Go keep the truck warm while I talk to your mom."

New life surged through Lucas at the prospect of starting the truck. He hurried away, the door slamming hard behind him.

Olivia stepped back, needing to put distance between herself and D. J. He smelled of cold and wood smoke, masculine and capable and far too calm in the face of her raging emotions. "What are you doing here?" she asked.

"Lucas asked me to meet him here. He was home alone and he was scared."

"He told you that?"

"No, he didn't tell me that. No thirteen-year-old boy is going to admit that. But I could hear it in his voice." He took a step toward her, his voice soft, as if he was struggling to control his anger. Another woman might have been afraid of his intensity, but Olivia knew he'd never hit her. For all his faults, violence wasn't one of them. "What are you doing leaving a kid that age home alone by himself?"

"My mother was supposed to be there. Besides, this isn't downtown Hartford, Connecticut. Eureka is safe, and you know Lucas—he's a responsible kid." She hated that he could make her feel so guilty when she hadn't done anything wrong.

"But he's still a kid."

"Don't tell me how to raise my child. I'm doing the best I can."

Some of the stiffness went out of his shoulders. "I know that. Don't you think I know how hard you work? And you've done a good job. But you don't have to do it all yourself anymore. I'm here and I can help."

"I don't need your help."

"I think you do. And even if you don't need me, Lucas does. A boy his age needs a man in his life."

She wanted to deny this, but how could she? Clearly Lucas did need a man to turn to. And he wanted to turn to D. J. She looked away, not wanting him to see the doubt in her eyes. "I don't know."

"It'll be all right, Olivia." She shivered at the sound of her name from his lips, like a caress on her fevered skin. "I may be a lot of things," he continued, "but I'm not going to hurt your son."

Maybe not physically, but what about emotionally, when he got tired of being around them and left again? "He can stay with you tonight, but just this one time."

"Why don't we say instead that anytime your mom can't be there when you work nights he can come stay with me?"

Pushing. He was always pushing for more. Still, if her

mother continued her relationship with Gerald Pershing, Olivia would have to make some arrangements for Lucas. "All right. I know Lucas would like that."

"I'd like it, too."

He smiled. That sweet, serious smile that made her insides feel like melted butter. "I have to get back to work now," she said.

"All right. I'll have him home after lunch tomorrow."

"What are you going to do?"

"Guy stuff. Don't worry. It'll be okay."

She watched him go, a knot of tears clogging her throat. He shouldn't be leaving like this—taking Lucas away, not to a place they shared, but to his own house. One where she couldn't go. Not because he wouldn't welcome her, but because she couldn't cross the chasm that separated them.

Her mother had said as you got older forgiveness was easier. But Lucille didn't understand. There were some things she just couldn't forgive.

CHAPTER SIX

Lucille woke with the sun in her eyes, the bedroom flooded with unaccustomed light. She smiled to herself, remembering the pleasure of the night before. She was pleasantly sore in places that hadn't been sore in a long time, but she'd been happy to discover everything still worked the way it was supposed to, and that she'd been able to please Gerald as much as he pleased her.

She rolled over, searching for him, but the place beside her was empty, though the pillow still bore the indentation of his head. The bathroom door was closed, so she assumed he was in there. Never mind. Arms over her head, she stretched like a cat, arching her back and feeling the pull on her muscles all the way to her toes. Then she lay staring at the ceiling, basking in a glow of happiness. Had her life ever been as perfect as it was right now? Olivia and Lucas were settled in, for a while at least. The city's financial difficulties were on their way to being solved. Even the weather was cooperating, with what looked to be a mild winter ahead, meaning they'd spend less on plowing roads and heating city buildings.

And Gerald. This handsome, sexy, and, yes, rich man

had come into her life and changed everything. "Gerald?" she called out. "I hope you're not in there getting dressed."

No answer. No sound of a shower either. She hoped he was okay. He'd seemed fine last night, but he wasn't a young man and maybe the exertion—well, she'd heard of men having heart attacks during or after sex.

She sat up and wrapped a sheet around herself, then tip-toed to the bathroom door. Not wanting him to catch her prying, she carefully put an ear to the door. No sounds. "Gerald?" She knocked. "Is everything okay in there?" No answer.

Heart beating faster, she grasped the doorknob. It turned easily and she pushed the door open and peeked inside. The room was empty. She opened the door farther and took a few steps to the sink. No Gerald. No towels on the floor or fog on the mirror or other signs of recent shower activity.

Scarcely breathing, she looked around the room. There was no toothbrush by the sink. No comb. No shaving kit. No sign that anyone lived here or used this room.

She lunged back into the bedroom and threw open the closet doors. Empty. The dresser drawers were empty, too, not so much as a spare handkerchief left behind.

She ran through the house, the sheet trailing behind her, her bare feet slapping against the cold wood floors. She raised the blinds on the front window to reveal what she already knew: His car was gone from the driveway.

Anger beginning to overtake fear, she found her purse where she'd left it by the sofa in the living room and retrieved her phone. She stabbed in Gerald's number and waited impatiently for the call to go through. It went straight to voice mail. "I'm sorry I can't take your call now . . ."

She hung up and typed in a text.

Gerald. What is going on? Is this your idea of a joke? Where are you?

Still clutching the phone, she returned to the bedroom and began to dress, pulling on the wrinkled clothes she'd worn last night—the new dress and shoes she'd bought for the occasion. The phone rang, surprising a shriek from her. But the number wasn't Gerald's.

"Have you seen Gerald?" Doug Rayburn asked.

"No, why? Have you seen him?" Even she could hear the shakiness in her voice and hoped Doug would blame a poor connection.

"Someone told me you had a date with him last night. We need to find him and ask him some more questions."

"Why? What's going on?"

"I decided it wouldn't hurt to check with the folks in Flower Mound and Peach Springs—see if he's really as great as he says he is. Everyone there says they've never heard of the guy or his Swedish investments or anything of the kind."

She sat on the side of the bed, her legs too weak to hold her. "He's gone," she said.

"What do you mean, he's gone?"

"I mean his condo is empty. No clothes. No suitcase, no car. He's gone."

Silence greeted this news. "Doug?" she asked. "Is everything all right?"

"No, everything is not all right. The bastard's taken our money with him."

"Can we cancel the bank draft?"

"We didn't give him a bank draft. We wired the funds directly into his account."

She closed her eyes. This couldn't be happening.

"Lucille? Are you still there?"

"I'm here." Though she wished desperately that she wasn't.

"What are we going to do? That was all the money we had in savings."

"I thought we were only going to give him part of the money, as a trial."

"That was the plan, but he convinced the banker we'd requested the wrong amount. Somehow he persuaded them to send it all."

She imagined Gerald now—so charming and earnest. Everyone believed him. Why wouldn't they?

"All that's left is a few thousand dollars in the operating account," Doug said. "What are we going to do?"

"I don't know. I don't know what we're going to do." But if she ever saw Gerald Pershing again, she was going to personally cut his heart out with a steak knife. Provided he even had a heart.

"Lucille, where are you right now?" Doug asked. "Are you at Gerald's condo? Did you, um, did you spend the night there?"

Shame flooded her, until she feared she might be sick. She pinched the web between her thumb and forefinger, hard. "I'm not going to answer that," she said weakly.

"Uh, okay. None of my business."

"No, it's not." She tried to make her voice crisp, protecting her dignity.

"You don't have any idea where he is?" Doug asked.

"No, I woke up this morning and he was gone. His condo is empty. He didn't leave so much as a toothbrush behind."

"Sounds like he planned his escape pretty well," Doug said. "Makes me think he's done this before. I asked Lou Aronson over at the Sheriff's Department to run Gerald's name through their computer, but they didn't come up with anything. Of course, it might not be his real name. It probably isn't."

"Right."

"I'm sorry, Lucille. This sucks any way you look at it."

"I have to go now, Doug. I'll talk to you later." She hung up the phone and pulled the sheet around her once more, gathering it the way she wished she could gather her dignity. On second thought, she wouldn't waste time cutting out the man's heart. She'd go right for cutting off his balls, so she could make sure he'd never make a fool of another woman the way he'd done her.

Olivia was surprised to find there was someone she could hate more than D. J. Surprised, too, that she could feel so much anger on behalf of her mother. Gerald Pershing had not only robbed the town of most of its funds, he'd turned her mother—the stern, strong, intimidating presence of Olivia's youth—into a pale, silent shadow of a woman, afraid to look anyone in the eye.

Olivia would like to find the man and burn his ears off with her angry words, but she knew she'd have to stand in line to do so. Everyone in town was up in arms over his deception—as much in anger over what he'd done to her mother as over the theft of the money.

Lucille had tried to resign as mayor, but the town council refused to accept her resignation. Though she blamed herself for what had happened, they'd pointed out she wasn't the one who voted to make the investment—they were. They'd called in the state police and the FBI, and were talking about hiring a private investigator to find Pershing.

Meanwhile, the chart for Bob's snowfall pool over at the Last Dollar was a blizzard of snowflakes, with everyone making their donation to the town coffers. The days grew colder as the calendar inched toward Halloween. And somehow, life went on. The world had shifted a little, but people kept up their routines and normal conversations in spite of the uncertainty that operated behind the scenes in the little town.

"I don't see what all the fascination is with zombies and vampires and such," Bob groused one afternoon in the Dirty Sally, as he scowled at the bat cutouts Olivia had taped up around the bar. "When I was a kid, we knew what Halloween was really for."

Jameso winked at Olivia. "What was Halloween for, Bob?" he asked.

"Don't smirk at me," Bob said. "Halloween is for playing pranks on people—the 'trick' in 'trick or treat.' "

"You mean turning over outhouses and putting cars on roofs?" Olivia asked. "I've read about stuff like that."

"Those kinds of things will do, for the unimaginative," Bob said.

"Then what did imaginative people like you do?" Jameso asked.

"One year when I was a kid we stranded the neighbor lady's cow on the roof. 'Course my dad found out and tanned my hide, plus made me muck out the neighbor's horse stalls for six months. When I was a little older we filled the mayor's car with about five thousand Ping-Pong balls. Once at the Merryvale mines, a buddy and I turned on the washhouse taps overnight and left the doors open. The place froze up like an ice skating rink. 'Course it was colder back then."

"Don't try any of that stuff here," Jameso said. "If you do, I'll never serve you another beer."

"I'm too old for such shenanigans. I'm just sayin' there hasn't been a decent prank around here since Murphy died."

"Jake was a great one for pranks," Jameso agreed.

"You remember the time he switched all the highway signs around?" Bob chuckled. "The locals didn't notice, but the tourists trying to get to Telluride kept ending up in Cassie Wynock's front yard. Poor old Cassie stood on her front porch with a shotgun, threatening to shoot the next person who drove up in her yard."

"Then there was the time he replaced half the pens at

the bank with trick ones that squirted water when you tried to write," Jameso said.

"Or the time he posed a store mannequin on a ledge up on Mount Garnet? Tourists kept calling to report a stranded hiker."

By this time both men were doubled over, laughing so hard Olivia half feared Bob might go into some kind of seizure. "Jake Murphy sounds like a laugh a minute," she said drily.

"Women never appreciate a good prank," Bob said.

"What else is there to do around here on Halloween?" she asked.

"You could drive out to look for the ghost lights," Jameso said.

"Ghost lights?"

"Up on Mount Winston," Bob said. "Big balls of light skip down the mountain. Sometimes there's just one of them, sometimes two or three or more. They bob around for a while, then disappear."

"That doesn't sound very scary to me," she said. "It's probably just a reflection or something."

"Or something is right," Bob said. "I think it's aliens up to no good."

"What are the aliens doing up on the mountain?" Jameso asked.

"They're stealing gold and silver and other precious metals to power their spaceships."

Was he serious? With Bob it was so hard to tell. "Okay, we know what the aliens are going to be doing for Halloween," she said. "What about the rest of us?"

"A few people have parties," Jameso said. "You can wear a costume to work if you want."

"Something sexy," Bob suggested.

"In your dreams. Besides, I'm working the day shift on Halloween."

"You can't do sexy in the daytime?" Jameso asked.

"There's no one around here worth dressing up for," she said.

Jameso put a hand over his heart. "I'm wounded."

"Get out of here, baby daddy." She flicked her bar cloth at him.

"You don't want to dress up for D. J.?" Bob asked.

"D. J. can kiss my ass."

"Anytime, darlin'."

Heat washed over her as D. J. strolled into the bar. "Why am I kissing your ass?" he asked pleasantly. "Lovely though it is."

She turned her back on him and retreated to the sink.

"I was telling Olivia she ought to dress up sexy for Halloween," Bob said.

"No need for a costume," D. J. said.

Coming from another man, the words might have sounded smarmy, or too glib. But D. J. didn't have a glib bone in his body. The fact that he could say things like that—and that his words sent heat curling up through her middle—made her furious, both at him and at herself for continuing to let him get to her after so many months.

She turned to face the bar once more, striking her best I-don't-give-a-damn attitude. "I was just saying the Dirty Sally should do something fun for Halloween."

"We could have a costume contest," Jameso said doubtfully.

"No, a ghost-story contest." She grinned, pleased with herself. "We can have an open mic and have prizes for whoever tells the scariest story and the funniest story."

"That's a pretty good idea," Bob said.

"It's a great idea." Jameso clapped his hand on her shoulder. "We'll make you one of us yet."

"What do you mean 'one of us'?" She drew back. "I'm not part of your prankster fraternity or anything like that."

"No, I mean part of the community. A local. This ghost-story thing could become a new tradition."

She bristled at the idea. She took it as a point of pride that she wasn't a joiner—no groups, clubs, or causes benefited from her presence. She had always preferred to fly solo. "Wanting to do something on Halloween besides sit at home and file my nails does not make me a Eurekian or Eurekite or whatever you call yourselves."

"I just say I'm from Eureka," Bob said. "If you have to slap a label on yourself, you probably aren't anything."

"Why ghost stories?" D. J. asked.

No one had asked him to butt in. Olivia wouldn't have answered the question at all, except Jameso took it up. "Yeah, why ghost stories?"

"Because it's Halloween." Shouldn't that be obvious? "Ghosts are traditional."

"Do you believe in ghosts?" Bob asked.

"You don't have to believe in them to think they're fun," she said.

"I believe in them," D. J. said. "And I don't think they're particularly fun."

His serious tone unnerved her. "When did you ever see a ghost?" she asked.

"I'm not talking about spirits in white sheets." His eyes met hers, bottomless brown and filled with a sadness that dragged at her like grasping fingers. "We all have things that haunt us."

She turned away, not wanting him to see the truth in her eyes. He couldn't know the things that haunted her— ghosts from the past she feared would never leave.

And those she feared would.

The ultrasound suite at the medical office building was painted a pale yellow, with a wallpaper border of zoo animals. The room was tiny, barely eight feet by eight feet, and Jameso paced relentlessly from one end to the other and back again.

"Will you please stop?" Maggie said. "You're making me more nervous than I already am."

"I can't help it." He halted and shoved both hands in the pockets of his jeans. "I've never done anything like this before."

"Well, neither have I." She squirmed. "When is that damned technician going to get in here?"

"A little testy, aren't you?"

"You would be, too, if they made you drink a quart of water, then wouldn't let you pee."

"Maybe I can distract you." He moved in as if to kiss her.

"Touch me and I'll pee all over you."

He drew back as the door opened and a very large woman in a hot pink smock wheeled in a table with a squat monitor. "Time for the baby's first pictures," she announced.

She raised the head of the table, pushed Maggie gently back, lifted the hospital gown Maggie wore, and squirted what felt like half a gallon of warm gel on her stomach. Jameso discreetly studied the charts on the wall, which depicted stages of fetal development. In the one labeled six weeks the fetus was a bean floating in a balloon-shaped stomach.

"Okay, Dad. It's safe to turn around," the technician announced. "Come stand over here by Mom so you can see the monitor."

Jameso did as he was told. "Where y'all from?" the technician asked as she fiddled with knobs on the machine.

"Eureka," Jameso said.

"Oh, y'all been in the news. The town lost all its

money to bad investments. Have you gotten any of it back yet?"

"Not yet," Jameso said.

"Guess y'all gone have to send everybody up in the hills with a pick and shovel to see if you can get anything out of those gold mines. I hear there's a lot of 'em up that way."

Jameso exchanged an amused glance with Maggie. "We'll make that suggestion to the town council."

"Send some of that gold my way if you find any. Okay, Mom, lie back and let's take a look-see at this baby."

As the technician traced a wand over her belly, Maggie suppressed a giggle. "That tickles."

The technician smiled. "That's what I love about this part of my job. It makes people happy."

A shadow passed across the screen. "What's that?" Jameso asked.

"That is your baby's head." She adjusted a knob, moved the wand, and a bean-shaped shadow swam into view. Maggie stared, mouth open in amazement, as the shadow moved and pulsed.

"You can see its heart." Jameso spoke in an awed whisper.

"And there's its hands and feet." So tiny, but she could see the beginnings of fingers and toes.

Something squeezed her fingers. She realized Jameso was holding her hand. She squeezed back, happier than she'd thought she could be that he was here to share this moment with her.

"Let's snap you a picture to take home and show everybody." The technician hit a button on the machine. "None of them will know what they're looking at, but most folks are polite about it and will ooh and aah for your benefit."

She retrieved the black and white photograph from the

machine and handed it to Jameso. "They're good to put in the baby book, if nothing else. You can freak out the kid with them when he's older."

"You can tell it's a boy?" Jameso asked.

"Do you see a penis in that picture? No, I cannot tell it's a boy. It might be a girl. A few more months we might be able to tell, if the baby cooperates and agrees to show us what's between its legs. In the meantime, just refer to it as 'the baby.' "

He nodded, still staring at the pictures.

"All right. I'll leave you to clean up and get dressed. Then I believe Mom is due for some blood work at the lab down the hall. And the restroom is right there through the door."

Maggie bolted for the facilities before the technician had even cleared the room. She returned a few moments later, feeling much better. "Apparently, I no longer have a name," she said as she pulled a sweater over her head. "I have a feeling I'm going to be 'Mom' for the rest of the pregnancy."

"That's not so bad, is it?" He handed her her jeans.

"I guess not. I'm still getting used to the idea." She stepped into the pants and pulled up the zipper.

"Me too. When she said 'Dad,' it took me a second to realize she was talking to me."

Maggie stared at the ultrasound photo. "This is really happening."

"Yeah, it really is." He sucked in a deep breath. "I hope I'm ready for this."

"I'm not sure anyone is ever really ready. But we'll do okay."

"At least you're going to have the fanciest nursery in Eureka County. Barb sent me more drawings yesterday. I have to put in a dozen electrical outlets and then stuff these plastic stoppers in all of them to baby-proof them. I told her it was too many outlets and she told me the baby needed them for monitors and diaper warmers and a ton of other electronic crap."

"Better to humor her," Maggie said. She stepped into her boots and bent to lace them. How many months before she wasn't able to do that anymore?

"Funny . . . that's what she told me about you."

"She told you to humor me?

He nodded. "She said you were in charge now and whatever you wanted, I should get, whether it was ice cream in the middle of January or rabbit fur slippers in June."

"Oh, please. That's ridiculous. You aren't my slave." Though the image of him dressed in nothing but a loincloth, ready to do her bidding, did have a certain appeal. . . .

"What are you smiling about?"

Her eyes met his. "Apparently, being pregnant makes me horny."

"It does?" He moved in closer. "Then maybe you shouldn't have gotten dressed."

"Jameso!" She pushed him away. "We're in an examining room. There are probably cameras. Not to mention someone will wonder if we don't leave soon."

"You're right. That table doesn't look very comfortable. But hold that thought until we get home."

"Aren't you supposed to be at work this afternoon?" She slung her purse over her shoulder and headed for the door.

"Olivia will cover for me if I'm a little late."

"You're incorrigible."

"Yes, and it's why you love me. Besides, you started it."

"No, you started it. That first night on my father's porch."

"You wanted to hit me over the head with a stick of firewood." He opened the door and they started down the hall toward the lab.

"I thought you were one of the most infuriating men I'd ever met."

"You still think that."

"Yes, I do. But you're never boring. For that, I'm thankful."

They stopped in front of the lab. "Today was nice," she said. "I'm glad you came with me."

"I wouldn't have missed this for the world." He held the picture out in front of him. "The debut of baby bean."

"I think you're holding it upside down."

He flipped the picture around. "How can you tell?"

"I think that's the head." She pointed at a dark space on the image.

"Maybe he has a big stomach." He held it out again. "I should pin this up at the bar. It's never too early to start showing off my progeny."

"Don't. I won't have all the barflies making fun of my bean."

He slipped his arm around her. "I'm probably going to screw up this fatherhood thing from time to time," he said. "But I'm going to do my best. I'm serious about that."

She rested her hand on his chest. His heart beat strong beneath her fingers. "Just be here. That's really all you have to do."

"I'm here."

That was all that mattered. He was here right now. She'd hold on to that and not worry about the future.

"What are you going to be for Halloween?" Olivia asked Lucas when she got off work on the 31st.

"Nothing."

"What do you mean nothing?"

"Costumes are for little kids."

"Tell that to all the adults who'll be in costume at the Dirty Sally tonight."

"You're not working tonight, are you?"

"No, but since you're going to your friend's house, I thought I'd stop by the saloon to hear the ghost-story competition. But I'll be home in plenty of time to know if you make your curfew."

He squinched up his nose as if he'd smelled something foul. "I don't see why I have to have a curfew on Halloween."

"Still, you have one, so don't forget it. What time does the party start?"

"Six thirty."

"Do you need me to give you a ride?"

"Nah, I'll take my bike." He pushed his chair back from the table. "I'd better go get ready."

Thirty minutes later, he bounded down the stairs, an old cape of Lucille's around his shoulders. He'd slicked his hair back with gel and stuck a pair of fake plastic fangs in his mouth. "I decided it would be dumb to show up without a costume," he said. "Since it's a party and all."

"Good idea." She resisted the urge to tell him he looked good. That might be all it took to send him back upstairs to change.

"Bye, Mom." He raced past, cape billowing behind him. The door slammed in his wake, rattling the glass in the windowpanes. Not that long ago he would have kissed her good-bye; maybe kisses were for babies, too.

The old floors creaked and Lucille came into the room, moving slow. She looked older and thinner, the light-hearted woman who'd dressed up for dates replaced by this careworn figure in an old skirt and cardigan. If Olivia ever met Gerald Pershing in a dark alley someday, he'd wish he'd never been born.

"Was that Lucas I just saw dressed as a vampire?" Lucille asked.

"Yes, he's going to a party at a friend's house. He won't say so, but I think he's pretty excited."

"He's fitting in well here." She sat at the kitchen table across from her daughter. "What are your plans for the evening? You should be at a party."

"I'm going over to the Dirty Sally for the ghost-story competition."

"I'd forgotten about that." She looked distracted, turned inward, as she often was these days. "Have a good time."

"Come with me," Olivia said.

"Oh, you don't want me tagging along on your night out."

Not all that long ago, that would have been true. Olivia would have been focused on the men she might meet, and having her mother along would surely cramp her style. But she hadn't seen a man who interested her in Eureka in weeks. "Come on," she said. "You'll enjoy it. And you can give me the lowdown on who's who among the folks who show up."

"Oh, I don't know." Lucille looked around, as if she might find guidance written on the kitchen wall.

"Come on." Olivia nudged her. "What are you going to do instead? Stay home and beat yourself up a little more?"

"Do I have to have a costume? I could wear a paper bag over my head. The way I feel, that wouldn't be such a bad idea."

"If you do, I'll wear one, too. We'll be twins."

That got a chuckle out of her.

Olivia felt a surge of relief. Things weren't so bad if her mother could still laugh. "You'll get through this," she said. "You've been through worse."

"Have I?"

"The two of us had some rough times. Now that I'm a mom I'm just beginning to see how rough." She had been every mother's nightmare: a smart-mouthed kid who thought she knew everything.

"You were not an easy child," Lucille admitted. "But I'm proud of the way you've turned out. And you don't have to worry about Lucas. He's a good boy."

"The trouble is, I remember everything I did when I was just a little older than he is," she said. "I know what kind of trouble he could get into." She'd tried everything—smoking, drinking, drugs, underage sex, shoplifting. Somehow, she'd survived, but it was a wonder Lucille didn't have more gray hair.

"Eureka isn't perfect, but it isn't the inner city," Lucille said. "And Lucas is smart—sometimes I think he's smarter than the two of us put together."

"He's scary smart," Olivia agreed. She patted her mother's arm. "So, will you come with me tonight?"

"Sure. Why not?"

CHAPTER SEVEN

The Dirty Sally had a larger than usual crowd for a Wednesday evening. Olivia and Lucille threaded their way through the crowd and claimed a table normally reserved for the bus tubs. Olivia stuck the tubs in the kitchen, then rejoined her mother at the table. "Is she this pushy at home?" Jameso asked from behind the bar.

"Worse," Lucille said. "She badgered me into coming here tonight."

"At least she's good for something."

"How's Maggie?" Lucille asked.

"Maggie is . . . hormonal." He shook his head. "I've learned to keep my head down and say, 'Yes, ma'am.' "

"Smart man."

They ordered beers, then turned to the stage, where Bob was fiddling with a mike stand. "Is this thing on?" he asked.

A chorus of yeses answered him. He slid one of the bar stools closer to the microphone and settled on to it. "I guess I'm supposed to get this competition started, so here goes. This story is about the haunted mine."

A hushed anticipation settled over the crowd. Bob

started off in a conversational tone. "Some people think of mines as holes in the ground you take rocks out of. They look at them the way you might look at a boulder or a pile of dirt—lifeless.

"But a mine is a living, breathing organism, I'm convinced. You spend enough time in one and you'll know what I mean. The air pressure in a mine constantly changes, as air flows in and out, the way breath flows in and out of a man. The walls sweat or dry like skin. Stay down there long enough and I swear you'll hear the heartbeat of the mine, steady and low as a pulse."

"Drink enough and you'll hear anything," someone called.

Bob scowled at the speaker. "You going to shut up and let me tell my story or not?"

"Tell your story and quit taking all night to do it," someone called.

Bob rested his hands on his knees and straightened his back. His voice carried over the assembled crowd. "I had a mining friend, Tate Moses," he said. "We worked together at the Miller Mine back in seventy-two, before they shut down. But like a lot of us, Tate had his own claim he worked on his days off. He called it the Pay Day, because he expected a big pay day from it before too long.

"During the time in question, Tate had decided to extend one tunnel of the mine, following a vein he thought would lead to a good quantity of gold. As the shaft got longer and deeper, he came across some bones. At first, he thought they were animal bones, but quick enough he realized they were human bones. He figured he'd run across an Indian burial ground. But he didn't tell a soul. The last thing he wanted was the state coming in and telling him where he can't dig and what he can't do on his own property. So he reburied the bones outside the mine and kept on digging.

"His next day off, he goes back to the mine, and all the bones are there, piled up in the tunnel. This makes old Tate hopping mad. He figures one of his buddies is playing a trick on him. So he reburies the bones, but this time, he scatters them—a leg over here, an arm here, a hand here and so on."

Olivia shivered. This was what she'd wanted, wasn't it? Grisly stories in keeping with the holiday? She hadn't counted on the local setting and Bob's authentic detail making the tales quite so realistic.

"The next day, everything's fine, and the next," Bob continued. "But the third day, the bones are back, all together in the middle of the tunnel.

"Tate is furious. He's determined to get to the bottom of this and find out who's trying to play him for the fool. He reburies the bones; then he hides in a little side tunnel, where he can see the goings on in the main tunnel. He plans to watch until he sees who the trickster is.

"He settles in for a long wait. He sits with his back against the wall and after a while, his eyes drift closed. He's worked hard all day, and he'd celebrated at the end of the day with a tot or two of bourbon.

"He may have drifted off, but a noise wakes him. He opens his eyes, but the inside of that mine is as black as the inside of a cast-iron Dutch oven with the lid on. He leans forward, straining his ears to listen. Then he hears it again—*scritch. Scritch.* Like nails scraping against rock.

"Scritch. Scritch." Bob lowered his voice. The crowd hushed, as if everyone was holding their breath. "The rocks shift, as if something heavy is dragging over them. Tate switches on his headlamp. At first, he doesn't see anything. He plays the light over the wall on either side of the tunnel. Then he searches lower, on the floor.

"The headlamp beam catches on a flash of white. Tate leans forward and recognizes a skull, the nose collapsed and the jawbone missing. He shines the light behind the skull and sees the rest of the bones—arm bones and leg bones and vertebrae, lined up in a semblance of order, but looking like they were put together by a tenth grader without a lot of knowledge of anatomy."

Bob leaned forward even more. By this time he had the attention of everyone in the room. Only the occasional clink of a glass or bottle cut through the silence. "By this time, Tate's heart is pounding so hard, he can hardly hear anything else. He wants to close his eyes and open them again and find out this is all a horrible dream—a nightmare. But he can't move. He's paralyzed. The bones aren't just assembled again, they're moving, crawling down the tunnel straight toward him.

"Tate can't do anything. He can't scream. He can't move. He can barely breathe. He sits there, overcome with terror, as the bones crawl past him. Just as they're even with him, the skull turns and looks at him with those empty eye sockets. Tate starts to shake all over, teeth chattering like he was caught in a blizzard.

"The bones move on. They finally collapse in a heap in the exact spot where Tate first uncovered them. Only then can Tate move.

"He runs screaming from the mine and then drinks all the rest of his bourbon. But the liquor won't kill the memory of those bones crawling toward him, or those empty eye sockets turned to him.

"The next day, Tate went back to the Pay Day and sealed off the tunnel. He paid a priest to come out and say prayers at the entrance. Then he worried that might upset the ghost even more, so he found an old Ute shaman and had him come out and say some words over the spot, too.

"The bones never bothered him anymore, but Tate lost his taste for mining. He preferred to stay aboveground after that, and let the dead stay below it."

The patrons of the Dirty Sally greeted the end of the story with hoots and whistles and stamping feet. Lucille leaned across the table toward Olivia. "I think Bob missed his calling when he chose mining instead of acting."

"It was a good story," Olivia agreed. "It'll be a hard one to top."

"All right, I've had my say," Bob said. "Who's next?"

"I've got a story to tell."

Olivia almost choked on her drink. She looked up to see D. J. taking Bob's place in front of the microphone. Dressed all in black, from his knit watch cap to his motorcycle boots, he presented an imposing figure. His grim expression did nothing to erase this impression.

He didn't look at Olivia, though he had to know she was there, just to his right, eyes fixed on him. He was like a bad accident she couldn't look away from.

"My story takes place in Iraq," he began. "A soldier—we'll call him Tim—is on guard duty. The night is moonless, and utterly silent—the most dangerous kind of night. Under cover of darkness, the insurgents will sneak up on the compound with suicide bomb attacks. Even innocent-looking civilians—women and children, even—could be deadly, so Tim can never let down his guard. He has to be constantly on edge, alert for killers."

She shivered. Is that what Iraq had been like for D. J.? He'd been a contractor, not a soldier, but still, he must have seen plenty of danger.

"The night is long," he continued. "Tim is out there alone and there's nothing to distract him from his own thoughts. And it's those thoughts that torture him, even more than his fear of dying or of failing to do his duty.

"Tim can't stop thinking about the woman he left behind in the States. They parted on bad terms, and he's weighed down with guilt."

Olivia looked away and pushed aside her empty beer glass, her hand shaking. Was D. J. talking about a made-up character? Or was he making a confession of his own?

"Over and over in his mind, he replays scenarios of what he could have done—what he should have said. He thinks about her all the time now. He's having trouble sleeping.

"But guard duty is worse. On this moonless night he's standing guard at the gate of the compound when he sees a woman walking toward him. She's wearing a pale blue burka that covers her from head to foot. 'Halt!' he tells her, then repeats the order in the local dialect. The woman stops and reaches up to push the hood of the burka away from her face.

"Tim stares at a woman who looks exactly like his lost love, the same blond hair and creamy skin. She's definitely not an Iraqi woman. She smiles and starts walking toward him again. He's not supposed to let anyone approach unless they have the proper credentials. But he's paralyzed and mute as the woman—his woman—walks toward him. She's smiling, but she doesn't say a thing. He calls her name, but still she says nothing.

"By this time, he's panicking. Is this some kind of trick? Is he losing his mind? 'Halt!' he shouts. He shoulders his weapon. The woman keeps coming. She's scarcely a yard from him. Still smiling, she reaches into her robe. All his training tells him she's going to detonate the explosives she's wearing. Tears are streaming down his face. 'Halt!' he screams, but she ignores him.

"He can't let her do this. He closes his eyes and squeezes the trigger on his weapon. The bullets tear into her, knocking her back. She lands in the street in front of him, a bloody rag doll. He drops his weapon and runs to her, kneeling beside her. The hood of the burka has fallen forward, shielding her face. He reaches up to push it back, but instead of the face of his beloved, he sees only a grinning skull."

Silence greeted the end of this tale. Olivia swallowed hard. Was this some twisted way of trying to make her feel guilty? Or was she too paranoid and this had nothing to do with her at all?

"That was seriously creepy," someone in the audience said, and a few people laughed, breaking the tension. Applause broke out. D. J. nodded. "Who's next?" he asked.

But before anyone could answer, the door to the bar opened and newspaper editor Rick Otis leaned in. "The ghost lights are back," he said. "They're putting on quite a show."

Glasses chimed and chairs scraped back as people headed for the door. Olivia and Lucille followed the others and stood in the street in front of the bar, looking up toward the pale outline of Mount Winston. "I don't see anything," Olivia said.

"There, over to the left." Lucille pointed.

Olivia looked along her mother's finger and saw a bloom of white light. The single orb shimmered in the night, then was joined by a second. The two balls of light skipped down the mountainside, swallowed up at the tree line. Then another orb appeared, and another. The display was eerily beautiful.

"Anybody want to drive up there with me, see how close we can get?" Rick asked.

"Don't do it, Rick."

Olivia started at the sound of her mother's voice. "Don't go haring off up there," Lucille said. "You won't find anything and you're liable to drive off the side of the mountain or something."

"Don't you want to know what's causing the lights?" Rick asked.

"No," she said. "We all need a little mystery in our lives."

"I'm with Rick. I don't like not knowing things." D. J.'s voice vibrated through Olivia, and she had to fight the urge to turn and look at him.

"Sometimes, all it takes to know things is paying attention," she said, raising her voice only slightly, so he'd be sure to hear.

"What do you mean by that?" He touched her arm so that she was forced to look at him.

He bore the same fierce, demanding expression she knew too well, a look that made her feel whatever she gave to him would never be enough.

"It doesn't matter now," she said, and pulled out of his grasp.

"Maybe I didn't pay enough attention before," he said. "But I'm paying attention now."

"It doesn't matter," she said. "It's too late." She'd had enough of dwelling on the past and letting things that should be dead and buried haunt her. She'd been telling the truth when she'd told him she didn't believe in ghosts. She wasn't about to start believing now.

"Did you see the ghost lights last night, Maggie?"

"The what?" Maggie looked up from her computer, mind foggy from spending the last hour trying to make sense of the town budget figures Doug had passed on to her. No matter which way she looked at them, the result was the same—Eureka was broke. And her job was to write an article breaking the news to the general public. Was it too late to change jobs?

"The ghost lights up on Mount Winston," Rick said. "They're these mystery blobs of light that show up from time to time—no one knows why. They put on a special Halloween performance last night."

"Is this another one of those quaint Eureka customs that's supposed to make up for the fact that you don't have a Starbucks or a Taco Bell in the entire county?" she asked.

He stared at her and shame washed over her. The filter between her brain and her mouth had gone missing lately. "No, I didn't see them," she said.

"People used to think that Murphy was responsible for the lights," Rick said. "They were the kind of practical joke he liked."

"So when he wasn't drinking or brawling, he was playing practical jokes. What a guy." She thought by now she'd come to terms with the fact that her father was less than the responsible, generous, superhero quality guy she'd fantasized about when she was a girl, but disappointment at how far he fell short of that image still pricked at her from time to time.

"People enjoyed his jokes," Rick said. "They were entertaining. Entertainment is hard to come by around here sometimes—seeing as how we don't have a Starbucks or a Taco Bell. We have to make do with coffee and tacos from the Last Dollar."

"Don't tell Janelle and Danielle I said that about Starbucks and Taco Bell," she said. She'd never be able to look the two café owners in the eye if they knew she'd expressed a preference for chain restaurant fare over the Last Dollar's homemade goodness.

"Are you all right?" he asked.

"I'm fine."

"Because you seem a little out of sorts. Are you feeling okay?"

"Other than morning sickness, constant fatigue, indigestion, and swollen ankles, I'm just peachy."

"Uh-huh. And things are okay with you and Jameso?"

"Great." Except she'd practically taken his head off last night when he asked if she wanted to go for a ride on his motorcycle. Didn't he think that sounded a little dangerous for a pregnant woman? Or didn't he think? "Why are you so concerned anyway?"

"Because if this is the mood you're going to be in for the rest of your pregnancy, it's going to be a long nine months."

"Seven and a half months." At his puzzled look, she added, "That's how long before the baby's born—seven and a half months."

"But who's counting? What's wrong, really? It's not like you to be so pissy."

Nothing's wrong and stop asking me about it! she wanted to scream. But even that wouldn't stop Rick. He was worse than a dog who knew a cat was on the other side of the door, refusing to give up.

"I'm on edge waiting for the results of the prenatal testing," she said. "They're supposed to be in any day now."

"And you're worried the results won't be good?"

"I'm forty years old, Rick. We're talking seriously old eggs here. The odds aren't in my favor."

"I think you need to go back to math class." He raised one finger, a professor in lecture mode. "While you might have a slightly higher chance of something going wrong, I'm pretty sure most women your age deliver perfectly healthy babies."

"And you know this how?"

"I read it in a press release. You'll be fine."

"But what if something *is* wrong?" She had to force the words out, though the question had been ping-ponging around her brain for days, like a hyper Jack Russell terrier.

"Then you'll deal," he said. "It's what people do."

"I'll deal? That's the best you can come up with? Because I feel so much better now."

"Would you rather I tell you you'll fall apart?" He shook his head. "You're not the falling apart type."

She hadn't fallen apart when she'd found out her husband of twenty years was cheating on her, or when he'd left her, or when she'd found out she had no more money, or even when the "inheritance" from her absent father had consisted of a cabin in the mountains, a ten-year-old Jeep, and a gold mine with no gold. "I guess you're right."

"Feel better now?"

Strangely enough, she did. "How come Jameso hasn't bothered to ask me why I'm being such a bitch lately, but you did?" she asked.

"He's probably assumed it's all his fault—the safe fall-back position for any guy in a relationship. And in this case, he's right. He's the one who put that bun in your oven."

"He could have asked."

"Cut the guy some slack. He's probably as freaked out as you are."

A tinny version of "Fire on the Mountain" sounded through the office and Maggie lunged for her phone.

"A Deadhead ring tone?" Rick asked. "Really?"

She ignored him. "Hello?"

"Maggie? This is Dr. Racine."

"Yes?" Her heart slammed painfully against her ribs.

"I have your test results. Everything looks great. You're on track to have a healthy baby."

"I am? I mean . . . that's great. Wonderful."

"Do you have any questions for me?"

She'd spent so much time preparing herself for bad news she had no idea how to handle good news. "No, I'm good. Thanks for calling." She hung up and stared at the phone in her hand.

"Everything okay?" Rick asked.

"Yeah, the tests came back fine."

"What did I tell you?"

She shoved back her chair. "I have to go tell Jameso." Not waiting for his answer, she grabbed her purse and headed for the Jeep.

She had no recollection of the drive to her house. She found Jameso in his living room, waxing his skis. "Expecting snow?" she asked.

"There's none in the forecast, but I'm hoping." He set aside the iron he was using to melt wax onto the bottoms of the skis. "What are you doing home in the middle of the day? Everything okay?"

"I heard from Dr. Racine. The test results came in."

"And?" He wore the pinched expression of a man bracing himself for bad news.

"Everything's fine. No sign of any problems."

His smile cut loose the last string that had been holding her together. She began to sob, big, hiccupy crying that made her feel sloppy and unattractive, but she couldn't stop.

"Hey, hey!" He gathered her into his arms and stroked her hair. "What's wrong?"

"I've just been so worried. And I've been such a bitch to you. I should have told you what was wrong instead of snapping at you."

"We're both the type to play it close to the vest when it comes to emotions."

Yeah. Just what every good relationship needed—two people who couldn't talk about their feelings. "Was Jake that way, too?" After all this time, she was still hungry for more details about her father.

"You know it. I was his closest friend and he never even mentioned you existed."

"Do you resent him for that?" she asked.

"I resent him for a lot of things, but that doesn't do any good," he said. "I'm trying to let go of the past."

"Yeah, it isn't always easy."

"Easier when you have a future to look forward to." He patted her back again. "I'm glad the baby's okay. I'll be honest, it still doesn't seem a hundred percent real to me, but I'm working on it."

"Right. As long as we're working on this being honest with each other thing, can I admit I'm terrified I'm going to screw this up? I mean, the whole baby thing. Who am I to think I can raise a child?"

"I think that's pretty normal," he said. "Babies are little, but they're huge, too, life changing."

That was definitely part of her fear. She'd had too many changes in her life in the last six months. Enough already.

"You'll be okay," Jameso said. "You have good instincts. My instincts, on the other hand, suck. But I'll do my best."

He was trying—that counted for something, right? She still couldn't see Jameso as husband and father material; he was too wild, too laid-back, too much like her father, who'd never really been a father.

But he was all she and the baby had right now. So they'd hang on and make the best of it, for the next eight months or forever, whichever came last.

If Lucille had had a regular city office, she could have locked the door and hung a sign saying the mayor was not in. But the only city official in Eureka who had an office was the secretary responsible for collecting money for building permits and trash pickup. The mayor and the town council conducted business from the storefronts and offices they manned for their "real" jobs.

Which meant Lucille was fair game for any citizen with a bone to pick with her from behind the front counter of Lacy's. So far no one had come in to read her the riot act about allowing a smooth-talking lothario to swindle the city out of all of its cash, but when she saw Cassie Wynock headed up the steps on Friday morning,

Lucille feared that stretch of good fortune was about to end.

"Good morning, Cassie," she said, when the librarian hurried into the store.

"I have a complaint," Cassie said.

Of course you do. When did Cassie ever not have a complaint about something? "Why is it no one ever comes to see me with compliments?" she wondered out loud.

"If you took this job because you wanted people to fawn over you, you deserve all the grief you get," Cassie said. "But people wouldn't have anything to complain about if government did what it promised to do in the first place."

"You'll have to take that up with the folks in Denver or Washington. We're not much in the habit of making promises around here." Even before Gerald had absconded with the town funds, the budget had been limited enough to prohibit any kind of extravagance. For the six years Lucille had been mayor, at least one town council meeting every fall consisted of a debate about whether or not they could afford new Christmas decorations for the town. The decision always ended up that they could not.

"You promised me you'd send someone to look at the shelves in the library that need replacing," Cassie said.

Lucille had a vague recollection of something about library shelves. She'd been in the throes of her most serious infatuation with Gerald at the time and dealing with Cassie's demands had been the last thing on her mind. Was that really only a few weeks ago? "In case you haven't heard, the town is broke," she said.

"Eureka has been broke as long as I've been alive. Yet you always seem to come up with money for the things you think are important. Well, I'm saying library shelves are important and it's time you realized it."

Cassie announced this—as she announced all her opinions—in the same tone of voice she might have used to berate a child for defacing library books.

Lucille leaned toward the older woman, palms flat on the counter between them to keep from reaching out and throttling her. "Don't talk to me like I'm ten years old or an idiot," she said. "I know how much money is in the town treasury, and it's $752.86. We don't have enough money to pay the light bill next month, or the plow drivers when the snow finally does fall, or the secretary's salary. So the library shelves are pretty far down on my list of priorities right now."

Cassie stared at her, wide-eyed. "Just what am I supposed to do, then?"

"I don't care if you have to prop the shelves up with old bricks. You're a smart woman when you're not looking down your nose at everyone. Deal with it."

Lucille braced herself for one of Cassie's notorious temper tantrums, but the librarian's response surprised her. "When I asked Doug how much money the town had left, he told me it was none of my business. I figured I'd get the truth from you, one way or another."

"This wasn't about the library shelves at all." Lucille had to admire Cassie's deviousness, though she still wanted to wring the woman's neck.

"Oh, the shelves still need replacing, but I can make them do for another year. I really wanted to see if it was true that you'd let what happened with your playboy lover turn you into some pitiful excuse for a woman."

"Playboy lover?" Lucille managed a laugh, albeit a bitter one. "You've been reading too many Hollywood gossip magazines. Gerald was a cheat and a swindler; I was just too stupid to recognize it."

"Not stupid," Cassie said. "But don't act like you're the first woman to ever be taken in by a man. All this proves is that you're no better than the rest of us."

Lucille wouldn't call the expression in Cassie's eyes compassion, but there was a measure of understanding there. She'd heard rumors about something going on between Cassie and Jake Murphy, and the mere mention of Jake's name was enough to upset the librarian; maybe she did have some inkling of what Lucille was going through. "I don't think I'm better than anyone else," Lucille said. "But I do have more responsibility to this town than the average citizen. This fiasco happened on my watch, and I've got to find a way to fix it."

"As someone once told me: You're a smart woman, you'll think of something." Apparently having gotten what she'd come for, Cassie turned to leave.

"Cassie?" Lucille gripped the edge of the counter, forcing herself to ask the question she needed to know the answer to. "Did you see through Gerald? Did you know I was making a fool of myself with him?" Was she the only one who hadn't recognized his true colors? Had her friends stood by and let this happen?

"All I knew was that he was a man. I don't trust any of them. You didn't do anything half the women in this town wouldn't have done, given a chance. Charm is a powerful persuader, even when we should know better." She left, the cow bells on the door jangling behind her.

Lucille rested her head in her hands, elbows on the counter. Gerald had been charming, all right. And she'd wanted desperately to believe every sweet word he'd said to her. Maybe her mistake hadn't been so much in trusting him—though that was definitely a mistake—but in avoiding any kind of romantic entanglement for so many years. She been waiting all this time for the perfect man to come along, and no such person existed.

All that those years of nursing the old hurt of her marriage had gotten her was another kind of pain. When she was young, she'd thought life would get easier as she got older and gained experience and wisdom. So much for that belief. She could shelve that one right up there with the idea that eating grapefruit made you lose weight or that tanning was good for your skin. All she had to count on now was whatever was in front of her at the moment. Which was an almost empty bank account and not a lot of ideas for filling it up.

CHAPTER EIGHT

The first week in November, Olivia collected her supplies and reported to the Last Dollar. "I'm ready to start on the mural," she told Danielle, who was manning the front counter.

"Super. We took everything off the back wall for you, but let us know if there's anything else you need."

Olivia had half expected the women to tell her they'd changed their minds. They didn't want an amateur like her messing with their restaurant. Trying to ignore the half a dozen diners who watched as she made her way to the back of the room, she set down her plastic tote of paints and brushes, and studied the blank wall before her. It looked a lot bigger than she remembered. Bigger than anything else she'd ever worked on, for sure; she was used to painting T-shirts and jewelry, not whole walls.

She took a deep breath. "You can do this," she whispered. She'd work on one section at a time. First up, sketch in the miner. She selected a pencil from her supplies, consulted the sketch she'd roughed out on a piece of notebook paper, and went to work.

Once the figure began to take shape beneath her hand,

she forgot about the diners watching or her worries about making the piece perfect. With the rough outline in place, she picked up a paintbrush, eager to see her idea fleshed out with color. At some point in the morning, Janelle brought her a glass of iced tea, and Danielle found a stool for her to lean against as she worked.

By lunchtime, the rough shape of the miner had emerged from the wall. "Well, look at that," a familiar voice behind her observed. "You've got talents besides putting a nice head on a mug of beer."

"Don't overdo the flattery, Bob. It's liable to go to my head."

"I was trying to be nice, so don't give me any of your smart mouth."

Was he really hurt, or just a good actor? Maybe a little of both. "Then, thank you," she said.

"This fellow looks pretty good." He took a step over to study the figure from a different angle. "You want me to get my costume from the Founders' Pageant and pose for you?" he asked.

"Why would I want you to do that?" she asked.

"It's clear as day that's me there in that drawing." He pointed to the sketch she'd tacked onto the wall.

Janelle paused on the way to refill water glasses at a table across the room. "I don't think it looks like you, Bob," she said. "The man in the picture is much younger than you."

He leaned closer and squinted at the drawing. "Of course it's me. You done a good job of capturing me in my prime. You wouldn't know it to look at me now, but I was a handsome devil. I made a real hit with the ladies."

"But, of course," Janelle said, and winked at Olivia.

Olivia turned back to her drawing, hiding her smile from Bob. "How's the snowfall betting going?" she asked.

"Don't let the state hear you call it betting," he said.

"To them that means gambling, and gambling is illegal unless you buy a license and give them their cut. This here is a contest with a donation."

"We've raised $250 so far." Danielle joined them.

"A drop in the bucket compared to all we lost," Bob said. "That won't even pay the diesel for one day of snow-plowing."

"So you think we're going to need snowplows this year?" Olivia asked. She thought of D. J., who was sitting idle, waiting for his first day of work. Lucas said he'd saved all the money he'd made in Iraq and was living off that.

"Oh, the snow'll get here sooner or later," Bob said. "And we'll need money to pay for plowing, not to mention streetlights and the library and maintenance and all the other things it takes to run even a little town. The town council and the mayor all agreed to waive their salaries, but since we pay 'em little or nothing as it is, that didn't help much."

"Any word on where that bastard Pershing ran off to?" Olivia asked.

"Not yet," Bob said. "But Reggie told me he asked a private detective he knows to follow his trail."

"I hope he rots in jail the rest of his life when they do find him," Danielle said. Olivia stared. Danielle was known for never saying an unkind word about anyone. She'd even been known to express sympathy for Cassie Wynock. She flushed now. "Well, it was horrible what he did to poor Lucille. And, of course, it was awful about the money."

"May not be much chance of him doing any jail time," Bob said. "People are saying if we handed the money over willingly, we can't charge him with stealing."

"I thought he talked the bank clerk into paying out more than the city authorized," Olivia said.

"He did, but nobody can prove that. We don't have anything in writing."

Olivia turned back to the mural, carefully sketching in the miner's hands. How dumb could these people get? Even she'd know not to hand over a bunch of money to a man who was practically a stranger, especially without a written record. Which didn't mean she thought her mother was stupid, but it had surprised her that someone her mother's age would be so gullible.

"I know what you're thinking," Bob said over her shoulder. "That we're all a bunch of dumb hicks. And maybe we were a little naïve. But the guy knew what he was doing. He knew just what to say to make us trust him. And he was a friend of your mom's."

She nodded. There was that. Everyone in town loved Lucille, so of course they'd loved Gerald, too.

"How's your mom doing?" Danielle asked.

Olivia leaned back against the stool. "She's sick over all of this." Guilt over the money was easy to understand, but Olivia knew something else was going on. Lucille was ashamed because she'd slept with Gerald and let him lead her on. Instead of blaming him for being a gold-plated bastard, she was faulting herself for not seeing through him.

"Well, you tell your mama when we do find Pershing, I've got some ideas for dealing with him," Bob said.

She could only imagine what back-country revenge Bob had planned. "I'll be sure to tell her."

"D. J. said he knows a hit man with the CIA who could take him out for us," Bob said.

She almost dropped her pencil. "D. J. said that?"

Bob nodded. "He sounded serious, too. He met some bad dudes over there in Iraq, I take it. I told him as much as it would please me to know the man was no longer around, it's more important to get our money back. Or as much of it as we can."

"I don't see how you're going to do that," Danielle said.

"I told you, I have some ideas. You tell your mother to stop worrying. I'm going to take care of things."

He sounded so certain, but what could Bob—who was known for his outlandish ideas—do to stop a professional con man like Gerald?

After Olivia had finished sketching in the miner, she headed home to eat supper before her late shift at the Dirty Sally. She found Lucille in the kitchen, staring at the directions on the back of a box of macaroni as if they were written in a foreign language. Olivia took the box from her hand. "Sit down, let me do that," she said.

Lucille sat. Or rather, she drooped into a chair. "Lucas is upstairs doing homework," she said.

"That's good." Olivia turned on the burner under the pot of water for the macaroni. "I saw Bob Prescott down at the Last Dollar. He said he's working on a plan to get the town's money back."

"Bob's always got a plan for something," Lucille said. "He means well, but usually his plans don't work out."

"At least he's trying." Which was more than she could say for her mother; Lucille seemed to have given up.

"Believe me, I'd get the money back if I could."

"I'm not talking about the money." She turned her back to the stove. "I'm talking about snapping out of it. So the guy talked you into bed and left you without so much as a kiss good-bye. It happens. Men are bastards. Life is easier if you just accept that."

Lucille scowled at her. "How did you turn out to be so cynical? Did I do that to you?"

"Life did that to me."

"I'm not so sure." Lucille picked up the salt shaker and rolled it between her palms. "After your father left I was pretty down on men. I think I passed that on to you."

"We're not talking about me. We're talking about you and Gerald. Quit grieving over him. He's not worth it."

"You think I'm grieving over him?" Lucille set down the shaker with a thump.

"Aren't you?"

"No, we had one night. And, yes, it was a good night. But I wasn't in love with him."

"Then why are you so upset?"

She sighed. "Shame. Embarrassment that I let my guard down. Guilt over what I've done to this town I love."

"The town council voted to give Gerald the money, not you."

"But they listened to him because I asked them to . . . because I vouched for him."

"But any two of the four could have disagreed and the money would still be sitting in the bank. So stop blaming yourself. Have you noticed no one else in town is? I haven't heard one person express anything but sympathy at the way you were taken in." It was amazing, really. She'd fully expected at least some people to come down hard on her mother—call for her resignation, maybe even sue her in court. Maybe folks grumbled in private, but even down at the Dirty Sally, second home to some of the worst curmudgeons in town, no one blamed Lucille.

"The sympathy's almost worse than anger. It makes me look pathetic and dumb."

"You're not dumb, but you're beginning to act pretty pathetic."

"I'm older and I don't bounce back from hurt the way I used to. Don't make the same mistake I did, Olivia."

"I'll keep that in mind if I ever meet any slick-talking rich guys."

"I'm not talking about Gerald. The mistake I made was that I wasted so many years keeping to myself when I could have found a good man. And there are some out there. I didn't have to spend all those nights alone . . . I chose to, for fear of being hurt. It was all such a waste."

The words surprised Olivia. Her mother had always been so independent, not needing anyone. "Are you saying any man is better than no man at all?"

"I'm saying we should take advantage of the opportunities that come to us and not hold ourselves back out of fear. If I'd had relationships with men all along, I might not have been so susceptible to Gerald's flattery. I might have learned to protect myself better. Or maybe I'd have already been involved and wouldn't even have been a target."

"I guess that's one way to look at it." Olivia turned back to the stove and dumped the package of macaroni in the pot of now-boiling water. She'd certainly thrown herself into dating after D. J. left—not that it had helped any.

"You know my secrets, now tell me yours," Lucille said. "What happened with D. J.?"

She stiffened. "You already know what happened. I loved him. I thought we'd get married, have children together. Instead, he decided to go to Iraq."

"Did you tell him how you felt?"

"He didn't ask. He just made this announcement that he'd taken this job and would be gone for six months to a year. What I wanted didn't matter." She'd waited for him to ask her opinion, to say something that would provide her an opening to tell him she didn't want him to leave, but he'd presented the idea as a done deal. He was going and what she wanted didn't matter.

"If you'd asked, he might have stayed."

Old anger flared. "I wasn't going to beg him. We lived together. We slept together every night. If he didn't know how I felt after all that, words weren't going to make any difference."

"Sometimes words do make a difference." Lucille's voice was gentle. "People make mistakes. I made a big one with Gerald. I think D. J. knows he made one with you."

"It's not just that he left."

"What else, then?"

Olivia hadn't told anyone the "what else." But maybe unburdening herself would help heal the wound. And she could trust her mother not to blab to anyone else. She glanced toward the stairs—no sign of Lucas. She lowered her voice. "I was pregnant when he left."

"A baby? But—"

"I miscarried two weeks after he left." The words sounded so stark, the first time she'd said them out loud. "D. J. never knew."

"Oh, Olivia." The two words carried all the sorrow and pain of a mother for her child. To Olivia, they were better than a warm embrace. "How awful for you," Lucille continued. "But if he didn't know, you can't blame him—"

"He should have known!" She wiped her eyes with the back of her hand, angry that she could still cry after all this time. "I'd been throwing up every morning for a week, and I even told him I'd missed my period. The man isn't dumb. He ought to be able to put two and two together. Instead, he runs off to Iraq."

"So you think he did know and he left anyway?"

She nodded, swallowing more tears. "How can you trust someone who's hurt you that way?" she whispered.

"That does take courage." Lucille's eyes met her daughter's. "But you've never been a coward, have you?"

"Neither have you."

Lucille nodded. "You're right. So we'll get through this. I've got to stop focusing on the past and think about the future. Since no one will let me resign as mayor, I guess I've got to pull myself together and run the town, even if we are broke."

"You've got a lot of people on your side. That counts for something."

"That means a lot. Especially knowing I've got you on my side."

"Yeah." She managed a rueful smile. "I never would have admitted this when I was a kid, but we're more alike than different."

"I couldn't be more proud of you. And whatever you decide to do about D. J., I'll stand by you."

"Thanks. I don't have any plans, but I'll let you know if that changes." The best she could say was that she no longer hated D. J. If only she could let go of hating some of the things she'd done before and after he'd left. Like mother, like daughter, she told herself. Sometimes letting go of the past was harder than facing the future.

As the baby grew inside Maggie, its presence in her life grew. How could a tiny baby, not yet born even, take up so much space—emotionally, mentally, and even physically? For instance, she had to make a place for this infant in the little house she rented in town. The second bedroom she'd been using for storage seemed the logical choice, but looking at it now with Jameso, she had her doubts. "It's an awfully small room," she said, contemplating the sloping ceiling and the one tiny window.

"Small for the plans Barb sent," Jameso said. "But it ought to be big enough for a baby. I mean, how much room do they need?"

"You need room for the crib and a dresser for clothing. A changing table would be nice, but I can make do with the top of the dresser. Somewhere to put diapers and a monitor. A humidifier for this dry air . . ." Everything she'd read in the half a dozen baby books Barb had sent her made her head spin.

"I can put up some shelves and stuff," he said. "It'll be okay."

"What about at your place? You need room for the baby there, too."

His expression grew wary. "Why do I need room for the baby there?"

"So he—or she—can stay with you sometimes."

"Why would he—or she—stay with me? I mean, babies need to be with their mothers. Won't you be breast-feeding . . . or something?" He said "or something" as if he was afraid to imagine what that mysterious other thing might be.

"I can pump breast milk for bottle feedings. And you'll want to spend time with your child to bond."

"I will?" He swallowed, Adam's apple bobbing. "I mean, sure, I will. But I don't think I need a whole room for the baby. It'll be easier if we keep everything here at your place."

He looked so flummoxed that she almost took pity on him—almost. "You've never spent much time around babies, have you?" she asked.

"No."

"No little brothers or sisters or cousins, or nieces and nephews?" He never talked about his family—one of the things that both annoyed and intrigued her.

"My sister is two years older than me. She's got a couple of kids, but we aren't really close."

"Why is that?" Being an only child, Maggie had often longed for a sister or brother. She'd fantasized about her mother remarrying, or her father reappearing with children in tow. She referred to Barb as the sister she never had, but it wasn't quite the same, having someone in the world who shared your blood and your memories of growing up.

"No reason. We just aren't close. So, you want the shelves here?"

He'd slammed shut a door she couldn't go through. This reluctance to talk about his family worried her. What demons lurked there that might affect her child? Did mental illness or alcoholism or drug addiction lie hidden in his bloodline?

Of course, she was one to talk, considering her father's penchant for abusing alcohol, and her suspicion that some mental imbalance had led him to flee his home and take refuge in his mountain hermitage. "We'd better wait until I get some furniture in here; then we'll know where the shelves will fit best. In the meantime, I have to figure out what to do with all this stuff." She surveyed the boxes, each cryptically marked with a single word: *Kitchen, Dining, Books.*

"You can store them at my place," he said.

"So you have room for my boxes, but not for a baby?"

"I can shove boxes into the crawl space. Certainly can't do that with a baby."

"You do know I'll need you to keep the baby sometimes."

"Sure. Of course, I'll do that." Though he didn't look or sound very confident.

"What will you do with the baby when you keep it?"

"I figured I'd just, you know, hold it. Keep it comfortable and . . . safe."

The earnestness of his expression and the tenderness with which he spoke the words untied another knot in the bindings around her heart. "Oh, Jameso, that's so sweet." She leaned against him and his arm went around her.

"I didn't say it to be sweet. It's just what I'd do."

"You're going to be a great dad," she said.

He flushed. "I'll do what I can, for you and the baby. I'll try not to mess things up."

"That's the best any of us can do."

"Yeah." He cleared his throat. "So you want to wait on the shelves?"

She laughed. "Yes, Barb said she had some ideas for the nursery."

"Barb has plenty of ideas. She sends me text messages and e-mails half a dozen times a day."

"She's almost more excited than I am. She and Jimmy are planning to visit for Christmas."

"I've got to meet this Jimmy guy. He must be something if he can handle Barb."

"He's actually very quiet—the strong, silent type. Very supportive. He pretty much lets Barb take the lead."

"I imagine if he didn't give Barb the reins, she'd yank them right out of his hands. So she's in charge of the nursery?"

"Yes, just do whatever she wants. It's easier that way."

"Definitely easier."

Too bad Maggie couldn't turn everything having to do with the baby over to someone like Barb. Then maybe she wouldn't feel so lost.

Big breath in. *Follow your instincts,* she told herself. *And take Jameso's advice. Hold the baby. Keep it comfortable and safe.* That's all any of them wanted, wasn't it?

CHAPTER NINE

Before she painted in the burro, bighorn, and other animals on the mural, Olivia decided she needed to do more research. She persuaded Lucas to accompany her to the library, where he helped her pick out several books. She was curious to see how the curmudgeon, Cassie, would respond to her and Lucas together, after her brusque send-off during Olivia's first visit to the library.

"Hello, Lucas, Ms. Theriot." Cassie greeted them formally at the front desk and accepted Lucas's library card. She studied the titles on their stack of books. They seemingly met her approval; she scanned them and handed them back.

"I'm doing more research for my mural," Olivia said, unable to resist goading the woman a little.

"I saw your work when I was in the café the other day," Cassie said. "I thought the pioneer woman was a nice touch. Women don't get enough credit for their contributions."

Olivia blinked, momentarily stunned by this unexpected praise. "Thank you," she said. "I'm glad you like it."

"I can't believe she said she liked my mural," Olivia

said to Lucas as they left the library. "She was so hostile last time I saw her."

"She isn't so bad, really," Lucas said. "I think she's probably had a hard life."

"Life is hard for almost everyone sometimes," Olivia said.

"Was it hard for you, growing up without your dad?"

The question startled and unsettled her. She and Lucas had never talked much about her past. He knew the basic facts, of course, but she'd always figured that, as a kid, he wasn't much interested in anything that had happened to her before he was born. Why the sudden interest? "My dad was around. I just didn't live with him all the time," she said. "I knew lots of kids whose parents were divorced, so it wasn't that big a deal."

But sometimes it had been. She'd carried a little girl's fantasy of the perfect dad, especially when she saw friends with their fathers. Sometimes she'd wished her mother would remarry, so that at least she could have a stepdad, but Lucille never dated while Olivia was living at home—at least not that Olivia knew about.

The thought occurred to her that maybe Lucas wasn't asking about her dad because he was curious about Olivia's childhood, but because he had regrets about his own. "Lucas, I'm sorry your father hasn't been a good dad," she said. "I tried to get him to see you, but some men just aren't good fathers."

He kicked at a rock in the road. "Yeah, well, I don't remember much about him, so I guess it doesn't matter."

"But you'd like a father to do stuff with. That's natural."

"D. J. does stuff with me."

"But D. J. isn't your father."

"I know that." He gave her a classic "I'm not stupid" teenage look that she remembered only too well directing at her own mother. "Let's go by his place," Lucas said. "I want to show him the books I got."

Refusing would probably start an argument, and she hated to destroy the closeness she felt to him today. Who knew how many more such times she'd have now that he was entering the turbulent teen years? And surely she could stand a few minutes in D. J.'s company. "All right."

They turned down the side street that led toward the rental where D. J. lived. "I know what I want for Christmas," Lucas said.

"And what is that?" She'd been thinking a new winter coat might be a good present, but he probably wouldn't agree.

"I want a twenty-two."

"A twenty-two?" she asked, confused. "Twenty-two what?"

"Not twenty-two what." He laughed. "A twenty-two. A gun. For hunting and stuff."

She stopped in the middle of the road. "You want a gun?" She stared at the young man before her. He was the same height as her now, and his hair fell in front of his eyes. Now that she thought about it, his voice had dropped to a deeper register sometime in the last few weeks. What had happened to her little boy—the sweet, innocent child who would never ask for a gun as a present?

"Sure, lots of guys at school have them."

"But you don't know anything about guns."

"D. J. can teach me. He shot guns in Iraq."

D. J. again! Had he put this idea into Lucas's head?

As they approached the house, she recognized D. J. in the front yard, standing next to—was that a dead deer?

"Where did you get that?" Lucas called, running ahead.

"I shot it up near Copper Springs. Hello, Olivia."

"You shot it?" She stared at the dead animal, strung up by its hind feet from a tree in D. J.'s front yard.

"Don't worry, I have a tag."

"But you're from the city. You don't hunt."

He laughed. "I'm discovering my inner mountain man."

"What are you going to do with a whole deer?" Olivia asked.

"Keep some of it. Give some away. I thought your mother might like some."

"You'll have to ask her." But Olivia had a feeling venison was in her future.

"Look at the books I got at the library," Lucas said. "We're studying the Civil War in school, so I got a biography of Robert E. Lee and one of Ulysses S. Grant."

"I read the Grant bio last year," D. J. said. "You'll like it."

"Are you coming to the Thanksgiving dinner?" Lucas asked. Apparently even school kids knew about the community Thanksgiving dinner—another Eureka tradition Olivia was going to have to get accustomed to. Lucille had informed her that, of course, they were all going, and they were going to contribute. Outvoted—since Lucas had enthusiastically agreed—Olivia had relented.

"I wouldn't miss a free feed," D. J. said.

"Mom is making mashed potatoes. From scratch."

D. J. looked at her. "Mashed potatoes for a hundred people?"

"Maybe enough for fifty." It was the one make-ahead-and-make-a-lot dish she knew she could handle, courtesy of a restaurant where she'd once waitressed, which had served up the Crock-Pot mix of potatoes, sour cream, and cheese as a specialty.

"Are they the ones with sour cream and cheese?" he asked.

She told herself she shouldn't be so pleased he remembered. "Yes."

"Then I'll definitely be there early."

"We'll save you a place," Lucas said. "You can sit with us."

She eyed her son. Was he playing matchmaker? She'd have to have a talk with him about that.

"Can I go in and play games?" Lucas asked. Perhaps this was another reason he'd been so eager to stop by D. J.'s place, to check out the latest video gaming system, which his mother and grandmother had refused to buy him.

"Sure."

He loped toward the house, long legs covering the distance in a few strides. As soon as the door slammed behind him, Olivia turned to D. J. "He asked for a *gun* for Christmas."

"And you think I had something to do with it."

"I know you did." She eyed the dead deer.

"It won't hurt him to learn how to shoot at his age. Lots of boys around here grow up around guns."

"He's not lots of boys. Lucas is smart. He has an IQ of 160. He's interested in science and history. He's going to go to college and do great things."

"He can do all that and still get a gun for Christmas."

"Not from me. And not from you either."

"I won't give him a gun if you don't want me to."

She hadn't expected him to acquiesce so easily. "Thank you for respecting my wishes," she said stiffly.

He took a step toward her. "Look, I know I should have asked you before I decided to go to Iraq. I was just feeling so bad about being out of work so long and not in a position to support a family. The chance to go away for a little while and make a lot of money seemed too good to pass up. I thought you'd see that I was doing it for us."

She held up her hand to stop him. "There's no sense going over this again. You made your choice, now we all have to live with it."

He started to say something else, but Lucas emerged from the house. "Mom! D. J.! Grandma is on television!"

They arrived inside to see the tail end of an interview with Lucille about the town's financial crisis. Olivia was struck by how drawn her mother looked. Older and smaller. But her words were calm and measured. "Eureka is not going to let this setback destroy us. The people here have always pulled together to help each other out. For instance, we're still having the Thanksgiving dinner as we do every year. We've got volunteers to do other jobs around town. We'll get through this together."

The cameras panned over the town—the Last Dollar, the Dirty Sally, Lacy's, the school, and the library. Trees were bare and everything looked a little forlorn and run-down.

"Eureka probably doesn't look like much to most people, but I like it," Lucas said.

"What do you like about it?" D. J. asked.

"I like that I can ride my bike everywhere, and that I know almost everyone now that I've been here a while. I like that Grandma is here." He paused, then added, "And kids here don't think I'm a loser."

"Of course you're not a loser," Olivia said.

He made a face. "You think that because you're my mom. In the city, I was a loser—a funny-looking brain who spent all his time with his head in a book. Here I have friends, and the teachers like me . . . well, most of them do."

"There are other places where you could have all that," Olivia said. "Bigger places with more opportunities."

"I don't want to move again, Mom." He set his lips in a pout.

"I didn't say anything about moving, just that you shouldn't limit your world to one small town." She wanted so much more for him—so much more than she'd ever had.

"Sometimes you can find everything you need in a small town," D. J. said. "If the people you love are there. And you're doing things that fulfill you."

Right. As if she was fulfilled behind the bar at the Dirty Sally.

Then she thought of the mural. She could lose herself in that work, mixing colors and adding shading and texture. If she could find a way to make art her work . . .

She became aware of D. J.'s gaze fixed on her, as if trying to read her thoughts. "Are you fulfilled driving a snowplow?" she asked.

"I don't know. I haven't done it yet. But I'm happy. This place is a good fit for me."

"For me, too," Lucas said.

Which left Olivia the odd person out. She didn't feel like Eureka fit. She didn't know if anywhere fit. A town wasn't like a sweater you put on, or a pair of shoes. "It's just a town," she said. "It's not the secret to happiness."

"You might be wrong about that." D. J. smiled, as if he knew a secret he wouldn't tell her. The look should have angered her; instead, it filled her with longing. All the moving she'd done, all she'd really been looking for was the place that fit. A home that felt right. What if such a place didn't exist for her? What if there was nowhere she could truly be happy?

"Sometimes when something doesn't fit, you have to alter it to meet your needs," he said. "Or you change your expectations."

"You accept less, you mean."

"No, I don't think you should ever accept less." His eyes met hers, deep and intense. "You deserve the best. You always have."

How did he know what she deserved? Or what was the best? If people got what they deserved, then, judging by her life so far, she hadn't qualified for much in the way of blessings. There was Lucas, of course—the best thing in her life, so far. But she'd fallen so short in all she wanted to give him. Eureka was the first real home he'd known, and even here they shared a house with her mother. She was almost thirty and she didn't have much education or anything like a career. None of that was what she called "the best."

"I guess I have a lot to look forward to," she said.

"I hope we both have good things to look forward to." He spoke as if he expected those things to happen to them together, that they'd be a couple again. That would never happen. You couldn't undo the past, and some wounds, she was sure, ran too deep to heal.

Lucille took Olivia's advice about stopping moping to heart and tried as much as possible to return to her old routine. Guilt and worry over the town's finances and her own role in the debacle made for many sleepless nights, but during the day she kept up a front of bravely carrying on. She was working behind the counter at Lacy's during the second week of November when the door opened and Bob, Doug, Paul, Junior, and Reggie filed in and arranged themselves in front of her like schoolboys called into the principal's office.

"If you're not too busy, Madam Mayor, we'd like to have a word with you," Bob said.

Had they come to ask for her resignation at last? "No, I'm not busy," she said. "I was printing out the turkeys for the place cards for the community dinner." Elementary-school children colored and cut out the pictures of turkeys to use as name tags and place cards at the long tables set up in the school gymnasium. The town provided a turkey and ham, and community members bought side dishes. Eureka might be broke, but that wasn't going to stop this tradition.

"It's good that we're still having the dinner," Paul said.

"Maggie's friend Barb Stanowski insisted on paying for the turkeys and Eureka Grocery is donating the hams," Lucille said.

"That's good, then." Paul glanced at the others in the party.

"Katya said to tell you she's sorry she couldn't be here," Doug said. "She's giving a massage over in Telluride today."

Lucille pushed aside the stack of photocopies. "What are you all doing here?" she asked.

They all looked to Reggie. "My private detective friend found Gerald Pershing," he said.

Lucille's chest tightened. She didn't want to hear Gerald's name. Didn't want to talk about him. But, of course, she had to. "Where was he?"

"He's been in Dallas the whole time," Doug said. "He's not even trying to hide."

"What did he say? Did you talk to him?" She pressed her lips together, wishing she could take back the words. Anything Gerald said would likely be a lie, and words would never justify what he'd done—to her and to the town.

"We haven't talked to him yet," Paul said. "We figure if we confront him, he'll deny he did anything wrong. We gave him our money to invest and as far as we know he invested it."

"He said it would be six months before we could expect a return," Junior said.

"But I think we all know we'll never get it back," Doug said. The others nodded.

"Can we press charges?" Lucille asked.

Reggie shook his head. "The state police and the FBI say not. There's no compelling evidence that he did anything wrong. He's probably smart enough to have manufactured some records showing he had the authority to take the money, and that he invested it somewhere."

"Then finding him didn't really do us any good."

"Except we have a plan," Bob said.

She looked at him, dismayed. "Now, Bob—"

"Hear him out, Lucille," Doug said. "He's got some good ideas."

That would be a first. She folded her arms across her chest. "All right. What is this plan?"

"We contact him, but only to inquire, friendly-like, how things are going," Bob said. "Then we mention that the town owns some old gold claims that have turned up some promising color. With the price of gold going through the roof, some companies are starting to reopen some of the old mines in the area, so our story won't sound so far-fetched. We'll tell him we're thinking about selling shares of stock to the public and can he help us make that happen?"

"Do you really think he'll fall for that?" she asked.

"Greedy people can't resist the allure of gold," Bob said. "If we have to, we'll salt the mine site with real gold and convince him there's plenty more where that came from. I'm friends with one of the engineers at a mine they're re-working over in Lake City and I can get copies of the assay reports from him to show Pershing. We'll sell him a bunch of worthless stock—enough to get back all the money we lost."

"And maybe a little more in interest," Junior added.

A fake gold mine? "It's crazy," she said. "He'll never fall for it."

"We think he will," Bob said. "Especially if you agree to help us."

A sinking feeling settled in her stomach. "Help you how?"

"You need to call him and get him to come to town so we can show him the gold mine and get the money in person," Doug said.

Lucille turned to Reggie. "Is this even legal?"

"We have to be careful," Reggie said. "We can't out-and-out lie . . . but we can lead him to make certain assumptions. Basically, we're trying to beat him at his own game. It's a little on the shady side, but he's not likely to file charges. If he did, his own illegal activities would be questioned in court."

"We want him to hand over the cash; then we want to tell him to his face he's been had," Paul said. "And that if he ever shows his face around here again, he'll lose more than his money."

"We want to scare him straight," Bob said. "Or straight to hell."

"You want me to call and talk to him?" Lucille couldn't believe what they were asking. "He walked out on me. He must know I'm furious with him."

"We're all furious, too," Bob said. "But if we can hide that, so can you. Play up to him. Tell him you miss him and want to see him again."

She stared. They couldn't possibly expect her to swallow her pride that much.

"We know it's asking a lot," Reggie said. "But it's all we've got. And we think he'll listen to you, either because he's got enough decency in him to feel guilty about the way he treated you or because he'll think you're still under his spell. Some men can't resist that kind of power."

"You want me to be desperate," she said.

"Well, Lucille, we are kind of desperate here." Bob leaned across the counter. "Without that money, we can't run the town."

"But a gold mine?" She shook her head.

"Everybody knows there's lots of mines around here," Junior said. "It's one thing we're known for. With the price of gold up so high, people are more interested than ever."

That much, at least, was true. At least once a month someone stopped by Lacy's and asked about mining. Some people still had the impression they could wander around anywhere in the mountains and prospect, then stake a claim to anything they found. Lucille had to explain that all the land in the area was either privately owned or held by the government, and someone had the mineral rights to all of it. The days of striking it rich by chance had disappeared long ago. But that didn't stop people from hoping and dreaming.

"I'll think about it," she said. "But I don't know if I can do it."

"There's no rush," Doug said. "We need time to plan this thing out. We've got to find a good location and come up with some fake documentation. And waiting a little while will lull him into thinking he got away with something."

How much time would she need to muster the nerve to talk to Gerald again? To face him and pretend he hadn't hurt her? "You're asking a lot," she said.

"We know," Bob said. "But you can do it. You're a mountain woman and no flatlander is a match for you."

How many times had she heard similar sayings? People up here prided themselves on being stronger, hardier, tougher, and yes, better than people who lived at lower elevations. They lived up here in spite of the hardships because they were special. A breed apart. Lucille used to believe all of that, but now she wasn't so sure. That cockiness might be one of the reasons Gerald was able to take them in so easily.

So maybe they weren't any smarter or tougher than flatlanders, but they could be more stubborn. It took hardheadedness to get through a winter up here. "You take care of the mine and I'll see what I can do about seducing Gerald."

"You can be there when we tell him he's been had," Bob said. "You can even give him the good news, if you like."

"As mayor, you should definitely be the one to tell him," Doug said.

"With pleasure." Seeing Gerald's face when he realized the tables were turned just might make this all worthwhile.

If Olivia had had her way, she would have done nothing but work on the mural at the Last Dollar every day. But her job, motherhood, and the demands of real life prevented that. As it was, she squeezed in painting between other tasks and worked at odd hours. Which is how she found herself perched on her stool in front of the painting after closing one night. She'd left Lucas doing homework with her mom. Janelle and Danielle bustled about in the café's kitchen, but she scarcely noticed them. They'd given her a key and told her to feel free to let herself in and out as she pleased.

She liked these late hours best, when she didn't have an audience to watch her work, and the quiet of the sleepy town settled around her. As the nights grew darker and colder, even the regulars at the Dirty Sally thinned out. The town was like a bear settling in to hibernate for the winter. Frost rimed the trees and the windshields of cars every morning, even if the anticipated first snowfall had yet to appear.

"Olivia, can you take a break for a minute?"

At Danielle's words, she looked up from working on the curve of the bighorn's horns. She was having trouble getting the texture just right. She'd consulted books for her sketches of the animals; she wished now she'd taken a photo of Jake Murphy's pet bighorn the last time she visited his cabin. Real-life models were always better to work from.

"Now would probably be a good time to take a break," Olivia said. "I'm getting a little frustrated."

"Come on back in the kitchen." Danielle motioned her over.

The café's kitchen was a clean, though crowded space dominated by a six-burner commercial cooktop and two commercial ovens. A marble-topped work island filled the middle of the room, over which hung an assortment of pots and pans. A pressed copper ceiling and hanging lights with copper shades gave the kitchen a homey, warm glow, and the space smelled of sugar and spice. "Hello, Olivia," Janelle said from her place at the work island. Today she had her blond cap of hair sheathed in a pink scarf, and she'd tied a green paisley apron over her T-shirt and jeans. "We need your help."

Danielle wore a similar apron and a chef's toque, tilted to one side atop her tied-back dark curls. "Taste this and tell me what you think?" She scooped something dark and fruity from a large pot on the stove and offered the spoon to Olivia.

Olivia blew on the steaming spoonful and touched her lips to the rim. The tartness of fruit mingled with the sweetness of sugar and a hint of unknown spice—cinnamon, maybe? She slid the spoon farther into her mouth. "It's delicious. What is it?" she asked when the spoon was clean.

"Do you really think it's good?" Danielle asked. "It's a cherry-cranberry pie filling I'm working on."

"We're making the pies for the Thanksgiving dinner," Janelle said. She nodded to a baker's rack across the room, lined with pie tins in various stages of completion. "Pumpkin, of course, but we like to offer something different, too."

"Something people will want to visit the café for more of later," Danielle said.

"I think you've got a winner," Olivia said.

"We thought so, too," Janelle said. "But it's good to

hear it from a third person . . . and we know you have good taste."

The compliment surprised her. "How do you know that?"

"Your beautiful art," Danielle said. "And you always dress nice, too."

Olivia glanced at her skinny jeans and high-heeled boots. "Thanks." Not that it took much to be fashionable in Eureka. She was positive her mother had clothes in her closet dating back twenty years—and she still wore them.

"The mural is looking great," Janelle said. She sprinkled the marble top of the work table with flour from a tin canister.

"Thanks." Olivia dropped the now-empty spoon into a pan of dishwater in the sink to her right. "I guess I should get back to work and let you two get back to your pies."

"You don't have to go." Danielle looked up from stirring her pie filling. Steam had curled the tendrils that had escaped her scarf into right corkscrews. "Stay and talk."

Janelle took a ball of dough from a metal bowl at her elbow and began patting it into a disk on the floured table. "I stopped by the school this morning to see how much space they had in their refrigerators and I saw that cute boy of yours," she said. "He was running an errand for his science teacher and he seemed pretty happy to be out of class when no one else was. He told me you're making mashed potatoes for the dinner."

"It's a recipe from a place I waitressed at for a while in Hartford," she said. "You make them ahead and keep them warm in a Crock-Pot. They're full of cheese and cream and all kinds of fattening stuff."

"Sounds delicious," Danielle said. She stirred the cherry filling one more time, then moved to the side of the stove and began cracking eggs into a bowl. "Of course, you can tell I love fattening food."

"Nothing wrong with a healthy appetite," Janelle said. She patted Danielle's backside fondly as she passed on her way to the walk-in cooler.

The two had such an easy relationship. They seemed so comfortable with each other and with themselves, though she'd never think of them as typical small-town types. "How did you two ever end up in Eureka?" she asked.

"We were living in New Mexico, in Santa Fe, and we came here on vacation," Danielle said.

"We hadn't been together very long." Janelle returned to the work table, a chilled marble rolling pin in hand. "So the trip was sort of a romantic getaway." She cast another fond look in Danielle's direction. "We met while we were waitressing at a restaurant in Santa Fe."

"From the first we talked about opening a place of our own, but Santa Fe didn't feel quite right to us." Danielle took up the story. "We came here for the hot springs—the Living Waters?"

"The nudist place?" Olivia had passed by there plenty of times, but she'd never gone in.

"Clothing optional," Janelle corrected her. "It's not what people think. It's just a bunch of folks who want to enjoy the warm water the way the native people did. You should try it. It's very relaxing."

Olivia wasn't sure she was ready to be that relaxed. "So you came here and liked it."

"We loved it," Danielle said. "There was just something about the mountains and the old buildings. We saw this place—the owner wanted to sell and move to Texas to be near his grandkids—the price was right, so we decided to take the risk."

"It didn't look anything like this, of course." Janelle made a face. "It was really just a greasy spoon."

"Emphasis on the grease." Danielle began beating the eggs. "We scrubbed for days getting everything clean enough to repaint."

"People were starved for good food," Janelle said. "So we were busy from the first day we opened our doors."

"And people didn't give you a hard time because you're a couple?"

"We didn't exactly wear signs that said, 'Kiss me, I'm a lesbian,'" Janelle said. "But most folks figured it out pretty quick. We didn't try to hide the fact that we loved each other."

"Some folks gave us a hard time." Danielle transferred the eggs to the bowl of a mixer and added pumpkin. "Somebody spray-painted vulgar sayings on our house, and somebody else burned down our chicken house. But we had friends who defended us."

"Jake Murphy, Maggie's dad, threatened to beat up anybody who harassed us, and he built us a fireproof brick chicken house." Janelle pressed the circle of dough into a pie tin. "Things calmed down after that."

"Small towns get a bad reputation for being cliquish and narrow-minded, but here people have learned to get along and either ignore or accept differences," Danielle said.

"I think they have to." Janelle ladled the cherry filling into the crust. The scent filled the room, making Olivia's mouth water. "We're all kind of stuck here together come winter, and it's easier if you know you can depend on your neighbor for help."

"I'm not crazy about the idea of being stuck here for the winter," Olivia said. "I mean, people can leave if they want, right?"

"Most of the time," Danielle said. "But when the big snows come, the passes on either side of town sometimes get blocked. Never for very long, but we've learned to order extra supplies for backup."

"Remember that year when the only thing left on the menu was eggs, pancakes, and pasta?" Janelle said.

"Bob was threatening to poach a deer just so we'd have something different to cook," Danielle said.

"You don't miss the city? Someplace bigger . . . more cosmopolitan?"

"Sometimes I'd love to be able to see a movie in the theater without having to drive thirty minutes." Janelle began rolling out a second crust.

"I miss being able to walk into a gourmet grocery and buy everything I need for a special dinner," Danielle said. "Here I have to order from a Web site and wait a week for anything more exotic than mushrooms and peppers."

"But this is home now," Janelle said. "Our regular customers are like our family. Where else can we have Thanksgiving dinner with everyone we know?"

"Is that really a good thing?" Olivia asked. "Presumably, whoever wrote that graffiti and burned your chicken house is somewhere in that crowd. And then there are sourpusses like Cassie Wynock."

"Cassie definitely doesn't approve of us." Danielle laughed. "But that's the thing about families. There's always some nutty aunt or skeevy uncle whom you don't really care for. But they just make everybody else look that much better."

"Aren't there ever people you wish you just didn't have to see again?" How much easier would Olivia's life be if she didn't run into D. J. every time she turned around?

"I think if someone bothers you, it's because you need to learn a lesson from them," Janelle said. "Everyone has something to teach us, about life, or about ourselves."

What lesson had D. J. taught her? Not to give your heart away to someone too insensitive to accept the gift?

Fat lot of good that education had done her. "What if you've learned your lesson and they still annoy you?"

"Then you haven't learned the right lesson." Janelle shrugged. "It's only a theory."

"Maybe some people are just here to annoy you," Olivia said.

"Everyone can teach us something. For instance, you have inspired me to explore my creative side. See." She indicated the pie crust she was decorating with cutout bits of pastry in the shape of flowers and leaves.

"You have a fierceness I admire," Danielle said. "People don't impress you. They have to prove themselves to you. That takes such strength, to see beyond the surface that way."

Was this her they were talking about? It was true that people didn't impress her, but she'd always figured that was because she was so unwilling to risk connecting with them. Distance always felt safer. "I never thought of myself as fierce," she said.

"I don't mean it in a bad way," Danielle said. "Just that you have good protective instincts. You're a survivor. Like that pioneer woman you're painting. After all, you came here with your boy by yourself and you're making a place for yourself, on your own terms."

"Eureka is the perfect place for that," Janelle said. "People here are more about breaking rules than following them."

"Which can make things interesting sometimes." Danielle added cinnamon and nutmeg to the pumpkin-pie filling in the mixing bowl. "Once the city tried to re-paint the parking stripes in front of the Dirty Sally so that they slanted the opposite direction. Something to do with controlling traffic flow. But it didn't work. Everybody ignored the markings and parked the way they always had."

"Good thing I'm painting a mural and not parking stripes," Olivia said.

"I hope the mural is just a start," Danielle said. "I hope you find other outlets for your art."

"Tourists would buy those T-shirts you paint, I'm sure," Janelle said. "And the jewelry you make. You wouldn't do much business in the winter, but you could do well in the summer, I think. And these days you can sell stuff on-line, too."

"The Internet has saved towns like this," Danielle said. "People don't have to go away to find work."

"They just have to work two or three jobs together," Olivia said. That went for non-artists, too. Look at Jameso, who taught skiing, tended bar, drove Jeep tours, and did odd jobs around town.

Danielle laughed. "Isn't that how it always is with artists?"

Olivia loved how they thought of her as an artist; that was a better compliment than saying she was fierce. "Maybe I'll try some of your suggestions. Thanks."

"Of course." Janelle transferred her finished pie to the baker's rack. "Only a few more pies to go. Will you be staying much later?"

"A little longer. I want to get this ram finished before I call it a night." And she wanted a little more time to absorb everything they'd said. Could she make it as an artist staying here in Eureka? Was that even what she wanted? Was she brave enough—fierce enough—to stay in one place long enough to face down D. J. and her own insecurities, and everything that had kept her moving from place to place all these years?

Was she brave enough to make Eureka, with its crazy cast of characters and at times claustrophobic lifestyle, into her home? The idea seemed as exotic and daring as welcoming all the crazy aunts and skeevy uncles into her living room for dinner, and learning to love them along with her dearest friends and relatives—maybe because it meant learning to love the crazy, skeevy side of herself. You didn't get much fiercer than that.

CHAPTER TEN

Maggie stared at the blank computer screen, willing the words to come. Was there any slower news time than the week of Thanksgiving? "Rick, maybe we should just run two pages of pictures of the kids coloring turkeys at the elementary school and call it good," she said.

"We promise the advertisers at least sixteen pages, so we have to come up with words to fill them." With these helpful words, he disappeared into his office and shut the door.

Maggie stuck her tongue out at him.

"Didn't your mother ever tell you not to do that in case your face froze?"

"Lucille!" Maggie stood to greet her friend. "Please tell me you've come to save me from a life of drudgery."

"I have. Can you take a break for a couple of hours and help decorate the school cafeteria for the dinner tomorrow?" She held out a large cardboard box. "I found a bunch of decorations in the back room of Lacy's, and some of the other women are bringing their contributions."

"I'd love to help." She shut down her computer and

grabbed her purse. "Anything to escape trying to get five hundred words out of the installation of the new sign at the bank drive-through."

Lucille handed Maggie a box. "Do you want to drive over to the school?"

"No, let's walk." Maggie shrugged into her coat and pulled a knit cap over her ears. "My doctor says exercise is good for me; plus, it's a nice day."

They stepped out into the crisp air. The sun shone in a cloudless, turquoise sky. If not for the bare trees, it might have been September rather than November. "I guess I'm glad the snow's held off," Lucille said as they crossed the street and headed toward the school. "It saves us the expense of plowing, but I can't remember a Thanksgiving without snow on the ground."

"More time for Bob's snowfall pool to bring in money," Maggie said. "It has to snow soon, right?"

"You'd think, but weather's doing weird things all over the country, so who knows?"

"Rick's got a whole front page planned when the first snow does arrive. That's how slow it's been this week . . . he's planning ahead."

"As mayor, I can appreciate when the town is quiet enough to not make any news," Lucille said. "Except, of course, for the continuing budget crises, which the press never tires of."

Maggie noted the tension around the older woman's mouth. Lucille had become the beleaguered face of Eureka in newscasts and newspaper and magazine articles that ran all over the United States, calmly explaining over and over how some "bad investments" had led to the emptying of the town coffers. "Has it been very hard for you?"

"I can't help feeling responsible, and it's more than humbling to have your personal foolishness written about and talked about all across the country. It was bad enough when the Colorado stations reported on it, but then the national news wires picked it up. Apparently a broke small town plays well with viewers."

"It's not that the town is broke," Maggie said. "People love hearing about how everyone has pulled together to keep things going. The Thanksgiving dinner is a great feel-good story. You don't look like a fool—you're a heroine for keeping the tradition going."

"It wasn't me," Lucille said. "A whole group of people came together to make this happen."

"If everyone is pitching in to hold the dinner this year, what did you do before?"

"The last couple of years we've had the dinner catered. Some people still brought special dishes, but the caterer did most of the work. We asked people to donate what they could, but the city picked up most of the bill."

"That must have been expensive."

Lucille nodded. "It was probably time to cut back, but I guess we'd gotten lazy. We wanted to keep the tradition going but didn't want all the work."

"I think people are enjoying the work," Maggie said. "Everyone in town is talking about the dinner. They're really excited about it."

"This is the way it was done years ago, with everyone bringing food to contribute. I think people missed that sense of coming together as a community and hadn't even realized it."

Tamarin Sherman and Shelly Frazier met them at the door of the school cafeteria and relieved them of their boxes. "Katya and Olivia brought orange and brown crepe paper streamers," Shelly said. "And I got butcher paper from the grocery to use on the tables."

"Cassie is here, too," Tamarin said. "She didn't bring any decorations; I think she mainly came to supervise."

The cafeteria was a buzz of activity. Katya and Olivia stood on ladders, taping festoons of crepe paper to the ceiling. Other women tacked construction paper pilgrim hats and cornucopias to the walls. Cassie was arranging a pile of pumpkins and gourds at the front of the room. "I've got a bunch of pinecone turkeys and little pilgrim dolls in these boxes," Lucille said. "I thought we could use them on the tables as centerpieces."

"We need to get the tables covered first," Tamarin said. "Maggie, can you help me with that?"

"Sure." She hurried to take one end of the industrial-sized roll of butcher paper. She and Tamarin rolled the paper down the length of one set of long tables, tore off the strip, and taped them in place.

"This is going to be the best Thanksgiving dinner ever," Shelly said as she helped Lucille unpack the boxes. "Everyone is going all out with the food. I heard Janelle and Danielle are baking forty pies."

"It's kind of nice, everyone pitching in this way to pick up the slack," Tamarin agreed. "It's more like when the dinner first started, back when the miners got together."

"Except we're liable to have a bigger crowd than ever this year, what with all the publicity in the paper and on the news stations," Katya said. "We don't want anyone to go away hungry, so everyone is bringing extra."

"I think it's disgraceful, having our problems broadcast to the world that way."

All heads swiveled toward Cassie, who had turned away from her pumpkin arrangement to scowl at Lucille. "It's one thing to lose all the town's money to that man, but you ought to have some pride and not broadcast our strained circumstances to the world."

"Cassie!" Tamarin hissed. "That wasn't Lucille's fault."

"Then whose fault was it? She's the one who's being interviewed on TV. She's the one who talked the town council into hearing her boyfriend's proposal. If it hadn't been for her, none of this would have happened."

The others exchanged horrified looks. *Someone ought*

to slap that woman, Maggie thought. But, of course, no one would. Lucille continued unpacking tissue-wrapped turkeys and dolls, as if she hadn't heard, though Maggie noticed the tips of her ears were bright red.

"She's embarrassing us all," Cassie continued, her tone growing more strident.

Olivia started toward the librarian, as if she would, indeed, slap her, but Maggie got there first. "Oh, shut up, Cassie!" she snapped.

It was the librarian's turn to flush red. "What did you say?"

"You're one to talk. As if you'd never been taken in by a handsome, smooth-talking charmer."

Cassie's expression grew even more sour. "I don't know what you're talking about."

"Don't you? I don't know what happened between you and my father, but clearly he sweet-talked his way into your good graces and then left you high and dry. It's why you hate him so much. Why you hate me." She met the shocked stares of the others. "Jake may have been my father, but I heard enough stories to know what he was like. What men can be like."

"That was a private matter," Cassie said. "It didn't affect the whole town, the way Lucille carrying on with that man did."

"Don't act so high and mighty, Cassie." Lucille looked up from her boxes. "Don't think I didn't notice you flirting shamelessly with Gerald. You all but admitted if he hadn't been so interested in me, you'd have done your best to reel him in."

"You're imagining things," Cassie said, but her face remained bright pink.

"The fact is, none of us are saints," Lucille said. "What's done is done, so instead of sniping at each other we ought to stick together. And do what we can to protect other women from men like him."

The others murmured in agreement. The words sounded good, Maggie thought. The problem was men—and women—weren't predictable creatures. She'd never have predicted her first husband would cheat on her after almost twenty years. "Sometimes you can't know what people are really like," she said thoughtfully. "Relationships are gambles. Sometimes you win and sometimes you lose."

"And some women are just stupid," Cassie huffed. She turned and practically ran from the room.

"Is she calling us stupid or herself?" Katya asked.

"Maybe a little of both," Lucille said.

"I'm sorry you had to hear that," Maggie said.

Lucille waved her hand dismissively. "Cassie doesn't bother me. If she judges herself half as hard as she judges others, she deserves your sympathy much more than I do."

Katya turned to Maggie. "Enough of sad subjects. I hear congratulations are in order."

Maggie flushed. She hated how her emotions were so close to the surface these days, but she supposed she'd have to learn to live with it, like living with morning sickness. "Thank you."

"Then it's true?" Tamarin asked. "You're going to have a baby?"

"Yes, it's due around the first of June."

"Maggie! You've been keeping secrets." Shelly embraced her.

"Not a secret. I mean, everyone will figure it out eventually." She smoothed her shirt over her still-flat stomach.

"How exciting!" Tamarin said. "What does Jameso think?"

She had no idea what he thought, only what he said. "He's happy. A little nervous, but then I am, too."

"You'll make a great mother," Lucille said.

Shelly looked wistful. "I wish I could have another baby."

"Not me," Tamarin said. "I was thrilled the day I changed

my last diaper. Now that my boys are old enough to dress and feed themselves, I'd never go back to sleepless nights and dirty diapers."

"Well, I won't be going back there either," Shelly said. "Charlie got snipped after Shanna was born. He said we had a boy and a girl and that was enough." She sighed. "Still, I miss babies."

"I'd love to have another baby one day," Olivia said. She'd been so quiet Maggie had forgotten she was there.

"You still have time," Maggie said "You're way younger than me and this is my first."

"I guess." She bent and pulled another paper-wrapped turkey from the boxes. "Let me help you with these, Mom."

Lucille patted her daughter's arm. *There's a story there,* Maggie thought. *A private one I'll never know.*

"Have you thought of names for the baby yet?" Tamarin asked.

"Maybe Jacob if it's a boy." Her father had been an ass-hole at times, but he'd also been a good man to many, and she liked to believe he'd done the best he could for her.

"Murph would have liked that," Lucille said.

"I'm having a hard time imagining my father as a grandfather," Maggie admitted. "He seemed like such a wild man."

"Wild men sometimes make the best fathers and hus-bands," Katya said. "When they decide to settle down, they have already sown all their wild oats. They are ready for the quieter life."

Maggie thought of Reg, with his biker leathers and long hair. He definitely seemed the wild-oats type. "Jake was sixty and he'd never settled down," she said.

"I don't think she's talking about Jake," Olivia said.

Maggie gave Katya a questioning look. "Do you mean Reg? I can see how he might have been a little wild be-fore you two go together."

"I didn't slow Reg down," Katya said. "Getting older did. But I was thinking of Jameso. I think he may surprise you."

"Maybe you're right." Maggie had certainly learned that life was full of surprises.

Talk turned to what everyone was bringing to the dinner. Maggie had signed up to contribute paper plates. "I'm not much of a cook," she admitted.

"I'm making mashed potatoes," Olivia said.

"From scratch?" Shelly asked.

"Of course. I've got to peel twenty-five pounds of potatoes tonight. I offered Lucas a nickel a potato if he'd help."

"Word to the wise," Tamarin said, "don't eat the sausage balls."

"The sausage balls?" Maggie asked.

"Bob brings them every year. He makes them out of his homemade venison sausage and jalapeno peppers. They're so hot they'll set your whole body on fire."

"There was a rumor going around that he brought the same batch every year," Shelly said.

"Oh, I don't think that's true," Lucille said.

Tamarin made a face. "They are starting to look a little petrified."

"I'll stay away from the sausage balls," Maggie promised, joining the others' laughter.

"We're lucky to have so much to choose from," Shelly said. "I did an article for the historical society newsletter a couple of years ago about the early Thanksgivings. The miners ate wild turkey, cornbread, and pumpkins, potatoes and parsnips they grew. That was it."

"And at the end of the meal they passed around jugs of homebrew and everyone took a sip," Tamarin said. "Even the prim old ladies."

"It was tradition," Shelly said.

"Not a tradition we intend to revive," Lucille said.

"People will have to settle for coffee and iced tea. The Elks Club is providing that."

"I'm kind of looking forward to this," Olivia said. "I've never been to a really big Thanksgiving feast. And Lucas is beside himself, dreaming about all the good things to eat."

"Do you realize this will be the first Thanksgiving we've spent together in seventeen years?" Lucille asked.

"That's so sweet," Shelly said. "And it's Maggie's first Thanksgiving with us, too."

This had been a year of firsts, Maggie agreed. Her divorce, finding out about her father, moving to Eureka, falling in love with Jameso. And now a baby. It was almost overwhelming.

"It is going to be a good Thanksgiving," Lucille said. "I guess hard times really do bring out the best in some people. It's a shame we can't get the good without going through the bad."

Without her divorce, or her father dying, Maggie never would have ended up in Eureka. She wouldn't have this baby now or all of these new friends. Looking back, she could say the pain was worth it, though she wouldn't necessarily choose to go through it again.

"We all have a lot to be thankful for," she said, squeezing Lucille's hand.

"We do," Lucille agreed. "Sometimes the difference between a blessing and a problem is just a matter of perspective."

Maggie told herself she should remember that next time she had doubts about Jameso or their future.

Thanksgiving morning, Olivia, Lucas, and Lucille carried four foil turkey pans full of mashed potatoes to the school. The kitchen was filled with volunteers setting out dishes, heating gravy and rolls, and preparing the meats. Olivia was surprised to see D. J. in his black watch cap and a long white apron, basting a turkey at the giant oven. He looked so at home there, so a part of things.

He was even newer to town than she was, yet he'd fit right in, transforming himself from city dweller to rugged mountain man seemingly effortlessly. You'd have thought he'd been born hunting his own food and splitting firewood, while she still felt out of place much of the time. When people bragged about surviving rugged winters, digging themselves out of blizzards and thawing frozen pipes, it didn't sound exciting and memorable to her—it made her want to pack her bags and flee south.

"Is D. J. a good cook?" Lucille asked.

"He made turkey for us last year." Lucas waved across the room. "Hey, D. J.! We'll save you a seat."

No! Olivia thought. But she couldn't voice her protest without upsetting Lucas and drawing a lot of unwanted attention. Maybe D. J. would be too busy cooking to sit with them.

Having deposited their contributions to the meal, she and Lucille followed Lucas back into the cafeteria. The cavernous room was filled with children scurrying about handing out name tags or decorating the butcher paper tablecloths with crayons. Mothers settled infants into high chairs borrowed from the Last Dollar for the occasion, while a group of old men claimed the spots closest to the serving line. The Elks Club and the Elks Auxiliary, dressed in crisp white aprons with red trim, took their places behind the serving dishes, and a half-dozen high-school girls scurried around with pitchers of tea, water, and lemonade, filling glasses.

Promptly at noon Bob climbed onto a chair and clapped his hands together to get everyone's attention. "We're going to get started in just a minute here," he said. "But before we do, I wanted to give y'all a little history on Thanksgiving in Eureka County. The first one of these here dinners was back in 1883, when the first miners came here. They were from Cornwall, England, from Ireland and Wales and Germany, and from the eastern states. They didn't have a lot in common but a thirst for adventure and gold. But they wanted to settle in to their new homeland, and they'd heard about this American custom of Thanksgiving.

"But there weren't a lot of women with them to cook a fancy meal, and they didn't have all that much food anyway. They decided to pool the things they had and have dinner together, to enjoy a little fellowship and toast their good fortune in coming to this beautiful place, where they all hoped to make their fortunes."

Someone started to applaud, but Bob shushed them.

"Come on, Bob, we're hungry!"

"Shut your trap, I'm almost done." He scowled at the assembled crowd until everyone quieted down again. "I just want to thank everybody who pitched in this year to keep the tradition going," he said. "This is really what it's all about . . . what it was about that very first year . . . everybody coming together to celebrate and enjoy each other's company. We divide up the work, share in the bounty, and nobody has to eat alone."

More applause this time. It rose and swelled to fill the room. Olivia's throat tightened. She took a hasty drink of water. What was wrong with her? She wasn't the sentimental sort. Thanksgiving was no big deal to her, that dinner with D. J. was the first time she'd even celebrated the holiday in years.

As if summoned by her thoughts, the man himself emerged from the kitchen and came to stand beside her. "This is pretty special, isn't it?" he said.

She nodded, afraid if she tried to speak she might get choked up. Damned emotions.

Reverend Adam Kinkaid stood now and cleared his throat. "Please bow your head for the blessing."

Olivia didn't pay attention to his words, merely let them wash over her in a soothing drone. It was odd to think of a whole town full of people in one place like this. The Dirty Sally and the Last Dollar and every other business was closed. Even the police officers were here; anyone passing through town could speed with impunity. She'd never been much of a joiner, but it felt good to be a part of this. Accepted.

"Amen," the reverend concluded, and another cheer went up from the crowd. People surged toward the serving line and the feasting officially began.

When Olivia returned to the table with her full plate she saw that someone—she suspected Lucas—had switched their place cards so that D. J. sat between the two of them, though she had made sure before that Lucas had the center position, a buffer between her and the man who still had the ability to upset her so.

"This looks cozy." D. J. came up behind her and set his own overflowing plate in front of his place card. He pulled Olivia's chair from the table. "Have a seat."

What could she do but sit? With so many people to accommodate, the chairs were very close together, so that when he sat their thighs almost touched and they had to be careful not to knock elbows. Every time he shifted in his chair, she felt it. As a result, she scarcely tasted the food, though Lucas and D. J. raved about everything.

"The mashed potatoes are delicious as ever," D. J. said.

"The turkey's good, too," she said automatically.

"Did you try the venison sausage balls?" He held up what looked like an eyeball-sized knot of leather. "They're really good. A little spicy, though. And a little chewy."

She choked and reached for her water glass.

"What is it?" He patted her back, none too gently.

"Oh, nothing."

Apparently satisfied she wasn't going to choke, he

popped the rest of the sausage ball into his mouth and chewed, a thoughtful look on his face. "Your mother looks like she's holding up pretty well," he said after a moment.

Olivia looked down the table to where her mother sat with Maggie and Jameso, Janelle and Danielle. "She's doing okay. I know having the press dig into her personal scandal has been hard, but most people have been supportive and that helps. And she's a really strong woman."

"I always thought you two didn't get along."

"We didn't, when I was younger." She laid down her fork and pushed her plate away. "I was a really mixed-up kid. After my dad left, she worked all the time and I spent a lot of time alone. I craved her attention, and the only way I knew to get it was to act up. Now that I'm a mom myself, I realize how much grief I gave her."

"It's good you could patch things up."

"Yeah, I guess so." Another of those good things coming out of bad that her mom had talked about? She wasn't ready to look at it that way. Bad things were just . . . bad. The good things were separate, not a result of the bad. You didn't have to have one to get the other. Life wasn't some big balance scale with tragedy and happiness meted out in even measure.

"The mural's looking good," D. J. said. "Are you almost finished?"

"Almost. I just need another few days. I should be done by next week."

"You should do more with your art. It's really good."

His praise warmed her and fueled her confidence. "I'm thinking about asking one of the gift shops if they'd be interested in carrying my painted T-shirts next summer," she said. She hadn't mentioned this idea to anyone before now, afraid she was reaching too far.

"That's a terrific idea. And maybe some of your jewelry, too."

She nodded, feeling light enough to float out of her chair. "I thought I could spend this winter making extra stuff."

He patted her knee, a friendly gesture that nevertheless made her light-headed. "You'll do great."

A commotion by the door saved her from having to answer. Sleigh bells jangled and people began to cheer. She turned in her chair and saw Santa, who looked suspiciously like Reggie Paxton, striding into the room with a flour sack over his shoulder. "Ho! Ho! Ho!" he shouted. "Merry Christmas! All the children gather round. I have something for you!"

Squealing and giggling, the children swarmed him. Olivia even spotted Lucas in the group. "Santa" handed a candy cane to each one. "Be good and I'll be back with more presents on Christmas Eve!" he shouted. "May you all receive gold nuggets instead of coal in your stockings!"

Everyone laughed, and some made comments about really needing that gold. Santa turned to leave, but the door flew open ahead of him. A driver from the highway crew strode in, white confetti dusting his orange wool cap and padded jacket. "Sorry to interrupt the celebration, folks," he said. "But I need all the plow drivers to report to the county barn. We finally got that snow we've been waiting on, and it's really coming down."

CHAPTER ELEVEN

Once the snow began, it showed no signs of stopping. It came down by the foot. Plow drivers had to work overtime keeping even the main roads clear. The county agreed to foot the bill for plowing for the time being, accepting an IOU from the city that Lucille only hoped they'd be able to pay. The bank fronted a loan to pay the town's two police officers, but that, too, was only a temporary fix. And every time she turned around, a new expense loomed.

"What are you going to do about Christmas decorations?" Cassie stopped Lucille on the street one morning to ask.

Lucille bit back a groan. The lighted candy canes and bells hung from every lamppost and street sign in town required hours of overtime from the park maintenance crew and a hefty monthly light bill. "I don't see how we can afford to put up the decorations this year." She felt like Scrooge, canceling Christmas.

"We have to have decorations for Yule Night," Cassie said. The annual nighttime festival was less than a week away. The Elks Club built a bonfire in the park, the various service organizations sold food and drinks, and local shops stayed open late to encourage Christmas buyers. The night was a big boost during an otherwise slow time in the local economy.

"I'm open to suggestions," Lucille said. "But it can't be anything that costs money."

She expected Cassie to launch into another tirade about Lucille's mishandling of local funds, but once again the librarian surprised her. "I always thought those bells and candy canes were tacky," Cassie said. "And they look more worn out and faded every year. My grandmother told me in her day they decorated with evergreen wreaths and red bows. Simple, but classy."

"That would look beautiful," Lucille said. "There's plenty of evergreens in the national forest we could use for wreaths, if people are willing to make them."

"The historical society can do that," Cassie said. "I'm sure the library has books that can show us how. But we'll need bows. Red velvet is nice."

"I don't suppose anyone has a few dozen yards of red velvet they'd like to donate," Lucille said. But the words sparked a dim memory. "On second thought, I might have something we can use. I think in the shop I have some draperies from a mansion in Telluride. We could cut them up for ribbons." Hey, if it worked for Scarlett O'Hara, surely it was good enough for Eureka. "I'd be glad to get rid of the things."

"We'll meet on Saturday at the library," Cassie said. "Bring your daughter and anyone else you can recruit. And we'll need men with trucks to help us hang everything." Not waiting for an answer, she left.

Lucille stared after her. How was it possible to loathe and admire one person so much? Say what you would about Cassie, she knew how to get things done. And she loved this town. Maybe more than anyone else.

"I can't believe Cassie volunteered to do this," Maggie whispered as she joined Lucille and Olivia at the library Saturday morning. "She's not exactly the volunteering type."

"She's happy to do anything where she can be in charge and take credit," Olivia said.

"True, but I'm grateful all the same," Lucille said. "It's one more problem solved." One in a very long list.

Cassie was definitely in her element. She'd ordered every man she could corral into the woods to cut bushels of evergreen boughs, and raided the thrift store for their stock of wire coat hangers, which she bent into wreath forms. She unearthed a coil of rope from somewhere, to use as the base for garland, then oversaw the wiring of the evergreens to the coat hangers and rope. She bossed and berated, coaxed and corrected until the pile of beribboned wreaths and garland stretched from one end of the library to the other. D. J. and the crew of plow drivers took over from there, festooning lampposts and street signs with the greenery.

Snow started to fall again while they were working, frosting the decorations, adding to their beauty. The businesses and homes in town had done their part to add to the festive mood, decorating with wreaths and lights and wooden cutouts of everything from manger scenes to Santa and his elves. "It has a wonderful, old-fashioned look," Maggie said, snapping a picture for the paper.

"Best of all, we won't have a light bill for these decorations," Lucille said.

"The Elks Auxiliary is talking about doing paper-bag luminarias all down Main Street for the Yule Night Celebration," Maggie said. "And the Presbyterian choir plans to dress up in Victorian outfits and go caroling."

"That night is a big one for the businesses down here," Lucille said. "Anything we can do to draw the tourists is good."

"Losing that money hurt, but I do believe it's brought us more positive publicity than bad," Maggie said. "We get calls at the paper almost every day asking about the little town run by volunteers."

"That's good, but volunteers can't pay for diesel to run the plows, or the salaries of policemen, or funds to repair water and sewer mains. For that we need cash."

"Any luck getting anything out of Gerald Pershing?" Maggie asked.

"Not yet. But Doug and Bob are working on a plan." So far their attempts to get in touch with Gerald hadn't been successful. They'd abandoned the idea of Lucille calling him directly, opting instead for the story that the town itself was looking for advice from the man who handled Eureka's other investments.

"Oh?" Maggie brightened. "What is it?"

Lucille laughed. "I can't tell you that. You're my friend, but you're also a reporter for the paper. We don't want any of this getting out until it's over and done."

"Can't you even give me a hint?"

"No, but when it's over I'll tell you everything. You can have an exclusive."

"I should hope so. The *Miner* is the only paper in the county."

Maggie started back toward the shop, admiring the festive decorations once more. Why hadn't they thought of this before? They'd never be able to go back to those tired old lighted candy canes now.

She'd reached the shop and was sorting the day's mail

when her cell phone rang. She checked the number. Doug. "Hello?"

"We got through to Gerald's secretary this morning and she's set up a phone meeting for us at one," he said. "We need you to be there."

So soon? She'd almost convinced herself that Gerald was never going to return their calls, that they were done with the man for good. She swallowed hard. "All right."

This was her penance for dragging the town into this mess, Lucille thought an hour later as she sat in Reggie's office above the Last Dollar Café. She had to sit here and remain composed while the man who had lied to her and embarrassed her and cheated the town lied some more. She had to pretend she didn't feel anything when she heard his voice, and that the night they'd spent together meant nothing. Well, it obviously had meant nothing to him, but that knowledge only made her feel sick to her stomach.

"I'm going to put him on speakerphone," Doug said as he dialed. He sat behind Reggie's scarred wooden desk, the others gathered around him. Lucille sat in the leather client's chair directly in front of the desk, hands in her lap, feet flat on the floor, determined not to let her expression betray anything. She was here in her official role as mayor, not as the scorned woman.

The secretary answered. Doug introduced himself and asked for Gerald.

"Doug! Good to hear from you," boomed the familiar, velvety voice. "How are things in Eureka?" He sounded so friendly, as if he'd last spoken with them only a few days ago.

"They're good. How are you?"

"I'm well. Busy as always. I hated to leave town so suddenly. I had an emergency back here at the office . . . you know how that goes."

Lucille felt the others watching her. She clenched her teeth until they hurt and refused to look at any of them.

"We're hoping you'll come back to visit us soon," Doug said. No wonder the guy was the first choice for the male lead in the community theater plays. He sounded so calm and friendly, as if he really meant the words. "Lucille says hello."

She gripped the arms of the chair, knuckles white.

"Lovely woman. I hope she got my note. I hated to run out when she and I were just getting to know each other, but this business couldn't wait."

There was no note. She'd looked everywhere for one, refusing to believe he could be so cold as to make love to her all night, then leave the next morning without a word. But, of course, he'd so clearly planned to do just that, having cleaned out his condo before she even got there. He'd realized that in the throes of passion she wasn't likely to notice missing toiletries in the bathroom. "Say hello to her for me," he said.

"I'll do that."

She wanted to scream. But, of course, she couldn't. She settled for glaring at the phone, letting anger burn away the shame.

"What can I do for you today, Doug?" Gerald asked. "I'm rather busy, but I can give you a few minutes."

"I was hoping you could give me some advice," Doug said. "Or rather, give *us* advice. I'm calling on behalf of the city. I guess you keep up with the price of gold these days."

"Yes, gold is a popular investment, though I still prefer technology stocks."

"Yes, well, Eureka owns quite a few mining claims that have been forfeited for back taxes. Most of them are probably worthless, but several of them have potential to be producing mines again, what with the development of new technology and the increase in the price of gold."

"You're saying you expect to take gold from these mines?"

The men exchanged glances. None of them missed the new interest in Gerald's voice.

"One of the mines is particularly promising," Doug said. "We've been doing some assaying and are very encouraged by what we see."

"How can I help you?" Gerald asked. "I admit I know nothing about gold mining."

"But you know stocks. Our plan is to sell shares in the mine in order to raise the capital we need for the technology and equipment to mine the ore and extract the gold. I was hoping you could tell us how to go about selling the shares."

"A public offering is a very long, involved process. It could take you two years or more to receive permission to trade stock."

Reggie had already explained all this to them, but Doug did a good job of conveying surprise and disappointment. "I had no idea. Is there anything else we can do? The gold's just sitting there, useless unless we can get it out. But we can't get it out without equipment and miners . . . I suppose if that Swedish technology stock pays off well . . ."

"There are other ways to raise capital," Gerald said. "You can solicit private investors."

"And you can help us with that, right? We'd be willing to pay you an appropriate fee."

"I might be able to help you. I'd want to know more about the project and the potential for profit. I never sell any investments I'm not confident will realize a good rate of return. I have a reputation to protect, after all."

The man was amazing. Even though they all knew he

was a liar and a cheat, he sounded absolutely convincing. Lucille saw doubt on the faces of some of the men.

"Why don't you come out here and see the mine?" Doug said. "We'd be happy to show you around, let you see our plans and the research we've done. We're excited about the project and we think it'll be a real moneymaker for everyone involved."

"My schedule is very full right now, but perhaps I could make some time. . . . I'll have to get back to you."

"Do that. We'd be happy to see you anytime. I won't keep you any longer. And thanks so much for your advice."

Doug replaced the phone in the receiver. "I think I need to go take a shower now," he said.

"Do you think he bought it?" Paul asked.

"Oh, I think he bought it," Junior said. "You could hear the greed in his voice."

"I predict he'll be out here before the end of the week," Bob said. "He won't be able to think about anything else. Gold does that to a man."

"If he comes out here, I'll show him the mine and make my pitch," Doug said. "But I think Lucille should be the one to persuade him to buy the shares."

"Take him out to dinner and act real friendly," Paul said.

"Seduce him, you mean." She was seeing a new side to her town council, and she wasn't sure she liked it. Apparently, they now saw her as some femme fatale.

"It's what he did to you, isn't it?" Bob said. "Turnabout is fair play."

"I don't know if I can do it."

Bob put a hand on her shoulder. "Sure you can. Don't think about what he did to you . . . think about taking back your dignity by cutting him off at the knees."

She could think of a few things she'd like to cut off of Gerald. "I'll try. But we have to get him here first."

"He's probably making reservations already," Reggie said.

Someone had said revenge was a dish best served cold. An icy day in December might be the ideal time to serve that particular entrée. "I don't suppose there's any truth to what you told him about the mines?" she asked. "Could any of them be re-worked to produce gold?"

"Not likely," Junior said. "Most of them never yielded much of anything in the first place."

"I've heard lots of talk about re-working some of the mines that were good producers once upon a time," Bob said. "When they shut down years ago it wasn't because there wasn't any gold left in them, just that the gold that was left was too hard to get to. They didn't have the technology and tools miners do today. But the mines the city owns were pretty much duds from the get-go. Not much hope there."

"I was just wondering," she said. "In case we can't get our money back from Gerald."

Bob cleared his throat and everyone turned to look at him. "As long as we're all gathered here, I'd like to make a proposal," he said.

"What's that?" Paul asked.

"Since we've got all this snow and the side streets aren't plowed, I think we should close off a route to traffic for a day and have a snowmobile race. Sort of a winter grand prix."

"Why would we want to do that?" Junior asked.

"Because it's fun. And because it would be another way to raise money for the town. The racers would pay to enter and local businesses could pay to advertise. We could make it an annual tradition. Y'all are always talking about wanting to find ways to get the tourists here in winter. I'm betting this would do it."

"It's a little late in the game to lure any tourists here this year," Paul said. "You have to advertise that kind of thing for months."

"So consider this year the trial run. See how things go and if it's a hit, we go on from there."

"It sounds dangerous," Lucille said. "We can't expose the town to liability."

"We're not talking Evel Knievel here," Bob said. "Make everybody sign a waiver. Put up barriers the crowds have to stay behind. Limit the number of racers, if you like. C'mon . . . don't you people know how to have fun anymore?"

Lucille exchanged glances with the other council members. "It does sound like fun," Junior said.

"I can draw up a waiver, though it won't necessarily stop a lawsuit if someone gets hurt," Reggie said.

After dealing with Gerald, Lucille felt reckless. "I don't have any objections, if Reggie will see to the legal paperwork and Bob and Junior will design a route that's least likely to expose racers and spectators to injury."

"I make a motion we allow the snowmobile races," Doug said.

"All in favor?" Lucille asked.

Everyone but Reggie raised his hand. Reggie shrugged and then put up his hand, too. "What the hell."

Lucille smiled. "I leave the planning to you gentleman."

"Is there really such a thing as Yule Night, or is it something people around here made up because there weren't enough holidays already this time of year?" Olivia frowned at the revelers who filed past the Dirty Sally. Eureka's Yule Night celebration was in full swing, complete with a bonfire in the park, horse-drawn sleigh rides, and strolling carolers.

"Isn't yule another name for Christmas?" Jameso drew a pint of beer and passed it across the bar to Bob.

"Yule's what the pagans celebrated at the winter solstice," Bob said. "Then the Christians came along and appropriated it."

Olivia tried not to look surprised. Bob might come across as a half-crazy old coot, but he was actually pretty smart, especially when it came to history.

"Mostly, it's an excuse for the stores to stay open late and encourage people to do their Christmas shopping here instead of ordering off the Internet," Jameso said. "Plus, it's a great party. Nothing wrong with that."

"What are you looking so sour about?" Bob asked. "You don't like Christmas?"

"Not especially, no." She waited for the sort of shocked protest she usually heard when she admitted she didn't care for America's most-loved holiday.

"It's a little much sometimes, isn't it?" Jameso said. "All that pressure to buy gifts and have a good time."

"Yes!" She whirled to face him, pleased to have discovered a kindred spirit. "All that forced gaiety and togetherness. It makes me want to gag."

"I thought maybe it would be better with a kid," he said. "I mean, a lot of stuff about the holiday is geared toward children."

Was he thinking of his own future child? "It's worse." She pulled a plastic bin from the refrigerator and began refilling the lime, lemon, and cherry container on the bar. "They want everything and you know no matter what you do, you're going to disappoint them."

"You two are just regular Scrooges, aren't you?" Bob shook his head.

"Bah, humbug," she said. "When was the last time you

had a really good Christmas—one like in the storybooks or TV shows, full of warm fuzzies and good cheer?"

"Maybe when I was really little?" Jameso shrugged. "I don't remember."

"But not when you were older, right? I dreaded Christmas when I was a teenager, shuffling back and forth between my parents. My dad had remarried and had new, little kids and I always felt like an afterthought . . . a couple of presents under the tree that my stepmother obviously bought at the last minute. Being with my mother was even worse. It was always just the two of us, so pathetic."

"So you had it rough as a kid," Bob said. "Get over it. You're grown up now . . . celebrate however you want."

"That's just it. All this"—she waved her hand to indicate the carolers and decorations and postcard-perfect snowfall—"all this tradition and sentiment have programmed us to want all those warm fuzzies and peace on earth. We're guaranteed to be disappointed no matter what."

"So you just don't celebrate?" Bob asked. "Ignore the holiday and hope it will go away?"

"I wish." She put the lid on the fruit with a resounding snap. "But I have a kid. I have to go through the motions for him."

"Last year, Murphy and I spent the holiday shooting off fireworks and getting drunk." Jameso looked sheepish. "When you're single, Christmas just reminds you how alone you are."

"Yeah." She rested her elbows on the bar, chin in hand, and watched a laughing family—mom, dad, and two little boys—stroll by. Last Christmas, she and D. J. had been together. He'd brought home a tree and they'd decorated it together. They'd seemed almost like a real family. It had been her best Christmas ever, but it hurt to think about now.

"What are you going to do this year?" she asked Jameso.

"I guess I'll spend Christmas with Maggie. Holidays like this seem important to her, so we'll do whatever she wants."

"So you're putting all the responsibility for the day on her. So like a man."

"Don't you give me that," Jameso said. "It's you women who are responsible for all this decorating and gift wrapping and celebrating. If it were up to men, we'd settle for a day off work and a stiff drink and call it good."

"Doesn't sound like a bad way to celebrate," Olivia said. She wasn't a big drinker, but she wouldn't mind a bit of oblivion on the one day of the year so soaked with sentiment and expectation that she was guaranteed to end up depressed.

The front door flew open, letting in a swirl of snow and the sound of sleigh bells and laughter. "Mom! Can I go with D. J. in the plow truck?" Lucas shouted.

"Shut the door," Olivia said. "And come here."

He did as he was told and came to stand in front of the bar. He was panting, as if he'd been running, and the transition from frigid outdoors to the warm saloon had fogged his glasses. "He has to plow the road into town and he said I could ride in the truck with him if you said it was okay."

"You know you're not supposed to come in the front door like that," she said, stalling while she processed his request. "The sign says twenty-one and older. You need to come in through the kitchen."

"I forgot. Can I go with him, please?"

"He's not going up on the passes, is he?" The bar patrons had filled her full of horror stories of cars being swept off the mountain by snow slides, or driving over the edge during whiteouts.

"No, he's just going to plow Main down to the intersection with the highway. He says you sit up real high in the truck and can see everything."

What they'd see in the dark, she couldn't imagine, but clearly the prospect of this special privilege elated Lucas. "All right, you can go. But you have to be home by nine-thirty. Grandma's closing her shop at nine and she'll be waiting for you."

"I will. I promise. Thank you. Bye!" He shouted the last as he raced out the door once more.

Maggie caught the door and came in. "Lucas is certainly excited about something," she said, unwinding a scarf from around her throat. Her auburn hair curled around her face and her nose was bright red from the cold.

"He's going to ride in the plow truck," Olivia said.

"Ah. That's better than a horse-drawn sleigh for a boy that age, I imagine. Hello, Jameso."

"Hello, Maggie." His smile was so warm and welcoming, Olivia had to look away, suppressing a sharp stab of jealousy. "Can I get you something?" he asked. "Coffee? Hot chocolate? I think we have some cider."

"Nothing, thank you. I had hot chocolate from the Friends of the Library booth. I just came in to get off my feet for a bit." She eased onto a bar stool. She looked tired, but good, Olivia thought. Her face was a little fuller than it had been a few months before, and her cheeks glowed from the cold. She'd be one of those pregnant women who looked more beautiful as the baby grew—all glossy hair and glowing skin. Not haggard and swollen, the way Olivia had felt with Lucas.

"Are you working tonight?" Olivia asked.

"Of course. Rick's driving the sleigh, so that leaves me to take pictures and interview shoppers and store owners."

"Our business has been good," Jameso said.

"I stopped by Lacy's and Lucille was busy," Maggie said. "And the Historical Society booth sold out of baked goods about a half hour ago. I guess we have a few more tourists than usual because of all the news stories."

"The shop owners will like that," Jameso said.

"Yes, and maybe some people will come back next year." She glanced toward the front window as a group of carolers passed, strains of "Jingle Bells" drifting in. "I can't blame people for wanting to visit," she said when the singers had moved out of hearing range. "Everything is so beautiful: the Victorian buildings, the snow and evergreens and candles. It looks like a movie set."

"I guess that's the idea," Jameso said. "Give people the perfect Christmas fantasy."

"But it's not a movie set, or a fantasy," Maggie said. "It's just the way it is here. Eureka is a special place. I hadn't been here long before I realized that."

To outsiders and newcomers less cynical than she was, Eureka probably did look perfect, Olivia thought. But every place had its problems, and its unpleasant people. It was naïve to pretend Eureka was different or special. Yes, the town had a few things going for it—the Thanksgiving dinner had been a lot more fun than she'd expected, and she'd been impressed with the way everyone had rallied around her mom. But that didn't make the town perfect or magical, or the people who lived here special.

"What do you want to do for Christmas?" Jameso leaned on the bar in front of Maggie.

"Oh, I don't know," she said. "Barb and Jimmy will be here, so maybe we could have dinner with them." She took his hand. "Just spending the day together will make me happy."

"You're an easy woman to please." He moved in closer and they kissed.

Olivia moved down the bar to give them some privacy, a familiar ache in her stomach. Sometimes she thought the hurt was from the baby she'd lost. What would D. J.

have done if he'd returned home to find her pregnant? Would a child have been enough to heal the rift between them?

The child would have been born around Christmas. Maybe that would have changed her feelings about the holiday and transformed it into a day of joy instead of sadness.

This year, the lost baby would be one more reason to dread Christmas. Being here among all the picture-postcard perfection made her sadness that much worse.

Bah, humbug indeed.

CHAPTER TWELVE

"Now that we have snow, we might as well enjoy it while we can." Jameso pulled a pack from the back seat of his truck and slipped it onto his shoulders.

When Maggie had accepted his invitation to "get out of the house for a while" she hadn't imagined he meant heading up to the top of Black Mountain Pass. She looked down at the snowshoes strapped to her boots. "I'd always imagined myself gliding gracefully along on skis."

"Not while you're pregnant. Too much danger of falling." He handed her a pair of ski poles. "These will help with your balance. Trust me, if you can walk, you can snowshoe."

"I'm not sure tromping around in the cold on top of a mountain pass is my idea of enjoyment."

"Come on. It's a beautiful day. And the doctor said exercise was good for you."

His enthusiasm was contagious and she had to admit, the day was sublime. The weather had cleared and the world around them was a frosted wedding cake, the dark pines dusted with powdered sugar. Sunlight sparkled on the snow, the air so clear and cold it practically crackled.

Colors were impossibly bright—the deep turquoise of the sky, the red of Jameso's parka, her own pink gloves and hat.

"Are you ready?" he asked.

"Sure. Let's go."

Snowshoeing turned out to be only a little awkward, requiring a wider stance and a shuffling gait. She followed him up a slight incline and around the curve. The snow was soft underfoot, light and fine as beach sand, crunching with each step. The sharp cold stung her cheeks, but the bright sun mitigated the bitterness. Maggie was soon winded, panting, but she felt gloriously alive nonetheless.

Jameso strode easily ahead of her, a tall, broad-shouldered figure in a red jacket and a black wool cap, more at home out here than most people were in their own living rooms. How had Maggie Stevens, a girl from the city, ever ended up with a man like him? She might as well have tried to tame a mountain lion.

He half-turned to look back at her. "You doing all right?"

"Just a little winded."

"We'll rest a little bit." He unzipped his parka and pulled out the tube of a water bladder and offered it to her. While she drank, he pointed to a cluster of buildings in a clearing below. "That's the old Blue Bird mine."

The buildings had the weathered, unpainted look she'd come to associate with the historic mine ruins that littered the mountains around Eureka. But these had a few modern touches—a rusting round-fender pickup truck on blocks beside one building, and the hulk of a yellow diesel tractor crouching in a shed.

"How long has the mine been closed?" she asked.

"I think it closed in the thirties, during the Depression. For a while the owners talked about reopening it, but nothing came of it."

"I heard a rumor the town is thinking of mining some of the old claims they own."

"I heard that rumor, too. I think Bob started it, which means there's probably nothing to it."

"Why would Bob start a rumor like that?" She'd learned the old man didn't do anything without a reason, even if his reasoning was sometimes a little skewed.

"Maybe he has a claim of his own he wants to sell and this is a way of getting people to think there's going to be a new gold rush in Eureka County." He shook his head. "I don't think those old claims are worth anything. Even if they are, where is Eureka going to get the money for the kind of technology you need to mine nowadays?"

"I guess not. It's an interesting idea, though. I mean, the French Mistress didn't have any gold in it, but the turquoise was a pretty neat find."

"Leave it to Jake to own the only mine in the county that was still worth anything."

"Maybe the town could sell the claims it owns to investors who have the money and technology to make them pay," she said.

"It's an idea. But first you have to convince an investor the mine could pay. Tough to do in this economy. Everyone's cynical." He zipped up his jacket. "You ready to go on? It's mostly downhill from here."

"Until we start back."

"You can do it."

"Yes, coach." But she grinned. Jameso was good at getting her to break out of her comfort zone and try new things—though having a first baby at forty was a bigger challenge than she'd ever imagined taking on. If she could do that, snowshoeing down a mountain pass seemed like a day at the beach in comparison.

At the edge of the clearing where the mine was situated, a sign proclaimed the area to be the property of the Eureka County Historical Society and warned against trespassing. "Cassie would have a fit if she knew we were here," Maggie said. The town librarian was also head of the historical society and regarded historical sites as her personal property.

"I'm tempted to tell her, just to see her reaction." Jameso led the way down what must have once been the main thoroughfare through the mine, past a tall house where tattered curtains flapped in glassless windows. "That was the boarding house for the miners," he said. He pointed to a smaller house farther up the canyon, with the remains of a green metal roof. "That was the mining superintendent's home."

"It's amazing how much of this has survived," she said, looking at the cables of a tram stretched overhead. Ore would have been transported in giant iron buckets along that tram, to the waiting mill on a slope above.

"There's talk of restoring all this and turning it into a mining museum," he said. "But the location's a problem. They'd have to build a road, and the state's not likely to grant a permit. It's tough enough to keep the highway open in the winter, much less a secondary road to a tourist attraction."

Wind stirred up whirlwinds of snow in the street and Maggie hugged herself, shivering. "Come on." Jameso put one arm around her shoulders. "Let's take a break out of the wind."

They moved to the shed that housed the yellow hulk of the tractor. Jameso took a thermos of hot tea and two almond butter and raspberry jam sandwiches from his pack and passed one sandwich and a mug of tea to Maggie. "My hero," she said, as she sipped the warm, sweet tea. It was all she could do to keep from moaning with pleasure at this unexpected indulgence. She'd taken off the snowshoes and sat in the driver's seat of the tractor while he lounged on the hood.

He grinned. "I'm lucky you're easy to please."

They ate in comfortable silence for a while. The shed wasn't warm, but out of the wind, cradling the mug of tea, she wasn't uncomfortable. "Does the tractor work?" she asked.

"It used to. A couple years ago Jake and I started it up and took it for a spin."

She pictured the two of them trundling through the valley on a wilderness joyride. She might have known her father had been involved in an escapade like that. "How did you two become such good friends?" she asked. "I mean, there was a big difference in your ages."

She'd asked the question before—each answer added another little piece to the picture of her father she kept in her mind.

"You don't really want to know," Jameso said.

"Of course I do."

"It's not a story that puts either one of us in the best light."

"I already know my father wasn't a saint." Jake Murphy had walked out on his family when Maggie was three days old and she hadn't heard a word from him until after his death. Yet since coming to Eureka to learn about him, she'd learned to pity him—and maybe even to love him a little. And to forgive him a lot.

"Yeah, and I guess you know all about my clay feet, too."

She said nothing, but waited, sensing he would talk if she gave him the time.

"I told you we met the first time up on the mountain."

"Yes." She recalled the tale. "You were target shooting and he joined you and shared your whiskey."

"Right. That really happened, but that's not really when we became such good friends. You might say that was how we first ended up on one another's radar. The friendship started a few months later."

"What happened?" She leaned forward, fascinated at

the developing picture of her father and his much younger friend.

"I was at a bar," Jameso said.

"Why am I not surprised?"

"Don't interrupt."

"Fine. You were in a bar."

"I tried to pick up this woman and she shot me down. Jake laughed and I told him to shut up or I'd punch him. I think I called him grandpa, but that only made him laugh more, which made me even angrier. I suggested we go outside in the parking lot. We did and he laid me out flat with one punch.

"Then he picked me up and took me back to his place and made coffee, and we stayed up half the night talking."

"Classic male bonding."

"I told you it didn't especially make either one of us look good. We had a lot in common."

"Anger and liquor."

Jameso nodded. "I hadn't been back from Iraq very long and I was pretty messed up. Jake helped set me straight. Part of it was seeing how he dealt—or didn't deal—with the demons in his own life."

"What happened in the war?" She'd asked the question before and he always refused to talk. But she'd keep asking, determined to break down the silence that was another barrier between them.

"I was in a convoy that was attacked and more than half the men in the group died. I had a bad case of survivor's guilt. When they sent me home I had nowhere to go."

"What about your family?"

"I stopped by to see my mom and sister up in Florida. My sister's married with two kids. Her husband made it clear he didn't think much of me. My mom is in a little one-bedroom apartment. I slept on the couch a couple of nights and I could tell I made her nervous. Like I was a bomb she was expecting to go off."

She waited and he rewarded her patience. He drained his tea mug and set it aside on the hood of the tractor. "I haven't seen my dad since I was sixteen. That's the last time he tried to hit me. For the first time I fought back, and I won. I told him if he ever laid a hand on me or my mom or my sister, I'd kill him. I think he knew I meant it, so he left and never came back." He glanced back at Maggie. "I learned later he had a shitty childhood, so he was just repeating all his father's mistakes with me. What if I do that with our child?"

"You won't." She leaned forward and squeezed his arm. It was like squeezing an iron bar, but beneath all his toughness, she had seen his tenderness. "You're a good man, Jameso."

He leaned forward, away from her touch. "There's a voice in my head that tells me I'm not good enough."

She swallowed past the knot of emotion in her throat and struggled to find the right words. "I think that voice talks to all of us sometimes. We have to learn not to listen to it."

He slid down off the tractor and began packing up the remains of their lunch. "You ready to go?" he asked. Conversation over. The words he had shared had been a gift; she wouldn't press for more.

"Sure."

They made their way out of the mining camp and back up the trail. Maggie felt closer to Jameso than she ever had, touched by the secret parts of himself he'd shared with her today.

Without her having to ask, he stopped halfway up so she could rest. He stood astride the trail, poles planted, face tilted up to scan the mountaintops above. Maggie had her camera in her jacket pocket, but she knew if she took it out she'd break the mood.

"I like being out here because the mountains make my

problems seem small," he said. "I can handle myself out here."

"You can handle yourself anywhere," she said.

"You'd be wrong about that." He turned toward her, but she couldn't read his expression behind the dark sunglasses he wore. "I don't always know how to handle myself around you."

"You've done all right so far."

"You turned down my proposal."

"Because I don't want you marrying me out of a sense of obligation."

"So you don't ever want to marry me?"

"Not until you prove it's what you really want."

He made a noise between a growl and a grunt, a sound that was equal parts anger and frustration. Maggie felt the warm closeness of the afternoon slipping away. She shuffled up beside him and slipped her hand into the crook of his elbow. "I'm happy with things the way they are right now," she said. "It's a beautiful day and I'm glad to be sharing it with you. That's enough for now, isn't it?"

He hesitated half a second, then patted her hand. "You're right. It's more than enough for now."

Olivia fussed with the hem of the tunic she'd fashioned from an old formal she'd found at her mom's shop. She'd ripped the dress apart for the material, a sky blue silk embroidered with tiny butterflies, and reworked it into an asymmetrical mini dress she was wearing tonight as a tunic over skinny jeans. Bright yellow high-heeled pumps—another thrift-store find—completed the look. "You don't think I look like I'm trying too hard, do you?" she asked as she studied her reflection in the mirror tacked to her bedroom closet.

"You look too fashionable and hip for Eureka," Lucille

said. "But I think that's probably the look you were going for, right?"

Olivia flushed. "Maybe. Maggie said she was going to take a picture for the paper."

Lucille patted her shoulder. "You look beautiful."

"You do, Mom." Lucas, wearing jeans and an over-sized desert camo T-shirt she suspected he'd swiped from D. J., stuck his head in the doorway of Olivia's room. "We'd better go or we're going to be late."

"They can't start without us," Olivia said, but picked up her coat.

She parked the SUV in the lot behind the Dirty Sally and they walked next door to the Last Dollar, but Olivia hesitated at the front door. "There are a lot of people here," she said, the butterflies on the tunic seeming to have migrated to her stomach.

"People have taken a real interest in this." Lucille reached around her and opened the door. "Go on in. This is your big night. Enjoy it."

At first no one noticed when they stepped inside the café. The aromas of fresh coffee and baking bread and grilled steak surrounded them. But as Olivia was hanging her coat on the pegs by the door, someone started applauding. Flushing, she turned to find a restaurant full of people—most of them familiar to her—clapping for her.

"Welcome, everyone." Danielle, a fuzzy teal sweater hugging her curves, joined Olivia by the front register. "This is a big night for us. We're celebrating the completion of our mural, painted by artist Olivia Theriot."

More applause. Olivia couldn't feel her feet as Danielle led her toward the back of the room, where Janelle waited with a pair of scissors. The girls had strung a wide pink satin ribbon across the back of the room. Janelle handed Olivia the scissors, then stepped back.

She turned to face the crowd. Bob sat nearby, with Reggie and some of the other Dirty Sally regulars. Another crowd of barflies stood just inside the front door with Jameso—apparently they'd emptied out the place to come watch her. Maggie was there with her camera, along with Rick, Tamara, and her husband, and so many other people she recognized, even if she didn't know their names.

D. J., however, was not there. She told herself it didn't matter, but her shoulders slumped just a little at the realization. "Speech!" someone called.

Right. She was supposed to say something. All the remarks she'd so carefully prepared earlier had vanished from her head, so she'd have to wing it. "I want to thank Janelle and Danielle for giving me this opportunity," she said. "They took a chance, hiring someone like me, without a lot of experience, for a project this big. I really appreciate it." More applause. She smiled. This wasn't so bad. "I also want to thank my mom, Lucille, and my son, Lucas, for all their patience and understanding while I worked long hours to complete this project. And thank you to Lucas for helping with my research. And to Cassie Wynock and Bob Prescott for their help in learning about the history of Eureka so I'd know what to paint. And thank you all for coming out tonight to celebrate with me." There, that was enough. She turned and snipped through the ribbon. The flash of Maggie's camera momentarily blinded her.

Then Danielle was hugging her. "It's so beautiful," she said. "Thank you so much."

Janelle embraced her then and pressed an envelope into her hand. "Here's the final payment," she said. "You did great."

Others came to congratulate her, and someone handed her a glass of wine. She hadn't realized she'd been scanning the crowd again until her mother moved in close. "D. J. told me to tell you he's sorry he couldn't be here," she said. "They had a big snow slide up near Robber's Roost and he's working to clear it."

"Oh." She had no idea where Robber's Roost was, but she didn't really care. "Well, I don't know why he'd have wanted to come anyway."

"He said to tell you congratulations."

Then Lucille moved away and another group of well-wishers came to offer hugs and handshakes. Olivia tried to pretend all the accolades didn't matter, but she couldn't stop smiling every time she glanced back at the mural. "Artist Olivia Theriot" was right there in black script in the bottom right-hand corner. Had anything ever looked so good?

When the picture of Olivia with the mural ran in the paper two days later, Jameso cut it out and tacked it up behind the bar. "I don't know if I can stand working with a celebrity," he teased.

"Oh, please." She swatted at him with her bar towel, but she couldn't quite hide her smile. This elation probably wouldn't last, but she was enjoying it while she could.

The door opened and a snow-covered figure entered. The man shook and snow flew, revealing Bob. "It's a whiteout out there," he said. He took his customary stool at the bar and Jameso drew a beer without waiting for him to ask. Bob drained half the pint, then set the glass on the bar with a hard thump. "Maybe we ought to start a new pool," he said. "Have folks guess how many days this season we'll be cut off from the rest of the world."

"Cut off?" Olivia asked. "What do you mean?"

"When the snow piles up, avalanches can cut off the passes at either end of town," Jameso said. "No one can get in or out."

"Can't they just plow the snow out of the way?" she asked.

"Not so easy when it keeps sliding down off the mountain," Bob said. "You have to wait until it quits snowing for a while, then get the big rotary plows from the state out to clear it. Sometimes they even have to bring in heavy equipment to shift trees and rocks off the road."

Olivia shuddered. She'd heard talk like this before, but she hadn't really believed it. People around here liked to exaggerate the hardships sometimes, as if that proved they were hardier and tougher than everyone else. "What if there's an emergency and somebody has to get out?"

"They just have to wait," Bob said. "You can't beat Mother Nature at her own game."

"Murphy and I skied out over Black Mountain Pass one year," Jameso said. "Not because we had to, just to prove that we could."

"Jake Murphy never had the sense God gave a goat," Bob said. "You could get buried in snow up there and nobody'd find you 'til July."

"Being crazy must be a requirement for living here," Olivia said.

"If crazy is not wanting to play by the rest of the world's rules, then maybe you're right." Bob shoved his empty glass forward. "I'll have another."

She pulled another glass of Irish Ale. She'd never thought of herself as a person who played by the rules, but maybe it was possible to take being different too far. People around here didn't show off their new cars—they bragged about how many miles they had on their old beaters, and how their ancient rust bucket pulled a tourist's new Lexus out of the ditch last week. Most nights one or two snowmobiles shared space with the trucks and cars in front of the bar, and last week the town council had officially closed Darter Avenue on the North End of town to vehicle traffic, designating the snow-covered slope as a "sleds and skis only" thoroughfare.

These people didn't just tolerate winter—they reveled in it.

"I'd just as soon the roads stay open until UPS has delivered all the stuff Barb ordered for the nursery," Jameso said, as Olivia slid the beer in front of Bob.

"I don't see why a baby needs a bunch of fancy stuff," Bob said. "I slept in a dresser drawer until I was two."

"Barb's driving me crazy. Every week she's got some new idea for a new color scheme or a new piece of furniture or gadget."

"What does Maggie say?" Olivia asked.

"Maggie's turned the whole thing over to Barb. I really think it's their way of keeping me occupied and involved, as if I'd forget about the baby without them reminding me of it every day."

"Would you like to forget?" Olivia asked. "At least for a little while?"

"No!" He flushed. "Okay, maybe sometimes I'd like to, but I won't. Finding out you're going to have a kid changes the way you look at everything. "

"Some men can't handle the responsibility," Bob said. "Jake was like that. When things got heavy, he left."

"What do you mean, he left?" Olivia asked.

"He skipped town when Maggie was three days old, so she never knew him."

"Lucas's dad and I split when Lucas was two. He never came back once to see his son."

"Well, I'm not like them," Jameso said. "I'm not going to desert Maggie or my kid. But she doesn't believe that."

He seemed to mean it, but how could he be sure? Olivia wondered. Maybe he'd freak out when the baby got here. "Did you know Maggie was pregnant before she told you?" she asked.

"No way. I mean, I guess I knew it was a possibility, but I never thought . . ." He shook his head.

Of course, he and Maggie didn't live together, and he hadn't known her as long as Olivia had known D. J., but maybe guys didn't pick up on these things the way she thought. Maybe D. J. really had been oblivious to all the hints she'd dropped.

The door opened again, ushering in another blast of cold, a flurry of snowflakes, and Junior Dominick, who dragged a large cardboard box covered in Christmas wrapping paper. "Where do you want me to put this?" he asked, straightening and brushing snow from his shoulders.

"There by the door will work." Jameso came from behind the bar to help him position the box.

"What's that for?" Olivia asked.

"The food and toy drive for the Santas," Junior said. "We've got a big list this year, what with the economy and all, so encourage folks to fill it up."

"The Santas?"

"The Elks puts together Christmas packages for anybody in need; then volunteers dress up like Santa and make the deliveries Christmas Eve." Bob joined them in front of the box.

"There's a tree at the bank with the kids' wish lists," Junior said. "Folks can pick an ornament off the tree, buy the stuff on the list, and deposit it here or in any of the other boxes around town. We need food for the Christmas dinner, too. And, of course, cash is always welcome."

"How many people are you collecting for?" Olivia asked.

"Last year it was thirty-five families," Junior said. "This year we might have as many as fifty." He turned to Jameso and Bob. "We need more Santas and drivers, so get over to the Elks Hall and sign up."

"I'd scare some poor kid to death if I showed up as Santa," Bob said. "But I'll help with the packing and stuff."

"You should come and bring Lucas," Junior told Olivia. "It's a great way to show kids the true meaning of the holiday."

"Sure, I'll do that." She'd make sure they got an ornament off the tree, too. Maybe that would help her look at the holiday in a better light—and take Lucas's mind off the gun he wanted.

The phone rang and she turned back toward the bar to answer it, just as a piercing shriek rent the air. "What the hell is that?" she asked, covering her ears.

"Emergency siren at the fire department," Junior said. He exchanged worried looks with the other men.

The door to the saloon burst open and Maggie raced in, the blare of the siren still echoing behind her. "There's been a big avalanche up on Black Mountain Pass," she said. "D. J. was plowing up that way and got pushed off the mountain."

Chapter Thirteen

While the others in the bar exclaimed and fired questions, Maggie watched Olivia. The younger woman was very pale—and very silent. "I'm headed up there now to try to get the story for the paper," Maggie said. "I just thought you all would like to know."

"I want to come with you." Olivia was already pulling her coat from behind the bar.

"All right," Maggie said. Clearly, she wasn't going to keep the girl away, and she probably didn't need to be driving, as upset as she looked.

Olivia waited until they were headed up the road to Black Mountain Pass in Maggie's Jeep before she spoke. "What happened?" she asked.

"I don't know everything, but the scanner message sounded like one of the avalanche chutes up on Black Mountain let loose, and swept the plow and the driver off the side of the mountain." Saying the words gave Maggie a sick feeling in the pit of her stomach. She glanced at her passenger. Olivia stared straight ahead, only the tightness around her mouth betraying her agitation. "Rick said this happens at least once a year," Maggie continued. "Most of the guys make it out okay."

"It's crazy," Olivia said. "He's crazy. Why would anyone take a job like that?"

"Because they're men and men are crazy?" Maggie smiled at Olivia's shocked expression. "I don't really think they're all crazy," she said. "But some of them do seem to enjoy testing the limits. Maybe it's a testosterone thing, liking risk and danger."

"He was in Iraq for six months," Olivia said. "Driving trucks in supply convoys. Maybe life here seemed too tame after that."

Maybe that was why Jameso liked hurtling down mountains on skis or flying through the night on his motorcycle, Maggie thought. Maybe regular life was too tame after fighting in a war. "It's none of my business, I know," she said, "but you and D. J. used to be . . . involved?"

Olivia fixed her with a cool stare. "Are you asking as a reporter?"

"No, I'm asking as another woman. As a friend."

Some of the stiffness went out of the younger woman's shoulders. "We lived together for about a year. Then he decided he'd rather go to Iraq than stay with me and we split up."

"And then he came to Eureka . . . looking for you?"

"Why do you think he was looking for me?"

"Nobody comes here by accident. And that would be too much of a coincidence, for both of you to end up in this remote small town."

She nodded. "He came looking for me. He said he was sorry and he wanted to try again. And you probably think I'm a coldhearted bitch for not taking him back."

"I don't think that. Saying 'I'm sorry' doesn't automatically make everything right."

"I hope he's all right." Olivia's lips compressed into a

thin line. "Then I can personally kill him for being so stupid."

Flares in the road warned them they were nearing the accident scene. Half a dozen cars and trucks—probably belonging to the Search and Rescue team—were parked along the shoulder leading to the summit of the pass, along with three county sheriffs' SUVs, light bars flashing. Maggie parked behind an old Dodge she recognized as belonging to Charlie Frazier, Shelly's husband. "Search and Rescue is here," Maggie said. "That's good."

The women climbed out of the car and trudged up the road. The sun had come out, bathing the scene in dazzling light, so that every snow crystal sparkled. Maggie squinted in the glare, even behind her sunglasses. The air smelled of diesel and pine. A pyramid of snow ten feet high blocked the highway, spilling into the canyon along the side of the pavement, where the road abruptly dropped away to nothing.

"I can't believe there isn't even a guard rail up here." Olivia hugged her arms across her chest and scowled at the canyon.

"I thought the same thing when I first came up here," Maggie said. "Then someone pointed out that guard rails wouldn't stop an avalanche, and they wouldn't allow the plow drivers to push the snow over the side."

"Is he really down there?"

"Let's find out." She approached the group of men and women gathered at the drop-off. Olivia trailed behind. As they drew closer, Maggie saw that someone, probably Search and Rescue, had strung a cable from a rock anchor, down into the canyon. "What's going on?" she asked Charlie, a stocky thirty-something with a ginger beard.

"The plow came to rest in a bunch of trees about thirty feet down, on its side," Charlie said. "We've got a couple men down there digging their way into the cab. We won't know much until they clear the snow." He shifted his gaze over Maggie's right shoulder. "What are you doing here, Olivia?"

"The driver, D. J., is a friend of hers," Maggie said.

"I'll have to ask you to step back, out of our way," Charlie said. His tone wasn't unfriendly, but it was firm.

They moved back a few steps. Maggie took a few photos of the avalanche and the men working. "It's freezing up here." Olivia stamped her feet.

The girl wore a stylish, but probably not very warm, denim jacket. "Do you want to go sit in the Jeep?" Maggie asked. "You could run the engine to keep warm."

"No, I want to be here when they bring him up."

Two other team members had a Stokes basket ready to haul up the injured man. Maggie prayed he was still alive. She hadn't told Olivia the other thing Rick had revealed to her—that the men who didn't make it out alive were usually in bad shape.

Both women turned at the sound of running footsteps. Lucille, her red wool coat bright against the snow, hurried up the steep slope to them. She stopped in front of them, red-faced and out of breath. "I came as soon as I heard. Olivia, are you all right?"

"Just dandy."

Lucille moved closer to her daughter but didn't touch her. Maggie thought again how different they were—tall Lucille with her raw-boned features and Olivia, delicate and gamine. Yet the women had the same mouth and the same firm set of their jaws.

"What's taking so long?" Olivia asked.

Maggie shook her head. She'd had her ears tuned for a shout from down below, some indication that they'd found D. J. alive.

A man she didn't recognize climbed up from the canyon and shook his head. "The cab's empty," he said. "He must have been thrown out . . . or jumped."

Olivia made a sound like a whimper and turned away.

"What are you going to do now?" Lucille asked the man.

"We'll start searching the canyon." He didn't add "for the body." Maggie's own imagination supplied those words. She scanned the vast canyon. The tops of dark green fir and spruce jutted from the snow, which looked soft and inviting, but she knew just beneath the surface lay jagged boulders. How could any man survive hurtling off the side of a mountain into that?

A wrecker arrived, the rumbling engine shaking the ground at their feet. Maggie looked up at the cliffs to their right, half-fearing another avalanche. But the snow clung there, silent and still. The driver climbed out and walked to the back of the rig and began spooling steel cable from the winch. "The plow doesn't look too damaged," Charlie told Lucille. "You should be able to get it running again without too much trouble."

"I'm more concerned about the driver than the plow."

"Of course. Still, with all our budget problems, not having to buy a new plow is a good thing."

Everyone watched as the wrecker driver climbed down, cable in hand. Fifteen minutes later he was up again. The winch groaned. Rocks shifted, and he began the slow process of hauling the wayward plow to the surface.

The diesel motor of the wrecker growled and popped. The winch groaned, and the scrape of metal against rock as the snowplow climbed made Maggie want to put her hands over her ears. Olivia kept her eyes fixed on the cable, scarcely blinking, giving no indication that the noise bothered her.

The wing of a plow blade emerged first, jutting up over the lip of the canyon like the talon of a prehistoric monster. Then the top of the cab came into view, a little dented, but surprisingly intact. The rest of the machine emerged quickly, until it sat upright on the road, listing a little to one side from a flat tire. The wrecker driver unhooked the cables, then returned to the wrecker to reposition it to load the plow onto the flat bed.

"I hope she's okay. She was my favorite machine."

The man spoke from behind them. Olivia gasped and they all turned to stare at D. J. He had a streak of blood on one cheek and one knee was torn out of his coveralls, but otherwise he appeared unhurt. "Where did you come from?" Maggie asked.

"I climbed up out of the canyon." He wiped his hand on his jacket. "I jumped free when the machine started to slide, and landed in a bunch of rocks. Knocked the breath out of me; then it took a while to figure out how to get back up here." He grinned. "That was a wild ride!"

Olivia walked toward him, eyes dark and huge in her pale face. Maggie raised her camera, ready for a shot of the big reunion hug. But instead of flinging herself at him, Olivia reached out and slapped him.

D. J. reeled and took a step back to keep from falling over. The sound echoed through the canyon. "Don't you ever scare me that way again!" Olivia shouted.

She stalked back down the road, toward Maggie's Jeep. D. J. stared after her, one hand to his cheek, which bore the clear imprint of her hand. Then he grinned, a goofy, half-out-of-it smile.

"What are you grinning about?" Maggie asked.

"Don't you see?" he said. "It means there's hope. She still cares."

D. J.'s reaction to Olivia's slap stayed with Maggie in the days following the accident. The ways couples chose to reveal their emotions would probably make a fascinating study for a psychology class, but with Christmas only a couple of weeks away, she was more focused on finding the right gift to show her feelings for Jameso.

Though she'd turned down his marriage proposal, she wanted him to know that she did love him—and she was glad he was the father of her baby. So she wanted to give him a gift that was special and would have meaning for him. That ruled out typical guy gifts like shirts or fishing lures or ski equipment.

She debated on books or music, but nothing seemed right. Barb was no help. "I'm giving Jimmy a contraption that monograms golf balls and a gift certificate for a massage," she said when Maggie telephoned and asked for suggestions. "Last year I gave him a round of golf at a course in Scotland—that was probably the best gift I ever gave him, but I don't want him expecting something that good every year."

"Jameso works at a bar. He has access to all the liquor he wants. And he has every piece of ski equipment known to man."

"Jimmy has tons of golf stuff, but he still likes it when I buy him something new. Just look at it like buying a gift for a bigger kid. Give him something he'd like to play with. You, for instance. All wrapped up in a red satin bow and nothing else."

"Yeah, I don't think so. When are you going to be here? Maybe you can help me shop."

"We're leaving the day after the party." The annual Stanowski Christmas bash was one of the benchmarks of the Houston holiday season, at least in the rarified circles in which Barb traveled.

"And Jimmy is okay with this? I thought he hated snow."

"He thinks he hates snow. He's never been around enough to know. Besides, I promised him we'd soak nude in the hot springs with the snow falling gently around us. He'd never pass up an opportunity like that. You do have snow, don't you?"

"Plenty. People tell me it's shaping up to be a record

year." Even now, when Maggie looked out the front window of the *Miner*'s offices, she could see a drift of white settling onto the already snow-covered streets and cars and buildings. "Jameso's thrilled at the skiing, and I'm just glad I don't have to drive far in the stuff."

"And you're not going near a snow shovel, I hope." Barb spoke sternly. Not for the first time, Maggie thought her friend would have made a great sixth-grade teacher.

"No, Jameso is taking care of all that." In fact, for a man who up until now had shown no hint of ever wanting to settle down and be responsible, he was amazingly attentive. He accompanied her to doctor's appointments and had let Barb bully him into creating her idea of the perfect nursery. "He seems happy about the baby," she added.

"So, are you going to marry him?"

Maggie squirmed in her chair. "He hasn't asked again." Marriage was a topic they were both clearly avoiding.

"Once wasn't enough? Really, Maggie, don't make the man work so hard."

"I think I'm worth a little hard work." She'd done most of the hard work in her first marriage, now she was ready to be wooed and won over, instead of hoping things would work out because a man got up the nerve to tell her he loved her.

"I'll deal with both of you when we get there," Barb said. "We're coming in on the twenty-third and staying through the New Year. I've booked us rooms at the Eureka Hotel. Do you know anything about it?"

"It's the only hotel in town." The nondescript, blockish building on the edge of town wasn't a chain but managed to look like one.

"I'll bring my own sheets. I have to go now. The caterer is on the other line. See you soon."

Maggie hung up the phone. She debated asking Rick what he thought she should give Jameso, but cringed when she imagined the laughter that would greet such a request. Rick was not the sentimental type, and he never tired of teasing her about what he saw as her unlikely matchup with her father's best friend.

Her gaze drifted to the picture of Jake that she kept on her desk. It had been taken at one of the Hard Rock competitions he'd won, and it showed a craggy, muscular man in a lumberjack shirt. He had an ax balanced casually on one shoulder and looked into the camera with a big, toothy smile. She liked the picture because he looked so happy. Though she suspected he'd come to Eureka to escape his demons, he'd found some measure of contentment here.

It was ironic, really, that she'd hook up with his best friend, a man young enough to be his son. Maybe in Jameso, Jake had seen the child he'd been too scarred, or afraid, to get close to. And maybe in Jake, Jameso had found a father to replace his abusive one. She knew Jameso missed his friend, much more than she missed the father she'd never known.

An idea hit her, as if she'd swallowed something warm and sweet. Smiling to herself, she hurried to the closet at the back of the room where they kept office supplies, old printer and copier parts, and the photo archives—shelves of cardboard boxes filled with black and white photos that dated from the days before they'd switched over to digital images.

She searched until she found the box with photos from the last Hard Rock competition her dad had won. The paper had done a two-page center spread of the festivities, so she had plenty of shots to choose from. She laughed at an image of Bob apparently instructing Junior Dominick on the art of driving a spike, both of them über-serious, while behind them, Jake made faces.

At last she found the photo she'd been searching for. Her memory hadn't let her down. It was a crowd shot of competitors and friends. Jameso and Jake stood by side by side. They were looking at each other, laughing, two friends sharing a moment.

She fished the photo from the box and slipped it into an envelope she found on another shelf. "Rick, I have to go out for a while," she said.

She drove to Lucille's house and was relieved to see Olivia's black SUV parked out front. Clutching the photograph inside her coat to protect it from the falling snow, she hurried up the steps and rang the bell.

Olivia looked wary as she opened the door, but relaxed when she saw Maggie. "Hey," she said. "Mom's not here. She's still at the shop."

"I didn't come to see your mom," Maggie said. "Can I talk to you for a minute?"

"Sure, come on in." Olivia held the door open and Maggie slipped inside. She brushed snow from her coat, then handed Olivia the envelope.

"Take a look at what I found in the newspaper archives just now."

Olivia sent her a questioning look but slid the photo from the envelope. "I recognize Jameso and a few other people," Olivia said. "So?"

"The man Jameso is standing next to is my dad, his friend Jake. I was hoping you could use the photo to paint a picture of the two of them for me to give to Jameso for Christmas. I know this is really last minute and if you can't do it, I'll understand." She held her breath. If this didn't work, she was back to square one.

"I can do it. Sure." Olivia studied the photo again. "They look a little alike, don't they? Maybe not so much physically, but they have the same attitude."

"God, I hope not," Maggie said. "My dad would never be mistaken for father of the year."

"Yeah, I heard he skipped when you were little."

"When I was three days old. Then, not another word until after he died."

"I don't think Jameso's like that. He seems really excited about the baby."

"Really?" Maggie moved to look over Olivia's shoulder at the photograph of the several years younger Jameso laughing. "It's hard to tell."

"Well, he's a man, so who knows what they're really thinking? But, yeah, I think he's looking forward to being a dad. A little nervous, but that's understandable."

"I think both of us are scared spitless sometimes. We have no idea what to do with a baby."

Olivia slid the picture back into the envelope and laid it on a table by the door. "You think I did? I was a sixteen-year-old punk rocker wannabe. I knew exactly zero about kids and didn't even think I wanted one. But there you go."

"So you were like me . . . a single mom?"

"The guy—Byron—and I decided we should get married. It's what everybody expected. Big mistake. We hung in there until Lucas was two or so; then I got tired of him beating up on me and left. I got divorce papers in the mail to sign months later. I should have hired a lawyer and sued for child support and whatever else I could get, but by that time I just wanted to be done, you know?"

"Yeah." Maggie nodded. She'd felt the same way by the time her own divorce had gone to court. She'd just wanted to be free of the marriage. Except for her rings and a collection of Steuben glass that she held on to for too long, she hadn't taken much in the way of reminders with her. When she'd finally gotten rid of the glass and the rings, it had felt like breaking the final connection, allowing her to really start over.

Steps pounded up the porch and they turned to see Lucas burst in the door. "Hi, Mom," he said, dropping his backpack in the hall. "Hey, Mrs. Stevens." He nodded to

Maggie, then turned back to his mother. "Can we ride to the school program with D. J. Thursday night?" he asked.

Olivia looked uncomfortable. "We can go in my car and D. J. can meet us there."

"But I want us to all ride together!" Lucas's voice rose an octave and his expression darkened.

"I really should be going," Maggie said, inching toward the door.

"No, you don't have to leave," Olivia said. She turned to her son. "Why is this so important to you?"

"Because D. J. is my best friend and I want to ride with him . . . but I want to be with you, too. Can't we just all go together?"

Olivia bit her lip. "All right, if it's that important to you."

"Thanks, Mom." He pulled her into a quick hug, then raced from the room. "I'm starving!"

"Sorry about that," Olivia said when she and Maggie were alone again. "So, don't worry about the painting. I'll have it for you before Christmas."

"I'll pay you, of course," Maggie said. "How much?"

Olivia looked around the foyer, as if the answer was pinned to the drapes or hiding under the table. "A hundred dollars?"

"I think a hundred and fifty sounds better," Maggie said. "I know you'll do a good job."

"Sure. That sounds great." She remained silent as Maggie shrugged back into her coat. "About D. J. . . ." she began.

"You don't owe me an explanation," Maggie said.

"No, but I want to tell you." Olivia twisted her hands together. "I guess I want to tell someone, and you strike me as a person who won't judge."

Maggie stopped buttoning her coat. "No judgment here."

Olivia sighed. "I guess it's pretty clear from the way I

acted the other day, after the accident with the snowplow, that I still have feelings for D. J. But they're a mix of good and bad. He let me down when I really needed him, and I'm not sure I can trust him. I don't want to hurt like that again."

"I hear you," Maggie said. "I've got a few trust issues of my own." She thought of Jameso, down on his knees before her with the ring in his pocket, looking like a man going to the gallows.

"Yeah, well, I just wanted you to know. I'm not blind or anything. I see that D. J.'s a good guy and he's trying hard, and Lucas loves him and everything. I get that. But it doesn't mean I can pretend nothing happened and we're now guaranteed a happily ever after."

Maggie reached out to grasp the younger woman's arm. "I understand. I really do."

A smile flickered across Olivia's face, then vanished. "Thanks. Love is never this tough in movies, is it? People fall in love and they just know they can get through anything together."

"Life is a little less pat than that." A lot of things could happen to kill love—that didn't mean it hadn't once been real.

Olivia straightened and took a step back, away from Maggie's touch. "Don't worry about the baby thing," she said. "You'll know the right thing to do when the time comes."

"Sounds like a good philosophy for life in general."

"I guess it does, doesn't it." She opened the door and Maggie stepped out into the snow again, and carefully picked her way to the Jeep. She still wasn't sure life was as easy as that, but she liked thinking she'd instinctively know what to do for her child, and that she'd know, too, when the time was right to make a commitment to Jameso.

Or not.

*   *   *

"Mom, hurry up! D. J. will be here any minute."

Olivia brushed mascara onto her lashes, concentrating on holding the wand steady despite the nervous flutter in her stomach. Why had she let Lucas talk her into riding with D. J. to his school program? Things would be so much easier if they went with her mom.

She was doing this for Lucas, not herself or D. J. or anyone else. This was his program, his night; she could ride to the program with D. J., no big deal.

She capped the mascara and studied her reflection in the medicine cabinet mirror. The relentless mountain sun lent color to her cheeks even in the dead of winter and the last of the platinum bleach had grown out, leaving her hair a softer, wheat-blonde. Add some stylish western threads and she could pose for a Ralph Lauren ad, holding the harness of a thoroughbred. Her hipster and punk friends from the city would laugh.

She sighed, then slicked on lip gloss and went downstairs. Lucas met her at the bottom step. "What took you so long, Mom?" He was practically jumping up and down with agitation. Thank God for that little-boy impatience, which reassured her this was her son standing in front of her; otherwise, she might not have recognized him. He'd seemingly shot up overnight, until he was as tall as her. He had his hair slicked back and wore black trousers, a white shirt, and a tie. Where had he gotten a tie? "We have plenty of time," she reassured him.

"You look really pretty, Mom."

She glanced down at the lavender silk sheath she'd found at a thrift store in Montrose. Too light and summery for the weather or the season, but she'd paired it with tall black boots and a fake fur jacket that gave the whole look an edge she liked. "Thank you."

"Yeah, very pretty."

She jerked up her head and found D. J. standing in the doorway. Dressed in khakis and a blue dress shirt, open at the throat, his worn leather bomber jacket instead of a sports coat, he looked impossibly handsome, less rugged than she was used to, but every bit as masculine.

"We'd better get going or we're going to be late," she said, and started past him.

"No rush." He put a hand on her arm as she passed. She stopped and looked into his serious brown eyes, and her knees threatened to give way beneath the intensity of his expression. The spicy scent of his aftershave overwhelmed her with memories of pressing her nose to the soft flesh at the crook of his neck to inhale his scent. *Get a grip,* she told herself. "What?" she snapped at him.

He released her. "Nothing. But I thought you might want to take your camera." He nodded to the little digital camera that sat on the table by the door.

She snatched it up and stuffed it into her purse, then stalked out the door ahead of them. This was the first time she'd seen him up close since last week on the mountain, when he'd come back from the dead to stand in front of her and all she could think was to slap the smug grin off his face. Afterward, she'd been ashamed of her reaction, but it was too late to take it back. The whole time, D. J. hadn't said a word, and he didn't seem inclined to say anything now.

They rode in Olivia's SUV—really D. J.'s. His name was still on the title, though he'd never asked for it back. He seemed content to drive around in the old beater truck he'd bought somewhere. She should probably offer— even insist—that he take the SUV back. But then what would she drive?

The school was lit up like a Christmas village. Most of the town must have turned out for the kids' program. A few snowflakes sifted over them as they climbed out of their vehicle. "You won't have to leave to go work, will you?" Lucas asked, his eyes wide with anxiety behind his glasses.

"I won't have to leave." D. J. put his hand on Lucas's shoulder. "I promise."

"Good. Well, you two go to the auditorium," Lucas instructed. "I have to go in the back way." Not waiting for an answer, he took off across the parking lot.

D. J. took Olivia's elbow and steered her down the crowded hallway. She wanted to protest, but she liked the feel of his hand on her arm. Steady and strong.

Lucille waved to them from the front of the auditorium and they squeezed into two seats she'd saved beside her. Though she'd lost weight and hadn't fully recovered from the whole fiasco with that Gerald bastard, she looked more cheerful, Olivia thought. Less pale and haunted. "Don't you two look nice," Lucille said. "Where's Lucas?"

"He went backstage. He's so excited and nervous he's making me nervous."

"You know he'll do great."

"What is he doing, exactly?" D. J. scanned the printed program they'd picked up on the way in. "He wouldn't tell me."

"He wouldn't tell me either," Olivia said. She found Lucas's name three quarters of the way through the listings, across from the words "The First Christmas." Lucas was acting in a nativity scene?

The lights dimmed and the school superintendent, Mr. Kinkaid, came onstage to welcome everyone and introduce the kindergarteners, who brought the house down with an animated rendition of "Here Comes Santa Claus" that was more shouted than sung.

From there the program progressed through the rest of the grades, with alternating spoken and sung performances. When the sixth graders sang "Silver Bells" Olivia closed her eyes and let the music wash over her. How odd that a song about Christmas in the city was just as beautiful here in the remote mountains.

"Don't fall asleep," D. J. whispered close to her ear.

She opened her eyes. "My butt is the only thing going to sleep."

At last the time arrived for Lucas's performance. "Our next presentation is an original piece written by eighth grader Lucas Theriot and performed by the eighth-grade class of Mrs. Desmet."

The curtains parted to reveal a stage set with a covered wagon against a backdrop of mountains and stars. One of Lucas's classmates, dressed in tall boots and suspendered trousers, lamented to a girl in an apron and sunbonnet that it was Christmas Eve and here they were, stranded on the road outside the town of Eureka, with no presents for the children and nothing but biscuits for their Christmas dinner.

Lucas, in miner's canvas pants, broad-brimmed hat, and an elaborate handlebar moustache, strode onto the stage. "What seems to be the trouble here, folks?" he intoned.

The man, joined now by a trio of children dressed in footed pajamas, explained the dilemma. "Santa will never find us here!" the smallest child wailed.

"We'll see about that," Lucas said, and exited stage left.

A girl paraded across the stage with a sign that proclaimed: FOUR HOURS LATER.

Lucas reappeared, leading a group of boys and girls carrying canvas sacks. Behind them came what must have been the tallest student in the class, dressed as Santa, complete with fake white beard and pillow-stuffed tummy. "Ho, ho, ho!" he shouted, and the stranded family climbed out of their wagon.

As Santa distributed gifts and good cheer, Lucas stepped forward on the stage. "Every year in Eureka, we

honor those first gift givers by carrying on the Santa tradition. On Christmas Eve, Santa and his helpers travel to
all the homes around the mountains, giving gifts and
spreading the spirit of Christmas."

Olivia applauded until the palms of her hands stung,
and blinked back tears. "He wrote that," she said, marveling. "He did such a good job."

She scarcely noticed the rest of the program, lost in a
fog of pride and marveling at the change in the shy, awkward boy who'd come to town seven months before.
Lucas was still bookish and sometimes awkward, but he'd
become much more outgoing. Judging by the crowd of
boys and girls he ran around with, he was even popular.

And then the show was over and she had no more time
to ponder all this. The noise level in the auditorium rose
ten-fold when the lights went up. Olivia was grateful for
D. J.'s bulk as they pushed toward the side door where the
students were pouring into the crowd. She stood on tip-
toe, searching for Lucas, and almost collided with his
teacher, Mrs. Desmet.

"You're just the people I've been looking for," Mrs.
Desmet said. She offered her hand to D. J. "I don't believe
we've met. I'm Sandra Desmet, Lucas's homeroom
teacher."

"D. J. Gruber." He shook hands.

"Let's step over here where we can talk." She guided
them into an alcove beside the stage. "We need a few
more people to help with the Santa deliveries on Christmas," she said. "I thought you two would be perfect."

"You mean what Lucas was talking about in his play,"
D. J. said. "The guys that go out dressed up like Santa on
Christmas Eve to deliver food and toys and stuff to down-
on-their-luck families?"

"Exactly." Mrs. Desmet looked pleased. "We especially need someone who can get to some of the more remote homes. I thought since you're a snowplow driver,

you'd be perfect for the job." She turned to Olivia. "And you'd go along as Mrs. Claus, of course."

"I don't think—"

"We always send at least one other person with Santa, to help with directions and carrying things," Mrs. Desmet continued. "Some of them dress as elves, but Mr. and Mrs. Claus together are even more popular. Please say you'll do it. It's only a few hours on Christmas Eve and the families appreciate it so much."

"Sure I'll do it," D. J. said.

Olivia couldn't very well say no now without looking bad. "All right." She could spend a few hours with D. J. helping others, couldn't she? "Lucas can go along as an elf," she added. And he'd act as a good buffer, lessening the tension between her and D. J.

"That would be lovely. Just show up by five o'clock on Christmas Eve at the school for your costumes and assignments," Mrs. Desmet said. "And thank you."

Olivia looked up to find D. J. grinning at her. "What?" she demanded.

"I'm trying to imagine you as Mrs. Claus."

"You're one to talk, Santa."

"Mom, D. J.? Did you see me? What did you think?" Lucas, his upper lip red from removing the moustache, appeared beside him. His hair was no longer slicked back and he was minus the tie, looking more like her little boy.

Olivia pulled him close in a hug. "You were wonderful," she said. "Your story was great."

"Mr. Prescott helped me with it. He knows all the local history."

Olivia would have to buy old Bob a beer and thank him.

"You were great," D. J. said, and Olivia couldn't help but notice how Lucas stood up straighter and practically puffed out his chest at this praise.

"Thanks," he said.

Olivia put her arm around Lucas's shoulders. "Let's go find your grandmother," she said.

"I saw her a minute ago near the door," Lucas said. "I told her I'd come get you two."

The crowd had thinned and they had no trouble walking up the aisle toward the doors. As they neared the exits, Olivia saw her mother standing with a silver-haired man in a fancy sheepskin jacket. She faltered, wondering if her eyes were playing tricks on her.

"Uh-oh," Lucas said.

"What?" D. J. put a hand on Olivia's shoulder and followed her gaze to Lucille. "Who is that with your mother?"

Olivia swallowed down a mix of anger and revulsion. "That," she said, "is Gerald Pershing."

Chapter Fourteen

"You're looking lovely as usual this evening, Lucille."

An icy chill swept over Lucille at these words, spoken in a deep, velvety, and all-too-familiar voice. Objectively, she'd known this moment was probably coming, but she hadn't prepared for it. She had never been an actress, but for the sake of her tattered dignity, she did her best to compose her expression as she turned to face Gerald.

"What a surprise," she said. "What brings you back to town, Gerald?"

"I've missed this place since I left," he said. "With my family scattered, and living alone as I do, I couldn't think of a better place, or better people, to spend the holidays with."

He smiled, a charming smile full of perfect white teeth and a wistful look around the eyes that would have melted her heart only a few weeks ago. "Eureka is a wonderful place to spend Christmas," she said. She probably should have added something about being glad to see him again, or similarly encouraging words to play along with the town council's plan to sweet-talk him into investing in their bogus mine. But she couldn't force the lie past her lips.

"Gerald!" Cassie descended upon them, all flirtatious smiles and fluttering lashes.

Lucille had never been so glad to see the librarian in her life. "Gerald, you remember Cassie Wynock," she said.

"Of course." He nodded, though his expression was cool. Cassie appeared not to notice.

"To what do we owe this pleasure?" she asked.

"I was just telling Lucille how I wanted to spend Christmas with the people who meant the most to me." He offered that winning, wistful look again. "And, of course, I wanted to take you all up on your kind offer to see this mine the town owns."

"You won't see much of a mine with all this snow," Cassie said.

"Oh, I don't think that will be a problem," Lucille said, trying to signal Cassie with her eyes to, for God's sake, shut up.

"Of course, the most important part of a mine is underground, where the weather stays pretty much the same all year," Cassie added, apparently getting the hint.

"Cassie is from one of the most venerable families in Eureka County." Lucille saw her chance to distract Gerald from more talk of the bogus mine. "At one time, the Wynocks owned most of the property in the area."

The expression in Gerald's eyes went from mild disdain to budding interest as he turned his attention once more to the gray-haired woman beside him. Never mind that Cassie didn't have anything left of her family's legacy but her grandmother's house and an outsized sense of entitlement, Gerald clearly thought he was in the presence of an heiress and turned on the charm.

"Such a pleasure to see you again, Miss Wynock." He took her hand in both of his and favored her with a look of such intensity that Lucille felt a surge of hot jealousy, in spite of all she knew about the man.

"The pleasure is all mine," Cassie simpered, clearly fallen under the con man's spell. Was she really so gullible?

"Is this man bothering you?" D. J., managing to appear even larger and more menacing than usual, loomed over them. Olivia and Lucas looked on, wide-eyed, behind him.

"Gerald, this is D. J. Gruber. D. J., this is Gerald Pershing." Lucille made the introductions.

D. J. glowered at the older man. Lucille tried to give him a reassuring look, but he ignored her. "Are you bothering these ladies?" he asked.

"On the contrary, we were having a pleasant visit until you interrupted." Gerald turned his back on D. J. and focused once more on Lucille. "I was hoping I could take you out for coffee," he said. "Or perhaps a bit of Christmas cheer?"

Lucille struggled to craft an answer that wouldn't appear too harsh. She'd agreed to go along with the council's plan and do her part to seduce Gerald into giving back at least part of the money he'd swindled from the town, but she couldn't face being alone with him again. Not yet.

"Grandma, don't forget you promised to help me with my project for school." Lucas, his voice half an octave higher and with the addition of a painful whine, inserted himself between his grandmother and Gerald. "I have to turn it in tomorrow and I can't do it without you."

"Aren't you out of school for the holidays?" Gerald asked, frowning at the boy, who someone managed to look five years younger and snivelingly pathetic.

"I was supposed to turn this assignment in last week, but I've been sick." He coughed moistly. Gerald wrinkled his nose in distaste.

"My teacher said I could have a little more time, but I

have to get it to her tomorrow or I'll fail!" The last word rose in a siren-like wail that made Lucille want to cover her ears. Over Lucas's shoulder, Olivia had her hand over her mouth, as if trying to stifle laughter.

Lucille put a hand on Lucas's shoulder and gave Gerald an apologetic smile. "As you can see, I have another commitment," she said. "Maybe some other time." Never would be fine with her.

"I'm free for coffee." Cassie spoke up.

For once, Gerald looked uncertain. Lucille could almost see the questions going through his mind. Did he risk offending one mark to latch on to a possible second?

"You should go with Cassie," she said. "I'm sure the two of you would find a lot to talk about."

"Yes, I'd love your advice on investing some funds I inherited from my late father," Cassie said.

Lucille gave her a sharp look. Was she serious? Or even more devious than Lucille had suspected?

Gerald's hesitation vanished. "Then I'd be pleased to spend time with you." He offered her his arm. "And, Lucille, I'll see you later."

Lucille nodded, anxious to be away from him. How was she ever going to manage the "intimate dinner" the town council had planned, where she was supposed to persuade Gerald to invest in the mine?

"Yes, see you later, Lucille," Cassie trilled, and carefully lowered one eyelid.

Lucille gaped, sure now that the world really had been turned upside down. Had Cassie Wynock *winked* at her?

"I could arrange for a snowplow to back over his car." D. J.'s voice was a low, angry rumble.

Lucille managed a smile. "As tempting as that is, you'd better not." She turned to Lucas. "You don't really have a project due for school, do you?"

"Nope, I just wanted to give you a good reason to get away from him."

"Thanks." She pulled the boy close. "You did a great job tonight."

"It was fun. Can I ride home with you?"

He looked innocent, but he didn't fool Lucille. Clearly, he was trying to arrange things so that D. J. and Olivia rode home alone.

"We'll both ride home with you," Olivia said. She turned to D. J. "Thank you for the ride over here."

"Anytime." He shoved his hands in his pockets and nodded to Lucille. "Let me know if you need anything."

"Thank you." Impulsively, she squeezed his arm. He was definitely one of the good guys. One of many in Eureka, she was finding out. She may have struck out romantically, but she'd hit the jackpot when it came to people she could count on in a crisis.

"Any word yet from the mayor's office?" For probably the fifth time that morning, Rick stopped in front of Maggie's desk at the *Miner* and posed the question she suspected half the town was waiting for the answer to.

"Nothing yet." This was the morning Reggie, Doug, and Paul were giving Gerald Pershing a private tour of the Lucky Lady, as they'd christened the hole in the ground chosen as the town gold mine. The site was an actual mine claim the county had taken for back taxes years ago, but as far as anyone knew it had never yielded so much as an ounce of gold dust.

"I hope they didn't get stuck in the snow." Rick stared out the window. Drifts piled on either side of the street formed white walls in front of the buildings and sidewalks. "That wouldn't make a good impression."

"D. J. plowed the road all the way up there," Maggie said. "I saw him coming back when I went out to start my car this morning." His route to the mine took him right past Maggie's place, so she'd had a freshly plowed path to work.

"I hear Bob salted it with some good-size nuggets."

"I hope he didn't overdo it," Maggie said. "Bob has a tendency to go overboard at times." He'd promised a few fireworks at the finale of the Founders' Day parade and ended up with a huge explosion that emptied the theater.

Rick turned away from the window. "What does a dude from Texas know about mining? He probably expects to see big nuggets lying all over."

Maggie hoped for Lucille's sake that Rick was right. Having Gerald back in town was placing a real strain on the mayor that was visible, at least to those who knew her well. She wore the tense, defensive expression of someone waiting for a blow.

"I saw Cassie with Pershing at the Last Dollar last night," Rick said.

"That sounds suspicious." Cassie knew what Gerald had done to Lucille—and to the town. Why would she want to have anything to do with the man? "I hope Gerald hasn't decided Cassie is his next target."

"I don't know," Rick said. "I'd say those two deserve each other."

"Rick!" Yes, Cassie could be unpleasant, but she was also a lonely woman who might be an easy mark for a man like Gerald Pershing.

"She probably knows about the town council's plan with the gold mine," Rick said. No one had broadcast the plan, but keeping a secret in Eureka was impossible.

"I hope she hasn't decided to share the information with Gerald for some twisted reason."

"If he doesn't bite, we'll know who to blame," Rick said.

The front door to the newspaper office opened and Lucille slipped inside, closing the door softly behind her.

She looked exhausted, dark circles shadowing her eyes, shoulders sagging. "Well?" Rick asked.

She frowned at him. "Hello, Rick. I came to talk to Maggie."

"What happened with Pershing?" He stepped between the two women, as if he intended to keep them separate until Lucille told him what he wanted.

"I can't tell you that," Lucille said. "You print anything about this in the paper and the deal will fall through. We might even end up in a lawsuit."

"I'm not asking as a newspaper publisher. I'm asking as a concerned citizen. I promise, I won't publish a word."

"I'll make sure he keeps that promise," Maggie said, peering around Rick at her friend.

Lucille hesitated, then nodded. "Doug said the mine visit went well. Gerald seemed really interested. Bob did a good job spreading the gold around, not making it seem too obvious. Gerald had done his homework. We were a little worried about that at first, because he said he'd asked some geologist at the University of Texas to examine the assay report Bob sent. But apparently everything checked out. Gerald is convinced the mine really does have the potential to yield some gold. He asked good questions and appeared satisfied with the answers the men gave him."

"What happens next?" Maggie asked.

Lucille slumped into a chair beside Maggie's desk. "Now I'm supposed to invite him to dinner and seal the deal."

"Why do you have to do that?" Maggie asked. "Can't the council just give him the paperwork and ask him to sign?"

"They thought it would be more convincing if they didn't do a hard sell. I'm supposed to use my powers of persuasion to make the deal seem too good to resist, all in the guise of asking his advice."

"They want you to seduce him," Rick said. "The way he seduced you."

Maggie glared at him, but Lucille's expression hardly changed. "Yes, that's what they want. But I don't think I can do it."

The front door flew open and Cassie Wynock bustled in, rattling the glass as she slammed the door behind her. "I thought I saw you come in here," she said, stalking toward Lucille as only a determined woman in sensible shoes can stalk.

"Cassie, I am not in the mood right now to talk about library shelves," Lucille said.

"I didn't come here to talk about shelves. I came to find out what happened this morning at the mine. Did Gerald bite?"

"Cassie, if you breathed one word of our plans to Gerald, so help me—" Lucille didn't finish the threat, merely drilled the librarian with a warning look.

Cassie waved away the threat and plopped into the chair beside Lucille. "I wouldn't give your little plan away. After what he did to this town, I'd like to see Gerald Pershing get his comeuppance as much as anyone."

Lucille blinked, probably as surprised as Maggie was. Cassie and the mayor were not usually on the same side of any argument.

"So what happened up at the mine?" Cassie pressed. "Did Gerald fall for the ruse?"

"I think so," Lucille said. "I'm supposed to talk with him more over dinner."

"At least you'll get a nice meal out of it," Cassie said.

"I don't think I can go through with it." Lucille rested her chin in both hands, elbows on her knees.

"Then let me do it," Cassie said.

Three heads swiveled to stare at the librarian. "What?" Cassie asked. "You don't think I can talk the old swindler into falling for the town's swindle?"

"But why would you?" Lucille asked.

"I saw you having coffee with Pershing last night," Rick said. "You two looked pretty cozy."

"We were a little worried you'd be his next victim," Maggie said. Well, *she'd* been a little concerned. She doubted Rick cared.

"I'm not as naïve as some people." Cassie nodded toward Lucille. "Gerald is handsome and charming, and no doubt has plenty of money socked away. But in my experience all men are liars and he's no different."

"Humph." Rick gave a snort of disgust and turned away.

"I wouldn't say all men are liars," Maggie said. "Though Gerald certainly is."

"Jake was a liar," Cassie said. "And your ex doesn't seem to have been overly concerned with the truth. Even Jameso lies. He probably told you he'd stand by you and the baby, didn't he? But that won't last. Boys like him, the ones who don't want to grow up, are the worst."

Maggie opened her mouth to make some searing retort, but all that came out was a choking sound. Her pulse pounded in her temples and her fingers ached. She looked down and was surprised to see she was holding the stapler, as if ready to bash Cassie over the head with it. "Shut up," she finally managed.

Cassie ignored the rebuke and stood. "I'll handle dinner with Gerald," she said. "After all, I am an actress." She lifted her chin and strode out of the office like a queen taking leave of her humble subjects.

"Bitch," Maggie said as the door closed behind Cassie's rigid form.

"She is," Lucille agreed. She straightened. "But in this case, she may be exactly what we need to deal with someone like Gerald. The two of them probably think more alike than we'd like to know."

"I can't believe she said all that, about men and—" Maggie shook her head.

"And about Jameso?" Lucille patted Maggie's arm. "She doesn't know what she's talking about. Jameso loves you and he's a man of his word. Those are two things I'm sure of."

But what can I be sure of? Maggie thought. She wasn't even certain how she felt about Jameso, never mind what his feelings were for her. She'd gone from newly divorced to torrid affair to expecting a baby fast enough to give anyone whiplash.

"So an old maid like Cassie thinks she's an expert on men." Rick shook his head. "If it weren't for the town needing the money, I'd wish old Gerald luck in taking Cassie for everything he could get."

"Cassie can't stand not being the queen bee in any situation," Maggie said. "In this case, she gets to play a starring role in the big drama . . . and if it works out she'll take all the credit for saving the town." Rick's reminder that Cassie really didn't have much experience with men had cheered Maggie. Cassie didn't even know Jameso very well, so how could she say he wouldn't stick with Maggie? She'd merely wanted to wound Maggie as one more way of getting back at Jake. "You should find out where she and Gerald are having dinner and spy on them," she said.

"I just might do that. Or I could send my ace reporter." He cocked one eyebrow at her.

"I was only joking, Rick. Whatever Cassie gets up to with Gerald, it isn't news."

"It may not be anything we can report, but it's important to the town. And I want to know what Cassie is doing. I don't trust her."

"If Cassie loves anything, it's Eureka," Lucille said. "She won't deliberately sabotage the council's plan."

"But Cassie is Cassie," Rick argued. "If Pershing says

or does anything to piss her off, she's liable to let him have it right there, fake gold shares be damned."

"Then one of us being there can't stop her," Maggie said.

"You could head off trouble. Distract her by spilling a drink or pretending to go into labor."

"I'm only three months pregnant."

"Then you'll think of something else."

"No, Rick, I cannot spy on Cassie. She'll never let me check out a library book again."

"Don't think of it as spying. Think of it as a night out on the town, paid for by the *Miner*."

"We don't even know where they're going." She tried one last protest.

"I'll find that out and let Jameso know. You be dressed up and ready to go tomorrow night."

She could refuse. Spying was not in her job description. But she didn't feel like making the effort. Rick was relentless and besides, part of her was curious to know what Cassie was up to. She didn't believe for a minute that Cassie was going out with Gerald in order to help Lucille. Cassie didn't go out of her way to help anyone but herself. So maybe Gerald had something she wanted after all. The question was, what was it?

Olivia had never seen so much snow. It towered in drifts pushed to either side of the narrow street and made mountains in the vacant lot behind the Dirty Sally, where D. J. and the other plow drivers dumped it by the truckload. Swirls of falling flakes obscured the horizon and made a white curtain out the front window of the saloon.

"Is it going to fall like this all winter?" she asked, turning back to the bar.

"Now that it's started, it doesn't show any signs of stopping, but you never know." Bob set his empty beer mug on the bar with a thump. "At least the snow sent most of the tourists packing."

"If not for the tourists, what would you complain about?" she asked. She refilled the beer mug and slid it toward Bob. "This one's on me."

"Well, that's mighty generous of you." He toasted her with the mug. "Thanks. And to answer your question, I'd find plenty to grouse about. Want to hear my opinions on the federal government?"

"No, thanks." Jameso lifted a beer keg into place beneath the counter. "Why are you giving away the profits to Bob?" he asked Olivia.

"He helped Lucas with his Christmas play. I appreciate it."

"Glad to see you can make yourself useful," Jameso said.

Bob ignored the jibe. "That's a sharp kid you got there," he said. "He asks good questions and he doesn't mind letting an old man rattle on about stuff that happened half a century before he was born."

Olivia took no credit for Lucas's brains. "He's always been that way," she said. "Wanting to know about everything. I don't know where he gets it."

"From what I've seen, his mom and his grandma are pretty bright themselves." Bob winked.

"You ought to take some credit for Lucas turning out the way he has." Jameso began emptying a rack of clean beer glasses, sliding them into the slots to hold them upside down over the bar. "I mean, good parenting means good kids, right?"

"I think most parents do the best they can and hope things work out," Olivia said. "I certainly didn't know anything about raising children when I had Lucas."

"I read somewhere that babies in the womb learn to recognize voices, so when they come out, they recognize their parents," Jameso said. "Do you think that's true?"

"How would I know?" Olivia asked.

"You're a mother. Don't mothers know these things?"

"I guess it's true." She remembered a newborn Lucas, his head tracking her by the sound of her voice before he could really see well.

"Makes sense to me that they respond to what they're used to hearing," Bob said.

Jameso racked the last glass. "I've been talking to Maggie's stomach a lot, just in case."

Olivia giggled at the picture of Jameso holding a conversation with Maggie's belly. "You're really excited about being a daddy, aren't you?" she asked.

He flushed a dark red beneath his beard. "Excited. Scared." He shrugged. "Hard to tell the difference sometimes."

Olivia pulled out the cutting board and began slicing lemons and limes, ready for the evening bar crowd. "And you really didn't know Maggie was pregnant before she told you?" she asked.

He frowned, dark brows coming together in a V. "How would I know that?"

"There are signs, you know. She was late with her period. Sick in the morning . . . stuff like that." Signs that had let her know right away that she was carrying a baby, even before the pregnancy test had confirmed the information.

"Guys don't pay attention to that stuff."

"Most guys would just as soon pretend all that stuff didn't exist." Bob took a long pull on his beer.

Both men looked so unnerved, Olivia almost laughed. She'd been so attuned to the changes in her own body, she hadn't imagined D. J. hadn't even noticed. Had he really had no idea she was pregnant when he decided to take off for Iraq?

The sudden tightness around her heart hurt, a wave of guilt and anxiety as a thought struck her with the force of an arrow. Had she been the one in the wrong here, letting him go off to Iraq without knowing about the baby? She'd assumed he was running away from his responsibilities, but maybe if she'd talked to him instead of assuming he would guess what was going on, she would have saved them all a lot of hurt.

CHAPTER FIFTEEN

To Maggie's surprise, Jameso agreed with Rick's plan to spy on Cassie and Gerald's dinner. "I wouldn't miss it," he said. "A fancy meal on Rick's dime and free entertainment, too."

"I'm still not crazy about the idea," she said. "But at least Cassie will have another woman on her side if Gerald tries anything."

"Cassie's probably hoping he'll try something," Jameso said. "She probably carries a sharpened letter opener in her purse and knows how to use it for more than opening the mail."

The note of respect in his voice made Maggie look more closely at him. "Are you afraid of Cassie?" she asked.

"Yes, ma'am. She once threatened to arrange to have a county garbage truck back over my motorcycle if I didn't stop racing up and down the street in front of her house at night. She made me believe she'd do it. She's a woman who takes revenge seriously, so Gerald is the one you ought to be worried about tonight."

Cassie had certainly held a grudge against Maggie's

father, Jake, long after he died. But considering how poorly the men in her life had treated her, maybe Cassie's bitterness was justified. Apparently, Cassie's father had used her as a glorified maid and nursemaid, and rumors were that Jake had led Cassie on in some way, possibly breaking her heart.

"I feel sorry for Cassie," Maggie said. "Even if I don't like her very much."

"She wouldn't appreciate your pity." Jameso maneuvered the Jeep into a parking space between piles of snow in the lot behind the restaurant in Montrose. Maggie started to push open her door, but Jameso stopped her with a hand on her arm. "Allow me."

Amused, she waited while he exited the car and came around to open the door on her side. He'd dressed up for the evening—well, he wore a white dress shirt beneath his leather motorcycle jacket, and he'd trimmed his beard and tried to tame the wild mane of his hair. In deference to the weather, she wore fleece-lined snow boots, wool trousers, and a fisherman's sweater that clung to the beginnings of her baby bump. She couldn't decide if she looked pregnant or like she'd eaten too many doughnuts.

The restaurant Gerald (or was it Cassie?) had chosen was a Victorian building that featured dark beams, weathered brick walls, and dim lighting. Jameso cursed as he knocked his head on a hanging lantern in the entrance that gave off the glow of a fifteen-watt lightbulb. "I don't see how we're going to find anyone in here," he muttered. "It's like a cave."

"Then they'll be that much less likely to see us," she said.

They followed the hostess to a table for two in a shadowy corner.

"What does it matter if they see us?" Jameso asked when they were seated. "We'll tell them we decided to have a romantic dinner together."

"Cassie will know neither one of us can afford this place." Maggie opened the leather-bound menu.

Jameso's eyes widened as he took in the prices. "I should have made Rick pay me up front," he muttered.

"Too bad I can't have wine," she said, studying the impressive array of vintages on the separate wine list. "We'd really make Rick cough it up."

"Humph." Jameso half-turned in his chair to survey the dining room. "Do you see them anywhere?"

"Over by the fireplace. Right under the elk head." The blazing logs cast a golden glow over the couple. Cassie wore an old-fashioned, lacy dress, pearl drop earrings, a silk flower in her hair, and too much makeup. She looked like an aging madam in some western melodrama.

"Is she really wearing red lipstick?" Jameso sounded horrified.

"Shh, she'll hear you."

He turned back to Maggie and lowered his voice. "I wish I could hear them. We need to be closer."

"No, we don't."

She studied the couple from behind her menu. Cassie was animated, hands waving, eyelashes fluttering. Gerald smiled charmingly and laughed at something she said. They looked harmless, but without any dialogue to provide context, their actions had an air of desperation Maggie hadn't recognized before. Gerald was a scammer, but was part of his scam the need to not be alone? And what about Cassie, relishing the chance to be the center of a man's attention—even if that man was a liar and a cheat?

"What are you looking so worked up about?" Jameso asked.

She lowered the menu. "I was thinking I shouldn't be so hard on Cassie," she said. "Lonely people will do a lot of things that don't necessarily make sense."

A waitress arrived to take their order—steaks with all

the trimmings, with stuffed mushrooms and Caesar salads. Maggie's mouth watered in anticipation.

When they were alone again, Jameso leaned across the table toward her. "You're not lonely, are you?" he asked. He looked wary, as if afraid of her answer.

"No, but I was in those months after Carter left."

"Are you saying you ended up with me because I was the closest warm body?"

She shouldn't enjoy seeing him look so uncomfortable, but she was pleased to know her answer mattered to him. "No, I didn't want to go out with you, remember?"

A little of the stiffness went out of his shoulders. "And why was that again?"

"You were too young. Not my type."

He grinned. "Too wild and dangerous."

Too irresponsible. But she didn't mention that.

A particularly loud burst of laughter from Gerald drew their attention. "I never knew Cassie was so amusing," Jameso said. "I can hardly remember ever seeing the woman smile."

"She's playing a part: the charming heiress." Since her debut in the Founders' Pageant this fall, Cassie had discovered a love of acting. And Maggie could admit the ordinarily dour librarian was doing a good job tonight. Gerald seemed captivated. "I think she's charming him," she said.

"Good. The better mood he's in the more likely he is to agree to the deal. The town can get some of its money back, plus the satisfaction of a little revenge."

The waitress delivered their salads and Maggie picked up her fork. "What if the plan backfires and Gerald goes to the police?" she asked.

"He won't." Jameso stabbed at his lettuce. "A crook won't risk an investigation into his own doings. Besides, offering stock in a speculative mine isn't against the law.

Reggie will make sure the town dances right along the line of legalities."

"I hope so."

They ate in silence, Maggie relishing every bite. When she finished, she pushed the plate away and sighed. Jameso smiled. "You enjoyed that."

"I'm enjoying this." She indicated the room around them. "It's nice to get away for some quiet time. Just the two of us."

"And Gerald and Cassie. But hey, I know what you mean. I should take you out more often."

"You should." But her smile let him know she wasn't overly serious. She didn't need fancy dinners or gifts from Jameso—she only needed him to be with her. She needed him to be a man she could depend on.

Their steaks arrived, fragrant and sizzling, and all conversation ceased while they paid tribute to the meal. Across the room, Cassie and Gerald enjoyed steak also and shared a bottle of red wine. The fire blazed and classical music played softly from hidden speakers overhead. A Christmas tree in the corner sparkled with hundreds of tiny white lights, and snow fell in a lacy curtain past the window. A warm haze of contentment settled over Maggie. She had good food, good company, and the sense that all was right in her world.

"I have to go out of town for a couple of days."

Jameso's words intruded into her pleasant fantasy. She blinked at him. "Go where?"

"Montana. I have some business I have to see to."

What business? Jameso didn't have business. And he never went anywhere, other than to Telluride to ski—except the time when he'd left town to avoid seeing her with her ex-husband. "But it's almost Christmas," she protested.

"I'll be back. I'll only be away a couple of days." He sounded very matter-of-fact, but Maggie thought he looked guilty.

"What kind of business?" she asked.

"You've never taken such an interest in my comings and goings before."

She flushed. This was true. She'd been very careful not to pry. She didn't want him to feel hemmed in. "I'm just curious why you'd need to leave this close to Christmas. And in this weather." She nodded toward the window.

"It's winter. You have to expect a little snow. I'll be fine."

"And this can't wait until after the holidays?"

"No, it can't. But I'll be back."

She pressed her lips together to hold back angry words. She didn't want him to leave, but she'd already made that clear, and what right did she have to ask him to stay? They weren't married, after all. They weren't even living together. And she'd been so careful not to interfere with his life that doing so now seemed shrewish.

"Gerald, are you saying I shouldn't invest in the Lucky Lady?" Cassie's voice rose, overly loud in the hushed restaurant.

"I merely think there are safer investments for a woman in your situation," Gerald said, not as loudly but still carrying.

"But you're going to invest in the mine, aren't you?"

"Shhh. Keep your voice down."

If anything, Cassie spoke more loudly. "You haven't answered my question."

"I'm considering investing," he said. "But I have more money to play with. I can afford to take certain risks."

"Yeah, he has Eureka's money," Jameso muttered.

Maggie shushed him and leaned forward to catch Cassie's next words. "Granddaddy's money is all I have to my name." Cassie simpered like a southern belle in a melodrama.

"Then your best bet is a stock fund. I have several I could recommend."

"But Granddaddy would so like the idea of investing in a gold mine. He made so much of his money that way, you know."

"Please keep your voice down," Gerald said again. He scowled and looked around him. Maggie dove under the table.

Jameso's head appeared beside hers beneath the table-cloth. "Are you all right?" he asked.

"I'm pretending I dropped a fork. I didn't want him to see me."

"Oh, was I talking too loudly?" Cassie's voice rang clear. "I get so excited at the thought of all that gold." She giggled. Maggie wondered how much of that giggle was acting and how much was due to the wine.

Gerald cleared his throat and Maggie risked sitting upright once more. "My understanding is that the town has only a limited number of shares to offer," he said.

"Yes, that's why I was all the more anxious to get in on the deal," Cassie said. "But you think stocks would be a safer bet?"

"Yes, I do."

"But what about the mine? I hate to think of some stranger, someone I might not trust, buying the town stock."

"You trust me, don't you?" Maggie didn't dare look directly at Gerald, but she could hear the smile in his voice.

"Yes, I do," Cassie said.

"I think I might invest in the mine," Gerald said. "It appeals to my sense of adventure."

"If I know you're going to buy the shares, I won't feel so bad letting the opportunity pass me by."

"Then I propose a toast." Gerald raised his wineglass and Cassie clinked hers to his. Maggie had to settle for water.

"That sounds promising," Jameso whispered. He picked

up the small menu the waitress had left. "Should we have dessert?"

"Definitely." If she couldn't have wine to calm her nerves, a heavy dose of chocolate would do.

"Hello, Maggie. Did Rick send you here to spy on me?"

Startled, Maggie sloshed water onto the table. She stared at Cassie, who stood by their table, looking pleased with herself.

Maggie glanced toward the table where Cassie and Gerald had been seated. Gerald's chair was vacant. "Where's Gerald?"

"He went to the men's room. I saw you two the moment you came in; luckily Gerald never noticed. So did Rick send you to spy on me, or did you have the idea on your own?"

"What makes you think anyone's spying on you?" Jameso asked. "Maybe I wanted to take Maggie out for a nice meal."

"I know Rick." She patted her hair. "What did you think of my little performance?"

"You were brilliant," Maggie said. It was true; she doubted she could have pulled off such an act with a man she despised.

"I was, wasn't I? Well, I have to go now. I don't want Gerald coming back and getting suspicious." She fluttered her fingers in a wave and hurried away.

Jameso stared after her. "That woman is a piece of work."

"I sort of admire her," Maggie said.

"You do?"

"She hasn't had an easy life. From what I gather, her father wasted the family money and Cassie had to look after him and her ailing mother. She clearly has pretensions of living a glamorous life but never was able to do so. Yet, she still has her pride. Outsized or misplaced, it

keeps her going and there's something to be said for that."
Pride could be armor and a shield, protection from hurt.

"Yeah, well, I still say she's a piece of work. And I
wouldn't trust her in a fight."

An odd expression to use, she thought. Was that how he
judged people—on whether or not he could count on them
to back him up in a fight? Clearly, her father had fallen into
the category of trusted co-combatants. A known brawler,
Jake had used his fists to back up his opinions and defend
his friends.

Maggie had never thought of herself as a fighter, but
she wanted to believe she'd stand by Jameso. Could she
count on him to do the same for her—not defend her with
his fists, but to stick with her for the long haul? It wasn't
the good times or even the bad times that truly tested a relationship, she thought, but the long, boring stretches
where the lure of something better glittered on the horizon. Some people ignored the temptation, but others ea-
gerly turned to it. Into which camp did Jameso fall?

Cassie and Gerald didn't linger over dessert. He solic-
itously helped her on with her coat, then escorted her out
the door, one hand at the small of her back. Cassie fluttered her eyelashes like a coquette.

"Think Gerald's going to get lucky tonight?" Jameso
asked.

"I don't even want to think about it," Maggie said.
Some things were better left unimagined.

"Do you want to do anything else while we're in town,
or are you ready to head home?" he asked.

"Your place or mine?" she teased. After all, they lived
next door.

He took her hand and kissed her palm, a tender gesture
that sent a shiver up her spine. "How about yours?"

"Yes." Suddenly, she was eager to be alone with him.
He was all the things she had objected to when they first

met: handsome and dangerous and dark and irresponsible. Yet somehow, crazily and inappropriately, she had fallen in love with him. She didn't trust the improbability of that love, didn't trust that it could last when other, more promising relationships hadn't.

Yet the very riskiness of her feelings made them that much more powerful and attractive.

"Do you really have to go away?" she asked.

"Only for a couple of days."

"Promise me you'll be back in time for Christmas," she said. "It's my first Christmas in Eureka and I want to spend it with you."

He squeezed her hand. "I'll be home for Christmas," he said. "I promise."

Lucille fixed her gaze on Gerald's fingers as he signed the documents that made him the owner of 100 shares in the Lucky Lady mine, at $1,000 a share. They were an old man's fingers, knotted at the knuckles and spotted by age, but the nails were neatly manicured, and the gold-nugget ring on the middle finger of his right hand was worth more than anything the Lucky Lady would ever yield. And those hands had touched her gently, in places no one had touched in decades. She shuddered at the memory, as much with regret as shame. If only he had turned out to be a different sort of man. . . .

"There you are, then. All the i's dotted and t's crossed." He pushed the papers away, reached into the pocket of his coat, and withdrew a folded check. "And here's the cashier's check for one hundred thousand dollars."

Lucille reached for the check, but he pulled it back. His eyes met hers, charm replaced by a harder look, an expression that made him both older and uglier, and more real than the polished façade he usually wore. "I want to make sure we're all on the up and up here," he said. "You wouldn't try to fool an old fool, would you?"

"What makes you say that?" She tried to look hurt, though she feared the words came out sounding more annoyed than wounded.

"I know the way I left the last time wasn't the most gentlemanly way to behave toward a lady." He leaned toward her and spoke in softer tones, as if the four other people in the room might not hear. "The truth was, my dear, being with you shook me to the core. I had to get away before my emotions got the better of me. I never believed in love at first sight, Lucille, but you have me questioning my beliefs."

She wanted to cover her ears, to refuse to let the treacherous words, spoken with such velvety fervor, seep into her brain. The man was a liar and a thief and the worst sort of swindler. If she needed more proof, here he was now, shamelessly attempting to seduce her once more, in front of the town council, no less.

He must have done this before, she reminded herself. He knew the exact words to say; the words to appeal to the lonely woman she hid from the world, words that echoed all the foolish fantasies she'd never even admitted to herself: fantasies of a love strong enough to bring a tough man to his knees, of two people destined by fate to be together. Dreams of a man who could not forget her.

Nothing in her life had given her the slightest proof that kind of love existed, yet some part of her she had seldom acknowledged refused to let go of the foolish hope that it did. Somehow, Gerald knew those fantasies existed. Not because she'd told him, but because he'd done this before. He'd used other women for his own purposes. She would not let it happen again.

"I'm sorry I misled you," she said, summoning the words—and the strength to say them—from somewhere deep within. She smiled, a cool, seductive smile. "We had fun together, but I never intended for it to be serious. I thought you knew that."

He hadn't expected this response. She could tell because he failed to keep a tight grip on the check. She plucked it from his hand and allowed a warmer smile as she studied it. One hundred thousand much-needed dollars for the town coffers.

"Thank you, Gerald. We'll put this money to good use."

He recovered quickly, the charming mask once more in place. He rose and shook hands with Reggie, Paul, Doug, and Junior. "When will you begin taking ore out of the mine?"

"We haven't established a timeline yet," Paul said.

"Probably have to wait until spring," Junior added.

Gerald frowned, a look that aged him, Lucille thought. "But you said the snow wasn't a problem . . . the temperature stays the same underground."

"Yes, but we have to think about the town's liability," Reggie said. "We can't have someone injured getting to and from the mine every day."

"And we've got to buy equipment, take safety precautions." Junior clapped Gerald on the back. "These things take time. After all, didn't you say it would be six months before we saw any return on the money we invested with you?"

"At least six months. And the markets have been quite volatile."

"Exactly. But the price of gold keeps going up, and that ore isn't going anywhere while we wait for the thaw."

This seemed to satisfy him. He turned to Lucille. "May I buy you lunch?" he asked.

"No, I don't think so."

"Dinner, then. I've discovered a wonderful new place—"

"No, not dinner either."

"Lucille, surely you're not holding a grudge against me. I tried to explain—"

She held up a hand to forestall any more romantic hogwash. "It's the holidays, Gerald. I'm spending them with my family. People who care about me. Whom I care about."

One eye twitched, the only sign that her words had hit home. The handsome, sexy man she'd once swooned over had vanished, replaced by this pathetic old fool who was desperate for the appearance of connections without real involvement.

"Then I'll ask Cassandra." The words held a challenge, as if he sought to make her jealous.

She held back laughter. "That's a wonderful idea." Though she suspected he'd find no greater welcome from Cassie.

He opened his mouth as if to say something else, but she cut him off. "If we have no more business, gentlemen, I have to get back to work." She picked up her gavel to adjourn the meeting, but before she could bring it down, the door to her office burst open.

D. J., black watch cap dusted with snow, goatee dripping with ice, surveyed them. "I didn't mean to interrupt," he said. "I just wanted to let you know the pass is closed."

"Which pass?" Reggie asked.

"Both of them. Avalanches on both sides of town. Took out the cell tower on Black Mountain, too. Until the state gets us dug out, we're cut off from the rest of the world."

"You mean I'm trapped here?" Gerald asked.

"Looks that way." Bob clapped him on the back. "Cheer up. You'll be able to watch the snowmobile races and enjoy a real small-town Christmas."

From the expression on his face, Lucille could tell that this was Gerald's idea of hell.

* * *

When word arrived at the newspaper that avalanches had sealed the passes on either side of the town, isolating them from the rest of the world, Maggie moaned in despair.

"It's not so bad," Rick said. He rubbed his hands together and grinned. "We've got everything we need to have a great Christmas here. The grocery and liquor deliveries made it through yesterday. Let the rest of the world get along without us for a few days."

"Jameso left town early this morning," she said.

"Where was he off to so close to Christmas?"

"He said he had business in Montana." Mysterious business. Or had that merely been an excuse to get out of town without her putting up too much of a fuss?

"Well, maybe the state will get the plows out here before Christmas," Rick said. "If not, I'm sure he'll be fine until the roads are open."

"Barb and her husband were supposed to drive in today," Maggie said. The thought of spending Christmas without her lover and her best friend was too depressing to contemplate.

She snatched up her phone and hit the speed dial for Barb's number. Rick retreated to his office.

The phone emitted its electronic beeps and buzzes, then fell silent.

"The police scanner says the slide on Black Mountain took out the cell phone tower." Rick emerged from his office and came to lean on her desk. "And the land lines are out, too."

She glared at the phone screen, the words NO SERVICE mocking her. "How is it possible in this day and age for a town to be cut off from civilization this way?"

"It's good to be reminded every once in a while that we don't need the rest of the world," he said. "Didn't anyone tell you this happens a couple of times almost every winter?"

She vaguely remembered some mention of the possibility, but it had seemed a wild fantasy, like the tales of her father's exploits—colorful and entertaining and not based in any reality she knew.

"How long is this going to last?" she asked.

"The pass could open up tomorrow or it could be two weeks." He shrugged. "It all depends on the snow. Might as well sit back and enjoy it. I hope you got all your Christmas shopping done."

He sat on the edge of her desk, arms crossed, hair mussed as usual, relaxed. How could he be so complacent? "Don't you worry we'll run out of food?" she asked. "Or fuel?"

"Most folks have learned to stock up, and they'll share with anyone who runs short. And you don't need much fuel if you don't have anywhere to go. There's plenty in town to keep us entertained. The snowmobile races tomorrow, for instance."

"What is Barb going to do?" Her voice quavered dangerously and she bit her lip, determined not to burst into tears in front of Rick, who would never let her hear the end of it.

"She'll have to stay somewhere else until the pass opens." He patted her arm. "The state patrol will help her find a place. It might not be the best Christmas she ever had, but it will make a great story to tell the folks back in Texas."

Maggie tried to smile, imagining Barb regaling her society friends with tales of her snowbound Christmas in the wilds of Colorado. Barb could make friends and have a good time anywhere. Meanwhile, Maggie was stuck in Eureka—alone.

"No sense moping." Rick stood. "Come on, I'll buy you lunch."

"I don't feel like eating," she said.

"The baby needs food. Besides, how often do you get a free meal out of me?"

"Twice in twenty-four hours, apparently, since you paid for dinner last night." She studied him critically. "Are you all right? You're not usually this free spending." In fact, Rick was known for his miserly ways.

"Guess I'm just feeling the Christmas spirit. Come on, get your coat. Sitting here moping isn't going to clear the passes or rebuild the cell tower."

He was right. She shrugged into her coat and followed him into the street. Fat flakes of snow drifted down over them, and for the first time since arriving in Eureka, Maggie wanted to curse the white stuff, which had blocked the roads and shut down the phones.

The Last Dollar was packed with half the residents of the town, who had apparently gathered to talk about the avalanches. Danielle, curves encased in a bright red sweater tunic and gray leggings, her black hair covered by a green and white knit hat with pom-poms dangling about her ears, rushed to envelop Maggie in a hug. "Come on in," she said. "Good thing we stocked up yesterday."

"What is your special today?" Rick asked.

"Today we have an avalanche special: a mountain of our homemade mashed potatoes, smothered in chicken and dumplings."

Reggie and Katya waved at them from a booth at the back. "Come join us," Reggie called.

"We just heard the news," Rick said as he slid into the booth next to Katya.

"I drove up to Black Mountain as far as I could go just now," Reggie said. "It's a mess. A solid wall of ice and trees and rocks as far as I could see. With the snow still coming down I was getting a little spooked about setting off another avalanche, so I came on down. But it will be a while before they dig us out of this one."

"I thought the highway department set off explosives to keep the snow from building up above the road," Maggie said. "Isn't that supposed to prevent avalanches?"

"It works when there isn't so much snow," Katya said. "But when it builds up by the foot, it has to go somewhere, and sometimes that somewhere is the highway."

"Was anyone hurt?" Maggie felt guilty that she hadn't asked this before.

"As often as the snow comes down over the road up there, there have been very few injuries," Reggie said. "It's remarkable, really. No one was hurt in either slide this morning."

"Chris, our UPS deliveryman, has been in four avalanches," Danielle said. "No one else will drive our route in winter, but he says he doesn't mind. He sits in his truck and waits for the county to come and dig him out."

"That's crazy," Maggie said.

"Do y'all know what you want to order?" Danielle asked.

"I'll have the special and iced tea," Rick said.

"Just the chicken and dumplings for me," Maggie said. "And water."

Danielle left and Rick continued the conversation. "Skiers and snowmobilers get caught in avalanches in the backcountry and a lot of them die," he said. "But some survive. Jameso told me once that the trick is to ride it like a wave and to swim to the top, if possible. The people who can do that make it out okay."

"Avalanche surfing."

"I surfed a snow slide once. Wildest ride I ever had in my life." Bob, bundled in insulated snowmobile coveralls, the black fabric repaired in several places with duct tape, stopped by their table. Instead of his usual ball cap, he wore a green knit cap and a pair of goggles pushed on top of his head. He looked like a mad scientist from an Arctic lab.

"You are so full of bullshit," Rick said calmly.

"Swear to God, it happened," Bob said. "Up at the Merryvale mines. Whole mountainside came sliding down underneath my feet. I started swimming to the top and popped out on the surface. Broke a leg when I slammed into a tree, but I survived."

Who could say if Bob was telling the truth or not? Maggie thought. He had a colorful story for every occasion; but then again, he'd spent a lot of time in these mountains. Maybe all his stories were true.

"You coming to the snowmobile races tomorrow?" Bob asked.

"Wouldn't miss it," Reggie said.

"How many racers do they have?" Katya asked.

"Six, last count," Bob said. "But I imagine we'll get some last-minute entries." He patted Maggie's shoulder. "If Murph were alive, he would have entered. You'll be there, won't you?"

"I guess I will," she said. After all, it wasn't as if she had anywhere else to go.

"You look a little shell-shocked," Bob said. "I guess this is a lot different Christmas than you probably spent last year back in Texas."

Last year, she and Carter had spent Christmas with Barb and Jimmy. Well, they'd had Christmas dinner at the Stanowskis' house. Carter had excused himself half an hour after the meal to deal with an "emergency" at the office. Though she hadn't been ready to admit it yet, Maggie had known something was wrong then. "My ex gave me a coffeemaker for Christmas last year," she said. "He gave his girlfriend a diamond necklace."

"Ouch!" Reggie said.

"It's all right." She hadn't thought about her ex and his new wife in months. The knowledge stunned her. She tried to summon a bit of her old hurt and rage, but the part of her that had once nurtured those emotions came up empty.

"I'm sure this Christmas will be much better," Katya said.

Would it? Without Jameso or Barb here, she wasn't sure. But she had friends around her and a picture-postcard setting in which to celebrate—none of which she would have imagined a year ago, sitting in tropical Houston. Nothing about her life was the same as it had been back then. And nothing about her was the same either. These mountains and these people had changed her, for the better she hoped. She rested a hand on her abdomen. More changes were happening every day. She didn't feel prepared, but like riding an avalanche, all she could do was go with the flow and hope she came out on top.

CHAPTER SIXTEEN

December 23 dawned cold and clear, the sun blindingly bright in a sky the color of the turquoise from the French Mistress Mine. "With the snow stopped, maybe they'll be able to open the roads soon," Maggie said as she stood with Olivia and Lucille in front of Lucille's house, awaiting the start of the snowmobile races. "Jameso will be able to make it home for Christmas."

"I hope so." Olivia adjusted the folds of the lacy wool scarf she'd draped around her neck. "For your sake and for mine. The bar's been packed with people who seem to think the best way to endure being snowbound is to pickle themselves in alcohol."

"Are there many people stranded on this side of the pass?" Maggie asked. "Where are they staying?"

"There were a handful of people at the hotel and a few folks staying with relatives," Lucille said. "There was a salesman from Cheyenne and a truck driver from Abilene. We put them up at the hotel. They're not happy, but they'll make the best of it. And, of course, Gerald Pershing is here. I don't think he planned on that."

"Oh?" Maggie had heard through the gossip grapevine that Pershing had handed over his check for the bogus mine shares yesterday morning. "Are you okay with that?"

"I'm certainly not going to let that old goat ruin my Christmas." Lucille snugged her coat more tightly around her.

The front door of Lucille's house opened and Lucas emerged. "Are the racers here yet?" he asked.

"Not yet." Maggie checked the time on her phone—at least she could still do that, even if she couldn't make or receive calls. "Bob said the races would start about ten. So any minute now."

"How many racers are there?" Lucas squeezed in between his mother and Maggie.

"Last I heard, seven, but that could change." Maggie turned to Olivia. "Is D. J. racing?"

"I have no idea."

"D. J. had to work this morning," Lucas said. He sneezed violently.

"Honey, maybe you should go back in the house," Olivia said. "You don't want to make your cold worse, standing out here in the wind."

"I'm okay." He sniffed. "Where are they racing?"

"Bob and Junior Dominick laid out the course," Lucille said. "They start at the county barn, just off the highway, then up Main, around Pickax, turn the corner, and head down this way to the finish line just down there." She indicated the stop sign half a block away, where Fourth Street intersected the main highway out of town.

"Too bad Jameso isn't here," Olivia said. "He'd love this."

"Yes," Maggie agreed. "He'll be annoyed they raced without him." Motorcycles, skis, snowmobiles—if it traveled fast and was dangerous, Jameso loved it. What drove some men to be such daredevils? Because he'd faced down death in Iraq, did he think he could keep on doing so forever? "I wish he wasn't so reckless," she added.

"No, you don't," Lucille said. "Then he wouldn't be the man he is."

Maybe Lucille was right. The first time Maggie had met Jameso, he'd ridden up on a motorcycle, a darkly handsome man in black leather, vaguely menacing. He'd seemed dangerous, but he'd been kind to her; the combination intrigued her, though she'd resisted her attraction for a long time. But the qualities that made a man an exciting lover didn't necessarily translate well to the qualities a woman needed in a husband and the father of her child.

She pulled her coat more tightly around her and peered down the street, pretending to watch for the snowmobile racers, but wishing she could see Jameso instead. He'd promised to be with her for Christmas; she couldn't blame him if the weather prevented him from keeping that promise, but then, he shouldn't have left her in the first place. Not when she'd all but begged him not to leave.

Lucas sneezed again, then leaned his head on his mother's shoulder. He was as tall as Olivia now, less spindly than Maggie remembered from when he'd first arrived in Eureka. "I probably won't be able to go with you and D. J. to hand out presents tomorrow night," he said.

"Maybe you'll be better by then," Olivia said.

He sniffed. "I doubt it. You and D. J. will have to go without me."

Olivia looked anything but pleased by the idea.

"Are you helping with the Santa project?" Maggie asked.

"Yes, Lucas's teacher asked us. They needed someone who could drive a truck to a couple of the more remote families, and since D. J. is a plow driver, he seemed a good choice. She said he needed a helper and I couldn't think of a way to get out of it without looking like a Scrooge."

"I bet you'll end up having fun," Maggie said.

Olivia looked doubtful.

"Good morning, ladies. Don't you all look lovely." Gerald Pershing, dressed like an old west gunfighter in a leather duster and Stetson, stood before them like a general surveying the troops. "Lucille, that scarf brings out the blue in your eyes."

"You'd better step back or you'll get run over when the racers come by," Lucille said, her face expressionless.

Gerald glanced down the street. Maggie thought she heard the whine of engines in the distance. "So kind of you to be concerned for my safety," he said.

"I'm not concerned for your safety as much as I'm concerned that we don't have an accident to ruin the race for everyone," Lucille said.

"Of course. You have to put your duties as mayor ahead of personal concerns." He paused, then added, "Perhaps I should pay a call on Cassandra this morning." He waited, as if expecting some reaction from her.

"Tell her I said hello. Now, if you don't mind, I'd like to see the racers."

Lucille started to turn away, but he took hold of her arm. "Don't do this, Lucille."

She didn't flinch, but looked him right in the eye. "Do what?"

"Be so cold toward me." He gave her his most charming smile. "I understand you might have some hard feelings over the way I left, but that's all behind us now. After all, we're going to be business partners, so to speak, working together on the mine."

"We're not going to be partners in anything," she said. "As for that mine, you'll get about as much return on your investment there as the town will on those technology stocks you sold us."

Maggie wished she'd had her camera ready to capture the confusion on Gerald's face. "What do you mean?"

"I mean, there is no gold in that mine. There never has been. Just like there was never any hope of a return on those stocks you sold us."

"You lied to me."

"We gave you some information and let you draw your own conclusions," Lucille said. "You believed what you wanted to believe, blinded by your own greed."

"That's fraud. I'll sue."

"Try it and I'll make sure every one of your shady dealings comes out in court. You'll end up in prison for the rest of your life."

Maggie suspected this threat was more wishful thinking than reality; if the town had any real evidence of criminal wrongdoing, they'd have turned Gerald over to the authorities long ago. But the words clearly shook the man. "I can't believe you'd do this, Lucille," he said softly. "After all we shared."

"After all you took from me." Lucille's voice shook. She swallowed, marshaling her emotions. "You may have thought I was just another lonely woman you could take advantage of, but you were wrong. I looked after myself for a lot of years and I'm not going to stop just because some good-looking charmer comes along. I hope this makes you think long and hard before you try to swindle anyone else."

She turned and caught Maggie watching the exchange. She winked, a saucy gesture that made Maggie smile. Her friend may have been battered by her experience with Gerald, but she wasn't broken.

Gerald also turned away, back stiff, head up, but he moved with the awkward gait of the shell-shocked and confused. He'd been bested at his own game and clearly didn't know how to handle it.

"What's the prize for the winner of the race?" Lucas's

question broke the awkward silence after Gerald left them.

"A bottle of brandy and a fruitcake," Maggie said.

"Fruitcake?" He wrinkled his nose.

"Janelle made it and it has so much brandy in it you can practically get intoxicated walking past it." Maggie had seen the fruitcake in question when she'd gathered details of the race for a story for the paper.

"I guess Janelle could make even fruitcake taste good," Lucas conceded.

The distant roar of engines grew louder as the racers turned the corner onto Fourth Street and headed toward the finish line. Half a dozen bullet-nosed snowmobiles were bunched in a tight group, rooster tails of snow fanning out behind them. The drivers, like colorful astronauts in red and blue and black helmets and insulated snowmobiling suits, hunched over their machines, gloved hands gripping the controls, barreling toward the crowd in front of the mayor's house.

"Who is that in the lead?" Maggie shouted over the roar of the engines.

"I think that's Charlie Frazier," Lucille said.

As the roaring machines flew by, Maggie thought she recognized a bit of Charlie's ginger beard beneath his helmet.

The racers shot through the stop sign and gradually slowed to a stop a hundred yards beyond, to the cheers of waiting supporters. The group on Lucille's porch moved toward the celebration. "Jake would have loved this," Lucille said, as Maggie fell into step beside her. "He would have won, too. He was such a competitor."

Maggie thought of the three trophies her father had won in the Hard Rock Days mining competitions, and the pictures of him competing—a big, ruggedly handsome man so clearly in his element. "I always missed him most at Christmastime," she said. As a girl, she'd daydreamed of her father arriving at last to visit her, loaded down with presents and apologies.

"I think he missed you, too," Lucille said. "He always had a hard time at the holidays. He drank more and refused all invitations. He said he'd rather be alone in his cabin, but I don't believe it."

"It was his choice," Maggie said. She still had a difficult time accepting that he'd known all along where she was and what she was doing, yet had never made contact. She remembered the letter he'd written but never sent, the one she'd found after his death. In it, he'd said that he hadn't intended to stay away from her forever, but he was never able to make himself go back—that the awful things he'd done in the war made him feel he didn't deserve to be around a baby like Maggie. He'd given her the cabin and the French Mistress Mine and this new life. That was something. Maybe not enough to make up for the years of hurt, but she could never hate him, only pity his inability to complete the connection while they were alive.

At the finish line, she joined the others in congratulating Charlie on his win, then took a picture of him kneeling in the seat of his snowmobile, the prize bottle of brandy in one hand, the fruitcake in the other. She was packing up her camera and notebook when the jingle of bells distracted her.

"It's a sleigh!" someone shouted.

Sure enough, two black Percherons, harnesses jingling, trotted down the snow-covered street toward the crowd, pulling a red and black sleigh festooned with more bells. Rick, a Santa hat perched rakishly on his head, stood and waved to the crowd. "Merry Christmas!" he shouted.

Maggie snapped a couple of photos, then raced to join the others around the sleigh. "Rick, where did you get this?" she asked.

"Ken and Darla Brubaker loaned it to me. They're out of town for the holidays and I promised to look after the horses. This is Boots"—he nodded to the horse on the left—"and Betty." Betty tossed her head and whinnied, bells jingling.

"Can I have a ride in the sleigh?" Lucas asked.

"Climb in. You too, Maggie, and Lucille and Olivia. I'll give a turn through town to anyone who wants."

The women and boy piled into the sleigh and pulled rough wool blankets over their legs against the stinging cold. Maggie laughed as they set off with a jerk.

"Now this is Christmas!" Lucille said, eyes shining. She grabbed Maggie's hand in her own. "Who needs cell phones when we've got this?"

Who indeed? From her vantage point high in the sleigh, she could almost believe she'd been transported back in time. The handmade decorations on the light poles and storefronts passed by at eye level, dusted with last night's snow, and the streets, cleared of traffic for the race, might have looked this way in 1920, or 1890 for that matter.

"Merry Christmas!" Rick called to passersby. Even the grumpy publisher had caught the Christmas spirit.

People said Christmas was a time for miracles. All Maggie needed was a little one—the roads opening to bring Jameso home to her. Then the holiday would be perfect. Perfection was a lot to ask for, she knew, but this was the one time of year when you might as well go for broke when it came to expectations.

"As far as I'm concerned, Christmas has come early," Lucille said as she watched the snow drift down over the quiet streets from a booth near the front of the Last Dollar. Rick had dropped her off here over an hour ago. She'd climbed down from the sleigh, feeling a good ten years younger, and almost giddy with joy and relief that they'd managed to recover at least some of the money Gerald had stolen.

"We haven't cashed that check yet," Reggie reminded her. Seated across from her, he sipped coffee and joined her in gazing out the window.

"No, but it's locked in the safe at my store, and with no phone service or DSL, Gerald can't stop payment or spirit the funds off elsewhere. As soon as service is restored, the bank has agreed to expedite the transaction."

"I don't like that he's still here in town," Reggie said. "And I'm not crazy about you admitting we scammed him."

"There's nothing he can do about it. And the look on his face when I told him was worth any trouble he might try to make. But he won't. He's too proud to admit in court that he was had." She pinched a bite off the wedge of fruitcake in front of her and popped it into her mouth. The rich, butter and brandy-soaked confection melted on her tongue with a burst of heat and flavor. "And right now he's busy trying to find some other woman to succumb to his charms. The last thing a man like him wants is to be alone at Christmas. Since I'm refusing to have anything to do with him, he's pursuing Cassie."

"How's that working out for him?" Reggie asked.

"Hard to say, but she's definitely taking advantage of his macho ego. Last I saw, she had him putting up decorations at her house, balancing on a ladder in the snow while she directed from the ground."

"Let's hope the old buzzard doesn't have a heart attack."

"If he does, we'll put the body on ice until after we cash the check."

Reggie looked shocked. "I did not hear that," he said.

Maggie stopped beside their table. "Can I join you?" she asked.

"Of course." Reggie slid over to make room for her. She peeled off her parka to reveal jeans, boots, and a red sweater that showed the slightest hint of a baby bump. She looked exhausted.

"Not sleeping well?" Lucille asked sympathetically.

She shook her head. "I'm worried about Jameso and Barb."

"They'll be okay," Reggie said. "Want some fruit-cake?" He slid the plate toward her.

She wrinkled her nose. "I wouldn't dare. That's got to be at least ninety proof."

"It'll make you forget your troubles." Reg slid the plate back. "But I suppose it wouldn't be good for the baby."

"Other than not sleeping, how are you holding up?" Lucille asked.

"I don't know what to do with myself. With no computers and phones, we've closed up the newspaper office. Half the stores in town have signs on the doors that say the owner is over at the Last Dollar or the Dirty Sally, not that I have any more shopping to do anyway."

Lucille had a similar sign on the door of Lacy's. "Something like this tends to heighten the sense of community," she said. "We want to gather together and eat and drink and wait out the storm."

"The snow looks like it's getting a little lighter." Maggie squinted out the window at the curtain of flakes that continued to fall, as steady as ever. "I wish I knew what was happening on the other side of those walls of snow up on the pass."

"You went up there?" Reggie asked.

"No, but Rick did and he showed me pictures. How is anyone ever going to get through that?"

"They'll have to get heavy equipment to clear snow and move trees; then the rotary plows can clear a path," Reggie said. "It'll take a while."

"Yeah, and who wants to be doing that kind of work at Christmas?" Maggie rested her chin in her hand, looking more glum than ever.

"You should come to my house for Christmas," Lucille said. "I usually go to the candlelight service at the Presbyterian church. Come with me . . . even if you aren't particularly religious, it's a beautiful way to welcome in the holiday. Afterward, we'll go back to my place and you can spend the night. Olivia will join us after she and D. J. finish their deliveries."

"She told me she got roped into playing Mrs. Claus."

"I'm hoping working with D. J. to help other people will open a way for them to settle their differences," Lucille said. "I've invited D. J. to Christmas dinner, just in case."

"What are you doing for Christmas?" Maggie asked Reggie.

"Katya and I have a tradition. We go skiing in the morning; then we go out to Living Waters for a soak. It's not exactly a Scandinavian sauna, but close enough."

The door to the café opened and Cassie sailed in, followed by Gerald, who was stooped over, a pained expression on his face.

"My goodness, Mr. Pershing, is something wrong?" Janelle asked.

"I believe I hurt my back moving boxes of decorations out of Miss Wynock's attic." He flashed a pained smile. "So kind of you to ask, dear."

"Oh, don't whine, Gerald. It's unbecoming. You'll be fine once we've had lunch." Cassie didn't even glance back at him. "Janelle, do you have any good steaks?"

"We just got in an order of grass-fed New York strips," Janelle said.

"That sounds perfect."

"Steak for lunch?" Gerald asked. "I was thinking some nice soup, maybe a salad."

"You promised me a nice lunch and I want steak. Oh, hello, Lucille." Cassie paused beside their booth and favored Lucille with a smug smile. "Gerald and I have been having such a wonderful time together."

Grimacing, Gerald straightened and slipped his arm around Cassie. "Yes, we have. Cassie has been showing me some of the family heirlooms. Such a distinguished family."

"Yes, I was telling Gerald how much my antiques are worth," Cassie said. "Some of the items are positively priceless."

Many of the items had been purchased in Lucille's own junk shop. "Oh, yes," Lucille said. "Cassie has quite the collection."

"Gerald's persuaded me to consider selling some of the more valuable items," Cassie continued. "After all, I really don't need so many old things sitting around. He feels he can get a very good price for them in Dallas."

"How thoughtful of him." Lucille managed to keep a straight face. What a shock Gerald was going to get when he showed up in Dallas with a truckload of cheap junk.

"He's been so wonderful." Cassie clung to his arm. "This afternoon he's promised to split firewood for me. There's nothing like a cozy fire on a snowy Christmas Eve, is there?"

"No, nothing like it." Though Cassie was doing a good job of playing the gloating new girlfriend, Lucille detected a glint of diabolical amusement in the librarian's gray eyes.

"Why don't we sit down now?" Gerald said. "Do you think Janelle and Danielle have any Scotch? Strictly for medicinal purposes."

"I have a feeling he won't be able to leave town fast enough," Maggie said softly as they watched Gerald shuffle across the restaurant in Cassie's wake.

"Yes, and Cassie will have a freshly stacked woodpile and a cleaned-out basement in the bargain," Reg said. "You have to admire her ingenuity."

"If it were anyone but Gerald, I might feel sorry for him," Lucille said. "But enough of that unpleasant topic. Please say you'll spend Christmas with us, Maggie."

"All right. And thanks. Hanging out with you and Olivia will definitely be better than sitting at my place by myself, worrying about Barb and her husband."

"They'll be fine." Lucille patted her hand. "And Jameso will be fine."

Maggie looked unconvinced. "This was going to be our first Christmas together."

"There will be others." Clearly, she needed to do something to keep the poor girl from sliding into depression. She stood. "Come on. I've got something that will make you feel better."

"What's that?"

"Let's head over to the school gym. They need people to help get the gifts together for Santa. If a couple of hours of wrapping gifts for children, not to mention eating Christmas cookies and singing carols, don't put you in the Christmas spirit, I don't know what will."

Olivia thought any child would have been forgiven for believing that Santa's workshop had somehow been relocated to Eureka, Colorado. Even though she knew local businesses, churches, and civic groups had been collecting presents, food, and even decorations for weeks, she blinked and fought the urge to rub her eyes when she stepped into the school gymnasium the afternoon of Christmas Eve. Every surface was covered with piles of wrapped gifts, boxes, and baskets of food, beribboned wreaths, strings of lights, and even stacks of freshly cut evergreens wrapped in twine. Volunteers swarmed around the piles like industrious elves, and half a dozen Santas in red velvet and white fur strode among them.

"There you are!" One of the Santas stopped Olivia as

she squeezed between a pyramid of canned hams and a mound of oranges in net bags. "You'd better hurry and change into your costume."

Olivia stared into the brown eyes of "Santa" and felt a jolt of recognition. "D. J.?"

"Just call me Santa." He grinned. "Pretty good costume, huh?"

The red velvet coat and pants, black boots, and white wig and beard, and the addition of some padding had transformed the burly plow driver into an imposing Santa Claus. "Yeah," Olivia said, still stunned. "I mean, the kids will love it."

"It's already starting to get dark out," he said. "I'd like to get going before too much longer."

"Over here, Mrs. Claus, and I'll show you your costume." A woman with a mass of blond curls and glasses on a chain around her neck took Olivia's elbow and steered her toward the restrooms just outside the gym. The stalls had been converted to dressing rooms, where Olivia changed into a white blouse, full red velvet skirt with a wide black belt, a gray curly wig with a mob cap, and rectangular granny glasses with clear lenses. "You can wear your own boots," the blonde said as she dotted Olivia's cheeks with rouge and whitened her eyebrows.

When Olivia turned to the mirror, she laughed out loud. She wouldn't have recognized herself. "You make a wonderful Mrs. Claus." The blonde patted her shoulder. "Now, go help Santa."

D. J. was waiting for her outside the restroom, pacing back and forth. "I'm ready," she announced. At least, she was dressed for her part. She wasn't sure anything could have prepared her for hours spent in the close confines of his truck cab. She didn't know what to say to him after so many months of nurturing her anger at him. Since Jameso had convinced her it was unlikely D. J. had known she was pregnant when he left for Iraq, she'd battled confusion and guilt. If she told him about the baby, would he be furious she'd kept the secret so long? Would he ever be able to forgive her for the way she'd treated him, or was there too much pain and misunderstanding between them to ever make things right again?

He studied her, then nodded. "Very sexy."

She laughed. "Yeah, as sexy as that Santa suit." Though all the fake beards and padding in the world couldn't tamp down the quiver in her stomach she felt at the prospect of hours spent alone with him.

"The truck's out here." He gestured toward a back entrance. "Already loaded."

She pulled on her coat and gloves—no need for a hat with the wig—and followed him outside. "Lucas still sick?" he asked as he held the door for her.

"He's not running a fever, but he has a cough and he says he feels awful."

"Bad luck to be sick at Christmas," D. J. said.

"I'm sure presents tomorrow will cheer him up." She halfway suspected her son of faking it, intent on more matchmaking, but she hadn't wanted to accuse him.

The back of D. J.'s old truck was piled high with boxes and bags, but it wasn't the gifts that made Olivia do a double take. The old beater was decked out from bumper to bumper with garland, tinsel, and ribbon. A wreath adorned the grill, and twinkling colored lights outlined the cab. "You decorated your truck?"

"It's Santa's sleigh tonight," he said, and held the passenger door open for her.

She climbed in and groped for the seat belt. "You're really into this, aren't you?" she asked.

"I want this to be a Christmas those kids will always remember." He slid into the driver's seat and cranked the engine. "Plowing the roads around the county, I've seen the way some of these families live. It's pretty rugged, especially on the old mining claims where we're headed. They don't have a lot of luxury in their lives. I want to make tonight special."

"That . . . that's really sweet of you," she said. She'd forgotten about this side of D. J.—the sensitive side that cared about other people. When they'd lived in Hartford, he wouldn't just give a buck to a guy on a street corner; he'd stop and escort him to the nearest coffee shop and buy him a muffin and hot cocoa.

She stared out the truck window, at the lighted, decorated businesses along Eureka's main street. Snow dusted the evergreen wreaths and garlands and frosted the red ribbons. Everything looked clean and orderly and prosperous. "I guess I don't think about there being poor people in Eureka," she said. "Everything seems so perfect here."

"There are poor people everywhere," he said. "Things are maybe cleaner and prettier and safer here, but you can't eat scenery."

"I guess not." But the scenery was one reason people lived here—the mountains and valleys drew them, despite the difficulty of making a living in such a remote location. She knew plenty of people who worked multiple jobs, and driving old cars and wearing secondhand clothes was almost a point of pride. People bragged about living on their own terms, even if it meant doing without some things.

"Even the poor people here look rich compared to some of what I saw in Iraq," he said. "There, whole families live in one- or two-room mud huts with dirt floors, dressed in rags, living on rice and tea. The Americans tried to help, but sometimes there wasn't a lot we could do."

"You've never talked about Iraq before," she said.

"You've never asked."

She hadn't wanted to know about the country that had pulled him away from her. She hadn't wanted to think about what he'd been doing while she mourned alone back in the States. "Was it very dangerous?" she asked.

"Two guys I worked with were killed by roadside bombs in the six months I was there. We'd drive these convoys, often at night, with maybe one or two Bradleys for escort. Every time you left, you never knew if you'd make it back."

She wanted to cover her ears, to keep on pretending he hadn't suffered during his time away. "I'm glad you made it back safely," she said.

He glanced at her, dark eyes beneath the artificially white brows intense. "From the day I stepped off the plane in Baghdad, I wished I'd never left. I thought the money would be so good, but there wasn't enough money to make up for all I missed while I was away."

She nodded, a pain in her chest, as if the jagged pieces of her broken heart were rearranging themselves. She wasn't ready for this; she didn't want to hear his confessions or make her own. She forced her gaze out the window, staring at the snow-covered road ahead of them. "How many families are we visiting this evening?" she asked.

He paused for a long moment before answering, but when he spoke his voice was calm, as if any interested stranger had asked the question. "We've got two families . . . one with two children, one with four. They're both up on Black Mountain, this side of the pass. I'll have to stop and put the chains on before we get there. The volunteers labeled all the bags and boxes with names, so when we get there it'll be easy to hand out everything." He glanced her way again. "I'm looking forward to seeing the kids' faces when we show up."

"That will be fun," she said. She meant it. Focusing on someone and something beside her own pain would be a welcome break. "I'm glad Mrs. Desmet asked us to help."

"Yeah, it kind of makes Christmas more special."

She nodded. This was definitely going to be a Christmas Eve unlike any other she'd experienced.

CHAPTER SEVENTEEN

Holidays had not really mattered to Jameso since he was a kid. Christmas was another day to be got through. Sometimes his mother or his sister would call and he would bluff his way through the awkward conversation, answering their questions about what he was doing with his life with reassurances that he was fine and no one should worry about him.

Last Christmas, he and Jake had climbed Mount Winston and skied down, then celebrated their achievement with a steak dinner and a bottle of good whiskey. They hadn't talked of anything important that Jameso could remember. Jake certainly hadn't mentioned his daughter. Had he thought of Maggie at all?

Sometimes Jameso had a hard time remembering that Maggie was Jake's daughter. She was gentle and open, where Jake had been so guarded and tough. But then she'd laugh and her eyes would crinkle at the corners, the way Jake's had, and Jameso would think of his late friend and feel sorry all over again that Jake, one of the bravest men he'd ever known, hadn't had the courage to get to know his own child.

Jake would have liked Maggie. He appreciated a strong woman who could be with a man but didn't have to lean on him. He'd have gotten a kick out of introducing his daughter to Jameso—and then he'd have whipped Jameso's ass for looking at her twice. The two men would have fought, then made up, as they had so many times before, and Jameso would have had to convince Jake that he was going to do right by his daughter.

Now Maggie filled Jameso's thoughts as he guided his truck over the snow-covered roads. Jake's friend in Montana had been very helpful, but slower than Jameso would have liked, requiring an extra day to do the job Jameso wanted. Which meant Jameso couldn't head back to Eureka until Christmas Eve.

He picked up the cell phone from the seat beside him and punched in Maggie's number again. The phone rang and rang, as it had all day, never even rolling over to voice mail. With a growl of frustration, he ended the call. He'd explain his tardiness when he saw her again. They'd be together for Christmas, and that was all that mattered.

A few years ago, when he was fresh back from Iraq, he'd tried to make things work with a woman. She'd been a lot like Maggie, the independent, understanding type. But she hadn't been understanding enough to deal with his distance and his rages, his drinking, and his inability to commit to anything, whether it was a job or a relationship. Their breakup, like everything in his life in those days, had been explosive and dramatic. He'd been almost relieved when it was over, the burden of trying to make things work lifted from him.

He tightened his grip on the steering wheel. He was a different man now. Watching Jake self-destruct had led him to cut way back on the alcohol. The rages had faded, and he was working on closing the distances and shouldering responsibilities. Only a few more miles to go, anyway, up Black Mountain and down the other side, then through town. If Maggie's Jeep was at the paper office, he'd stop there. He hoped she'd be pleased and surprised, and not angry at his late arrival.

The truck groaned its way up the switchbacks toward the top of Black Mountain. No traffic passed him from the other direction. Was everyone else already settled in for the holidays? He'd expected a few skiers making a last dash for the resort in Telluride, or families on their way to Grandma's house. Yet he had the road to himself, driving in the fading daylight, with intermittent snowfall. He glanced at the phone again. No service. He'd never understood how the top of a mountain studded with cell towers could be a dead zone.

He rounded the curve of another switchback and stared ahead at the pair of railroad crossing arms lowered across the pavement. ROAD CLOSED, the sign between them read. Leaden cold settled in the pit of his stomach as he applied the brakes. So this was why the road had been so deserted. He must have failed to see the signs warning of this closure while he was fiddling with his phone.

He brought the truck to a stop with the grill almost touching the arm of the highway gate. Leaving the engine running, he climbed out and went to stand at the gate. Snow came almost to the tops of his boots, and his breath froze in his beard, but he scarcely felt the cold. The sun hung low in the afternoon sky, the fir and pines casting long shadows over the unbroken sea of snow ahead, like fingers stretching toward him. He couldn't tell where the road ended and the mountains began. Probably somewhere up ahead an avalanche, or a series of avalanches, had buried the pass. The state had big rotary plows that could chew through the walls of snow, but on Christmas Eve no one was in a hurry to do so.

He turned to look back the way he'd come. A 200-mile detour could take him around to the other side of town, and the other mountain pass that also might be blocked by snow. Every winter Eureka was shut off from the rest of the world like this once or twice, as many as half a dozen times. It was an inconvenience people put up with; one more thing that made them unique, tougher than the rest of the world, more independent.

He'd never minded the blockages before. He had everything he needed right there in Eureka. But he'd never been on this side of the pass before, barred from the things he wanted by forces much bigger than himself.

He climbed back into the truck, turned it around, and drove halfway down the switchback to a parking area on the right. A popular backcountry trail started here, unused and blocked by snow this time of year. Jameso nosed his truck in next to the Parking sign and switched off the engine. Then he pocketed the keys, slipped his cell phone into his pocket, and pulled on his jacket, hat, and gloves. From the bed of the truck he pulled out a backpack, cross-country skis, boots, and poles.

He and Jake had skied over Black Mountain Pass two years ago on a lark. No reason Jameso couldn't do it again. He'd made a promise to Maggie, and he wouldn't let a little snow prevent him from keeping it.

The Eureka Presbyterian Church was packed for the Christmas Eve service. Maggie stood shoulder to shoulder with Lucille and Tamarin Sherman, watching the flickering flame of her candle, amid a sea of other candles, and choking back tears as the strains of "Silent Night" filled the air around her. She didn't consider herself a particularly religious person, but standing here with the smell of beeswax and evergreens and Tamarin's sweet perfume filling her senses, the magic of the night moved her. She felt loved and cherished by these people and this place; the knowledge that her child would feel this same love started a fresh flood of tears. She sniffed and Lucille handed her a tissue.

"Thanks," Maggie whispered, and dabbed at her eyes. "And thanks for inviting me here tonight. I think I needed this."

As they filed out into the achingly cold night, Danielle sidled up to them. "Stop by the Last Dollar before you go home," she said. "Some of us get together every year to toast Christmas."

"Sounds good," Lucille said. "I could use a shot of something to warm me up."

"I think the cold is invigorating." Maggie pulled her coat more closely around her and turned her face to the sky. "And look at those stars. We didn't have stars like this in Houston." Thousands of them twinkled against the pitch black sky, like silver glitter scattered by an exuberant hand. She'd never known so many stars existed before she came to Eureka.

The fact that she could see them so clearly tonight meant the clouds had cleared. It had stopped snowing. Tomorrow, or the next day, the plows and heavy equipment would arrive to clear the passes, and Jameso and Barb would make their belated way to her. They'd celebrate Christmas late, but they'd be together. That was all that really mattered.

She and Lucille and several others followed Janelle and Danielle, Reggie and Katya over to the Last Dollar Café. Bob waited for them at a table near the door, a bottle of Jack Daniels open in front of him.

"Hello, Maggie," Bob said as she moved past him. "I was just sitting here thinking about how Murph and Jameso and I sat here last Christmas and toasted the holiday together."

Maggie's throat tightened at the mention of Jameso. "Dad's probably looking down on us now," she said. *But where is Jameso?*

"And Jameso's probably stuck in a hotel in Durango, cursing the snow that's keeping him away." Bob lifted his glass. "To Jameso."

"He is coming back, you know," Lucille whispered as she and Maggie settled into chairs at the table next to Bob's. Reggie had volunteered to fetch drinks, and tea for Maggie.

"I know." She absently smoothed her sweater over the slight swell in her belly. "I mean, I was worried he wouldn't when he first said he was leaving, but he didn't act like a man who was running away. He really does want to do the right thing for me and the baby. I'm worried he'll try something foolish."

"Like what?" Lucille asked.

"I don't know. My father was his best friend. They did some crazy things together."

"Last year, on Christmas Day, they climbed Mount Winston and skied down," Bob said.

"I remember the year they moved the Christmas tree from in front of the library to the Dirty Sally." Janelle set a cup of tea in front of Maggie. "When it came time for the saloon to open, the tree was blocking the door. No one could get in or out until they moved it."

"It wasn't easy either," Bob said. "They'd wired it in place."

"One year Murphy set off fireworks on Mount Garnet at midnight on Christmas Eve," Reggie said. "He forgot to wear ear plugs and he couldn't hear anything for three days."

"The Forest Service and the Department of Wildlife threatened to fine him or haul him off to jail," Bob said. "For Halloween the next year, Murph stuck a pair of mule deer antlers to his hat and lit up sparklers all over them. He told everybody he was an endangered species, so they had to buy him a drink."

"Jake did good things, too." Danielle settled into a

chair across from Maggie. "One year he heard about a family in one of the mining camps that the Elks Club Santas had missed. Jake got together presents and a Christmas dinner on his own and took it to them."

"He found me and got me to open the store at nine o'clock on Christmas Eve," Lucille said. "I helped him find clothes and gifts for the whole family. I offered to contact the Elks and see if they could help, but he wouldn't hear of it. He wanted to do it all himself."

The stories continued, of Jake's exploits and good deeds, his outrageous behaviors and touching kindnesses. Maggie let them flow over her. Since coming to town, she'd been hearing these stories about her father. They made her feel closer to him.

And tonight, they made her feel a little closer to Jameso, too. She closed her eyes and said a silent prayer that he was all right—safe in that hotel room in Durango.

"I hope Olivia and D. J. are all right."

Lucille's words surprised Maggie into opening her eyes.

"Why wouldn't they be all right?" Reggie asked.

"They went to deliver gifts up on Black Mountain," Lucille said. "I thought they'd be back by now."

"Maybe they are back," Bob said. "They could be at D. J.'s place, having their own celebration."

Lucille smiled. "I hope you're right. I think they really love each other, though Olivia is too stubborn to admit it." She sipped her drink, a small glass of Bailey's. "She takes after her mother that way."

"Christmas is a good time to kiss and make up," Janelle said. "Maybe that will be their Christmas present to each other."

Someone asked how Lucas was feeling, and someone else asked Bob about the Christmas play he'd helped Lucas write. But Maggie was only vaguely aware of these peripheral conversations. She'd focused all her attention on the sensation in her belly—like the flutter of a butterfly's wings or a flower suddenly opening. She sat up straighter, concentrating—waiting.

"What is it?" Lucille's voice broke through the fog. "Maggie, are you all right?"

She nodded.

"What is it?" Danielle asked. "Is it the baby?"

The flutter came again, a goldfish swimming in her belly. Maggie rested her hand on her stomach and the fluttering stopped. "I think I felt the baby move," she whispered.

"Oh, Maggie." Lucille covered her friend's hand with her own.

"That's wonderful," Danielle breathed, eyes shining.

"Our first Christmas miracle," Janelle said.

"It's not a miracle the kid moved," Bob said. "Babies are supposed to move."

"Since when are you an expert, old man?" Lucille nudged him.

"I'm just saying, it's not a miracle. A miracle is when something happens that's not supposed to happen."

"All babies are little miracles," Janelle insisted.

To Maggie, this baby was a miracle. A year ago she'd spent Christmas as an unhappily married, soon-to-be-divorced, thirty-nine-year-old childless woman. She'd been sure her life was over. Now here she was, carrying her first child, with a new home, a new job, and a new circle of friends who loved her.

Jameso was part of that miracle, too. If her father really was watching them tonight, she sent up a silent plea that he would keep Jameso safe, and bring him back to her and to their unborn child. That was the only Christmas present she really wanted, the only Christmas miracle she needed.

* * *

The weathered gray wood of the little house blended into the darker gray of the rock against which it sat. If Olivia had passed it on a hike, she would have thought it was a relic of old mining days. But when D. J. stopped the truck in front of it, the door burst open and four children ran out, followed by a man and woman. The woman smiled shyly and waved while the man looked grim.

"Santa's here! Santa's here!" the children shouted, dancing around the truck.

"Ho! Ho! Ho!" D. J. boomed in a credible imitation of the Christmas saint. "Merry Christmas!"

"Merry Christmas!" Olivia called, smiling past her nervousness and climbing out to help D. J. carry in the bags of gifts and boxes of food.

The front room of the house was small, made smaller still by eight people crowded into it. A tall fir, still smelling of snow and woods, was planted in a bucket of sand in the corner opposite the wood stove, and D. J. headed to it, a black plastic trash bag full of presents slung over his back in a fair imitation of Santa's pack. "Who wants to help me give out the presents?"

"I do! I do!" The tallest child, a boy of eight or nine, jumped up and down and waved his hand.

D. J. beckoned him over. "Christopher, you can help me give out the gifts to your brother and sisters."

Wide-eyed, Christopher nodded.

D. J., Olivia, and the boy handed out two bags full of wrapped presents—dolls and Legos, a harmonica and a handheld video game, new shoes and jeans and shirts. Olivia pressed a box containing a sweater into the mother's hand and the woman began to cry. The father looked stunned at a pair of new work boots.

But the children captured most of Olivia's attention. The oldest girl danced around the room hugging a pink quilted parka trimmed with fake fur, and the youngest clutched her doll to her chest and gaped at them. D. J.

knelt beside her. "Do you like your dolly, Nina?" he asked.

She nodded, then, still holding the doll, threw her arms around his neck. "I love you, Santa," she said.

"I love you, too," he said, and patted her back. When he stood, Olivia thought she caught the glint of tears in his eyes, and she had to blink hard to clear her own vision.

They left with a chorus of "Merry Christmas!" and "Good night, Santa!"

Neither of them spoke until D. J. had turned the truck around and made his way down the steep driveway to the road, which itself was only a snow-covered dirt track. "That was intense," he said.

"You were wonderful with those children," Olivia said.

"I like kids." He chuckled. "Did you see how big their eyes got when I called them by name? They thought I really was Santa."

"I never knew you liked children so much."

"I like Lucas." He hunched forward, peering at the road.

"I mean little children."

"Well, sure. Kids are great." He glanced at her. "I wish I'd known you and Lucas when he was a baby."

How would her life have been different if she'd known D. J. then? What if he had been her husband, or one of the boyfriends who'd followed the breakup of her marriage, instead of the losers who had come and gone, always leaving her and Lucas alone?

The chains on the tires crunched loudly on the packed snow, but even with chains, she felt the back tires spin in several places. D. J. hunched over the steering wheel, knuckles white. "How far is the next family?" she asked.

"They're up near Black Mountain, just off the highway. I plowed up that way this morning to make sure we could get through."

The house was even farther up a narrow, winding drive, almost to the tree line, crouched against a boulder taller than the roof. Two children lived here, solemn twins who stared at Santa and his bounty with slack mouths, until their mother persuaded them to come closer. She took photos of the boys perched, one on each of Santa's knees. Settled there, the children didn't want to leave, and opened their games and clothing and toys seated there, with Santa exclaiming over each gift with a tenderness that made Olivia's heart feel too full to speak.

They parted with many cries of "Merry Christmas" and headed back toward town in full dark, the headlights of the truck illuminating a world of black and white— white road and white mountain, studded with black trees against a blacker sky, sparkling with more stars than she had ever seen. She had thought it would be awkward, spending so much time alone with D. J., but seeing him with the children had eased the stiffness between them. She felt more at peace than she had in months, grateful to be here, in this place and in this moment, with him. He didn't feel the need for idle conversation the way some people did. He was content to focus on the driving and leave her in peace to think. "It's so beautiful up here," she said.

"I like to come up here before the sun's up to plow," he said. "It's hard to believe this is even the same world as Connecticut or Iraq." He shifted the truck into a lower gear and the engine growled. "I wish I had my plow truck now. Even with the chains, the back of this truck wants to fishtail around going downhill."

"But you plowed up here this morning, right?" She clutched the dash as the truck slid sideways once more.

"Yeah, but the wind has drifted the snow in places." He straightened the truck again and they crept downhill. "It should be better once we reach the highway," he said.

She nodded, too nervous to speak. She stared out the

windshield, willing the highway to appear. But all she saw was white snow and black trees.

"We're almost there." D. J. nodded toward the road ahead of them. "The intersection with the highway is up ahead."

"Great." The highway would be wider and smoother, with pavement instead of dirt underneath, and it wasn't as steep. They'd be safer once they reached the highway.

"I'm not going to risk riding the brakes through the turn," he said. "There's no one up here, so we'll just coast out into the lanes, then straighten out."

"All right." The plan made sense to her. She braced herself, nervous, despite the fact that she knew there was no traffic up here this time of night. They were almost at the barricades where the road was closed due to the avalanches. And who would be out on Christmas Eve?

No person was out, but a trio of bull elk, crowns of antlers shining white in the moonlight, chose that moment to cross the road in front of them. D. J. stomped on the brakes, cursing, and the truck fishtailed wildly. The elk bounded into the woods and the truck careened down the steep, narrow road, coming to rest skewed sideways in the ditch at the bottom of the slope, headlights shining up into the trees.

D. J. shut off the engine. Olivia gripped the dash and braced her feet against the door to keep from sliding down against it. She stared into the darkness, the tick of the cooling engine and her own labored breathing the only sounds. She started when the headlights switched off, plunging them into blackness. Already icy fingers of cold crept into the cab. "What are we going to do?" she asked, trying to keep her voice from wavering.

"I can walk into town for help."

"Don't leave me." She stretched out her hand and clutched his arm. "I'll go with you."

"You aren't dressed to walk far. It must be twenty below out there."

"I'm not dressed to sit here waiting for you either." She unbuckled her seat belt and dragged herself across the seat toward him. "How far is it to town?"

"Seven or eight miles."

"You'll freeze."

"No, I won't. I can walk eight miles."

"In your regular clothes, maybe, but in a Santa suit? You don't even have a coat. That velvet isn't going to keep you warm for long."

"I've got an old work coat behind the seat. I'll be all right."

"Don't leave me. Please." To hell with pride. The thought of sitting here alone, not knowing what was happening to him, terrified her.

He pounded the steering wheel with frustration. "Let me think," he said.

She hugged her arms across her chest and tried not to shiver. Her eyes had adjusted to the darkness and she could see more now—the shadows of trees on the paleness of snow, and the tracks of animals in the whiteness.

"There's a cabin not too far up the road here. A summer place, empty this time of year, but we can break in if we have to."

"How far?"

"Less than a mile." He leaned over the back of the seat and pulled out a bundle of army green. "Put this on." He shoved the cold fabric toward her.

She thought about protesting, but why waste time with arguing? And her jacket wasn't doing a very good job of keeping her warm. She'd worn tights under her skirt, but what she wouldn't have given for a pair of insulated snow pants.

She opened the door and slid out, sinking to her knees in snow. It overflowed the tops of her boots and trickled to her ankles. Grunting in frustration, she kicked her way out of the drift and met D. J. at the truck's back bumper. He was rummaging through a toolbox and pulled out a hammer, wrench, and screwdriver. "In case I have to take the cabin door off its hinges," he said.

"There's probably a key," Olivia said. "People always hide a key."

They walked up the road side by side, in the tracks the truck had made coming down. If not for the bitter cold, Olivia might have enjoyed the walk. The moon and stars bathed their path in silvery light, and the only sounds were the crunch of their boots on the snow and the huff of their breathing.

But the cold stole any chance of enjoyment after too many minutes. She could no longer feel her feet or her face. "How much farther?" she asked, puffing along behind D. J.

"We still have a ways to go. Are you going to be all right?"

"Of course." She didn't have a choice. She had a son and a life to get back to. Not being all right wasn't an option.

Since when had a mile been so far? She supposed the fact that they were climbing in the dark, through snow, made the distance seem so much farther. Gritting her teeth, she plowed on. One foot in front of the other. She wouldn't give up and she wouldn't complain. She forced herself to think of warm things—a cozy wood fire, a bed piled high with quilts, a bowl of steaming soup.

D. J. scanned the side of the road with a flashlight until he found the row of reflectors on a tree that marked the entrance to the drive leading to the cabin. He stopped and handed Olivia the light. "Shine this ahead of me. I'll walk in front and break trail."

"All right."

He patted her shoulder. "You okay?"

"Sure." Every part of her ached from the cold, and she hadn't been able to feel her feet for some time. What if her toes were frozen? Would doctors have to amputate, so that she'd never be able to wear high heels again? What a stupid thing to worry about right now, but she had no control over her random thoughts. D. J. was probably just as cold or colder. After all, he'd given her his coat. They'd be warm soon, she told herself.

She'd imagined a short walk up a snow-covered driveway, but as soon as they stepped off the road, she sank in snow halfway up her thighs. The ground beneath the snow was steep and uneven. D. J. plowed ahead, trying to stomp down the snow and make a path, but she kept slipping and falling.

"Maybe I could carry you," he said, as he helped her up again.

"Dammit, I can walk!" She struggled to her feet once more, tears freezing on her face.

"Don't cry." He brushed at the tears. "We're almost there. Don't be afraid."

"I'm not crying because I'm afraid!" She glared at him.

"Then why are you crying?"

"Because I've been so stupid!" Her voice rose on the last word, a wail in the still night.

D. J. frowned at her. "You're not stupid."

"I am. I've wasted so much time. When you went away I said I hated you. But I was lying to myself." The words came in a rush, half speaking, half sobs. She clutched at his arm. "I never stopped loving you, but I was too proud to show it."

He pulled her close, into his warm embrace. "I know," he said softly. "And I never stopped loving you. That's why I was willing to wait."

She closed her eyes and rested her head against his chest. She wanted to stay here like this all night, but, of course, that was impossible. She looked up at him. "D. J., there's something I have to tell you."

"Shhh." He put a finger to her lips. "It can wait." He took her hand and pulled her forward. "We need to keep moving. Let's find a place to get inside and get warm."

Cold. So cold. Jameso's jaw hurt from clenching it against the chattering that shook him. Sharp pain stabbed at his fingers in his thick gloves, and he could no longer feel his toes. Frost hung heavy in his beard and wind-blown snow dusted the shoulders of his coat. He felt heavy and so tired, but he forced himself to keep moving: slide one ski forward, reach out to plant his pole, slide the other ski forward, plant the second pole.

His headlamp sent a thin beam of blue-white light in front of him, showing a world as white as a blank sheet of paper. Fields, walls, and mountains of snow stretched in every direction in disorienting, vertigo-inducing whiteness. Had he reached the top of the pass yet? Had he descended to the other side? The whiteness had stolen his sense of direction, his feeling for up and down. All he could do was keep going. Keep moving.

"At least when we did this before we had sense enough to do it in the daylight."

He started at the familiar, booming voice, and turned to see a figure skiing alongside him. Like Jameso, the man wore a heavy parka, dusted with snow, and had a knit cap pulled low over his ears and a scarf wrapped around his face. But that voice . . .

"You've been this cold before, remember?" the ghost skiing next to Jameso continued. "That night you helped me with the ghost lights up on Mount Winston. Damn, we like to froze our asses off skiing around up there, waving those lanterns . . . all to give the folks in town a thrill."

"That was cold," Jameso said. "But not like this. This

year when I did the lights there wasn't even any snow. It was almost easy climbing in the dark."

"Keeping the tradition alive." The ghost chuckled. "I like that."

Jameso shook his head, as if to clear it. It wasn't a good sign if he was hallucinating Jake Murphy this way. Did it mean he was freezing to death? That the end was near?

"What the hell made you think this was a good idea anyway?" Jake asked. "You could be sitting in a warm bar in Durango, drinking a toast to Christmas. Instead, you're out here trying to freeze to death."

"I have to get to Maggie." Jameso faced forward once more and quickened his pace. Things were bad if he was hallucinating dead men.

"There was a time I would have kicked your ass for looking at her twice, much less knocking her up."

"I'd like to see you try, old man." He and Jake had had their share of brawls, and they always ended in a draw. Jake was bigger, but Jameso was younger and that made them about even.

"I didn't come out here tonight to beat you up."

"Then why did you come out here?"

"Maybe I just felt like a midnight lark in the snow."

Jameso grunted. Was it his imagination or was he moving downhill now? He must be over the pass. The knowledge renewed his energy. Downhill meant toward town. Toward Maggie.

"Maggie's happy about the baby, right?" Jake asked.

"She's happy." At least he was pretty sure she was happy. Maggie kept her own council, one of the things he admired about her. She told him what she wanted him to know but didn't feel the need to share everything.

"If the baby is a boy, she should name it Jake."

"Like the world needs another you," Jameso said. His voice was hoarse from the cold and the words came out in a croak, but what did it matter since he was talking to a ghost?

"Maybe you have a point. And maybe she wouldn't want to name her kid after me."

"It's not like you ever did anything for her."

"I'm still her old man. And if I ever hear of you treating her bad or letting her down, I *will* come back and make you sorry you were born."

"You're one to talk." Anger at his old friend rose, and he stoked it. Anger had heat and strength to drive him on. "All she ever wanted was for you to be there for her and you couldn't even give her that."

"Go ahead and call me a bastard. I know what I am. But whatever she thinks, she was better off without me around."

"I don't believe that, and Maggie doesn't believe it either."

"All you need to believe is that you shouldn't be like me."

"Then why did you do it? How could you walk out on a helpless baby that way?" He shook, not from cold, but with rage. He thought of the tears Maggie had shed in his presence over her father—and all the tears she must have cried before. All for a man who had left her when she needed him most.

"I wasn't punishing her, if that's what you think. I was punishing myself." Jake stabbed a ski pole into the snow so hard it sunk halfway to the handle. He pulled it out with a grunt. "I'd done so many bad things . . . killed so many people in Vietnam who didn't deserve it. I didn't deserve to be around an innocent little child, to poison her with my presence. I didn't deserve to be around good people."

Jake's voice cracked with pain, and even though Jameso knew this wasn't real, that this was only some ice-fueled illusion, he felt that pain. "I didn't do bad things," he said quietly. "But I saw a lot of bad things, over in Iraq. I lived when others didn't. It made me afraid to get close to people."

"War does that. Sometimes life does that. But you've got to figure out how to beat it, for Maggie's sake. And for the baby's sake."

"That's what I'm trying to do. That's why I'm freezing my ass off up here right now."

"You can do it. Be there for her, I mean. And you won't freeze your ass off tonight. Is that a light up ahead?"

Jameso leaned forward, squinting into the whiteness. He could make out the black outlines of trees and a soft glow beyond that. He pushed harder, breath coming in ragged gasps. The glow solidified into a square of golden light, shining in the window of a cabin. "I'm going to make it," he said, and turned to grin at Jake.

But there was no one there. He was alone again in the night, with the Christmas silence all around him.

Lucas's idea had been to fake a cold so that his mom and D. J. would have to go off together to deliver the presents. He hoped they'd talk and maybe, since it was Christmas and all, they'd figure out whatever was wrong between them and decide to get back together. Everything had gone pretty smoothly, too, except he'd ended up with a real cold, which kind of sucked. Especially at Christmas.

Grandma had offered to stay home from church with him, but he was thirteen, a teenager, so it wasn't as if he needed a babysitter. "I'll probably just go to bed early," he'd told her. Except he wasn't really sleepy, and he didn't feel that sick; he just had a stuffy head and a little bit of a sore throat. Mostly, he was bored. And a little lonely. This was his first Christmas in a real home and he'd thought things would be a lot different.

He wandered down the stairs, into the big front room they hardly ever used. His grandmother called it the parlor. She and Lucas had set up a Christmas tree there—a real fir tree Bob had cut from the woods for them. It must have been close to ten feet tall, the tip brushing the high ceilings. That was another first for him; when his mom had bothered to have a tree it had been a little artificial number, set on a table in the corner of whatever apartment they'd been living in at the time.

Lucas stared at the big tree in front of the bow window, refusing to blink, letting his eyes lose focus until the tree became a blurry arrangement of softly glowing lights, like those Impressionist paintings he'd read about. Finally, he had to blink and bring the tree back into focus. And the piles of presents underneath. He dropped to his knees and picked up a box wrapped in red paper. For his mom from Grandma. Probably clothes or something. Grown-ups always seemed crazy about clothes. He figured his mom would probably get him a new coat, since his was ripped and a little tight. She probably thought that was a great present, but he needed the coat anyway. A present should be something you didn't necessarily need, but you wanted it anyway.

He wanted a gun—a .22 he could take hunting. D. J. thought it was a good idea, but Lucas wasn't sure he could talk Mom and Grandma into letting Lucas have it.

He looked out the window, at the snow softly falling once more. The flakes looked pretty, dancing in the soft glow from the porch light. What were Mom and D. J. doing right now? Had they made up yet? They loved each other— why couldn't his mother see that? Or why wouldn't she admit it?

He left the tree and pulled on his too-small coat, then went out onto the porch to watch the snow and to watch the street for his mom and D. J., or Grandma. They ought to be home by now, shouldn't they?

The street was quiet. Empty. No cars. No people out walking their dogs. No movement in nearby houses. He shivered. What if he were the only person left alive? What if zombies had killed and eaten everyone else?

Movement in the window of a house down the street caught his eye and he breathed a sigh of relief. He knew there really weren't such things as zombies, but still . . .

The figure in the window moved away. That was Miss Wynock's house. She was probably down there all alone; she didn't seem to have many friends. He wasn't sure she wanted any, but he didn't think she was so bad. He shoved his hands in his pockets against the cold and started down the street toward her.

He'd ring the bell, tell her Merry Christmas, then leave. She wouldn't even have time to be mad at him for disturbing her. But when the big oak door creaked open, he forgot what he was going to say. The old librarian stood there with her hair piled on top of her head, wearing pink lipstick and dangly earrings like his mom liked, and a long, sparkly silver dress. She looked almost pretty. "I . . . I didn't mean to interrupt anything," he stammered. "I just . . . I just wanted to say Merry Christmas."

He turned to leave, but she put her hand on his shoulder, stopping him. "Come in, Lucas. You aren't interrupting."

What could he do then but follow her inside? The house was a lot like his grandmother's, at least the way the rooms were arranged. But these rooms were crammed full of old furniture and books and clocks and enough old stuff to furnish a museum. He guessed the house was a kind of museum. Cassie led him into the dining room, where candles in a silver candelabra shone down on a table set with china and silver. "It has always been a tradition in the Wynock house to dress for dinner on Christmas Eve," she said. "You're just in time to join me."

She indicated a place at the table, which was set for four. "Are you expecting other guests?" Lucas asked.

"No, but I like to be prepared in case someone stops by."

"Is Mr. Pershing here?" He'd seen the old guy hanging around the place earlier, hanging lights in the big tree out front.

"Gerald? Oh my goodness, no. I sent him away as soon as he finished splitting the last of the firewood. He wasn't very happy with me, but I persuaded him it would be in his best interest to go. Living alone, I know how to defend myself." She nodded to a pearl-handled pistol that rested on the table by the door. Its barrel was polished silver, engraved with lacy filigree. "Now, do have a seat. We don't want dinner to get cold."

He pulled out the chair and sat, then wondered if he should have offered to hold her chair for her. He'd seen that in a movie once and it sounded like the kind of thing she'd expect. But she said nothing, merely slid into her own chair and reached for a bottle of wine at her elbow. She filled her glass, then hesitated and filled Lucas's.

He stared at the pale golden liquid in the glass. He'd never had wine before. He and his friend Ryan had sneaked a couple of beers out of the back of the Dirty Sally once, but Lucas hadn't been impressed with the experience.

"Just one glass," Cassie said, as if reading his mind. "Sip it very slowly. After all, it's Christmas Eve."

She removed the domed cover from a platter and transferred what looked like a whole, miniature chicken to his plate. "Cornish game hen," she said. She added some brownish rice and green peas to the hen on his plate and motioned he should begin eating.

The chicken was scrawny, but it tasted okay. "It's good," he said.

He sipped the wine carefully. It was sour and sweet, too. Not great, but not terrible. He watched Cassie out of the corner of his eye and tried to copy her movements, the way she held the knife and fork, how she set aside the utensils between every bite. He didn't want her complaining to his mom or grandmother that he had horrible manners.

"When I was a girl, we'd have a dozen or more people gathered around this table on Christmas Eve," she said. "My father and mother had so many friends . . . famous people like the governor, doctors and lawyers, and wealthy businessmen. Everyone wanted to gather at our table during the holidays." She looked around the table and smiled, as if seeing it full of distinguished guests.

Lucas's stomach hurt, thinking of her all alone in this house, setting the table for guests who never arrived. He took a drink of wine, forgetting to sip, but the tart liquid helped some. "Did you have brothers and sisters?" he asked.

Her gaze came more in focus and she studied him. "No, I was an only child. Like you."

He dragged the tines of his fork through the peas. "It's lonely being the only kid at Christmas," he said.

"Yes, yes, it is." She stared into her own wineglass. The house was so quiet Lucas could hear a clock ticking somewhere across the room. He wondered if he ought to leave now. Mom would be worried if she came home and he wasn't there.

"What do you want to be when you grow up, Lucas?"

The question was one adults often asked kids, but the way she stared at him so intently, Cassie seemed truly interested in his answer. "A historian, maybe," he said. "Or an archeologist. Or a policeman. I'm not sure." It wasn't as if he had to decide right this minute.

She nodded slowly and refilled her wineglass. "Whatever you choose, don't let others stifle your dreams," she said. She sipped the wine, then pushed her half-full plate away. "I wanted to go away to college and my parents convinced me to wait. I was needed at home. I was always needed at home, so I never went away. I wanted to go into politics or the foreign service, to be a diplomat and travel the world, but I let them convince me to become a librarian instead. It was more practical. More suitable."

"You could travel now," he said.

She shook her head. "I'm too old."

"You're not that old. You're not much older than my grandmother, are you?"

"I'll never be the girl I was." She sighed dramatically, as if she were acting in a play.

"You can be whoever you want to be." Lucas pushed aside his own plates. "That's what adults at school always say anyway. Do you think they're lying?"

She didn't answer. She held her wineglass in one hand and stared into the distance. He wondered if she'd forgotten he was there. "I'd better go now," he said. He stood. "Thank you for the dinner."

"Good night, Lucas. Merry Christmas."

"Merry Christmas."

She didn't move from her chair, so he saw himself out. When he stepped onto the porch the cold air hit him like a slap across the face, but it felt good. He could still taste the wine on his tongue, and he savored the taste as he trudged down the side of the road through the fresh snow. Even without streetlights, the road stood out clearly, the banks of snow on either side glowing white as if illuminated from within. The snow had stopped and the sky cleared, and thousands of stars shone overhead—the sky was almost white with them.

He stopped in the middle of the street and stared up at the sky, like a little kid searching for Santa Claus. But he didn't care about Santa, or about the cold, or even that he was alone on Christmas Eve. He thought about how big the world was, and how lucky it was that he was standing here right now, in the place where he was the happiest he'd ever been. He didn't know if he believed in God, but just in case such a being existed, he sent up a little prayer of thanks. "Merry Christmas," he whispered to himself, then started walking home again.

By the time they reached the cabin and D. J. found the key above the door lintel and let them in, Olivia was so cold she was sure she'd never be warm again. She collapsed onto the old sofa in the room and watched, only half-aware, as D. J.—still dressed as Santa—knelt before the black iron stove and built a fire. As the first golden flames licked at the wood she felt a spark of life return, and she sat up to lean toward the welcome blaze.

"There's tea and some canned soup we can heat up on the stove," he called from the cabin's little kitchen area.

She said nothing, staring into the fire. Was it possible for a brain to freeze? Hers felt encased in ice, too numb to function on more than a primitive level.

D. J. moved in front of her, setting a pan and a kettle on the stove. *I ought to get up and help,* she thought, but didn't move. Firelight silhouetted D. J.'s tall frame and broad shoulders. He'd taken off the Santa jacket and padding to reveal a red, waffle-weave thermal top. He might have been a miner, home after a day's hard work. But were miners ever this strong and sexy? Maybe so . . .

She closed her eyes, only for a second, and the next thing she knew D. J. was seated beside her, shaking her awake. "Drink this," he said, putting a warm mug in her hand. "You'll feel better."

She sipped the sweet, hot tea, and a low moan of delight escaped her. "Soup'll be ready in a bit," he said. He settled back on the sofa, his arm still around her. She had no willpower left to fight the urge to curl against him, head on his shoulder, so she surrendered, and his arm wrapped around her more tightly.

"I can't think of anyplace I'd rather be right now," he

said. "Or any better Christmas present than being alone with you."

The tears that stung her eyes surprised her, and she blinked furiously. He gently took the mug of tea from her hand and set it on the low table in front of the sofa. "Look at me," he whispered, and put one finger under her chin to tilt her face up to his. He kissed not her lips, but her cheek. "Why are you crying?"

"Because I've done something so awful." She couldn't hold back the tears now, and her words came out as sobs.

"No." He held her tightly and rocked her back and forth. "Nothing you've done has been awful," he said.

She wanted to stay here like this forever, letting him croon to her and comfort her. But she didn't deserve that comfort. Not yet. She forced herself to push away from him. "I have to tell you," she said. "You have a right to know."

He studied her, his face very pale against the darkness of his beard. She knew he was bracing himself against something horrible. "What do you want to tell me?"

"When you left for Iraq, I was pregnant."

He frowned. "Pregnant?"

"I should have told you, but I was angry. I thought you should have known. You should have seen the signs. I thought you did know."

"If I'd known, I never would have left."

"I was stupid. And afraid." Afraid if she had told him it wouldn't have made any difference. Pretending he'd known and left anyway had somehow hurt a little less.

"What happened to the baby?" His voice was strained, the words pinched off and distant.

"I lost it. A few weeks after you left. A miscarriage."

"Oh, honey." He pulled her into his arms once more. "I'm sorry you had to go through that without me there." Something splashed on her cheek and she realized he was crying. She buried her face in his shoulder and sobbed, all the grief and worry of the past months pouring out of her. He held her while she wept and she thought he cried, too. How foolish they'd both been. How much time they'd wasted.

At last she had no more tears. They sat together on the sofa, rocking in each other's arms, until D. J. suddenly bolted up. "The soup!" he said, and rushed to pull the burning pan from the stove. Smoke poured from the charred contents. He raced to the door and threw the whole thing into the snow.

Olivia burst into laughter and he joined her. It felt good to laugh together. Healing. "I can open another can," he said.

"Maybe later. I'm not hungry right now." Not for soup. She held out her arms and he came to her.

He kissed her lips, then pulled back.

"No," she protested.

"I just have to get rid of this ridiculous wig." He grasped the mop cap and tugged, and it and the gray wig came free. Olivia reached up and took out the hairpins that confined her real hair, and it fell down around her shoulders.

"That's better." He smiled and kissed her again. His lips moved down to her neck and the tops of her breasts as he peeled away the ridiculous Mrs. Claus costume. She traced her hands across his shoulders and back, rediscovering the once-familiar contours of muscle and bone. "I've wanted you so much," he whispered, his voice trembling.

"Yeah," she answered, too moved to speak. "Yeah."

They made love slowly, cautiously, as if they were both afraid of shattering this wonderful, fragile dream. Olivia felt feverish with need, and her skin burned wherever he touched her. How would she ever be cold again? When he slid into her, she cried again, tears of joy and triumph and love. "I love you," she cried. "I never stopped loving you."

"I know," he said. "In my heart, I've always known." Then they didn't speak again, focused on emotions too big for words.

Later, they fell asleep in each other's arms. As she drifted off, Olivia thought it was probably past midnight. "Merry Christmas," she whispered. He didn't answer, and that didn't matter. They were together. It was Christmas. She'd never hate the holiday again.

Olivia awoke to a heavy, thudding noise. She burrowed out from under the blankets D. J. had piled on them and sat up. D. J. sat also. "What the hell?" They stared at the door, which shook with the force of the blows.

D. J. climbed over her on the sofa and reached for his pants. Olivia grabbed the ridiculous Mrs. Claus dress and pulled it over her head. "Maybe a search party from town came to rescue us," she said.

"Maybe we didn't need rescuing." He headed to the door. "Who is it?" he called.

The muffled answer was unintelligible. D. J. jerked open the door and a figure all in white stumbled into the room and fell to its knees on the floor. D. J. knelt beside the intruder, who appeared to be a man, covered in snow and ice. "Help me get him out of these frozen clothes and over to the fire," D. J. said.

Together, they peeled off the man's pack, hat, and gloves. Olivia brushed snow and ice from his beard and face, and a pair of familiar eyes stared back at her. "Jameso!"

He tried to speak, but his teeth chattered so badly the words were unintelligible. "Get closer to the fire," D. J. said, taking hold of Jameso's arm. "Olivia, bring those blankets over here, and could you make a cup of tea?"

While Olivia fussed with blankets and tea, D. J. stripped Jameso of his remaining clothes and laid him out in front of the fire. She found empty Lexan water bottles—the kind people took camping—in a cabinet over the sink and filled them with hot water from the kettle on the stove. "Put these around him," she said, handing them to D. J.

"Good idea." He tucked the bottles at Jameso's feet and stomach. "What the hell were you doing out there on a night like this anyway?"

"G—got to g—get to Eureka," Jameso gasped. He tried to sit up, but D. J. pushed him back down.

"You're not going anywhere right now," he said. "You'll be lucky if you don't lose fingers or toes to frost-bite."

Olivia knelt and held the cup of tea to Jameso's lips. "Drink some of this," she said.

He sipped the tea and made a face. "Needs whiskey," he said.

Olivia laughed. "We looked, but apparently the owners of this cabin are teetotalers."

In a few minutes, Jameso was able to sit up and hold the teacup himself. Olivia moved to the sofa and put on the rest of her Mrs. Claus costume, while D. J. dressed once more as Santa. "Is this some kinky Christmas fantasy I don't want to know about?" Jameso asked.

"We were delivering Christmas presents for the Elks and the truck got stuck." D. J. sat on the sofa next to Olivia. "What's your excuse for turning yourself into an abominable snowman?"

"I was on my way back from Montana and the road was blocked, so I decided to ski the rest of the way. My skis are out there on the porch."

"You decided to ski, in the dark, over an avalanche-blocked mountain pass, just for fun?" D. J. looked skeptical.

"It wasn't dark when I started, and I've done it before, a few years ago. With Jake."

"At least you made it here before you froze," Olivia said. She tried to sound cheerful. After all, she was glad Jameso was all right, even if he had interrupted her reunion with D. J.

As if sharing her feelings, D. J. slipped his arm around her. Jameso noticed the gesture. "I see you two decided to kiss and make up," he said. "As soon as my clothes are dry I'll be out of your hair."

"None of us are going anywhere until morning," D. J. said. "We're lucky we found this cabin when we did."

"You can stay, but I have to get to Eureka." He struggled to his feet, clutching the blanket around his waist. "Where did you put my clothes?" He spotted them draped across the back of a chair and headed toward them.

"Jameso, don't be stupid," Olivia protested. "You can't go back out there."

"I promised Maggie I'd be home by Christmas and I have to keep my promise."

"It's another eight miles into town, at least," D. J. said. "If you don't get lost in the dark or fall into a snowbank or ski over a cliff, you'll freeze to death."

"No, I have a plan." He dropped the blanket and pulled on long underwear bottoms. "There's a steam tractor at the old Blue Bird mine. This is one of the miner's shacks for the mine. We can start the tractor and drive down to town. It's got tracks . . . it will get through anything."

"A tractor that's been sitting at an abandoned mine for years is junk," D. J. said. "It's not going anywhere."

"It'll start. Jake and I fired it up just a few months before he died."

"From everything I've heard, this Jake character had more than one screw loose," D. J. said.

"He was crazy," Jameso said. "But he wasn't stupid.

And he saved my ass more than once. I think he was looking out for me tonight anyway."

Something in his voice made Olivia think this wasn't just a casual remark. "What do you mean?" she asked.

He shook his head. "It was probably nothing. The cold making me hallucinate."

"What happened?" she asked.

"I thought I saw Jake out there tonight. Skiing with me. Guiding me to this cabin."

When D. J.'s eyes met Olivia's, she saw his skepticism. "People say all kinds of things can happen on Christmas Eve," she said. "How far away is this tractor?"

"No!" D. J. said. "We are not leaving a warm, safe cabin on a crazy fool's errand like this."

"It's not far," Jameso said. "Less than a mile. There's an old mining road through the trees right behind this cabin that leads right to it. Once we get the tractor fired up, we'll be warm and safe in the cab all the way to town."

"We aren't going anywhere," D. J. said.

Jameso shrugged into his coat. "Suit yourself. You can stay here. I don't blame you if you do. But I have to go. I have to keep my promise to Maggie."

"You're crazy." D. J. stood, as if intending to block Jameso's way, but Olivia took hold of his arm.

"We should go with him," she said.

D. J. stared at her.

"He might need our help starting the tractor," she said.

"You want to help him with this crazy plan?"

She nodded. "It's Christmas and the man is in love. We have to help him."

Maggie tried to embrace the Christmas spirit that filled the Last Dollar—not the alcoholic kind, though plenty flowed from the bottles Bob and Rick passed around, but the sense of friendship and community that warmed her in a way no liquor could. Even if Jameso couldn't be here, she had plenty to be thankful for this holiday season. The baby growing inside of her was a miracle she couldn't even have contemplated last year at this time, and though a lot of things about the future frightened her, her life looked a lot more hopeful than it had just twelve months before.

"This is a wonderful Christmas!" Katya, face glowing and eyes shining as much from the hefty shot of bourbon Bob had poured into her eggnog as from the holiday spirit, lifted her mug high. "We should get snowed in at Christmas more often."

"To friends." Danielle lifted her own glass, which sparkled with champagne from a bottle someone had opened.

"To friends," they repeated. Maggie sipped her tea—unadulterated—and caught the worried gaze of Lucille across the room. She made her way through the crowd—half the town must have joined their impromptu party—to stand by the older woman. "Something wrong?" Maggie asked.

"I'm worried about Olivia and D. J. They should have been home by now." She turned her head to check the clock that hung on the wall beside the door. Maggie was amazed to see it was almost two. "I should get back to the house and check on Lucas."

"He's probably asleep," Maggie said. "And maybe Olivia and D. J. are already home."

"Maybe. But I'd think they'd have seen the crowd and stopped by here." She sighed and looked into her empty glass. "You're right. I worry too much."

"I do, too. I know good and well Jameso is holed up in a hotel room somewhere, perfectly fine, but I can't help fretting."

"He'll be back, Maggie. Jameso has his faults, but he's not going to run out on you and the baby."

"I know." Saying the words made her feel calmer, because she knew they were true.

"What are you two whispering about over here in the corner?" Rick joined them, a Santa hat askew on his head.

"We're talking about you, of course," Lucille said.

"Only good things, of course." He threw one arm heavily over Maggie's shoulder. "Some of us are taking the sleigh out for a midnight run. Want to come?"

"You still have the sleigh?" Lucille asked.

"Sure. It's parked in the county barn around the corner, right between the snow plows." He grinned. "I couldn't leave the horses out in the cold, but I didn't want to take them all the way back out to the ranch, so Junior and I fixed up a place for them, with blankets and hay and everything."

"And now you're going to make them go out in the cold to haul a bunch of us around," Maggie said.

"They don't mind. It's what they do. And can you think of a better way to see in Christmas?"

"I can. They all involve a nice warm bed," Lucille said.

"I'm sorry, Madam Mayor. I just don't think of you that way."

Lucille stuck her tongue out at him. "Let me get my coat. You can drop me off at my house as we go by."

"What about you, Maggie?" Rick turned to her.

"Why not?" She set aside her teacup. "A sleigh ride sounds fun."

They waited in the snow for Rick to bring the sleigh around: Maggie, Katya, Reggie, and Lucille. Stars spangled the sky above and snow blanketed the sleeping town. No one disturbed the silence; Maggie had never known such peacefulness. The whole world seemed hushed with expectation. Waiting.

Then the jingle of sleigh bells rang clear in the midnight stillness and the sleigh turned the corner and hove into view, the two Percherons high-stepping and tossing their heads, Rick standing in the driver's seat and waving.

"Merry Christmas!" he called, reining to a stop in front of them.

They piled into the sleigh's two seats and pulled scratchy wool blankets over their knees. With a jolt, the sleigh started forward, gliding through the unplowed street. Strings of lights outlined the windows, doors, and rooflines of most of the businesses in town, and in front of the library the town tree glowed, the glitter-and-Styrofoam decorations crafted by schoolchildren sparkling like jewels.

"We should sing," Katya said.

"Some of us shouldn't," Lucille protested, but Katya had already started a credible "Dashing through the snow," and Reggie, Rick, and Maggie joined in.

Their voices rang through the night, and on the chorus even Lucille joined in. "Jingle bells, jingle bells . . ."

"Whoa! Whoa there!" Rick pulled the sleigh to a stop in the middle of the street.

"What is it?" Lucille asked. "Why are we stopping?"

"Is something wrong?" Maggie asked. She pushed off the blanket and stood.

"Just a real Christmas miracle," Rick said. He pointed ahead of him with the whip. "Look up there."

Maggie stared at the glare of a single headlight approaching. But the light was too high up to be attached to a car, and the engine sound was like no automobile she'd ever heard.

"It sounds like a train," Lucille said. "And is that steam?"

"You can't have a train without tracks," Reggie said.

"It's not a train," Rick said. "I think it's an old steam tractor."

Maggie's heart skipped a beat, then started to pound. She clutched Lucille's arm. "It's the old steam tractor from the Blue Bird mine."

"I heard about that thing," Rick said. "But who the hell is driving it into town on a night like this?"

"It's Jameso," Maggie said, as sure as she'd ever been of anything.

The tractor was close enough now they could make out the hulking shape and yellow metal cab. Steam poured from the smokestack, but Maggie couldn't make out anything past the dark glass of the cab.

"He'd better stop or he'll run over us," Lucille cried. The horses whinnied and danced sideways as the monster machine trundled forward on rubber treads.

But with a rumble and a jerk, the tractor ground to a halt a few feet from the sleigh. The passenger's door popped open and a tall man dressed like Santa, minus the fuzzy white beard, hopped to the ground.

"It's D. J.," Lucille called.

The man reached up and helped a woman—Olivia—to the ground. Maggie glanced at them, then refocused on the driver's side. The door opened and it was as if a corresponding portal opened in her heart, letting out all the pent-up pressure and anxiety. "Jameso," she whispered, as he climbed down the steps to the snow.

She didn't remember climbing out of the sleigh, didn't remember running to him, but suddenly she was in his arms, the strength of his grip around her the most comforting sensation. "I knew you'd come," she said, kissing him over and over.

"I told you I'd make it home for Christmas," he said.

"I don't know why you ever had to go away." Now that he was here, she felt the need to scold, if only as a way of gaining control of her emotions.

"I had to get this." He reached into his pocket and pulled out a small box and pressed it into her hand.

She stared at the ring box. "Jameso, I—"

"Go on. Open it."

She did as he commanded and stared at the gold band

studded with colored stones. "The gold is from one of Bob's claims," he said. "I got him to sell it to me. The turquoise is from your mine, the French Mistress. The diamonds are from some estate jewelry Lucille had in her shop. I had a jeweler Jake knew in Montana make it up for me. Just for you."

She stared at the ring—so beautiful, and unlike anything she'd ever seen. He'd gone to so much trouble to get it. "I don't understand," she said. She'd already turned down his proposal and refused one ring.

"I wanted to show you how special you are to me. How much I love you." He kissed her, his lips cold against hers, the stubble on his cheek abrading her skin. Yet never had a kiss been sweeter. "Marry me, Maggie," he said. "I won't be happy until you're my wife."

The child inside her stirred and she almost laughed, she was so happy. "Yes," she said softly. Then louder. "Yes, I'll marry you."

They kissed again, a deep, warming kiss she felt all the way to her heart.

"Is this a Christmas miracle?" Lucille tapped Maggie on the shoulder.

They broke apart and Maggie laughed. "Yes." She showed Lucille the ring in its box. "Congratulations." Lucille enveloped Maggie in a hug; then everyone crowded around, adding their good wishes.

"What are you two looking so smug about?" Rick asked D. J. and Olivia, who stood arm in arm, a little apart from the others. Olivia merely smiled and shook her head.

Then the door of Lucille's house burst open and Lucas, a coat pulled on over his pajamas, bounded into the street. "Hey, Mom!" he called. "Where have you been?"

"My truck got stuck in the snow and we had to hitch a ride home on this." D. J. gestured to the tractor.

"Cool." Lucas put one arm around his mother and hugged her.

"I have something important to ask you," D. J. said to the boy, his face solemn.

"Yeah?" Lucas looked wary.

"Would it be all right with you if I married your mother?"

"For real?" A grin split the boy's face. "I'd say it was about time." He turned to his mom. "You'll say yes, won't you?"

Olivia looked D. J. up and down, as if considering. "I guess I'll say yes," she said. Before she could add more, he silenced her with a kiss.

"What do you think you people are doing, standing here in the street, making such a racket?" Cassie, dressed in a formal gown and pearls, her old wool coat thrown over her shoulders, marched toward them through the snow.

"Merry Christmas, Miss Wynock," Lucas called. "My mom and D. J. are getting married. And so are Jameso and Maggie."

Cassie sniffed. "I don't know why they couldn't wait until a decent hour to make the announcement."

Jameso pulled Maggie close once more. "You ready to go home?"

"How will we get there?"

"The steam tractor will take us."

Maggie eyed the huffing, growling monster. "Are you sure it's safe?"

"Safe enough."

"I suppose my father would approve. No doubt he'd have been with you tonight if he could."

"He was with me." He spoke quietly, his face serious.

"Jameso, you don't mean . . ."

He shrugged. "Maybe I was hallucinating from the cold, but I'd swear Jake was there. He led me to the cabin where D. J. and Olivia were holed up. He saved my life. And he brought me back to you."

She closed her eyes against stinging tears. She wasn't one to believe in the fantastic, but she could believe every word Jameso said. He had no reason to lie to her, and she'd heard so many fantastic stories about her father already that he seemed capable of anything. For a man who had abandoned her as a child, he'd given her so much—a new home and friends and family. And now he'd brought the man she loved safely back to her. She had all she ever wanted—the best Christmas gift anyone could have given her.

Big changes are afoot in the small town
of Eureka in Cindy Myers's

A Change in Altitude

With local Maggie Stevens's baby on the way—not to
mention her wedding to Jameso Clark in the works—
spring in Eureka promises to be a time of rebirth in more
ways than one. To add to the excitement, and to refill the
town's depleted coffers, Lucille, the mayor, has wooed a
movie producer to Eureka, throwing folks into a tizzy—
and inspiring some to reach for the stars. As if that
weren't enough, the bogus Lucky Lady mine the town
partially sold turns out to *really* have gold in it—and possibly a ghost to boot. But with each silver lining, there
seems to be a cloud. . . .

With Eureka's financial future at stake, Lucille will
have to wrangle Lucky Lady's greedy half-owner to re-
gain control. Meanwhile, just as Jameso is getting comfortable with the imminent role of husband and father, his
wayward sister, Sharon, comes to Eureka to escape a
troubled marriage. Can the residents of Eureka find the
courage to stand up to ghosts of all kinds and get their
beloved town back on its feet in time to welcome their
newest addition—and celebrate the gifts of spring . . . ?

Turn the page for a special excerpt!

A Kensington trade paperback and e-book on sale now

CHAPTER ONE

"Mo-oooom!" The cry rose and fell with the intensity and pitch of a siren's wail, and Sharon Franklin felt the same flood of adrenaline and worry that had once been her response to her infant's wail.

Only now the infant was thirteen years old and glaring at her with the disdain only a teenager can muster.

"What's wrong now?" Sharon asked, her hands tightening on the steering wheel of the Honda Civic. She'd been behind the wheel so long she feared her fingers would remain permanently bent, as if she were always trying to hang on to something that wasn't there.

"You can't be serious about staying here." Alina, bangs she'd been growing out falling forward to half-cover one eye, glowered out the side window of the car at a row of false-fronted buildings on a dirt side street. "If you were so set on living in East Podunk, we could have stayed in Vermont."

We could have stayed in Vermont with Dad and Adan, Sharon completed the thought, and her eyes burned with tears she refused to let fall. "You know we couldn't stay in Vermont," she said softly.

Alina glared at her but said nothing. Sharon turned the car down the side street and slowly rolled past a coin laundry, a hardware store, and a place that advertised hunting licenses, firearms, and fishing tackle. A skinny old man in canvas trousers and a brown plaid shirt emerged from the hardware store and openly stared as Sharon eased the car down the street. A shiver rippled up her spine as she felt his eyes on her. Maybe she'd made a mistake coming here. Maybe she and Alina would have been better off in the city. San Francisco, maybe. Or Dallas . . .

"Where are we going?" Alina asked.

"I'm just getting a feel for the layout of the town." She turned left, onto another unpaved street, past a park and a trim white house with lilac bushes flanking the front door and a sign that indicated the library.

"We should go in the library and ask about Uncle Jay," Alina said.

Sharon slowed the car and considered the idea. "My brother was never much of a reader," she said.

"Yeah, but librarians know things. I'll bet the librarian knows everybody in a small town like this. And they might have telephone books and stuff."

"You're right. That's a good idea." She stifled a sigh. Was she ready for this? Not just yet. "Let's eat first. I think better on a full stomach." The coffee and stale muffin she'd had at the motel this morning were a distant memory. And she could use another hour or two to gather her failing courage. When she'd set out on this journey, it had seemed like such a good idea—the strong, right thing to do for her and her daughter.

She wasn't feeling very strong right now. She wanted someone else to tell her what she should do.

"Do you think they'll have anything I can eat?" Alina wrinkled her nose. She'd become a vegetarian last year—a perfectly reasonable choice, Sharon thought, but her father and brother had given her nothing but grief about it.

She had struggled all the way across the Midwest, eating mostly salads, French fries, and baked potatoes.

"I'm sure they'll have something," Sharon said.

"Where is there to eat in this town anyway?" Alina looked around. "Uh-oh."

"What?" Sharon followed her daughter's gaze to the black and white sheriff's department cruiser that had pulled in behind her. The officer switched on his rotating overhead lights and she groaned, a surge of adrenaline flooding her with a rush of nausea and dizziness. Was he going to give her a ticket for idling her car in the middle of the otherwise deserted street?

She watched in the side mirror as he approached the car. He was young with short blond hair and dark sunglasses. His brown shirt and pants fit closely to a trim body. She rolled down her window and managed a weak smile. "Hello," she said.

"Hello, ma'am." He touched two fingers to the brim of his Stetson, a salute that was almost courtly. "I saw you stopped here in the street and thought you might need some help. Are you lost or having car trouble?"

"Oh, no. I'm sorry, I was just trying to get my bearings." Her smile was more genuine now. "I just got to town."

"Welcome to Eureka. I'm Sergeant Josh Miller, with the Eureka County Sheriff's Department." He offered his hand and she took it for a brief, firm squeeze.

"I'm Sharon Franklin. And this is my daughter, Alina."

"Hi," Alina said. "We're looking for my uncle, Jay Clarkson. Do you know him?"

Sergeant Miller rubbed his jaw. He had big hands, with short, square fingers. "The name doesn't ring a bell. But then, I've only been in town a month myself, so I don't know a lot of people yet."

That was good news anyway, Sharon thought. There was a time when Jay would have been on a first-name basis with most law enforcement in their town. And not in a good way. "It's nice to meet another newcomer," she said. "We're thinking of relocating here."

"Where are you from?"

"Vermont."

"I've never been there, but I hear it's pretty. Different mountains, though."

Different was exactly what she wanted. "The Green Mountains are less rocky and, well, greener. But this looks pretty."

"It's a good place to live." He had a kind smile, though she couldn't read his eyes behind his sunglasses. She could use a little kindness, so she chose to believe the emotion was genuine. "Is there anything else I can help you with?" he asked.

"Is there any place to eat that would have vegetarian food?" Alina asked.

"The Last Dollar Cafe has pretty much any kind of food you like," he said. "And it's all good." He pointed ahead. "Just go to the corner here and turn left."

"Thank you. It was nice meeting you."

"Same here." He took out a card case. "Here's my card. If you need anything that's not an emergency, you can reach me on that number."

"Thanks."

He hesitated and her heart pounded. For a fleeting moment, she was afraid he might ask for her number. She'd heard about western towns where the men so outnumbered the women that any single female was immediately popular. The last thing she wanted in her life right now was romance.

"I guess I'll see you around," he said. He tipped his cap again and walked back to his cruiser.

Relieved, Sharon rolled up the window, put the car in gear, and carefully pulled away. "He was nice," Alina said.

"Yes."

"Cute, too."

"He was nice looking." More importantly, he'd been a friendly—but not too friendly—face in a place that was foreign to her, the first to welcome her to what she hoped would be her new life. She pulled the car into a space in front of the Last Dollar Cafe. Was the name a sign? She wasn't down to her own last dollar yet, but it wouldn't be long. "This looks good, huh?" The cedar-sided building had green shutters, leafy shrubs across the front, and planters full of flowers on either side of the door.

"Let me get my camera." Alina pulled this most treasured possession—a fancy, multiple-lens digital camera—from its case on the floorboard at her feet and slung the strap around her neck. "I might see something good to photograph."

Inside, the café was an attractive, homey place, with tables covered with red-checked cloths and booths with red vinyl benches. A colorful mural filled the back wall, and the other walls were filled with antiques—old skis, skates, and kitchen utensils. A hand-cranked coffee grinder caught Sharon's eye; she'd had one like it back home.

A pretty dark haired young woman greeted them. "Hello. Y'all can sit anywhere you like."

They chose a booth against the wall. The young woman brought silverware wrapped in paper napkins and two glasses of water. "The menu is on the wall." She indicated a large chalkboard covered in writing in colored chalk.

"Do you have a veggie burger?" Alina asked, her expression guarded.

"We have a great veggie burger," the young woman said. "And killer sweet-potato fries or onion rings. Or I can get you a salad."

Alina made a face. "I've had enough lettuce to last me

a lifetime. But the veggie burger sounds good. And sweet-potato fries."

"I'll have the same," Sharon said. "And iced tea."

"I'll have a Coke," Alina said.

"Sounds good." The young woman left and Sharon sagged back against the booth and closed her eyes.

"Are you okay, Mom?"

Sharon's eyes snapped open and she pasted on a confident smile. "I'm fine. Just tired of driving." That was true; they'd been in the car most of four days now. But she was also worn out with worrying—not just about this trip across the country to find a brother she hadn't seen in years, but all the worrying of all the months before that leading up to the decision to leave and come west.

A few moments later a tall blonde brought their drinks. "What brings you two to Eureka?" she asked.

Sharon opened her mouth to say they were just visiting, but Alina answered first. "We're here to visit my uncle. We're thinking about staying, though. If Mom can find a job. Is it nice here?"

"It's pretty nice," the young woman said. "Danielle and I—that's the dark haired woman who waited on you—we weren't sure what to think when we first came here a few years ago. We'd never lived in such a small town. But it feels like home now. I'm Janelle, by the way."

"I'm Alina." Alina offered her hand. Amazing what the promise of a veggie burger could do for a sullen teen. "This is my mom, Sharon."

Sharon took the offered hand and smiled weakly. "Hello."

"Who's your uncle?" Janelle asked.

"Jay Clarkson," Alina said. "Do you know him?"

Janelle looked thoughtful. "The name doesn't ring a bell. Danielle!" She called over her shoulder. "Do we know a Jay Clarkson?"

"I don't think so."

"Anybody else know that name?" Janelle addressed the half dozen other patrons in the restaurant.

After some murmuring and brief discussion, it was decided that no one knew of a Jay Clarkson.

Sharon felt hollow. Defeated. Had she driven all the way across the country on a fool's errand?

"We thought about asking at the library," Alina said. "But Mom says Uncle Jay isn't much of a reader."

"Well, I hope you find him. And enjoy your stay in Eureka, however long it ends up being. It's kind of quiet now, but things really pick up come summer."

"Is there a motel in town?" Sharon asked. She'd planned on asking Jay if they could stay with him, but if he wasn't here . . . She was suddenly so exhausted that the thought of getting in the car and driving to the next town was almost enough to make her burst into tears.

"There is. The Eureka Hotel, up by the highway. It's not fancy, but it's clean. We've got a bed-and-breakfast opening this summer, but it's not ready yet."

"The hotel is fine. I'll check it out." She hoped the rooms were cheap. The wad of cash she'd stuffed in her suitcase before she left was getting alarmingly thin. She'd have to find a job soon. She'd counted on Jay to help with that; living here, he'd know who would hire her, where she and Alina could live. . . . But if he wasn't here . . . She fought back the sick, panicked feeling that had threatened to overwhelm her whenever she allowed herself to think of her and her daughter alone. Really alone—something she had never been in her life.

Danielle brought their food, and the aroma of burgers and fries revived Sharon some. She told herself she'd feel better when she'd eaten. She would find Jay, and he would help them. End of story.

"Oh, this is so good," Alina said after a few minutes, pausing to sit back. She took a sip of Coke. "Maybe this place isn't so bad after all. I like Janelle and Danielle."

Sharon nodded. "I was really hoping someone would know where to find Jay."

"When was the last time you heard from him?" Alina asked.

"I talked to him on the phone right before we moved last time."

Alina's eyes widened. "You haven't heard from him in five years?"

"Your father thought it was best to keep to ourselves." Joe had been big on self-sufficiency. That, and his increasing paranoia, had led him to sever relationships with their families and most of their friends.

Alina took a long drink of her soda, then dragged a sweet-potato fry through a pool of ranch dressing on her plate. "He listened to Wilson too much," she said. "Wilson was paranoid that the government was opening all our mail. But Dad isn't that stupid."

Sharon said nothing. Joe wasn't stupid, but he had his own share of paranoia, grown worse since they'd moved next door to his best friend—pretty much his only friend now—Wilson Anderson, a man who trusted no one.

She turned her head to study the mural on the back wall of the café. A miner and his mule stood against a backdrop of majestic peaks, while a stern-faced pioneer woman did laundry in front of a log cabin. On the other end of the painting, a breechcloth-clad Native American crouched beside a stream, watching a rainbow trout.

Janelle stopped by to refill Sharon's iced tea. "Can I take a picture of your mural?" Alina asked.

"Sure. A local artist, Olivia Theriot, painted that for us a few months ago," she said. "She works part time at the bar next door, the Dirty Sally, but she has T-shirts and jewelry and stuff in a shop up on the square."

"Cool," Alina said.

"Maybe you ought to stop in the Dirty Sally and ask

about your relative," Janelle said. "If he's not the library type, maybe he's the bar type."

"Definitely the bar type," Sharon said. At least when she'd last seen him, her brother had been a hard-drinking, motorcycle-riding, authority-defying rebel. Maybe he was in jail somewhere.

Janelle moved away. Alina slid out of the booth and went to take pictures of the mural. Sharon stared out the window beside the booth, which looked out onto a neat backyard, complete with a chicken coop and bare raised garden beds.

"Are we going to ask about Jay at the bar?" Alina asked when she returned.

"I don't know." Sharon pushed her almost-empty plate away. "Maybe he isn't here anymore."

"We can't come all this way without at least asking." A whine crept into Alina's voice. "I'm tired of riding. Let's stay here for a day or two, check things out. At least we'll eat good." She nodded to the chalkboard menu. "They have vegetarian lasagna, vegetable soup, stir-fry with the option of tofu instead of chicken, and macaroni and cheese."

Sharon suppressed a smile. Apparently, the way to her daughter's heart was through her stomach. "We'll stay a couple of days," she said. "And we'll keep looking for Jay."

After all, she was running out of options. She needed to find someplace to settle, in case Joe decided to make good on his threats to come after her.

"Have you seen my key chain?" Olivia Theriot asked, as she combed through the box of miscellaneous junk that had collected beneath the cash register at the Dirty Sally Saloon. "It's a real aspen leaf, encased in resin. D. J. gave it to me."

"Are your keys still attached to it?" Fellow bartender Jameso Clark looked up from the draft beer he was drawing.

"No, I have the keys. But I noticed last night the leaf was missing. I was hoping it had fallen off here and someone had found it."

"I haven't seen it." Jameso finished filling the glass and set the beer in front of Bob Prescott, who sat at the bar eating a bacon cheeseburger.

"Maybe you lost it at the house," Bob said.

"Maybe so, but I looked there." Olivia made a face. "I'm losing everything these days—my favorite pair of earrings, pens, and now my keychain. I think I'm just stressed out with the remodeling and everything."

"How's that coming?" Jameso asked.

"Slow." She and her boyfriend, D. J. Gruber, had bought the old miner's house in a foreclosure sale last month. They'd gotten a sweet deal, but now they spent every spare moment trying to make the place livable. "I can't wait until we can move in together. Maybe then I'll stop misplacing things." D. J.'s rental house was too small for the two of them and her teenage son, Lucas, so she lived with her mother, Eureka mayor Lucille Theriot. Besides, getting their own place and fixing it up together was symbolic of her and D. J. starting over. She was a big believer in symbols. D. J. said that was the artist in her. Lucas just said she was weird.

"Maybe you have a pack rat," Bob said.

"We do not have rats!" She shuddered. Mice were bad enough, but rats were enough to give her nightmares.

"Not a regular rat, a pack rat." Bob set down his burger. In his seventies, he was the picture of the grizzled miner, right down to his canvas pants, checked flannel shirt, and scraggly whiskers. Olivia suspected he cultivated this image carefully. "They're bigger and hairier than your average rat, and they like to collect things and stash them in their nests."

"They're harmless," Jameso said.

She tried to push away the image of a giant, hairy rat wearing her favorite earrings and changed the subject. "How's Maggie?" she asked Jameso. Maggie Stevens, a reporter at the local paper, had moved to town about the same time Olivia had come to Eureka, and had started dating Jameso not too long after.

"Pregnant."

She laughed. "That doesn't answer my question. How's she feeling?"

"She feels fine," Jameso said. "But between the wedding plans and getting Barb's B and B ready to open this summer, she's driving me crazy."

Olivia tried to hide a smile and failed.

"What are you smirking about?" Jameso asked.

"Those two love ordering you around," she said. Barb Stanowski, Maggie's best friend, lived in Houston but spent a lot of time in Eureka. Right now, she was remodeling another of the town's old homes into a fancy bed-and-breakfast inn. "I think they like the idea of domesticating the wild man." Before Maggie had arrived in town, Jameso had a reputation as a hard-partying free spirit, a handsome rogue who refused to settle down. Now that he and Maggie were engaged, with a baby on the way, he'd definitely changed.

"Yeah, well, I'll be glad when the B and B opens and the wedding's over and things settle down." He bent and began detaching the beer keg beneath the bar. "You got the last beer out of this one, Bob."

"I hate to tell you, but with a new baby in the house, your life will be anything but settled," Olivia said. "Have you and Maggie found a place to live yet?"

He scowled. "No, and I don't want to talk about it."

"Maybe you don't have a packrat." Bob, having finished his burger and drained the beer, pushed his empty plate and glass away. "Maybe you have a ghost. What house did you buy again?"

"It belonged to a woman named Gilroy. She was moving to Florida to live with her daughter."

He nodded. "That's the old McCutcheon place. I wouldn't be at all surprised if it didn't have a ghost. They say old man McCutcheon murdered his wife when she tried to run off with a traveling insurance salesman, and buried her body in the back garden. Of course, they never found the body, but could be she's haunting the place. A woman would like fancy earrings and such."

"Oh, shut up, Bob. Save the tall tales for the tourists." She didn't believe in ghosts. "I'm just losing things because I'm stressed. I'll have to be more careful."

"Don't go scaring her with your ghost stories, Bob." Jameso hefted the empty beer keg to his shoulder. "I have to change this out. Be right back."

As he exited out the back, the front door to the saloon opened and a woman and a girl entered. The woman was of medium height and thin, with dark brown hair falling well past her shoulders. The girl—her daughter, most likely—also had dark hair, worn in two braids on either side of her heart-shaped face. "Can I help you?" Olivia asked.

The woman looked around the almost-empty bar, then finally rested her gaze on Olivia. She had dark circles under her eyes and looked exhausted. "I'm looking for a man named Jay Clarkson," she said. "Have you heard of him?"

Olivia shook her head. "I don't know anyone by that name." She turned to Bob. "Sound familiar to you?"

Bob shook his head. "No, and I know everybody. What do you want with this Clarkson fellow?"

She and the girl were already backing toward the door, like wild animals frightened by the questions. "Don't go," Olivia said. "Maybe we can help you."

Jameso emerged from the back room with a fresh keg and Olivia turned to him. "Jameso, do you know—?"

But he was staring at the woman, his face the color of copy paper. "Sharon!" He lowered the keg.

"Jay!" She took a few steps toward him, then stopped. Jameso was frozen in place. "Aren't you happy to see me?" she asked.

"Sure. Of course." He shoved both hands in the front pockets of his jeans. "I'm just surprised. I thought you were in Vermont."

The woman pressed her lips together and took a deep breath, nostrils pinching, then flaring. "I've left Joe." She glanced at the girl, who had hung back, though she kept making furtive glances in Jameso's direction. "It's a long story. Jay, I'm just so glad to see you. I've been asking around town and no one knew you. I—"

"Jay?" Olivia said.

"It's Jameso now," he said, his voice strained. "Jameso Clark."

"You changed your name?" Sharon asked.

He put one hand on the bar, leaning on it. "It's a long story."

The woman crossed her arms over her chest. "I have all the time in the world. Why don't you tell me?"

"Yeah." Olivia copied the woman's pose. "Why don't you tell us?"